THE SINISTER REALM

THE SINISTER REALM

THE QUEST OF DAN CLAY: BOOK THREE

T.J. SMITH

Tate Publishing & *Enterprises*

The Sinister Realm
Copyright © 2010 by T.J. Smith. All rights reserved.

This title is also available as a Tate Out Loud product. Visit www.tatepublishing.com for more information.

No part of this publication may be reproduced, stored in a retrieval system or transmitted in any way by any means, electronic, mechanical, photocopy, recording or otherwise without the prior permission of the author except as provided by USA copyright law.

The opinions expressed by the author are not necessarily those of Tate Publishing, LLC.

Published by Tate Publishing & Enterprises, LLC
127 E. Trade Center Terrace | Mustang, Oklahoma 73064 USA
1.888.361.9473 | www.tatepublishing.com

Tate Publishing is committed to excellence in the publishing industry. The company reflects the philosophy established by the founders, based on Psalm 68:11,
"The Lord gave the word and great was the company of those who published it."

Book design copyright © 2010 by Tate Publishing, LLC. All rights reserved.
Cover design by Kandi Evans
Interior design by Joey Garrett

Published in the United States of America
ISBN: 978-1-61663-101-7
Fiction: Fantasy: Action: Folklore
10.03.29

THIS BOOK IS GRATEFULLY DEDICATED TO:

the Holy Spirit for enlightenment,
my mother—Jean—may she rest in peace,
my father—Robert—for his inspiration,
my siblings and their spouses for their encouragement,
and
Reverend James Spahn for his friendship over the years.

ACKNOWLEDGMENTS

I extend my gratitude to family members and friends who offered the encouragement to ensure that *The Sinister Realm* became a reality. Specifically, I acknowledge Reverend Joseph Blanco, Archbishop Charles J. Chaput, O.F.M. Cap., Sharon Doerflinger, Bill Egan, Reverend Monsignor Thomas Fryar, Reverend Monsignor Michael Glenn, Reverend Andreas Hock, Niharika and Wesley Joe, Judy and Tim Keilman, Robert Linn, Francis X. Maier, Nancy and Michael McKee, Betty Jane Nelson, Rose Mary Nelson, Deacon Charles Parker, Jr., Religious Sisters of Mercy of Alma, Kathleen and Richard Riley, Caroline Rose, Celeste Thomas, Virginia Thomas and Thérèse Wright.

—T.J. Smith

TABLE OF CONTENTS

1.	BLIND FAITH	8
2.	ASCENT TO SUPREMACY	18
3.	DISPELLED DOUBTS	30
4.	BLOODCURDLING THOUGHT	48
5.	LOOKS ARE DECEIVING	64
6.	THE SMELL OF EVIL	77
7.	THE MESSENGER OF ILL TIDINGS	91
8.	A WALK THROUGH TIME	107
9.	THE UNIMAGINABLE	122
10.	THE RIPPED PAGES	139
11.	HAUNTING VISIONS	157
12.	THE RESURRECTION	172
13.	BODILY INVASION	191
14.	THE UNSEEING ADVERSARY	206
15.	THE STONEHEARTED SISTERS	219
16.	SELF-INFLICTED PUNISHMENT	239
17.	THE IMAGE AND LIKENESS OF GOD	251
18.	THE NEANDERTHALS	269
19.	THE RISE TO PANDEMONIUM	292
20.	PHANTOM CHILDREN	314
21.	CANOPY CHAOS	333
22.	GUARDED GRIN	352

CHAPTER ONE
Blind Faith

Unlike Sam White who intentionally entered the tree to rescue Brad Blaze, Nancy Clay suspected that her sons deliberately broke their promise and crossed over to the parallel world through the belly of the spirited tree. She was torn between extreme anger with her sons' disobedience in venturing to the oak the previous night and agonizing distress for their safety. Though she knew they could defend themselves—since witnessing their resourcefulness and bravery when battling the creatures during the dinner party—she couldn't suppress her maternal instincts for their well-being. She placed her conflicting emotions aside and continued her walk to the church parking lot, arm in arm, with Sara Somer. En route, she tried to convince herself that Dan and William were in the peaceful parallel world.

•

Nearly the exact moment when Dan experienced the eerie sensation of passing through the tree, he was shocked by something stepping on his hand. The two events happened so quickly and nearly simultaneously that he couldn't say with certainty which incident happened first. Flat on his back, he opened his eyes and saw a human foot trample his hand into the ground. He shut his eyes to refocus his vision and opened them a second time. The foot was gone but was followed by another foot stepping on his other hand.

Although the area was in near darkness, dim light permitted him to notice that while the object was a human foot, it wasn't like any he had ever seen. The foot—with its definite proportions, obvious weight, and visible outer limit—was almost transparent. At the sight, he gasped. Seconds later, he moaned. Another foot had stepped on his ankle. He raised his head and watched the being step off his ankle and onto his chest. He groaned. *What the*—he thought.

A blinding light filled the area. He witnessed a throng of semi-transparent beings rushing at him—or so he thought. He jumped to his feet, as quickly as the crossover effects from the oak would permit, and darted from the path of the charging mob to a boulder close by. The see-through beings dashed past Dan. The explosion of light faded.

Free of the stampede, Dan leaned against the large rock to catch his breath. Experiencing a pounding headache, he touched the back of his head and discovered that his recent knock against the church pew—before being thrown into the oak—had drawn blood. With the present situation demanding his undivided attention, he wiped his bloody hand on his pants, reached into his pocket, and grabbed his flashlight.

"Not again. Why don't flashlights ever work for me?" he mumbled. He flipped the switch off and on, but with no luck. He tapped it against the boulder. A beam of light burst forth, but quickly faded and died. After several more failed attempts, he shoved the flashlight into his back pocket.

In minimal natural light, he glanced behind and saw a stonewall that was covered with gnarled branches and teeming with insects. One branch dweller dropped from the deadwood; he cringed. The water bug was more than three inches in length. The insect scurried to the safety of the limbs. The moist atmosphere was conducive to their propagation as the multitudes bore out. While not poisonous or life threatening, the squirming of thousands of insects gave the illusion that the wall was moving and had come to life. Dan turned from the sight and scanned the area of his confinement.

Though he could see only several feet ahead, he wondered, *Is this the parallel world?*

Another explosion of brilliance filled the area.

He took a further survey of his rock prison. He was perplexed with the transparent beings who were rushing in the opposite direction. Another visual sweep confirmed his suspicions that he was in an enormous cave. So large, in fact, that he couldn't see its distant side, even in the intense but short-lived light. The ceiling soared roughly fifty feet and was adorned with countless stalactites that perpetually released mineral-rich droplets to the ground.

Three water bugs climbed his pants.

He wildly shook his leg. Unsuccessful in dropping them, he brushed them to the floor where they raced to the wall and buried themselves among the dead branches. Seeing more water bugs at his feet, he jumped on top of the boulder and resumed his surveillance of the cave in the fading light.

He suspected that the transparent inhabitants were human. But at the same time, he harbored some doubts. During the latest beam of natural light, he noticed that unlike the rest of their bodies, the beings' eyes were not transparent. Still sitting on the rock, he easily looked through one cave dweller and into another being behind it. *How come I never saw these semi-humans in the parallel world?* he thought.

He was still comparing the two worlds when another blaze of light filled the cave. His eyes were immediately drawn to a large dirt mound where the glow originated. A golden chest materialized atop the incline. Intrigued, he jumped from the boulder. The ground shook unexpectedly. Thousands of partially transparent beings were dashing in the direction of the dirt mound. The cave dwellers ruthlessly competed against one another in pursuit of the prized golden chest.

Then it hit him. This must be why the inhabitants retained their eyesight. As he watched the quest for the prize unfold, he observed the lead inhabitant—now only inches from the golden chest—extend his see-through arm to claim his reward. The chest vanished.

After a period of darkness, another burst of light exposed the prize on a cave wall alongside a pool of stagnant water. The semi-humans raced from the dirt mound to the wall where the golden chest was wedged among the dead branches.

I wonder what's in the chest, he thought. *Maybe a priceless treasure; or maybe it holds the key to a plush and carefree life.* Before he knew it, he was in the midst of the cave dwellers darting to the golden chest. Questions about the inhabitants' ability and agility—not to mention

Dan's curiosity if they were penetrable—were quickly answered. He was savagely pushed in all directions by the beings in their relentless quest of the valued object. As a cave dweller reached for the prize, the golden chest vanished with the light. With the temporary halt of the stampede, silence permeated the damp cave. Dan and his co-inhabitants anxiously awaited the next burst of radiance.

He surveyed the dim area and spotted the cave's exit only a short distance from where he stood. *My way out,* he thought.

The passageway was roughly six feet high and equally as wide—large enough for him to walk through with ease. Moreover, the escape path was free of the gnarled branches and the unsightly water bugs.

He had taken only two steps in the direction of the exit when he was distracted by another surge of light. His thoughts switched from the passageway to the golden chest that had reappeared on top of a large rock. In his reckless dash to the boulder—together with thousands of other potential possessors—he thought, *Wow, Mom, Dad, and William would be so excited if I grabbed the golden chest and fulfilled all our family's dreams.* He quickened his pace and rammed his way near the front of the mob. *William has probably been thrown into this miserable place too, along with Father James and Sam,* he thought. *I mean, I saw the tree limbs grab William and Father James in the church.* A sobering reality hit him as he questioned inwardly, *What's wrong with me? Why am I obsessed with the golden chest when my brother and friends could be in danger?* He redirected his attention and focused on the exit which—thanks to his recent sprint to the golden object—was now a great distance away.

Halfway into his passageway retreat, he stopped. *Could William, Sam, Father James, and Brad Blaze be somewhere in this cave?* he thought. As he looked about, his thoughts continued, *This place is enormous. It'll take hours, if not days, to search every inch.* He turned from the exit and began what he feared most—advancing into the isolated regions of the shadowy cave. With each burst of brilliance at regular intervals, he scanned the area for any beings that were not transparent. With the ability to look through one being and into another, it took only a few minutes for him to realize that there were countless semi-humans quarantined in the cave. As much as he dreaded exploring the remote areas, the likelihood of his friends being in danger forced him to extend his search.

After what seemed a four-hour hike and inspection of the terrain, he decided to intensify his efforts—but at a great personal risk. "William! Sam! Father! Brad!" he yelled.

There was no response.

Sadly, within moments of his screams, he heard and clearly felt something drop to the ground. The fact that it knocked him and a handful of semitransparent beings off their feet, he feared something large was aware of his presence. As he watched the fallen inhabitants rise without speaking a word, he suspected they were incapable of screaming or even talking.

Quite unintentionally, Dan had drawn the attention of an unseen predator to himself.

"Come on," he whispered nervously. "Where's the burst of light?" He spun in all directions, hoping that no creature would come into view. Unlike his previous trip to the parallel world, he was totally defenseless. The weapons were in Sam's bag—wherever he was.

A flash of light finally brightened the cave.

Dan took full advantage of the brief illumination by scanning the rock world for as long as the light endured. No predator was seen, though he felt the ground move and sensed he was being watched. He convinced himself that his co-travelers were not in the cave and faced the exit, confident that a hushed approach would not attract the attention of whatever creature inhabited the cavernous world.

With another surge of light, he spotted not only the passageway a couple hundred feet ahead, but also took in another unlimited view of his surroundings for the unknown predator. Once the brightness faded, he resumed his fast trek in minimal light. *If a creature inhabits this place, I wonder if it will exit the cave,* he thought. *And what's on the opposite side?*

Another dazzling display of light sent numerous semitransparent beings in the opposite direction of the lone traveler to the relocated golden chest. With the cave dwellers far removed, he reduced the distance between himself and the exit in the fading light. After three more explosions of radiance, he was only feet from safety. He made a charge for the passageway, but ran into a rock wall and was knocked to the ground. The exit—like the golden chest—had vanished.

While flat on his back and madly brushing off water bugs that had clung to him during his collision with the wall, he was momentarily blinded by another flash of light. With the arrival of the intense glow, he eyed an object coiled around a stalactite overhead. The exit reappeared in the distance. He jumped to his feet.

The cave darkened.

With no light for the next three minutes, a nerve-racking silence pervaded the hollow ground. The inhabitants remained at a standstill, awaiting the next burst of brightness. Amid the calm, Dan heard a brushing movement and then a snap. With another blast of light, he spun and saw a hundred-foot-long anaconda cracking the spine of a semi-human only paces away. Another question was answered—the transparent beings were unable to scream even in unbearable pain.

The moment Dan's eyes met the yellow eyes of the serpent, the creature released its constrictive hold on the cave dweller, arched its head, and slithered in the direction of the newest arrival.

Almost certain that the passageway would shift the moment he tried to step through it again, the only alternative was to remain motionless and face imminent death. However, recalling his brother's and friends' safety, he decided to take his chances and bolted to the relocated exit.

A second anaconda which only recently was wrapped around a hanging rock fell to the ground.

In his race to the passageway, he trailed several semitransparent men who had witnessed the attack of their cave mate and were now dashing to the exit to escape the two serpents. For a fleeting moment, the threat of death overpowered the beings' desire for wealth. Unfortunately, like his attempted escape minutes earlier, the inhabitants ran into a stone wall. The passageway relocated even farther away.

With two anacondas on the hunt, Dan concealed himself within the throng of beings that were running in the opposite direction of the exit in pursuit of the golden chest which had materialized moments earlier. In the midst of being jabbed and knocked about, he racked his brain to think of an escape. Unfortunately, since the exit moved with every attempted breach, he feared it would be only a matter of time before he became the anacondas' next warm meal.

Another crash to the ground didn't go unnoticed. A second snap followed. *God no, not a third serpent,* he thought. Sadly, the latest collision was clearly felt. He suspected that the newest predator was close by.

Darkness filled the cave.

With the next bolt of light, he ran with the mob while constantly surveying the area for three serpents. Thankfully, the latest charge of the crowd headed in the direction of the new exit. *But what good is that if it'll vanish upon contact?* he thought. *There has to be a way through the passageway. Since it relocated on me and the semitransparent beings, there must be something we share that's forcing the exit to move.*

Another snap drew him from his thoughts. A cave dweller fell to the ground only seconds before Dan spotted a pair of yellow eyes glowing in the darkness. His latest dash within the multitudes had placed him within feet of the recently discovered exit. He spun from the approaching serpent. While turning, he tripped over a semitransparent corpse and fell on his back. He looked behind and was grateful that the exit was still in place and only six feet distant. Another burst of light caused him to jerk his head forward and face the anaconda that was rapidly closing in on him. Consumed with terror, he feverishly crawled backwards on his elbows. He completely dismissed the exit from his thoughts and remained engrossed with eluding the aggressive snake. Before he realized what had happened, he had cleared the passageway.

The anaconda, however, intensified its efforts.

Dan continued his backward escape several more feet until he hit a rock wall. He was trapped. As the serpent made its final side-to-side motion and was lunging its head to the passageway, the opening vanished. Still seated and pressed against the stone wall outside the cave, Dan passed out and fell to the ground.

Several minutes later, he awoke to movement on his shoulder. He jolted to a seated position. A rat fell from his shoulder and scurried up the rock cavern.

Dan staggered to his feet in bewilderment. The enormous open cavern that he had entered, while only several feet across from where he stood, widened ahead of him until it was nearly a hundred feet from wall to wall and equally as high. The main cavern was so immense that it assumed a Gothic appearance. Without warning, the entrance to the side cave that he had just left reappeared beside him. The anaconda on the opposite side, still craving its warm meal, sprang in Dan's direction. It was instantly repelled with the exit's disappearance.

I wonder how I was able to escape, he thought. *Maybe it had something to do with not eyeing the exit; maybe crawling backwards without looking at the opening set me free.* He ended his speculations by attributing his path to safety to blind faith.

"But I don't feel safe," he mumbled while peering ahead in the poorly lit cavern with no idea where it led. Like before, his brother's and friends' safety summoned the courage he needed to adventure into the unknown.

Nearly thirty minutes into his walk—although it was only a guess since he wasn't wearing a watch—the distance between the cavern walls drastically diminished until barely twenty feet separated them. Deciding to rest, he sat on the ground and leaned against the rock wall. Immediately, the ground shook. He bolted to his feet. Loathing the idea of encountering whatever lived in the open cavern, he raced ahead in near darkness. With no side caves or openings in the walls, he had no choice but to keep running. In the dim light, he glanced behind and caught sight of a five-foot-long crab with its four pairs of legs and two oversize anterior pincers pursuing its human prey. At once, Dan discovered reserved energy and darted even faster until he spotted a pool of water a short distance ahead.

Knowing he didn't have the luxury of time, since the colossal crab was quickly reducing the distance between them, he quickly scanned the murky water for predators before he was directly upon it. Seeing nothing in his hurried visual search, he jumped into the water.

Within seconds, he was chest deep in the pool and barely halfway across when he heard a splash to the left. He froze. Ominous ripples slowly approached. Though overly curious with what had dropped into the watery terrain, he was careful to turn only his head in the direction of the disturbance. There was nothing there. Certain that the crab wouldn't hesitate plunging into the water, he dashed for the distant shore.

"Please God, no," he whispered. He had stumbled and wedged his foot between two rocks on the water's bed. The teenager was an easy target. Before leaning forward to pull his leg free, he offered a quick backward glance and saw the king crab rushing into the pool. The ripples from the first intruder passed beyond Dan. He suspected that the unknown creature which had fallen into the water was nearby. In desperation, he submerged himself to free his foot from the rocks. From below the surface, he gulped water. He had looked behind and saw the legs of a creature—walking atop the water—intersecting the path of the giant crab.

The combat between the crab and the unidentified cavern dweller was violent. Even below the surface, the thrashing water caused Dan to lose his balance and fall forward with his foot still stuck between the rocks. After shaking his leg and nudging the rocks with his hands, he came up for air.

From the water's surface, he watched the crab thrust a deadly pincer at an enormous water spider. As the arachnid turned to dodge the crab's oncoming claw, Dan gasped. The fact that the spider was nearly four feet long didn't shock him as much as the fact that it was unlike anything he had encountered in the parallel world or could ever have imagined. It had a human face. During the spider's passing glimpse at the partially submerged teenager, Dan sensed it recognized its own kind. He refocused his efforts on freeing his foot while the spider and crab resumed their mortal battle.

The king crab tried to submerge its adversary, but the spider was quick to sink its fangs into the soft underside of the crab. It was partially paralyzed. With the motionless crab floating atop the pool, the spider temporarily abandoned its prey and walked upon the water toward Dan.

He stood perfectly still and attempted to remain as inconspicuous as possible. However, curiosity eventually consumed him. He looked over his shoulder.

A twitch from one of the crab's legs sent the spider racing in its direction to deliver another venomous bite. The spider dragged its victim to its den.

After several more tugs, Dan broke free. He raced through the water to the distant shore as fast as his twisted ankle would allow.

Nearly exhausted, he wanted nothing more than to rest, if only for a few minutes. But the grim reality that the water spider might return—not to mention the fact that his friends might also be encountering similar unearthly creatures—forced Dan to continue his exploration of the strange world.

He had walked nearly two miles, while constantly searching the cavern walls for openings, when the pain in his ankle became unbearable. He lowered himself and rested against the rock wall.

CHAPTER TWO

Ascent to Supremacy

AFTER SEVERAL MINUTES MASSAGING HIS ANKLE, DAN REMOVED his boot and sock. He looked ahead and was surprised to see a glowing torch wedged in a cavern wall. Though grateful for the light, at the same time, he was fearful knowing that something or someone lighted the torch and would probably return to reignite the flame once it died. He tried not to think of the likely encounter with the light keeper and directed his efforts at easing his pain. He wrapped his sock around his sprained ankle, replaced his boot, and staggered to his feet. Before resuming his hike up the open cavern—or tunnel—he took another look behind. He needed the assurance that the water spider was not on the offensive. Seeing nothing and hearing no movement, he turned and headed up the tunnel in search of his brother and friends.

In the midst of scanning the area for predators and side openings in the cavern wall, he noticed that the distance between the walls narrowed even further until the pathway was only three feet across—barely wide enough to walk through without rubbing his shoulders against the rock perimeter. Even worse, the path through the partially lit tunnel had taken a gradual decline, forcing water droplets from the ceiling to converge in the lower realms of the tunnel. Within minutes, he was wading through knee-high muddy water with no visual end in sight.

What was I thinking? he thought. *Why didn't I grab the torch?* Hoping he'd discover another one ahead, he continued his trudge through the stagnant water. A bite on his partially exposed ankle, the constant howling of wind through the narrow passageway, and the occasional sounds of life forms on the stone walls forced him to increase his pace—as much as his injured ankle would permit. After what he imagined to be a thirty-minute hike, he spotted another flicker of light in the distance.

He paused to catch his breath and suffered several more bites on his leg. Despite the fact that only minimal light filtered down the narrow cavern, it was enough for him to see that the passageway was widening—ever so gradually—to the point where his stride was now unhindered from his shoulders brushing against the walls. With a slight incline on the footpath, the murky waters gradually receded until it was just ankle deep. A short distance up the path, he was walking on moist soil between cavern walls that were now five feet apart and bathed in light.

He raised his pant leg. Five leeches were stuck to his calf. After several unsuccessful attempts at removing them by hand, he limped to the torch ahead, yanked it from the wall, and grazed the flame to his leg. Although the pain was excruciating, the blaze dislodged the parasites which fell to the ground and burrowed out of sight. Freed from the bloodsucking worms, he leaned against the cavern wall, extended the torch, and surveyed his new surroundings.

The ceiling must be twenty feet high, he thought, *and the walls—* His inspection ended abruptly when he spotted an unusually small opening ahead. He pushed himself from the wall. With the torch in hand, he hobbled to the newest entrance. During his approach, a dilemma seized him. As much as he feared entering the unknown side cave, he knew he had to search for his brother and friends in every conceivable place. That meant investigating every inch of the hollow world, including the latest discovered opening.

He dropped to his knees, extended the torch through the hole in the wall, and peered inside. Seeing no anacondas, he took a deep breath and crawled into the cave. Inside, he was pleased that the entire area was immersed in light that originated from a large hole in the ceiling roughly twenty feet above. Certain that he would need the torch upon his exit, he drove it into the moist soil at the cave's entrance.

He rose to his feet and took a panoramic view of the new inner rock world. This particular side cave, though also imprisoning a multitude of humans, was different from the cave of his confinement. Most notably, the inhabitants appeared normal—they were solid and not semitransparent. His scan of the surroundings was cut short by the rowdy cheers of humans who were staring at the hole in the ceiling. Immediately below the opening stood a wooden ladder that extended from the ground through the hole above. Dan watched in disbelief as human after human jostled each other to reach the ladder in their quest for the opening overhead. With each attempt, however, as an inhabitant climbed the ladder and neared the glowing hole, the rungs of the ladder split down the middle and dropped the climber twenty feet.

Dan remained motionless as several more humans attempted the seemingly impossible feat. Sadly, the results were the same—that is, until he saw a male climber clear the opening. A scream was heard within the hole. The overhead cry was so piercing that it was heard easily over the applause and cheers of the inhabitants below.

What's happening? Dan thought. He watched another human grab the first of four ladder rungs and begin his ascent. Dan's attention was redirected from the ladder to the throng of onlookers below the opening who were savagely elbowing one another for the next place in line.

"What am I doing?" he whispered. He removed his stare from the unruly mob and walked among the humans in search of Sam, Brad, Father James, and possibly William.

Although he hadn't actually seen his brother tossed into the oak, he knew the limbs had grabbed him in the church. He could only guess that his brother, like himself, was hurled into the oak.

The cave dwellers were extremely savage as each made his or her way to the towering ladder which was constructed of two thick vertical supports. Dan offered another passing glance. He halted his search efforts and watched a male inhabitant plummet twenty feet. Before he even hit the ground, another human was cheered on as she gripped the first rung.

Dan took one step forward. While eyeing the woman stretching for the second rung, he tripped over a partially embedded stone. He grabbed the arm of an inhabitant to avoid a fall. The cave dweller's arm was cold and clammy—nothing like he had expected. Dan hit the ground. As he lay on his stomach, he looked ahead and saw a wave of inhabitants racing in his direction. He madly crawled from their path and reached safety at a cave wall where he rested and massaged his ankle. He scanned the area for his friends.

Seeing no familiar faces, he reached above, grabbed a knotted branch that was rooted in the wall, and pulled himself up. The branch snapped from the wall. Though baffled that it was dislodged so easily, he discarded it to the ground.

Unknown to Dan—since his back was facing the wall—the newly created opening slowly crumbled until a large hole was exposed on the cave wall.

He continued his scan of the lit cave and plotted a route that would ensure minimal physical contact with the rowdy inhabitants.

Three spiders landed on Dan's shoulders. He bolted several feet while jerking frantically to drop the unwelcome hoppers. In his spastic movements, he turned and witnessed thousands of jumping spiders leaping from their inner cave encasement. He spun again, darted from the approaching spiders, and crashed into an inhabitant. Both hit the ground. Within seconds, Dan was covered from head to toe with the eight-legged critters. Even though he wasn't bitten, the sensation of hundreds of spiders crawling on him was mental anguish. After shaking the spiders from his face, he jumped to his feet and raced as fast and as far away from the spiders, ignoring his throbbing ankle.

Screams were heard.

He looked behind and saw six cave dwellers prostrate on the ground and covered with spiders. It was only then that he recalled his natural science class several months ago where he learned that certain arachnids thrive on dead skin cells. This memory, coupled with the fact that he distinctively felt the cold touch of an inhabitant just minutes earlier, caused him to suspect that the cave dwellers were not living—at least not in the traditional definition of the word. *This also would explain why the inhabitants on the ground near the wall are in agony whereas I didn't feel any physical pain under the weight of the spiders,* he thought.

One by one, other cave dwellers at the wall fell to the ground amid high-pitched screams. Even though their cries were deafening, they failed to distract the many humans below the ladder from their rallying cheers for the next climber.

Dan slowed his pace and ultimately came to a complete stop. He watched a man climb the ladder. As the cave dweller grasped the second rung, he nearly lost his grip. He quickly regained his hold, pulled himself up, and reached for the next rung. With nearly all eyes focused on the climber, a thunderous roar of excitement filled the cave when he pulled himself through the opening and vanished from sight. An overhead scream was heard. Another man leaped for the first rung.

The cries at the rear cave wall grew in intensity.

Although the spectators below the ladder were preoccupied with the climber, Dan's focus was drawn to the shrieks behind that were now relentless. He eyed a man on his knees reaching for a boulder and then lifting himself from the ground. Dan retched when the man stepped into full view. Obviously in extreme pain, the man's lower body—from his waist down—was nothing but a skeleton, whereas his upper torso remained relatively unscathed. A handful of spiders jumped onto his chest and continued their feeding frenzy. The man collapsed to the ground.

"My gosh!" exclaimed Dan. "What is this place?" He switched his gaze from the inhabitants who were being flayed and made a quick scan of the area. *If my friends are in this cave, God forgive me for abandoning them*, he thought.

The screams from behind reached fever pitch. Though Dan sensed he wasn't in any mortal danger with the spiders, nevertheless, their rapid advance in his direction drove him closer to the cave's exit. The thud of a climber crashing to the ground redirected his attention to the imposing ladder.

"Is that—" Dan whispered. He spotted a man wearing a familiar red plaid shirt and standing at the base of the ladder. He postponed his retreat to the cave's exit and approached the ladder.

"Sam!" he yelled.

The man made no sign of acknowledgment. He was absorbed with his leap for the first rung.

Dan yanked the cave dweller in his direction. "Sam!" he exclaimed. "It is you!"

ASCENT TO SUPREMACY

The man made no comment or act of recognition. He spun and stared at the first rung.

Dan stepped between his friend and the ladder.

The man pushed the teenager to the ground. His wide-eyed gaze on the ladder remained unchanged.

Before Dan could jump to his feet, the man had secured the first rung.

"Sam, what are you doing?"

The climber ignored the question and ascended to the second rung.

"The exit is that way!" Dan pointed to the small opening in the rock wall.

The man stretched for the third rung.

"Sam, we have to get out of here—now!"

Without warning, the rungs split down the middle and tumbled the climber to the ground. He jumped to his feet and raced to the ladder for a second attempt.

Dan jumped on Sam's back to frustrate his advance. His ploy worked. Another man secured the first rung.

"What's your problem?" screamed Sam. He threw Dan from his back to the ground. "You cost me another climb on the ladder."

"Sam, the exit is over there," insisted Dan. He pointed again to the three-foot-high opening in the cave wall.

Sam offered only a glimpse at the exit. He quickly focused on a man in a blue shirt ascending the ladder. While observing the climber's progress, he shouted, "Besides, I can't exit that way!"

"Why not?"

"I just can't!" Sam shouted.

"It's safer than climbing a ladder that leads to who knows where," said Dan.

Sam looked at the cave's exit again and then Dan. "If I go through there, then I'll have to bow or even worse, crawl in the dirt!"

"So, what's wrong with that?" asked Dan.

"I'll tell you what's wrong with that," snapped Sam. "I refuse to stoop to anyone or anything anymore. Nearly my entire adult life, I've been looked down upon." He raised his sights to the ladder whose uppermost vertical supports remained hidden within the opening and said, "But up there—that's my long-awaited chance to look down on others. Once I'm up there, people finally will look up to me!"

"Sam, what's gotten into you?" Any lingering doubts Dan had about the man's identity vanished. He squeezed Sam's arm. "There are plenty of people in Lawton who look up to you and respect you—me, for one."

Sam jerked his arm from Dan's grip. "That's not good enough!" he shouted. He pointed to the lit opening. "Up there, I'll be revered by the cave dwellers below. Besides, I know I can do it. I don't need anyone's help. I can do it alone."

"Sam, you're not making any sense. Just because—"

Dan's remark was drowned out by the applause of the cave dwellers who witnessed the man in the blue shirt disappear beyond the opening.

Another overhead scream was heard.

"Sam, this place isn't normal," said Dan. "Something's not right. We have to get out of here!"

Shrieks from the back of the cave commanded Dan's attention. He spun and watched dozens of inhabitants collapse to the ground amid an onslaught of jumping spiders. He turned to face Sam, exclaiming, "Our way out is through the wall, not through the ceiling! Why are you so arrogant? There's nothing wrong with bowing. And there's certainly nothing wrong with tasting a little dirt. It never bothered you before."

Sam grabbed Dan's arm and yelled, "You've obviously got a lot to learn!" He shoved Dan away.

A female climber stood on the first rung.

Puzzled with Sam's unnatural and unexplained obsession with the climb, Dan tried to think of something to lure his friend from the cave. He stepped in front of Sam again and posed, "What about finding Brad Blaze? Isn't he the reason you entered this world in the first place?"

Sam watched the female climber stand on the second rung. "I never even knew the man," he mumbled.

"And what about Father James?" asked Dan. "Has he helped you so little over the past several weeks that you'd turn your back on him and let him die in this wretched place? After all, he was one of the first Lawtonians who welcomed you with open arms."

Sam lowered his gaze from the ladder and glared at Dan. "What? Father James is here?"

Dan—sensing that he may have been indirectly responsible for the priest's abduction to the unknown world—cast his sights to the ground. "I think so."

Sam grabbed Dan by the throat. "Why on earth did you lead him here?"

Dan broke free of Sam's grip. "I didn't lead him here," he defended. "He, William, and I were in the church the night of your leap when the oak limbs exploded through the windows, captured the three of us, and threw us into the tree."

"Your brother's here too?"

"I think so. I was tossed into the oak after Father James. Though I never actually saw William thrown into the tree, I saw the limbs grab him in the church. So I'm sure he's somewhere in this world."

"Well, where are they?" asked Sam.

"I don't know." Dan looked to the flayed cave dwellers and recounted, "I ended up in another cave a couple miles back that had a golden chest and a few anacondas. But somehow I escaped." He switched his weight from his injured ankle. "I searched the cave for you and the others, but I didn't find anyone." He took a sweeping view of Sam's rock prison. "Have you seen the others in here?"

Sam remained fixated with the opening in the ceiling. "No, I just materialized in that spot." He pointed several feet away, but never removed his overhead stare. "And I'm not aware of anyone else appearing since my arrival."

Dan was determined to release Sam from his fascination with the ladder. He grabbed his shoulder and reported, "I did a quick search of this cave, but I didn't discover anything—except jumping spiders at the back wall."

Sam lowered his gaze to the ground. "Spiders! I hate those disgusting things." He turned to face Dan. "Sorry I choked and shoved you earlier. I don't understand my attraction to this ladder."

"I don't either," admitted Dan. "It's like something's taken possession of you." Impatient to leave the hollow ground, he grabbed Sam's arm and pointed him in the direction of the cave's exit.

"I wish I knew why I was so determined to climb through the opening in the ceiling." Sam stepped away from the ladder. "I just don't get it."

"I'm sure we'll figure it out later. But for now, we need to find the others."

At the exit, Dan bent over and snatched his burning torch from the ground. "Hey wait a minute!" he exclaimed. "Where's your backpack with the lances? We'll need them."

"Dan, this is a peaceful world now. We won't need the weapons."

"Trust me, I could have used them a couple times already. The anacondas in my cave were abnormally aggressive."

Sam looked around the rock world trying to recall where he left his backpack. "There it is!" he eventually shouted while pointing to the ladder's base. "I dropped it on the ground when I arrived. I'll be only a minute."

Dan was convinced that his friend would become re-enchanted with the ladder. "Sam, crawl through the opening," he ordered. "I'll grab the bag."

"But it'll take just a minute." He took two steps nearer the bewitched ladder.

Dan grabbed his arm. "Get through the exit. I'll be fine."

Sam dropped to his knees and unwillingly crawled through the exit.

With his torch in hand, Dan neared the ladder. While grabbing the backpack, he inadvertently brushed the flame against the ladder's right vertical support.

An overpowering screech came from the ceiling's opening. The ladder rungs split down the middle and dropped a female climber.

The shriek forced a curious Sam to re-enter the cave where he witnessed one of the upright supports collapsing to the ground within only yards of his friend.

Before the dust from the collision had settled, Sam and Dan eyed the vertical beam lift itself off the ground, revealing a twenty-five-foot-long walking stick with the shreds of a blue shirt dangling from its mouth. Since the creature landed between the teenager and the cave's exit, Dan had no choice but to flee into the deeper recesses of the rocky confinement with the torch and backpack in hand.

Though weaponless, Sam darted into the haze to rescue his friend.

Despite the fact that the walking stick was a slow mover, its six-foot stride made it an unrivaled adversary.

Dan dashed in the direction of the feasting spiders which had devoured the flesh from nearly fifty cave dwellers.

Several yards from its prey, the creature slowed its pace when it found Dan trapped against a wall.

Dan pulled a lance from the bag before dropping it and the torch to the ground.

Each of the creature's three lunges was deflected by the weapon.

Under the cloak of the dusty haze, Sam crept behind the walking stick. "Throw me a lance!" he shouted.

The creature turned its head and spotted another potential meal.

With the beast's head directed at Sam, Dan tossed his lance which landed several feet from his friend. With the predator still focused on a motionless Sam, the teenager pulled another weapon from the backpack and targeted the creature's neck. Unfortunately, only a flesh wound was inflicted.

The beast shrieked and jerked its head in Dan's direction. A running charge was made at the teenager who turned and leaped through the crumbling wall and into the nest of jumping spiders.

Sam took advantage of the beast's interest in his co-traveler. He raced to the grounded weapon and hurled it into one of the beast's eight legs.

The walking stick suspended its attack on Dan and turned to confront its new mortal enemy.

With the beast's back facing the rear wall, Dan bolted from the inner sanctuary and grabbed another lance from the backpack.

Hearing shuffling from behind, the creature rotated its head once more.

With precision, Dan impaled its neck. The creature fell to the ground—atop several flayed inhabitants—in a pool of blood.

"Awesome shot!" yelled Sam.

"Come on!" shouted Dan. "Let's get out of here!"

THE SINISTER REALM

Sam yanked the lances from the carcass while Dan snatched the torch and backpack.

En route to the exit, the men nearly hit the ground when the second vertical support crashed to the cave floor.

Only now, Dan and Sam realized that the walking sticks had interlocked four of their legs on one side to form the ladder rungs, while the legs on the opposite side were cleverly concealed—flush against the supposed vertical supports.

The travelers kept a close eye on the area below the ceiling's opening during their sprint to the exit. They hoped to increase the distance between themselves and the charging carnivore.

At the exit, Dan wasn't surprised when his friend refused to drop to his knees. "Sam—go!" he yelled.

Sam remained standing, staring below at the small opening. "I can't," he whispered.

Dan looked behind at the rushing creature. "Do it!" He knocked Sam to the ground and pushed him through the exit.

Once Sam was on the opposite side, Dan was only a second behind. Barely two feet separated the head of the walking stick from Dan's boots.

The instant Dan cleared the exit, Sam kicked him away from the opening.

The flesh-eating creature rammed its head through the passageway.

Sam thrust a lance into its neck.

The tenacious creature attempted another snap at the teenager who lay on the ground only feet away.

Sam dislodged the embedded spear and sank it into the beast a second time, robbing it of its life.

"Thanks," said a breathless Dan.

"Don't mention it." Sam pulled the spear from the expired creature. After helping Dan to his feet, he apologized for his unexplained delay in crawling through the exit which nearly cost them their lives. "I don't understand my attraction to the living ladder or why I hesitated crawling through the opening," admitted Sam.

"I don't know either," replied Dan. "But there's got to be a logical explanation." He grabbed the torch from the ground and posed,

"For some reason, raising yourself through the ceiling's opening was more appealing to you than lowering yourself to the dirt and crawling through the exit."

Eager to change the embarrassing subject, Sam looked up and down the open tunnel. "So which way do we go?"

Dan pointed to the left. "That way," he directed. "The right leads to the cave with the golden chest and the anacondas. Trust me; I don't want to revisit that place."

Sam noticed a troubled look on his friend's face. "What's on your mind?"

"Things aren't right in this world," said Dan.

"What do you mean?"

"Well for starters, I've never heard of anacondas being so aggressive; I mean, overly hostile," explained Dan. "And I know that walking sticks in our world have three pairs of legs, not four."

"But we're not in our world," reminded Sam.

"I know. But I still sense that something's not right."

With each bearing a weapon, the explorers headed up the cavern in search of Father James, Brad Blaze, and possibly William.

CHAPTER THREE

Dispelled Doubts

IN THE TRAVELERS' WORLD OF BIRTH, THE FAMILIES STOOD in the church parking lot discussing the grim reality that their children were missing again along with Father James.

"Sara, I'm sure Cindy's fine and that we'll find her soon," assured Nancy. Knowing that her friend was in no condition to drive, she offered, "You ride home with Jeff and me and the Parkers. We'll try putting the pieces together over a warm breakfast." She glanced at Sara's car that was haphazardly parked against the street curb. "We'll get your car later."

"Where can Cindy be?" asked Sara. "She promised she'd never enter the tree again. She promised!"

"Shh," consoled Nancy. She rested Sara's head on her shoulder in a display of comfort. "We'll get to the bottom of this. But in the meantime, I want you to stay at our house today and away from the silence of your own home."

Sara struggled to voice her acceptance, but only cried.

The drive to the Clays' house was uncomfortably quiet. Each parent was engrossed in the possible location of their children and their safety.

"Our children promised they'd never step foot inside the tree," reminded Nancy.

Silence filled the car.

"But for argument's sake, let's say they did," she continued. "Then

I'm sure they're in a peaceful world. After all, before Sam made his leap, he told us it was exactly that—peaceful."

None of the passengers voiced their agreement or denial of her claim.

"If they entered the tree—which I seriously doubt—they were probably having such a good time with Ceremonia and Salvus that they missed the full moon departure earlier this morning," suggested Nancy. She looked out the car window and inconspicuously wiped a tear from her cheek before concluding, "If they stepped into the tree, I'm sure they'll return next month."

Again, stillness prevailed until Jeff pulled into the driveway.

Nancy pushed her own worries aside and tried to console Sara as she helped her to the front porch. "Come inside, Sara. We'll talk over a cup of coffee and breakfast."

The ladies stepped into the foyer.

Nancy sensed that her home had embraced a deadly silence since rushing to the church earlier that morning. Her entire world had been turned upside down in an hour. Although she couldn't describe the feeling, it was identical to what she experienced when learning of Dan's initial disappearance to the parallel world. Deep down, she suspected that her sons might be in danger, but she never disclosed her unconfirmed fears to Sara or the Parkers who were seating themselves on the living room sofa in a dazed state. She excused herself and entered the kitchen where she reheated the breakfast.

Jeff opened the dreadful conversation by relating to his guests how he discovered his boys' disappearance earlier that morning. "Nancy and I thought they may have walked to the church before sunrise to welcome Sam back from his journey."

"Did they say they'd be meeting Sam at the church?" asked Marie.

"Not exactly," he mumbled. Jeff rose from a recliner, approached the latest family portrait hanging above the mantel, and remarked, "But since the boys have spent so much time with Sam since their return from the parallel world, it wouldn't surprise me if they headed to Saint Augustine's. As a matter of fact, when Sam was leaving the house for the church the boys asked if they could walk with him to the tree. Nancy and I said no, since we suspected they'd be tempted to visit Salvus and Ceremonia."

Tom watched Jeff stare at the family photo. He knew his neighbor was finding it difficult reliving his sons' disappearance. "Jimmy and Cindy headed to the movie theater last night," Tom explained. "Ever since Jimmy's return from the parallel world, Marie and I have insisted that he let us know where he's going when he leaves the house at night and made him promise he'd call if he was running late. Up until last night, even we were surprised that Jimmy was true to his word. We always knew where he was. I guess we're still terrified for his safety, even though we're sure he can take care of himself." Tom rose and neared Jeff at the mantel. "I guess it's our parental instincts that refuse to admit Jimmy's capable of fending for himself—just as Dan and William are capable of doing."

The ladies remained seated on the sofa. Marie put her arm across Sara's shoulders and comforted, "I'm sure that Cindy and Jimmy are fine." Believing it would be good for Sara to express her feelings, Marie handed her a tissue and urged, "Tell us how you discovered Cindy was missing."

Sara blew her nose and cleared her throat. "I came home very early this morning from an out-of-town meeting," she began. "Since I was excited to see Cindy, I raced down the hall and threw open her bedroom door. I was stunned with the empty room and the made bed. I immediately suspected the worst. After searching the house and calling Cindy's friends, I drove to your homes to see if she was there." Sara leaned forward and rested her head in her hands. "Anyway, after no one answered at either house, I drove downtown. You can imagine the thoughts that went through my head when I saw flashing lights on a patrol car near the church and a crowd of spectators gathering nearby. And, well you know the rest of the story."

Nancy entered the living room and told her guests that breakfast was ready.

As Sara neared the open kitchen doorway, she paused and recalled the previous homecoming dinner party where her daughter bravely defended her and the Parkers from a troll in the kitchen. Refusing to dwell on the past and determined to find Cindy again, she conquered her emotions and stepped into the room.

DISPELLED DOUBTS

During the meal, the families agreed that they would resume their morning visits in the church to pray for the safe return of their children, Sam, Brad Blaze, and Father James.

"I wonder who will celebrate Mass in Father James's absence," posed Marie.

"I'm not sure," replied Jeff. "But I guess we'll find out tomorrow."

The remainder of the meal witnessed each parent recounting a story of the group's initial trip to the parallel world and how their children worked together to outsmart the savage creatures. Though no one admitted the obvious, it was unmistakable that they were trying to instill hope that their loved ones would return safely again.

After several hours of mutual support—both at the breakfast table and in the living room throughout the afternoon—the Parkers excused themselves, but not before offering Sara a ride downtown to her car.

Sara accepted.

As the Clays escorted their guests to the front door, Nancy and Jeff reminded them that they'd meet the next morning in church. Nancy grasped Sara's hand and strongly advised that she spend the night after picking up her car.

Sara politely declined the offer saying that she'd rather sleep in her own home.

"I understand," said Nancy. "But if you change your mind, there's a room here for you."

"Thank you," she replied. "I'll see you in the morning at church."

The next day proved unseasonably muggy. While grabbing their umbrellas, Jeff knew his wife was deeply troubled. Neither parent could believe they were childless again and praying for another miracle. He placed his arm around her. "They're resourceful kids. They'll be fine."

"I know they will," she said, "with heaven's help."

As expected, the church parking lot was nearly full for Sunday Mass. Jeff was helping Nancy from the car when he spotted Sara's sedan parked closest to the church doors.

The Parkers pulled into the lot.

"Good morning," greeted Jeff, once Tom and Marie stepped from their car.

"Morning," they replied. "Is Sara here?"

"Yeah." Jeff pointed to her car.

The Parkers stepped alongside the Clays.

"I wish Sara would have stayed with you and Nancy or at our house last night," said Tom.

"I know," agreed Jeff. "But given her condition, I think it's best that we don't force her to do something she's not ready to do."

"I suppose you're right," Tom conceded. "During our drive, Marie and I were wondering if there will even be a priest this morning since Father James only recently disappeared."

Jeff rested his hand on Tom's shoulder. "Let's step inside," he directed.

With several window openings boarded up, the interior of the church had lost much of its grandeur that the parishioners had taken for granted for many years.

The families neared the fifth pew where Sara was deep in prayer.

"Good morning," whispered Nancy.

Sara raised her head from atop her folded hands.

"May we join you?" asked Nancy.

"Of course." Sara slid a few feet to the left.

After greetings were exchanged between the families, all implored silently the Almighty's protection on their missing children and friends. A bell chimed, signaling the beginning of Mass. All rose from their kneelers.

To the group's astonishment, Father Andreas Schmitz—the priest in residence for a brief period at the parish two years ago—entered the sanctuary. Since Nancy knew that she and the other families would have to persuade him not to cut down the oak, she was grateful that the priest was someone she knew.

Immediately following the Mass, Nancy reminded the families that before they began their prayers below the statue of Saint Michael they had to speak with Father Andreas about the tree.

Speculating—although not entirely certain—that the oak would be the answer to their children's safe return, the families agreed.

Father Andreas stood at the church doors speaking briefly with his parishioners as they stepped from the House of God. Once the worshipers left, the group approached him.

DISPELLED DOUBTS

"Good morning, Father," greeted Nancy.

"Morning...um...Nancy, is it?" he asked.

She extended her hand to welcome him to the parish. "Yes Father. You have an excellent memory."

"I try to remember the names of all my parishioners, both present and former." After a moment's hesitation, he expressed, "Even though I just arrived at the parish, I've heard of your tragic misfortune. I'm so sorry."

"Thank you, Father," Nancy expressed.

Still holding her hand, he added, "Tell me, have there been any developments on the whereabouts of your children or Father James?"

"Actually Father, that's what we wanted to speak with you about," interrupted Jeff.

"How's that?" he asked.

Nancy suspected that her husband didn't know how or where to begin. She released her hand from the priest and asked, "Father, do you believe in the paranormal?"

"The paranormal?"

"Yes," she confirmed.

"Well," he explained, "during my years at the seminary, students were briefed on various phenomena. But we were warned that delving too much into such matters could stunt or even kill one's faith life. Why do you ask?"

Nancy knew that he should know the whole story and not simply bits and pieces. She suggested that the group sit in the last pew.

Once updated, the priest stood and glared at the parents. "I've heard some pretty outlandish stories during my priesthood, but this one is beyond probability. You actually expect me to believe that Father James, Sam White, Brad Blaze, and your children may have entered a parallel world through the oak tree on the church's front lawn?"

"Father, I know it sounds bizarre," admitted Tom. "Heck, even I had serious doubts when I first learned of the tree. But the injuries our children suffered confirm their stories."

"Please Father, all we're asking is that you not remove the tree in case they entered the oak again," implored Nancy.

The priest glanced from face to face. He failed to detect any falsehood in their eyes. "All right, I won't cut it down," he reluctantly agreed. "I'll do as you asked for the potential safety of your children and Father James."

"Thank you, Father," said Marie.

"But just because I agreed to let the oak stay for the time being doesn't mean that I believe your story," stressed the priest.

The parents weren't bothered by his skepticism. The tree was staying; that was all that mattered to them.

The group stepped from the pew.

"Father, when our children and Sam disappeared the first time, Father James encouraged us to pray every morning after Mass for their safe return," informed Jeff. "Actually, he led us in prayer."

The priest knew what he was asking. "Yes," he offered, "I'll lead you in prayer for their safe return from wherever they may be." Concerned that his earlier comment may have been misinterpreted as uncaring, he emphasized, "Look, I don't mean to be judgmental about your claim that your children entered a parallel world through a tree. But I can't emphasize enough the dangers to your faith life if you explore the paranormal."

"We understand, Father," said Jeff. "I only hope you never learn the truth of our story firsthand."

Not wanting to pursue the conversation further, the priest disregarded Jeff's warning.

As the families knelt below the heavenly statue, their children's stories of the heroic acts of the archangel and how he guarded them on their initial journey brought indescribable comfort to the parents. Despite the fact that no one was certain whether or not their loved ones had stepped into the oak, they maintained their unconfirmed suspicions and prayed for their protection.

In the midst of her meditation, Nancy sensed something different about the statue. The cause of her concern, however, escaped her. Her visual inspection of the marble artwork was interrupted by Father Andreas asking her to lead the next decade of the rosary.

Shortly before 9:30 a.m., the group ended their prayers and headed to the back doors.

"Thank you, Father," said Nancy. Her appreciation was supported by the entire party.

DISPELLED DOUBTS

"You're welcome," he replied. "I'll be here tomorrow morning if you'd like me to join your prayer group."

"Oh yes, that would be great," blurted Nancy.

"Then I'll see you tomorrow." He bid farewell and walked to the sacristy.

At Sara's request to have a few private words with the women during their drive home, Jeff and Tom stepped into their vehicles and drove from the parking lot.

Within minutes, the women were also driving up Main Street with Sara behind the wheel. Though initially deep in thought, a discussion regarding the next full moon inevitably developed.

"If our children entered the oak and are in the parallel world again, do you really think it's a peaceful world this time?" asked Sara.

"At this point, we don't know with any certainty that they entered the tree," reminded Nancy. "But if they did, then yes, I think they're in a peaceful world." Although Nancy still entertained doubts about the children's safety—especially after seeing a demonic face at the base of the oak—she refused to share her deep-rooted concerns. *Why needlessly worry anyone if there's no proof the children entered the tree or that they're in any danger,* she thought.

Seated in the rear seat, Marie leaned forward and proposed the harsh reality. "Even if it's a peaceful world, it's still possible that our children could injure themselves and be unable to reach the tree before the next full moon."

The car swerved onto the road's shoulder. Sara's sharp tug on the steering wheel pulled the car back onto the roadway. Marie toppled in the back seat while Nancy grasped the dashboard for dear life. Marie's remark obviously had disrupted Sara's concentration.

"I'm sorry, Sara," apologized Marie once sitting upright. "I didn't mean to upset you, but we have to be realistic."

A pause followed as the passengers regained their composure.

The silence was ultimately broken by Marie, stating, "It's nice that we're trying to be hopeful, but we also need to weigh the facts. For example, why hasn't anyone mentioned the blood near the Communion rail? I, for one, can't get the thought out of my—"

"The blood in the church could have been anyone's!" shouted Nancy. She was fearful of a head-on collision. "And it could have been caused by anything. I seriously doubt that the blood at the Communion rail was our children's."

Nancy's logic eased Sara's overactive imagination.

Another moment of silence flooded the car before Marie explained, "Nancy, I mentioned earlier the possibility our children could be injured for a reason."

Nancy turned sideways in the front seat to view Marie. "Why's that?" she asked.

"It might be a good idea that our husbands make the journey next month through the tree—like Sam went in search of Brad Blaze—in case our kids can't make it home," explained Marie.

Nancy was struck to the core. She knew that Marie had a legitimate point. Though she would fear for her husband's safety, she wanted nothing more than to have her sons back home again. She gathered her thoughts and compromised, "I have faith in our kids and in their ability to defend themselves. I mean, they more than proved it at the homecoming dinner party. So I don't think it would be wise to ask our husbands to take the trip during the next full moon. Let's give our kids at least until that time to return home. If they don't return next month, then we can discuss your option with our husbands for the following full moon. Remember, Marie, we don't have any proof that they stepped foot inside the oak."

Marie rested back in the seat. "I suppose you're right. Maybe we should give our kids until the next full moon to return. But I can't promise you that I won't discuss the possible trip with Tom."

"I'm sorry if I seemed cross with you," apologized Nancy. "It's just that I don't think it would be prudent to ask our husbands to endanger their lives, especially since we don't know for sure where our kids are."

"I understand," said Marie. She stared out the window at the high school, mumbling, "I only hope they come home soon."

Sara turned the corner onto Beacon Lane and pulled into Nancy's driveway.

"Sara, come on in," invited Nancy.

"Thanks, but I'd like some time alone."

"I understand," said Nancy. "But if you want to talk, you've got my phone number."

Nancy and Marie stepped from the car and entered their homes. Sara drove away while tapping the horn.

Nancy had no sooner opened the front door when the telephone rang. She dashed to the kitchen.

"Mrs. Clay?" was heard from the other end of the line.

"Yes, this is she."

"This is Officer Moore."

"Did you find someone?" blurted Nancy.

"No. We haven't uncovered any new leads. Actually, I'm calling to see if Officer Nelson and I could meet with you and your husband tomorrow morning to fill in a few questions on our police report."

"Yes—yes of course," said Nancy, "anything to help find our boys." Moments later, she concluded by agreeing to meet with the officers at 9:30.

Jeff slipped into the kitchen through the back door.

After informing him of the phone call and that there were no developments in the case, Nancy told him that two police officers wanted to meet with them in the morning.

"Absolutely," he said. "I'll take off as much time from work as they need."

"Thanks honey." She stared out the window, asking, "What were you doing in the backyard?"

"Raking a few leaves. It helps keep my mind off—you know."

"But there can't be that many leaves since it's only—"

The phone rang.

Nancy lifted the receiver. The screen door slammed behind her husband.

"Nancy, it's Marie," came from the other end of the line.

"Is anything wrong?" asked Nancy.

"I don't know. Did you get a phone call from the police?"

"Yes, just moments ago. Why?"

"Officer Moore just phoned me and asked if she and another officer could meet with Tom and me tomorrow morning," explained Marie.

"They want to meet with Jeff and me tomorrow morning also," said Nancy. "I suspect they want to talk with our families separately to see if our stories contradict."

"Should we tell them the truth about the tree?" asked Marie.

"I don't know, especially since we're not sure the oak is the culprit this time," reminded Nancy. "Why don't you and Tom come over for dinner tonight around seven o'clock. We'll discuss it together. In the meantime, I'll invite Sara. I'm sure she'll receive a call from the police as well."

"That sounds like a good idea. I'll see you tonight." After apologizing for needlessly alarming her and Sara during their drive from the church, Marie said good-bye.

Nancy hung up the phone but remained in the kitchen. She had a hunch that Sara would call any moment.

Within seconds, the phone rang.

"Hello," greeted Nancy.

"Nancy, it's Sara."

"You got a phone call from Officer Moore, didn't you?" questioned Nancy.

"How'd you know?"

"The officer already called Marie and me," related Nancy.

"What do you think they're after?" asked Sara.

"Probably just gathering more information, which is why I think you and the Parkers should have dinner with Jeff and me tonight to discuss what we should and shouldn't say."

"What time do you want me over?" asked Sara.

"Stop by around seven," invited Nancy. "But feel free to come over earlier if you want to talk."

"Thanks. I'll be there shortly before seven."

After hanging up the phone, Nancy struggled to calm her nagging thoughts about what should and should not be revealed to the police. She spent the duration of the morning and afternoon hours cleaning the house and making meal preparations for the evening's guests.

Jeff stepped into the kitchen through the back porch door shortly before 5:00. "Hi honey," he greeted.

Nancy closed the oven door. "Hello dear." She raced to the refrigerator to gather seasonings. "Would you mind setting the table for me?"

DISPELLED DOUBTS

"No problem." He noticed five sets of dinnerware on the counter. "Are we having company tonight?"

Engrossed with readying the house and meal for her guests, Nancy had neglected to tell her husband. "I'm sorry," she apologized. "I forgot to tell you that I invited the Parkers and Sara over for dinner. After Officer Moore contacted us about our meeting tomorrow morning, she called Marie and Sara to schedule separate appointments with them. I thought it would be a good idea to have them over to discuss what we should tell the officers."

"That's fine." He watched his wife pull five napkins from a holder. "What do you mean what we should tell the officers?"

She grabbed a bowl from an overhead cabinet and turned to her husband, clarifying, "I mean, should we tell them about the oak or not?"

"I don't know. On the one hand, I don't think we should since we're not certain the kids are in the parallel world. But then again, I don't like withholding anything from the police." He carried five plates from the counter to the table. "Maybe we should ask the Parkers and Sara what they think."

"Part of me wants to tell the truth about the oak," Nancy confessed. "But the chances that the police will believe our story are slim to none." After placing the glasses on the table, she concluded, "Let's see what the others have to say. Tom seems pretty levelheaded."

Between periodic checks on the meat over the next two hours, Jeff and Nancy relaxed in the living room and reminisced about their sons' last adventure. Several times during their laughter and tears, Nancy debated mentioning Marie's suggestion that Jeff and Tom make the journey in the near future. However, each time the thought surfaced, she dismissed it, rationalizing that if she put her husband in needless danger she'd never forgive herself. Deep down, she knew that her boys would look out for each other. She only hoped they would return safely.

During Nancy's fifth and final trip to the oven, a knock was heard at the front door.

"I'll get it!" yelled Jeff from the living room. He darted into the foyer where he welcomed Marie and Tom.

"Thanks for the invite," expressed Marie. "I think it's a good idea that we're all on the same page before we meet with the police tomorrow morning."

"Yeah," agreed Jeff. "We need to have our facts straight." He was just closing the door when he saw Sara pulling into the driveway.

"Hello Jeff," greeted Sara as she stepped onto the porch.

"Come on in, Sara. Make yourself at home," he offered.

Sara entered the living room where the other guests had already made themselves comfortable on the sofa.

Nancy stepped from the kitchen, asking, "Can I get anyone something to drink?"

"May I trouble you for a glass of water?" asked Sara.

"It's no trouble." She looked at Tom and Marie.

"No thanks, we're fine," said Marie.

Moments after Nancy returned with a glass of water, Jeff approached the fireplace and turned to face his guests, saying, "Nancy suggested that we meet tonight to discuss what we should tell the police. More specifically, should we tell them about the oak or not?"

"Personally, I think the police should know—just in case our children entered the tree," voiced Marie. "If nothing else, they'll keep a close eye on the oak and make sure it's not removed. I know Father Andreas promised he wouldn't cut it down, but it sure wouldn't hurt having the police keep a watchful eye on it too."

"I agree," seconded Sara. "Even if our children didn't enter the tree, I think the police should be told of its dangerous qualities—if for no other reason than to prevent other people from falling prey to it."

Nancy bent over and lit a candle on a side table. "I also think we should tell the police," she said. "It's reached the point now that whenever I see the officers I feel like I've betrayed them. It still bothers me that we had to make up stories where our children were once they returned from the parallel world. And remember, the police devoted many hours in their search."

Tom shared Marie's opinion; Jeff supported his wife's reasoning.

Nancy returned the matchbook to the drawer and concluded, "Then I guess it's settled. We'll tell the police the truth tomorrow."

DISPELLED DOUBTS

She took a few steps nearer the kitchen and announced, "I think the pot roast is ready."

As Nancy and Jeff expected, within minutes of finishing the meal, Sara thanked her hosts and excused herself. The Parkers soon followed.

The next morning, shortly after the Clays had returned from prayers at the church, a knock was heard at the front door. They welcomed the police into their home and suggested they meet in the kitchen over a cup of coffee.

"Nancy and Jeff, have either of you noticed anything peculiar about your sons' behavior during the past few weeks?" asked Officer Moore.

"No," they replied.

"Do you have any reason to suspect that they were planning a trip of some kind—say with their friends?" she continued.

"No, there was nothing out of the ordinary," assured Nancy. She rose from the table and approached the counter. She stared out the window to the backyard and blurted, "Officers, there's something you should know."

"What's that?" asked Officer Moore.

Nancy turned to face the policewomen and related her sons' journey to the parallel world through the oak in the forest. Throughout her twenty-minute account, she unknowingly paced the kitchen floor.

At the conclusion of her story, Officer Moore slammed her notepad on the kitchen table, shouting, "Look, the police department is sorely understaffed. We don't have time for this garbage! How dare you waste headquarters' time with such stories!"

"But officer, it's the truth," insisted Nancy.

"And is there anyone who can verify these parallel world stories?" demanded the policewoman.

Nancy lowered her head, acknowledging, "The only people who can support our story are missing."

Officer Moore rose from her seat, glared at the Clays, and warned that their withholding information in the past—as ridiculous as it may have been—was still grounds for impeding an investigation.

THE SINISTER REALM

"When you learned the truth of where your sons were, why didn't you report it to the police?"

"Because we knew how absurd it would sound," admitted Jeff. "Since our boys were home, we didn't see the need to bother the police further."

Officer Nelson followed in the steps of her partner through the living room to the front door.

The Clays trailed.

Before reaching for the doorknob, Officer Moore turned and faced the Clays. "Even though you refused to share facts with us in the past, it's our sworn duty to serve and protect. Having said that, we'll continue with our search for all missing persons in this case. But I warn you, if you keep any information from this moment forward—"

"We promise to notify you on anything and everything," interrupted Jeff.

"Then I expect to hear from you if you remember anything unusual," concluded Officer Moore.

"Yes. Thank you, officers," said Nancy.

The police stepped onto the porch and headed to the Parkers' house.

Nancy peered through the living room window and waited until the police had left the Parkers' home. Each officer bore a look of frustration. It was obvious to Nancy that Tom and Marie had also divulged stories which the police found troubling and unbelievable.

After concluding their interview with Sara, the officers decided to inspect the church again.

The police were welcomed at Saint Augustine's by Father Andreas who inquired about any leads in the case. After being informed of the dead end in the investigation, the priest excused himself and returned to the rectory.

As the police walked up the center aisle, a reflection on the floor—beneath a pew—caught Officer Moore's attention. She discovered a key and key chain.

In the process of gathering the broken stained glass from the floor and covering the window openings with wood, the mainte-

DISPELLED DOUBTS

nance crew had failed to spot the key that was resting against a pew's vertical support.

The policewoman placed the key in a plastic bag and dropped it into her pocket as potential evidence of a crime scene.

As Officer Nelson neared her partner, she received a call on her portable radio of a disturbance at Gogat's Bed-and-Breakfast.

En route to the church doors, Officer Moore pulled the plastic bag from her pocket and noticed a red marking on the key. Given her extensive experience in crime scene investigations, she knew it was blood. *But whose,* she thought, *Father James's or an alleged church burglar?* The moment the church door closed behind her and her partner, she tried inserting the key into the lock. It was not a match.

"Whose key is that?" asked Officer Nelson.

"I found it under a pew and thought it might be Father James's key." She returned the evidence to her pocket. "We better get to Gogat's."

Once a man was apprehended for attempting to use a stolen credit card at the bed-and-breakfast, the policewomen delivered him to headquarters.

After informing Officer Nelson that she had a few more questions for the Clays, Officer Moore asked her partner to process the man while she paid a visit to Nancy and Jeff.

Officer Nelson agreed.

Since Jeff had taken off work the remainder of the day, he and Nancy were just sitting down for lunch when a knock was heard at the front door. Jeff stepped into the foyer. "Officer," he greeted.

Curious who the visitor was, Nancy poked her head through the kitchen doorway. Seeing the policewoman, she stepped alongside her husband.

"Good afternoon, Nancy," said the officer. She shoved her hand into her pocket. "After visiting with you this morning, my partner and I decided to inspect the church again for possible overlooked evidence." She pulled the key from her pocket. "I found this under a pew. I checked it against the church door, but it wasn't a match. I know it looks like any other key, but—"

"That's Dan's house key!" Nancy blurted.

"Are you sure?" questioned the officer.

"Yes. That's his high school key chain," she claimed.

The officer pointed the key in the direction of the keyhole. "May I?" she asked.

"Of course," permitted Nancy.

The key slipped easily into the lock.

"Unfortunately, I must keep this as potential evidence," insisted the officer.

"We understand," replied Jeff.

As the policewoman pulled the key from the lock, the clock in the hallway chimed noisily. She dropped the evidence.

Nancy bent over, picked it up, and spotted the dried blood. She immediately imagined the worst. Her hands trembled as she returned the house key to the officer. Nancy left the foyer, sat on the living room sofa, and rested her head in her hands.

Jeff recognized his wife's reaction. He took the key from the officer for a closer look. Even though it was only a drop of blood, the hellish nightmares of their sons' first journey flooded back. He handed the key to the officer and neared his wife.

Nancy raised her head. "So our boys were in the church," she exclaimed. "But how did blood get on Dan's key if it was found under a pew like the officer said and not near the Communion rail where there was a pool of blood?" She grabbed a tissue from the table and blew her nose. "And who on earth would harm and then kidnap a priest and our boys in a church?"

On seeing Nancy's emotional distress, an idea crossed Officer Moore's mind for the first time. *Could the families be telling the truth?* she thought. As difficult as it was for her to believe such tales, nothing would prevent her from visiting the oak during the next full moon. She excused herself, but not before asking if there was anything she could do for the Clays.

"Thank you, officer," responded Jeff. "But we need some time alone."

"Of course." She turned and stepped onto the porch.

With the fact confirmed that the boys were in the church the night of the last full moon—and in proximity to the oak—the possibility that they jumped into the tree seemed more likely to Jeff than a burglary and a possible kidnapping. After all, he was well aware of his sons' obsession with the oak. The key, however, puzzled him. *If the boys entered the church before their leap into the tree,* he thought, *why did Dan leave his house key behind, how did it get splashed with blood, and where was Father James? It wasn't like him to neglect his parish responsibilities by jumping into the tree.* The likelihood that Jimmy and Cindy met up secretly with his sons also seemed disturbingly probable. While calming his wife, he dreaded what he knew he had to do. He handed her another tissue and stated, "I should notify the Parkers and Sara." He walked into the kitchen and reached for the phone.

CHAPTER FOUR
Bloodcurdling Thought

IN THE UNKNOWN WORLD, SAM AND DAN WALKED UP THE POORLY lit cavern with an added degree of caution.

"So where do you think we are?" asked Dan.

"I haven't the foggiest idea." Sam scanned their bleak surroundings. "But I'm pretty sure it's not the parallel world."

In his gut, Dan suspected that Sam was right. But to ease his worries and suppress his overactive imagination, he proposed, "Maybe we're in a huge underground cavern in the parallel world that we never discovered during our first trip."

Sam sensed uneasiness in his friend's voice. "I guess anything's possible," he said. "But for now, we shouldn't worry about where we are as much as finding our friends and getting back home."

Dan stopped in his tracks and leaned against the cavern wall. The pain in his ankle had returned.

"So what happened to your leg?" asked Sam.

Dan carefully lowered himself to the ground, explaining, "A being from the first cave stepped on my ankle. Then I got it wedged between some rocks."

Certain that any information could shed light on their whereabouts, Sam prodded, "Tell me about your cave."

Dan rubbed his ankle. "It was crowded with thousands of invisible beings who kept chasing a golden chest that disappeared and then would reappear minutes later in a different spot."

A confused look draped Sam's face. "If these beings were invisible, then how could you see them?"

"I guess invisible isn't the right word," admitted Dan. "They were more...um...I guess semitransparent. I mean, I could make out their physical dimensions. But even though their bodies were see-through, their eyes seemed normal."

"What do you mean?" asked Sam.

"Their eyes weren't transparent like the rest of their bodies. If I had to guess, I'd say their eyes were normal so they could see the golden chest."

Sam was curious. He squatted alongside his friend and asked, "What was inside the golden chest?"

"I don't know. I only know that I also fell victim to its attraction and tried to snatch it away. But after a couple failed attempts, I thought of you, William, Father James, and Brad. I can't explain it, but for a while I was more interested in the chest than in finding my brother and friends."

"It sounds a lot like my fixation with the hole in my cave's ceiling," compared Sam. "I can't explain it either. But when I was below the opening, nothing else mattered to me—not even finding Brad Blaze which is why I took this trip in the first place."

"I think you may be right," admitted Dan.

"About what?"

"This probably isn't the parallel world," conceded Dan, "since we never experienced these kinds of obsessions even before the parallel world was peaceful."

Sam suspected that Dan was finding it difficult accepting the fact that they could be somewhere even more sinister than the parallel world. He placed his arm around his friend's waist and helped him to his feet. To ease Dan's load, Sam insisted on carrying the backpack. He handed Dan the lit torch and remarked, "This may not be the parallel world, but we'll escape this place as well. I promise."

"Yeah, I'm sure we will."

The travelers had advanced only a few paces up the tunnel when Sam rested his hand on Dan's shoulder. "So how certain are you that William's here?"

"Pretty sure. I know he was grabbed by the limbs in the church, so I suspect he's here somewhere. I don't know where else the branches would have thrown him."

"In my cave, you mentioned that the limbs captured you," reminded Sam. "That's what I don't get. On the church lawn, I simply stepped into the oak and walked through it like we've always done."

"You mean you weren't attacked by the limbs?" asked Dan.

"Attacked?" blurted Sam. "No, I just stepped into the tree."

"Maybe the new oak has supernatural qualities that the first oak didn't have," suggested Dan. The teenager saw a questionable look emerge on his co-traveler's face. "Look Sam, I know I saw Father James and William grabbed by the limbs. The tree also captured me and threw me into its base. Believe me, I didn't just walk through it and neither did Father James nor William." He lowered his torch-bearing arm. "I also know that Father James was injured when the limbs grabbed him."

"What do you mean?" asked Sam in a worried tone.

"When William and I were being yanked and thrown about by the limbs, I remember Father James yelling at us to get out of the church. I looked near the Communion rail and saw a pool of blood where he had been kneeling."

Sam placed his back to his friend to conceal his expression. Father James's safety and friendship meant a great deal to Sam. "If Father James is here—and if he's been injured as you say—we need to find him right away."

Dan stepped to Sam's side, claiming, "I'm sure he'll be okay. But like you just said, we need to find him right away."

Sam shook his head. "So now we're looking for Father James, Brad Blaze, and possibly William."

"Yeah, I think so."

"What about Jimmy and Cindy?" asked Sam.

"What about them?"

"Are they in this world too?"

"No, they weren't in the church with William and me," replied Dan.

Sam tightened the straps on his backpack. "That's good, since it means we'll be out of here that much sooner."

The march resumed.

"Speaking of which, how long do you think we've been here?" asked Dan.

"That's a good question. But I can't imagine we've been here too long since I'm not hungry and I haven't had to use the bathroom." He glanced at Dan's wrist. "I see you're not wearing a watch either."

"No. When William and I sneaked out of the house the night you entered the tree, I didn't bother with a watch. I thought we'd be home in a few hours."

Sam came to an abrupt stop and grabbed Dan's arm. "You mean your parents didn't know you left the house?"

Dan escaped Sam's grip. "It's not like William and I knew we'd be thrown into the tree and into this hellhole," he defended.

Sam rested his hand against the cavern wall, mumbling, "My God, your parents are living another nightmare." He stared at the rock ceiling in the torch's poor light. "What were you and William thinking?"

"Sam, don't think I haven't thought about my parents and what they're going through," he snapped. "William and I had no idea that the tree had somehow turned aggressive or that we'd be in danger by praying in the church for your safe return." He raised the torch and peered up the tunnel, advising, "The sooner we find the others, the sooner we can leave this rock world."

The men resumed their hike in an awkward silence. "Look Dan, I didn't mean to be overly critical with you back there," Sam eventually replied. "I appreciate the fact that you, William, and Father James were praying in the church for me. I just wish that Father James hadn't been injured and that the three of you hadn't been thrown in here. And your parents—"

"Sam, I didn't take offense at your remarks," interrupted Dan. "But you've got to believe me. Father James, William, and I didn't willingly step into the oak. I had no idea we'd ultimately be missing when we left the house for the church. The last thing I wanted to do was put my parents through another nightmare."

Sam dropped the backpack and attempted to ease his friend's mind. "I'm sure that Cindy and Jimmy are comforting your parents at this very moment."

"I hope so."

Sam reached for the backpack.

"What's inside the bag?" asked Dan.

"What I packed in your basement before I left," reminded Sam.

He opened the backpack and displayed more than a dozen lances, his revolver, spare bullets, a flashlight, and a bag of food that Nancy had packed for his one-night trip.

"Why all the lances?" asked Dan.

"Like I explained to you and the others before this trip, if I miss the full moon, I'd like to take in a little rabbit hunting in the forest—presuming we find the exit to this cavern and assuming this is the parallel world. If I lose a lance or two, I'll have plenty in reserve. Besides, they don't take up much room."

Dan reached for Sam's flashlight. "This will come in handy, especially since mine hardly ever works."

"But we need to use the torch for as long as possible to conserve the batteries," stressed Sam. "We'll use the flashlights when the torch burns out."

Dan returned the flashlight to the backpack, along with his own flashlight.

The march resumed.

"By the way, how'd you escape the anacondas without a weapon?" asked Sam.

"How'd you know about the anacondas?"

"Don't you remember?" asked Sam. "You told me about them at the base of the ladder in my cave."

"Oh yeah," recalled Dan. He ran his lance along the cavern wall while disclosing, "That was odd too."

"What do you mean?"

"The entrance—or exit—to my cave kept moving each time I tried to walk through it, just like the golden chest kept moving," compared Dan. "At one point, I was on the seat of my pants and inching backwards to escape an anaconda when suddenly I found myself in the open cavern. The next thing I knew, the entrance relocated just when the snake was making its final lunge."

"But why didn't the passageway move when you were crawling though it?"

"I don't know," replied Dan. "Maybe leaving the cave—without looking at the exit—had something to do with it."

"Well, I'm sure there's a logical explanation, just like I'm sure there's a logical explanation why I was so preoccupied with the ladder."

BLOODCURDLING THOUGHT

Dan raised his weapon to shoulder height. "Anyway, this lance would have come in handy against the anacondas and the giant crab. No lie, Sam, the crab was at least five feet long if not longer."

"What crab?"

"After I fled my cave, but before entering yours," Dan recalled, "I sat and leaned against the cavern wall to ease the pain in my ankle. The ground suddenly shook." He paused to spit cave dust from his mouth. "Since I had no intention of meeting whatever creature was racing up the tunnel in my direction, I darted as fast as I could. At one point, I looked back and saw a king crab closing in on me."

Sam looked back to make sure they weren't being followed. "So how'd you escape without a lance?"

"I ran as fast as I could, until I reached a pool. I knew I'd be a dead man if I lingered behind, so I plunged into the water." He held the fading torch upside down to intensify the flame. "To make a long story short, I got my foot stuck between rocks in the pool. As I was trying to free myself, a huge water spider—probably four feet long—dropped into the pool and fought the king crab. The last thing I saw was the spider dragging the crab away."

Sam glanced behind a second time. "The spider wasn't after you?" he asked.

"I don't think so. But it was unlike anything I've ever imagined."

"What do you mean?"

"It had a human face," clarified Dan.

"A human face?" exclaimed Sam. "What do you mean a human face?"

"Just that, which is why I suspect it didn't attack me. Maybe it thought I was part of its species."

Sam slowed his pace and admitted, "I know you don't want to hear this, but the more stories I hear about your encounters and the longer we're in this cavern, the more I'm convinced we're not in the parallel world—evil or peaceful."

With each step, the distance between the cavern walls gradually diminished until they were barely ten feet apart.

Dan stopped and turned the torch upside down again to brighten the flame.

The teenager had taken only one step further when Sam grabbed him by the arm and warned, "Let's be careful. I have a bad feeling about this narrow tunnel."

"What do you mean?" asked Dan.

Without removing his sights from the restricted tunnel, Sam cautioned, "I don't know—just something I sense."

Dan extended the glowing torch to arm's length. "I don't see anything unusual ahead, though the ground seems a little bumpy. There are a lot of dirt clods."

"What about the walls?" prodded Sam.

Dan waved the torch from side to side. "There's not a lot of distance between them, but nothing's hanging from them if that's what you're asking." Only now sensing that something was different about the tunnel ahead, Dan took a loud gulp, "But we really don't have a choice. If we backtrack, we'll end up at the two caves that we've already searched. If William, Father James, and Brad are in this world, then they're ahead of us through this tunnel."

With each man carrying a lance—and Sam the backpack—Dan took the first step into their cramped surroundings with a death grip on the torch.

Sam immediately trailed.

Only a short distance into their hike, Dan switched the torch to his left hand and his lance to his right in case he needed to drive back a hungry creature.

Sam, meanwhile, repositioned the backpack on his shoulders without loosening the tight grip on his weapon. "So how did you find my cave?" asked Sam in an effort to ease the escalating tension.

Dan turned slightly to face his friend, saying, "After freeing myself from the rocks in the water hole, I dashed up the open cavern. Since I wasn't sure if the water spider would change its mind and hunt me down, I hiked for as long as I could on my twisted ankle. In the end, the pain became so bad that I had to rest against the wall. Eventually, I was on the move again. It was then when I spotted the opening to your cave." He came to an abrupt standstill. Sam bumped into him.

"What's wrong?" blurted Sam.

"I thought I heard—nothing," said Dan.

With each step, the tunnel grew even darker. The torch struggled to illuminate an area only feet ahead.

"What'd you hear?" whispered Sam.

"It was nothing," Dan insisted. "Let's keep moving."

Sam stopped to inspect the walls. He soon found himself several feet behind his friend. In the poor light, he took one step forward. He was instantly seized by the ankles and collided with the ground. "Dan!" he screamed.

Skeletal arms had exploded from two dirt clods, grabbed Sam's ankles, and were pulling him below the surface.

Sam jabbed his lance at the arms, but the weapon was useless.

The bony creatures were unscathed by the tip of the spear.

Sam delivered a second stab.

Not even a scratch was inflicted on the skeletal arms as they continued pulling themselves and Sam below the surface.

Dan dashed to the scene, dropped his lance and torch, and fought to free Sam from the enclosing ground. He quickly realized that he was making no headway against the unseen predator that was pulling his friend further below the surface. He pressed his back against the cavern wall for leverage and resumed his rescue efforts. He was relentless. His determination paid off.

Sam was slowly pulled from the soil.

Without warning, a skeletal arm burst from the wall and wrapped around Dan's neck. He released his grip on Sam and madly tried to remove the arm from his throat. But the creature's grasp proved more than a match for his waning strength. As he eyed the burning torch on the ground, he also noticed that the modest advance he had made in freeing Sam was quickly reversing. His friend was now waist deep in the soil.

With his head pinned against the wall, Dan extended a leg to drag the torch within reach. With some success, the torch was pulled nearer the wall. One final jerk of his leg landed it within arm's reach. He snatched the torch, raised it over his shoulder, and touched it against the skeleton. The arm quickly receded inside the wall. Dan was free. He crawled to Sam and wrapped his arms around his co-traveler's upper chest. After several minutes of gaining and losing ground, the skeletal arms released their grip on their victim. Dan pulled his friend to safety.

"What—" Sam paused to catch his breath. "What was that?"

"I guess these mounds of dirt aren't what they seem," replied a short-winded Dan. Aware that Sam had been too preoccupied with his own deadly predicament to see how he freed himself from the arm in the wall, he related the story and concluded by guessing that the skeletal arms were probably fearful of heat.

Hundreds of dirt mounds lay ahead with no end to the tunnel in sight.

"I think we should rest here for a while and catch our breaths," suggested Dan. "We'll need to be alert and focused when we hike ahead."

"I think you're right." Sam looked behind and admitted, "I just wish there were another way out of here."

"So do I, but our friends are ahead, not behind," said Dan.

After a several-minute respite, the men were on the move with Dan in the lead, waving the torch in all directions before taking a step.

Unbelievably, the travelers had advanced a couple hundred feet without disrupting a clod. Still, there was no end to the passageway.

"How far does this tunnel go?" complained Dan. "I was in a narrow tunnel before, but I don't remember it being this long."

A cold breeze was felt.

"Did you feel that?" asked Sam.

"Yeah," said Dan.

"That means there's an opening ahead," speculated Sam.

A stronger draft swept through the tunnel.

"Oh no," mumbled Dan.

"What's wrong?" demanded Sam.

"The flame—it's going out!" blurted Dan.

"What?" Sam peered over his friend's shoulder.

Dan turned the torch upside down to resurrect the dying flame. But this time, there was no rebirth of the fire.

The flame died, leaving the men in near darkness amid hundreds of dirt clods.

Dan blew on the extinguished flame, but with no results. "Sam, do you have a lighter or matches?"

"No." He checked his pockets to confirm.

"Your flashlight!" yelled Dan.

"Of course." In darkness, Sam fumbled for it in the backpack and handed it to Dan.

With a flick of the switch, the tunnel was instantly aglow. The men gazed about and discovered that the cavern was only four feet wide and marred with hundreds of mounds.

"Just make sure we don't step on any clods," warned Sam.

"I'll be careful." Dan directed the beam ahead and inched up the tunnel.

Sam trailed immediately behind.

Nearly thirty minutes later, Dan exclaimed, "I see light ahead!"

"Take it slowly," advised Sam. "We don't want to—" He bumped into Dan.

"What are you doing?" snapped Dan who narrowly missed a mound.

"Sorry. My foot skimmed a clod a few feet back," explained Sam. "I wasn't going to wait around to see what happened next. I already know."

Dan peered up the tunnel. "See, there's light ahead," he exclaimed.

"Yeah, you're right." Sam took a backward glance at the mound he had grazed. "The sooner we get out of here the better."

"Let's take our time—and don't be running into me," warned Dan.

Fifteen minutes later, the flashlight was switched off. The men stepped from the narrow tunnel and into a lit open cavern with walls nearly a hundred feet apart and the ceiling soaring fifty feet.

"We made it!" exclaimed Dan.

"Good job." Sam snatched the flashlight from Dan and dropped it into the backpack. "Let's save the batteries and use the natural light."

"That's fine," replied Dan. "Should we take a break or move on?"

"I think we better continue our search for the others, especially since we don't know how long we've been in this world or when the next portal will open," said Sam.

As the explorers advanced, an eerie thought crossed Dan's mind. "Sam, we don't know what we're looking for."

"What do you mean?"

"I mean that in the parallel world we knew to look for the oak at a certain spot in the forest," Dan clarified. He halted his stride and offered a bewildered look to Sam. "But here—in this maze of caves—there's only dead gnarled branches and no trees. Where's the portal? What does it look like?"

Sam also had stopped in his tracks. With his eyes downcast, he was completely mortified that he had overlooked something so crucial to their escape.

"Sam!" yelled Dan.

Sam shook his head, mumbling, "I wish I had an answer." He removed his backpack and sat on it. "When you were thrown into the oak, what was the first thing you saw when entering this world?"

Dan sat alongside his co-traveler. "I remember being hurled into the tree and then—"

"Then what," interrupted Sam.

"And then, I woke up to semitransparent beings stepping on me."

Sam rose from the backpack and neared a cavern wall. "Think Dan. Do you remember anything else—regardless of how insignificant it may seem."

"No. That's all I remember." He stood and approached Sam. "What do you remember after stepping into the tree?"

"Not much more, I'm afraid." Sam retraced his steps to the backpack. "I remember feeling the oak to see if it was soft. Then I walked into it. The next thing I remember, I was standing below the ladder in my cave."

"But there's got to be something we're overlooking," claimed Dan.

Knowing they needed to cover as much ground as possible, Sam grabbed the gear. "Look, I'm sure that something will come to mind before the thirty days are up. But in the meantime, we need to keep moving and searching for the others."

"What's the point in finding them, if we have nowhere to go?" grumbled Dan.

Sam yanked Dan's arm. "That's enough!" he shouted. "That kind of hopeless talk will get us both killed!"

Dan broke free from his grip and walked on. Several paces ahead, the teenager exclaimed, "Oh great!"

"What now?" asked Sam. "What's up ahead?"

"No. It's not that."

"What then?" pressed Sam.

"I just had another horrible thought."

"What?"

"What if we're not meant to leave this place? It's obvious that we don't know what we're looking for."

Sam had no immediate response. He eventually broke the awkward silence and offered a glimmer of hope. "Maybe one of the others saw something that will lead us out of this world." He rested his hand on Dan's shoulder. "Sorry I snapped at you. It's just that...well...I still can't believe I neglected something as important as the portal."

"You don't have to apologize. But if our friends may have the answer, then all the more reason to find them right away."

The explorers resumed their fast trek up the spacious tunnel in silence. Each was mentally replaying his entry into the foreign world. Each was trying to remember a piece of crucial evidence that would lead them home.

Sam broke the lengthy stillness. "Look Dan, I feel horrible that I took my frustrations out on you back there."

"I said it's okay."

"No, it's not okay," snapped Sam. "I know that you can take care of yourself. But since I'm the senior member here, I feel responsible for you which makes the fact that I can't remember anything about my entry into this world all the more irresponsible."

Dan eased his friend's conscience. "Sam, I appreciate your looking out for me, but the fact that you can't remember anything about your entry isn't your fault. I can't recall anything about my entry either." His eyes lit up. He spotted another torch wedged in a wall fifty feet ahead. He darted to the torch, looked back, and yelled, "You're probably right. Maybe one of the others will remember something!"

Sam tried to match Dan's pace.

"Come on!" shouted Dan. He pulled the torch from the wall. "Time is still on our side."

Sam reached the teenager's side.

"Oh great," grumbled Dan.

Sam remained silent. He also saw the situation. A short distance ahead, the ceiling nose-dived. The search for their friends and answers demanded they continue their hike on their stomachs.

Sam minimized their troublesome situation by joking, "It's a good thing we're not Jimmy's size."

To Dan, the area ahead reminded him of a crawlspace in a house.

"Let's switch," suggested Sam. "I'll take the lead with the torch and you follow with the backpack."

"Sam, I'll be fine."

It was too late. Sam had dropped the backpack, ripped the torch from Dan's hand, and was racing to the stony crawlspace. He rested on his knees and extended the torch inside the dark opening. "Wow, it's going to be a tight fit."

"I wonder how far it goes," posed Dan.

"I guess we'll find out." Sam crawled inside the opening on his stomach.

Dan was immediately behind. Given the low clearance, he had no choice but to drag the backpack and lance at his side.

The initial twenty feet proved backbreaking until their stomach muscles and backs became fairly acclimated to their tight surroundings.

Sam heard mumbling behind. "What'd you say?"

"Nothing!" shouted Dan. "I was just praying that my hour of death wouldn't be in this dreadful shaft."

With each forward movement, the men surveyed their right and left. They knew that—at least on earth—small rodents and reptiles thrived in close quarters. They were soon visited by several water snakes.

Though Sam knew the snakes were harmless, they were still unwelcome. "Hey Dan! We have a few visitors."

"Now what?"

"Relax," said Sam. "They're harmless water snakes. The worst they will do is rub against you for warmth."

"Are you sure?" posed Dan. "Remember, this isn't earth."

The fact that they were in a foreign land initially slipped Sam's mind. He now eyed the slithering creatures with extreme caution.

Within seconds, a snake curled around Sam's arm. No bite was

BLOODCURDLING THOUGHT

delivered. The creature released itself almost as quickly as it coiled around him.

"They're harmless!" yelled Sam.

"Are you sure?"

"Yeah." Sam turned in the body-hugging shaft and watched the departure of the snakes. He froze while eyeing the expanse behind Dan. "What the—"

A glowing mist that was clearly visible against the rear darkness had entered the shaft and was drifting slowly in their direction.

"Hey Dan," alerted Sam, "it's probably nothing, but a white mist just entered the passageway behind you."

Dan twisted his neck and saw the intruder. "What is it?"

"Probably just vapor," guessed Sam. "But let's not take any chances. Let's pick up our pace." In the distance, Sam spotted the exit to the crawlspace. "The tunnel ends about fifty feet ahead! I think we can make it in plenty of time before the mist reaches us."

Three water snakes had slithered beyond Dan and were approaching the glowing mist.

With his body pressed against the rock floor, Dan felt vibrations. He jerked his head and gasped. The snakes were flipping wildly in the glowing mist. Almost immediately, they were engulfed in a ball of fire. "Sam—move! That's not vapor!" yelled Dan.

Sam also turned and witnessed the combustion.

At a rapid pace, the men crossed a record amount of rock in a short period of time. Sam was only feet from the tunnel's exit when Dan screamed for help.

Sam spun as fast as he could in the limited confines, dropped the torch on the rocky surface, and scrambled to his friend, shouting, "Hurry!"

"I'm stuck!" screamed Dan.

"On what?"

"The ceiling! It's too narrow; I can't get through!"

Within seconds, Sam was face to face with Dan. "Give me your arms!" shouted Sam. Once clasped, he ordered, "Inhale—press your face to the ground!" Sam pulled while keeping an eye on the mist that was closing in on his trapped friend. "Again!" he yelled.

With a third pull, Dan budged. Unfortunately, he also groaned. The mist had touched his legs.

"Inhale!" screamed Sam.

The fourth yank freed Dan from the low ceiling. Sam pulled him from the glowing mist. Without losing a moment's time, he dragged his injured friend from the path of the slow-moving creature.

With the torch and backpack left behind, Sam lifted Dan from the crawlspace, placed his arm around his waist, and helped him up the open cavern. He glanced behind; the mist was still advancing. A side cave was spotted only ten feet ahead and alongside a burning torch. Almost certain their chances of survival would be better in the unknown cave than in the tunnel with the mist, he helped Dan inside. Only feet inside the entrance, the men waited and watched the haze resume its death journey up the cavern.

The explorers were safe—for now.

Sam placed Dan on his back and tapped his cheeks. "Dan, stay awake," he pleaded.

The teenager opened his eyes and mumbled, "What was that?"

"I don't know," replied Sam. "Let's take a look at your legs."

Although the soles of Dan's boots were charred, thankfully, his jeans suffered only slight burn holes.

Sam raised Dan's pant legs. Scorch marks were clearly visible on his calves and ankles. But as bad as it was, Sam counted his blessings. He knew that his friend could have suffered the same fate as the snakes. "Why didn't I bring a first-aid kit?" he whispered. His thoughts were drawn to the backpack that was abandoned in the rock shaft. Convinced now more than ever that the weapons would be crucial to their survival, he had no choice but to leave Dan and recover the bag. "Dan," he said, "I'll be back as fast as I can. I need the backpack."

Before Sam rose to his feet, Dan grabbed his arm. "The mist—be careful," he warned.

Sam removed his weak grip. "It's all right. The mist is gone." He stepped to the side cave's opening and poked his head inside the open tunnel to confirm that the mist had floated away and wasn't lurking around the corner for an ambush. *After all, this isn't earth,* he thought. With no trace of the haze, he dashed to the crawlspace and grabbed the scorched bag of weapons. Unfortunately, the discarded torch was lifeless. He re-entered the side cave and examined Dan's injuries more closely.

"How bad is it?" asked Dan.

Sam placed his hand on his friend's forehead and checked for a fever. "Look, I'm not going to lie. You've got some nasty burns. I'm sure it's just a matter of time before blisters appear."

Dan attempted to rise.

"Whoa, rest now," ordered Sam. He pressed on Dan's chest to keep him flat on his back. "I'm afraid there's nothing I can do for your burns without a medicine kit. Time will be the cure."

Dan sensed unwarranted guilt on the part of his friend. "Sam, you had no way of knowing we'd end up in danger," he reminded. "Heck, you didn't even know you'd have a co-traveler. It's not your fault that you didn't bring a first-aid kit."

"Be that as it may, I—"

"I'll be fine. I've endured worse," interrupted Dan. He raised his sights to the ceiling, saying, "I wonder what inhabits this cave."

"Don't dwell on that now," ordered Sam. "You rest here while I explore the cave for the others." He took a wide scan of their new surroundings, grabbed a lance from the backpack, and escaped Dan's view.

Within minutes, Dan's pain won out. He placed his head on the backpack and fell into a light sleep.

CHAPTER FIVE

Looks Are Deceiving

SAM ADVANCED DEEPER INTO THE UNEXPLORED CAVE. HE WAS awestruck. The third inner rock world boasted countless stalactites projecting downward from the hundred-foot ceiling and stalagmites that soared from the stone floor. Both mineral deposits were so overpowering that one could easily mistake the ceiling for the floor and vice versa.

Hundreds of torches along the cave's perimeter bathed the dwelling in a warm glow that added to the beauty of the stone confinement. For several moments, Sam remained motionless, captivated with the grandeur of the inner realm. His hypnotic stare was suddenly disrupted by a loud crash.

A stalactite had plunged to the ground.

Immediately, screams were heard in the distance.

He dashed up an incline and froze at its peak. Looking below, he watched in horror as a group of fifty or more men and women assaulted one another alongside a clear pond.

With a bird's-eye view of the hollow ground, he noticed hundreds of similar-size ponds. The light from the torches reflecting off the pools of water enhanced the brilliance of the cave. To Sam, the dwelling was heaven. But oftentimes, looks are deceiving.

Before descending the slope, he noticed an imposing waterfall against a distant cave wall. It also was breathtaking. Once at the base of the incline, he approached the closest group of cave dwellers surrounding a pond. He was baffled that they had ended their skirmishes so quickly and were now on their hands and knees looking intently at the water. He stood several feet behind the group and cleared his throat to steal their attention. The inhabitants remained motionless, refusing even to raise their heads. After two more unsuccessful attempts at distracting the pond gazers, he yelled.

They failed to respond.

Are these people deaf? he thought. He took only three steps nearer the cave dwellers when he gasped. Their legs were severely decomposed. Some inhabitants were even missing their lower limbs. What little clothing remained was either rotten or overgrown with skin. And what little hair clung to their scalps was infested with maggots. Their foul odor would have discouraged any potential inquisitor, but Sam was in search of answers—answers about his location and that of his missing friends.

He held his breath and advanced the few remaining feet to the water. Enamored with an attractive woman's reflection in the pond, he thought, *She's absolutely stunning.* Her unmatched beauty forced him to his knees alongside her where he attempted to exchange greetings. With no reply, he extended his hand and rolled her chin in his direction.

"My God!" he shouted. He fell to the seat of his pants and scrambled backwards.

The woman's actual appearances were nothing like her reflection. Her facial skin was nearly eaten away. The bits and pieces of flesh that remained were home to a colony of flesh-eating worms. Perhaps most repulsive was her left eye which dangled from its socket.

As Sam remained on the ground panting, the woman wasted no time redirecting her sights to the water. She attempted to touch her reflection. The moment her shriveled hand was within an inch of the pond's surface, a stream of water burst from the pool and struck her face. Her prolonged moan confirmed to Sam that she was enduring intense pain. Another blemish was added to her rapidly fading facial features.

Sam jumped to his feet and was offering a sweeping glance at the pond when he discovered that the same scenario was being played out by all the inhabitants, including the men.

A middle-aged man who was positioned on all fours at the opposite side of the pond also bore bizarre physical disfigurements. Even though he retained both eyes, his nose had been ripped from his face.

Sam walked around the water's edge, squatted beside the man, and noticed that although his actual looks were revolting, his reflection was quite handsome.

The man also made a futile attempt to touch his reflection. He was instantly repelled by an explosion of water from the surface.

Obviously, these people have no idea what they actually look like, thought Sam. *They're so infatuated with the deceptive beauty of their reflections that they're oblivious to their real looks and to their horrid physical abnormalities.*

As Sam prepared to take his leave, a creak was heard in the distance. He stared ahead and watched a stalactite surrender to the power of gravity and crash to the cave ground. Within seconds, brawls arose around the ponds. As he stared at the pool beside him, he came to understand that the collision of the hanging rock with the floor had created ripples on the water's surface which distorted the reflections of the dwellers. Once their perfect images were erased from the pool's surface, the inhabitants refocused their attentions from the water to one another. With their false self-images from the reflecting pool etched in their minds, each believed that he or she was the most beautiful. A mere glance at their unsightly neighbor disturbed them greatly. Blows were exchanged. To the inhabitants, someone as hideous as the person squatting beside them had no right to exist or at the very least should not be in their company.

As Sam stared in disbelief, he suspected that since the cave dwellers had remained on their hands and knees—fixated with their reflections—for a long period of time, they were probably unable to rise to a standing position, even to battle their fellow pond gazers. To him, the scuffle on all fours reminded him of a hound going for the throat of its victim. To him, they were no longer human.

The fights were brutal. Chunks of decaying flesh were ripped from faces, insect-infested hair was yanked from scalps, and limbs were pulled from their sockets. Those who suffered the misfortune of dislocated arms madly shoved them back into their sockets before the ripples vanished. Their arms were crucial in their attempts to touch their reflective beauty.

As quickly as the fights began, they ended. A great calm settled upon the water's surface. The cave dwellers resumed their previous positions, spellbound with their perfect reflections.

At the cave's entrance, the recent clamor and the collapse of the stalactite stirred Dan from his sleep. He grabbed the lance at his side and struggled to his feet. Like Sam, he was mesmerized with the cave's false splendor. Knowing that he had to find their friends, he remained spellbound with the interior's brilliance for only a few moments longer before beginning his search of the new cave for William, Father James, and Brad. He stood atop the incline and was amazed that the inner regions of the cave were even more spectacular than the area near the entrance. The countless reflecting ponds added a touch of mystique. He saw movement at the center of the enormous cave. *That must be Sam, since the inhabitants seem to be motionless at the edges of the pools,* he thought. As he descended the slope, his thoughts continued, *I wonder why the cave dwellers are so entranced with the water and refuse to enjoy the other beauties of the cave.*

Sam continued his quick search scanning the ponds' reflections for familiar faces. A flash of light drew his attention to the distant waterfall where a woman materialized alongside a pond.

She immediately dropped to her knees, leaned forward, and was captivated with her youthful image in the pool.

Suspecting that the area nearest the waterfall was the point of entry for the newest arrivals, Sam darted to the cascade in search of his friends.

As Sam was heading to the waterfall, Dan was nearing the center of the cave. To his disappointment, Sam was nowhere around.

Another commotion followed within seconds of another hanging rock crashing to the ground.

Dan froze at the melee. Suspecting that his friends could be in the midst of the feuds, he increased his frantic search.

With no luck locating his friends at the waterfall, Sam abandoned the area and retreated to the farthest recesses of the hollow ground until he was at the back of the cave.

Dan's ongoing exploration landed him away from the center of the cave and closer to several small ponds adjacent to the waterfall.

Two inhabitants jumped to their feet and engaged in deadly combat.

"What the heck," Dan whispered. He, like Sam, suspected that the upright cave dwellers were the newest arrivals. He raced closer to the waterfall as fast as his leg injuries would allow. Sadly, his friends were nowhere in sight.

As the waters calmed and the dwellers were returning to their previous positions, Dan heard, "Get out of my sight!" It wasn't what was said, but how it was said. He recognized the voice. As he neared the pond in question, he was stunned. "Cindy?" he mumbled. *But she wasn't in the church*, he thought. He stepped closer to the woman and sat on the ground alongside her. "Cindy?" he said again.

The woman offered no response.

Whereas most inhabitants were obsessed with their deceptive facial beauty, this particular woman was engrossed with flexing her toned upper arms and admiring her muscular structure in the pool's reflection. Her facial expression that was mirrored on the water's surface confirmed that she was pleased with her image.

"Cindy?" Dan said again. With no reply or reaction, he grabbed the woman's arm.

She immediately broke free of his grip.

Dan tugged her face in his direction to disrupt her spellbound gaze. In the brief moment he had to look at her—before she jerked her sights back to the pond—he could have sworn it was Cindy Somer. As the young woman remained entranced with her reflection, Dan ordered, "Come on, we have to get out of here!"

Again, there was only silence.

Dan squatted behind the woman, placed his arms around her, and dragged her from the pond's edge.

In a heated rage, she elbowed him in the legs.

Intense pain forced Dan flat on his back.

The woman scrambled back to the water on her hands and knees.

Another attempt was made to release her from the captivating power of the pond. Sadly, the results were the same. Nearly convinced it was his friend, Dan recalled her unusual strength and determination in the parallel world and admitted that he'd be no match for her, especially in his present condition. He made a mental note of the pool's location and left the young woman in search of Sam. *Maybe with his help, we can free her,* he thought. He grabbed his lance and had advanced only several feet when he looked back at the young woman. She was reaching over the pool's edge to touch her athletic image when a blast of water shot from the pond and targeted her face. She groaned in agony.

As much as Dan hated the idea of leaving her behind, he knew he had to find Sam as soon as possible. He raced to the center of the inner rock world where he had last seen Sam from the incline at the cave's entrance. He lingered at the spot, hopeful that his friend would eventually return to the area. The wait proved to be mental torture. Though he knew it was best to stay put and wait, he also realized that the woman whom he believed to be Cindy was in grave danger. He imagined that the longer she gazed at the pond, the more difficult it would be to pull her from her trance. He was absorbed in his dilemma when he spotted a man walking upright only a short distance ahead. "Sam!" he yelled.

There was no reply.

"Sam!" he screamed again.

"What?" echoed throughout the cave.

Dan nearly jumped out of his skin when something landed on his shoulder from behind. He spun and saw Sam lifting his hand from his shoulder.

"I told you to rest at the cave's entrance," admonished Sam.

"Cindy's here!" he shouted.

"What do you mean Cindy's here?"

"I'm almost sure it was her." Dan pointed near the waterfall. "Over there," he directed.

Sam suspected that his friend's pain was influencing his judgment, especially in a cave that was riddled with distortions. "How can she be here? Was she in the church?"

"Well no. But you have to believe me—it's Cindy!"

"Maybe it's someone who just looks like her. After all, everyone supposedly has a twin in the world," reminded Sam.

"I'm serious. I really think it's Cindy," Dan insisted.

Even Sam was surprised with his friend's persistence. "Did you speak with her?"

"Not exactly."

"Why not?" asked Sam.

"When I tried to pull her from the pond, she knocked me in the legs and—"

"And what?" prodded Sam.

"She elbowed me in the legs and I fell to the ground," replied a mortified teenager.

Though still entertaining doubts about his friend's discovery, Sam was more concerned for his safety. "I want the truth, Dan."

"Yeah."

"How bad is the pain in your legs?"

"That's not important right now," maintained Dan.

"It is to me," snapped Sam.

"Okay, it's pretty painful. But not as painful as knowing that Cindy could spend the rest of her life staring at her reflection."

A strong, warm breeze was felt from the waterfall.

"What was that?" asked Dan.

Sam looked over his companion's shoulders to the waterfall. "I'm not sure."

The unexpected blast of air presented the perfect opportunity for Dan to mention a nagging feeling he'd had since descending the slope at the cave's entrance. "Sam, I've sensed something that I can't shake."

Sam suspected that he was referring to the likelihood of finding their friends. "I'm sure we'll find the others," he asserted.

"No Sam, it's not that."

"What then?"

"I've got a gut feeling that...well...like we're being watched," divulged Dan.

Sam remained silent.

Dan followed his friend's gaze from pond to pond. "It's probably nothing, but—"

"Of course we're being watched," interrupted Sam. "There are thousands of beings here."

"That's not what I mean."

"I know that's not what you meant," admitted Sam.

"It's just that—"

"I've sensed it too," interrupted Sam. "I didn't mention it because I didn't want to needlessly alarm you. But you're right. I can't shake the feeling either."

A stronger breeze roared within the rock chamber.

The gust eventually subsided.

"Where did you see this woman?" asked Sam.

Dan had just turned from his friend and pointed to the waterfall when a vine exploded from a crack in the rock ground and coiled around Sam's calf.

Pond skaters—long-legged insects that thrived alongside water sources and were known for their voracious appetites for skin tissue—scurried along the length of the plant stem.

"Get 'em off!" yelled Sam.

Dan spun in Sam's direction and witnessed his friend's crawling predicament. Though Dan quickly severed the plant's shoot with his lance, eight bugs climbed Sam's pant leg. With several brushes of the spear, the pond skaters dropped to the ground and scurried to the nearest pool.

Repulsed with the lingering sensation of crawling insects on him, Sam moved at a fast pace away from the area in the direction of the cascade.

"Were you bit?" asked Dan who tried to match Sam's fast clip.

Aware that his stride was exhausting the limping teenager—not to mention that they were beyond the pond skaters' range—Sam slowed his pace. "They got a piece or two of me, but I'll live. Thanks."

"Don't mention it."

Within minutes, the men were standing at the area where Dan had previously seen the young woman.

"Which pond was it?" asked Sam.

Dan scanned the pools. "That one!" He took several steps forward and knelt on the ground beside the young woman. "Look Sam." He jerked the inhabitant's face in his direction.

Sam got a quick glimpse of her facial features before she snapped her gaze back to her reflection.

Dan looked up at Sam. "See, I told you."

Sam raised a hand and cupped his chin between his thumb and index finger. He still had doubts. "Dan, how can this be Cindy if you said she wasn't in the church with you?"

"I don't know. Maybe she was tossed into the oak later that night. But it doesn't matter. We have to get her out of here."

Sam stooped and leaned in for a closer look at the woman's face. "I don't remember Cindy having a blemish below her right eye."

"Oh come on, Sam," replied Dan in an annoyed tone. "She could've got that mark from her journey here or—" He recalled the pond water striking her face earlier. "Or maybe it's from the water that splashed her just a few minutes ago. For all we know, this water may have corrosive qualities." He looked at the pool's surface and then back at Sam. "As you keep reminding me, we're not in our world."

"But what if we take her from this place only to find out later that she's not Cindy."

"I know it's her," claimed Dan. "And if by some freakish accident we find out it's not … well … is it wrong to rescue someone from their miseries?"

Sam reluctantly agreed. "All right, we'll take her with us. By the way, during your earlier wanderings, did you see anyone who looked like William, Father James, or Brad?"

"No." Dan crawled behind the woman and prepared to drag her from the pond. "But if they're in this cave, then I'd suspect they'd be huddled around one of these ponds closest to the waterfall."

"What makes you say that?" asked Sam.

"Because during an earlier brawl, I saw two inhabitants fighting in an upright position in this general area. I figured that the recent arrivals probably still had the ability to stand."

"Yeah," agreed Sam. "I also saw something that suggests the newest arrivals probably enter this spot first."

"What do you mean?"

"Earlier in my search, I saw a flash of bright light that materialized a woman in this vicinity." Sam paused to scratch his calf that received a bite from a pond skater. "Nevertheless, before we pull this woman from her gaze, we should search the neighboring ponds for

LOOKS ARE DECEIVING

our other friends—just to make sure. Once we leave this cave, I don't plan on returning." He helped Dan to his feet.

While the woman remained enthralled with her reflection, the men separated and explored the sixteen ponds nearest the cascade.

A strong wind swept through the cave again. The gale, however, was more powerful than the previous blasts. Dozens of torches at the back of the cave were extinguished.

"Whoa!" exclaimed Dan. The wind nearly knocked him off his feet.

The men reunited at the pond where the cave dwellers remained spellbound with their reflections. "Any luck?" asked Sam.

"No. I didn't recognize a single face."

"All right then. What's your plan for releasing this woman?"

"I'll drag her away," explained Dan.

"That's it? That's your plan?" replied Sam in a cynical tone.

"Well yeah, but I'll need your help. She's pretty feisty."

Sam noticed a look of pain on Dan's face when he lowered himself alongside the woman. He helped him to his feet. "You lead the way," he ordered. "I'll pull her free."

"Okay. But I'm warning you, she's got a wicked fight in her."

Sam squatted and wrapped his arms around her waist. "One, two, three!" he yelled before pulling her from the pond's edge.

The woman screamed, punched, clawed, and bit as she fought to release herself from Sam's grip.

Another mighty wind whirled throughout the cave.

Sam released his hold on the woman and watched the falling water of the cascade thrust outward.

Dan witnessed the same phenomenon.

The men froze.

A pair of green eyes glowed behind the waterfall.

The woman—unbothered with the looming danger—raced to the water's edge.

"Dan, stay perfectly still," whispered Sam.

An enormous frilled lizard poked its head from beside the gushing water.

Sam hoped for a major distraction; Dan hoped for a miracle.

The lizard—towering nearly twenty feet—exposed its ten-inch

fangs before flaring its massive folds of skin that encircled its neck and head.

The men retreated two steps.

Dan received his miracle when the creature stepped alongside the waterfall.

The movements of the oversize beast—nearly sixty feet in length—triggered tremors that created fast-moving ripples in the ponds. At once, thousands of cave dwellers were engaged in battle.

Sam took advantage of the chaos. "Run for the entrance!"

"But Sam!"

"Now!" he ordered.

The large-scale infighting among the inhabitants confused the giant lizard. The intensifying clashes were too much for its underdeveloped brain to process.

Regrettably, the violent and widespread clashes separated the men. Sam was forced to flee to the darkness at the back of the cave.

Dan dashed to the entrance. He came to a sudden stop when he realized that he had left the young woman at the water's edge fighting with a pond mate. *What am I doing?* he thought. *I can't leave her in the creature's path.* He retraced his steps to the pool and discovered that Sam was nowhere in sight. He took a quick sweep of the area and caught sight of his friend stepping into the darkness at the back of the cave.

The frilled lizard expanded its folds of skin and made the loudest hissing sounds Dan had ever heard. The creature flattened a handful of cave dwellers in its charge at Sam.

Dan knew he had to remain as inconspicuous as possible. He dropped to all fours, grabbed the combative Cindy look-alike, and dragged her several feet away.

She screamed hysterically.

The creature poked its head from the rear shadows and took several steps in the direction of the young woman's screams which were heard easily over the pond brawls.

Sam—who remained concealed in the darkness while watching Dan's attempted rescue effort—yelled to distract the beast.

The frilled lizard halted its advance on the two escapees and remained motionless. It alternated its cold-blooded stare between the darkness at the rear of the cave and the fleeing teenagers.

Totally oblivious of the beast, the woman continued struggling with Dan. She needed her reflection.

Dan had to act quickly to subdue her. The instant the lizard directed its stare to the rear darkness he punched the woman in the jaw. She was out cold.

"Run for the entrance!" yelled Sam.

"We're not leaving without you!"

"Go—now!" shouted Sam.

Thinking he'd deliver the woman from harm's way and then return to help Sam, Dan crept backwards in the direction of the cave's entrance while dragging the woman and his lance.

Sam's shouts were purposely nonstop to distract the lizard which was keenly eyeing Dan's slow retreat.

Once at a safe distance, Dan lowered the woman to the ground behind the safety of a boulder. He raced over the incline to the backpack at the entrance. Dan knew that many lances would be needed to take down the colossal lizard. He opened the bag and was rummaging through its contents when he hatched an idea. He raced back to the boulder that concealed the woman and yelled to capture the beast's attention.

The lizard pulled its head from the darkness and took four steps closer to Dan.

A loud bang echoed throughout the rock chamber—then another.

The frilled lizard had no time to react to a stalactite dropping from the ceiling and piercing its skull. The lifeless creature swayed before collapsing to the stone floor.

With great care, Sam walked around the dead beast.

Dan raised his arm from the boulder and displayed the smoking revolver. The bullets had dislodged the hanging rock.

"Great shot!" yelled Sam.

However, his praise went unheard, thanks to the rebirth of clashes—the result of the creature's crashing contact with the rock ground.

Sam was soon standing at the boulder beside Dan. The men looked down at the unconscious woman.

"So you really think this is Cindy?" asked Sam.

"Yeah, I do. No offense Sam, but I don't put much stock in your theory that everyone has a twin in the world. I just don't understand how she got here." Once the revolver was slipped between Dan's waist and jeans, he and Sam carried the woman over the incline and through the cave's exit where they placed her on her back.

Within the safety of the open cavern, Sam stared at her. "I wish I shared your optimism, Dan. But even though she looks a lot like Cindy, we can't forget that we're in a strange world where even stranger things can and have happened." He rested his hand on the woman's forehead. "For Cindy's sake, I hope this isn't her."

As Dan was returning the revolver to the backpack, he noticed a scrap of paper sticking out of the woman's front pocket. He removed it, read it, and shook his head.

"What's wrong?" asked Sam. He ripped the paper from Dan's hand and read the printed words aloud, "Starlight Cinema." He held the paper closer to read the fine print. "I don't get it. I don't understand."

"You had just left for the church that night when Jimmy called and asked if William and I wanted to see a movie with him and Cindy." Dan lifted the woman's head and rested it in his lap. "Look at the date on the ticket stub," he directed.

"August thirtieth," replied Sam.

"The last full moon," reminded Dan.

The woman opened her eyes.

CHAPTER SIX
The Smell of Evil

THE YOUNG WOMAN INITIALLY SCRUTINIZED HER NEW surroundings before returning her gaze to the men leaning over her. "Dan? Sam?" she whispered.

"Yeah Cindy," said Dan.

Any lingering doubts Sam had about her identity vanished into thin air.

Cindy scrambled to the cave's entrance. She had cleared the entry by only a few feet when Dan lunged at her and knocked her to the ground.

"Let me go!" she screamed. "I need my reflection!"

"Cindy!" yelled Dan. He struggled to pull her from the side cave. "You have to resist the temptation. You don't belong here!" He suspected that a diversion would mitigate her abnormal attraction to the ponds. "Where's Jimmy?" he shouted.

She continued fighting his hold.

Sam rushed into the cave. "Was Jimmy with you?" he shouted.

Each man sustained several bites and a boot in the face before dragging a hysterical Cindy back into the open tunnel.

Sam shook her shoulders. "Cindy! Cindy! Was Jimmy with you?"

The distraction worked.

An exhausted Cindy gradually redirected her attention from the cave's interior to her traveling companions. "Yes," she eventually replied. "Jimmy and I went to a movie."

"Then what?" prodded Dan.

She looked inside the cave.

Dan yanked her face away. "Where did you go after the movie?"

"Jimmy insisted on walking past the church on our way home," she related. "He wanted to see if the tree was soft."

"Did you see anything out of the ordinary at the church?" prodded Dan.

She stared inside the cave again. "When we got to the church, we saw the oak limbs smashing through the church windows." She redirected her gaze to Dan. "First we saw you thrown into the tree, then we saw William hurled—"

"So William's here?" blurted Dan.

"I don't know," she mumbled.

"And Jimmy?" asked Sam.

"He was walking to the tree when a limb fell from the sky. It grabbed him and threw him into the oak."

Sam displayed a doubtful look at the teenagers. "I don't get it," he said. "The original oak in the forest wasn't aggressive at all. And the night I entered the tree on the church grounds, I simply walked into it—just like we've done in the past."

"Sam, I can't explain it either, but you've got to believe us," claimed Dan. "We didn't just step into the tree. We were thrown in."

Cindy further detailed. "After Jimmy disappeared in the oak, I was running out of a limb's path to get help when I was grabbed by a branch. The next thing I remember, I was staring at my reflection in a pond."

Sam scratched his scalp. "So now we're looking for Father James, Brad Blaze, William, and Jimmy?"

Cindy scanned the vast tunnel. "I don't remember the parallel world looking like this."

Sam helped her to her feet. "Dan and I aren't totally convinced this is the parallel world."

"Then where are we?" she asked.

"We're not sure," said Sam. "But one thing's for sure—we'll not figure it out by standing around here." Suspecting that Cindy had not recovered enough from her ordeal to bear a weapon, Sam refused her request for a spear. "Dan and I each have a lance. We'll be fine."

Surprisingly, Cindy didn't press the issue.

Sam snatched his lance from the ground and swung the backpack over his back while Dan grabbed his weapon and a torch. The three explorers set out in search of their friends and answers.

The initial leg of their journey was covered in complete silence as the transworld travelers surveyed their mysterious surroundings. Each was looking for something that he or she remembered seeing in the parallel world.

Eventually, Cindy broke the stillness. "Sorry about—you know."

"What's that?" asked Dan.

She ended her stride. "I don't know what my infatuation was with the ponds back there. It was weird. It was like something had control over me. Part of me wanted to run from my reflection, but I couldn't."

Dan sensed her shame. He revealed that he and Sam also had experienced similar obsessions in other side caves.

"You did?" she asked.

"Yeah," replied Dan. "After I was tossed into the tree, the next thing I remember, I was chasing a golden chest that kept disappearing and then reappearing at another spot in my cave. Just like you, something had control over my will power to escape the cave."

"Was anyone with you in your cave?" she asked.

"Oh yeah. There were thousands of beings. But no one I recognized." He glanced at Sam and clarified, "He was in a different cave."

Cindy was curious how Dan had escaped the mental bonds of his confinement. "But how'd you free yourself?"

Dan tugged on her arm and motioned that they should continue their hike. "I'm not sure," he eventually replied, "though I do remember thinking about Sam, Father James, William, and Brad. I had a feeling they were probably somewhere in this world and needed help." He came to a standstill.

"What's wrong?" asked Cindy.

"It's weird. I just realized something," said Dan.

"What?" inquired Cindy.

"As soon as I stopped thinking about myself and the golden chest—and started thinking about my friends' safety—I was free from my fixation with the chest. Maybe my selfless thoughts set me free."

THE SINISTER REALM

Sam took four steps back and pulled Dan by the arm. He was determined to cover as much ground as possible.

"Sam, did something like that happen to you?" asked Cindy.

"Come on, we have to keep moving," Sam ordered. He was trying to avoid the painful subject.

Cindy was not dissuaded. "Sam, what happened to you?"

Reluctantly, he replied. "After I stepped into the tree, I also found myself among a throng of beings in a large side cave. But unlike your caves, I was consumed with climbing a ladder that extended to an opening in the ceiling. The only thing that mattered to me was earning the respect of the other cave dwellers."

The group came to a sudden stop.

"What was that?" whispered Cindy.

Sam glanced about. "Just a breeze."

Fairly certain they were exploring an uncharted world, the travelers were overly suspicious of any unexplained noise or movement.

"It was just the wind," reiterated Sam to ease his friends' worries.

"Hey look!" shouted Dan. He pointed to a burning torch embedded in a cavern wall.

The three approached the distant torch.

"Sam, how'd you escape your cave?" asked Cindy.

"I was fortunate that Dan had entered my cave and saw me at the base of the ladder. He used the same tactic on me as he did on you. He diverted my attention from my fascination with the ladder to our friends."

"How did he do that?" she asked.

"He told me that Father James was injured and that the priest and William were probably somewhere in the vast network of caves. Anyway, that's all it took. I can't explain it, but before Dan arrived, I was totally obsessed with the opening in the ceiling." He cleared his throat. "It was only when we focused on leaving the cave that we realized the ladder wasn't an ordinary ladder."

"What do you mean?"

Dan resumed their story of escape by explaining that after he had accidentally brushed a torch against one of the ladder's vertical supports it fell to the ground and then raised itself off the cave floor, revealing a giant walking stick.

THE SMELL OF EVIL

"No—please," implored Cindy. "Don't tell me we're dealing with more creatures."

"It's okay," assured Sam. He pulled the newfound torch from the wall. "We have our weapons and a second torch. We'll be fine."

"And not a moment too soon," declared Dan.

Within seconds of Sam yanking the torch from the wall, Dan's torch died. Their painstaking efforts to reignite it from the new torch were useless. The flame refused to rise again.

Dan tossed the useless piece of wood to the ground.

The rescue party resumed their mission with Sam and his torch taking the lead.

"So what happened to the walking stick?" demanded Cindy.

"Actually, there were two," corrected Dan. "But they're long dead. Just as we were—" He paused. "Wait a minute. Didn't you see the frilled lizard in your cave?"

"The what?" she blurted.

"A giant frilled lizard that hid behind the waterfall," said Dan.

Cindy shook her head. "Like I said, the only thing I remember seeing was my reflection in the pond. So what happened to the lizard?"

"Dan was brilliant," exclaimed Sam. "The moment the lizard stepped below a stalactite, he aimed the revolver at the hanging rock. It dropped like a spear into the beast's skull."

"Quite the gunman," complimented Cindy.

"Not really," played down Dan.

The hike resumed beneath the glow of Sam's torch.

During the group's silent advance, Dan thought it was the perfect time to ask the crucial question. "Cindy, after you were thrown into the oak, do you remember anything about your entry into this world?"

"Not really. Why?"

"You don't remember seeing anything odd or—"

"Cindy, you should probably know it now," interrupted Sam.

"Know what?"

"Remember during the second half of our trip in the parallel world how we were looking for the oak tree?"

"Of course. How could I forget?"

"Look around," directed Sam. "There aren't any trees here. And I seriously doubt we'll see any on this trip."

The revelation hit Cindy to the core. She looked at the cavern walls and up the tunnel as far as the torchlight would permit. "Then what are we looking for? Where's the portal?"

Sam drew the torch closer to her face and promised, "I'm sure we'll eventually find the portal. But in the meantime, are you sure you don't remember anything unusual about your journey through the oak or your arrival in your side cave?"

She stopped in her tracks, lowered her eyes, and shamefully admitted that she couldn't remember a single object or event after being pitched into the tree and appearing beside a pond.

"Sam, since no one remembers anything about their entries, then I suggest we continue searching this cavern world for our friends," proposed Dan. "Maybe we'll stumble upon a clue in the process."

Sam nodded. "You're right. Let's continue looking for the others. Maybe one of them will recall something about his arrival into this world."

Dan stared at the ground and tapped his feet. "Sam, this isn't right."

"What's not right?"

"The ground—it doesn't feel like rock anymore," revealed Dan. "It feels gritty and loose."

Sam and Cindy tested the ground. They also sensed something was different.

"What do you think it is?" asked Cindy.

"I'm not sure," replied Sam. "Maybe the constant breeze and the moisture droplets have loosened and eroded the rock flooring."

Though Cindy and Dan doubted his theory, they said nothing.

"I'm telling you it's nothing," assured Sam. "Come on, we need to keep moving."

The three continued their march up the cavern which was graced with a twenty-foot-high ceiling.

Cindy made an attempt to reduce the growing tensions by opening a conversation. "So Sam, how long do you think we've been in this world?"

"It's difficult to say. But I can't imagine we've been here longer than—" He turned to Cindy. "Are you wearing a watch—you know—one that also shows the date?"

"No. But maybe Jimmy or one of the others is."

The breeze in the tunnel quickly grew in intensity to a forceful wind.

Before anyone asked the obvious, Sam maintained that it was simply a strong wind and nothing more.

Cindy stepped alongside Sam and the torch. "I don't think we've been here too long. I mean, I'm not hungry and I haven't had to go to the bathroom."

"And I don't need a shave," added Sam.

"What about you, Dan?" she teased. "What about your six whiskers?"

"Very funny. If you must know, my facial hair—"

A loud crash was heard from behind.

The explorers spun in fright.

Sam extended the flame to arm's length. He and his friends witnessed a stalactite rocking on the tunnel floor. Without warning, the loose ground on which the huge rock had landed collapsed.

"Run!" yelled Sam.

The group bolted ahead.

While racing up the tunnel at record speed, Sam took a quick glance over his shoulder. To his astonishment, the unstable ground behind the travelers was crumbling rapidly in their direction. The wind killed the flame. In darkness, he tossed the torch.

The three continued their sprint into the shadowy unknown.

Regrettably, the buckling ground quickly overtook their slight lead.

The floor collapsed beneath Sam who was lagging behind the racing teenagers. Moments later, Cindy and Dan also plummeted thirty feet into a dark chasm before its hurricane-force updrafts slammed them against the cavern ceiling.

The travelers hit the rock ceiling with incredible force. Miraculously, they narrowly missed several stalactites. With great pains, they rolled onto their backs, pressed their heels against the ceiling, and inched their way forward with their front sides facing the bottomless abyss and the driving winds.

"Dan!" yelled Sam.

The intensity of the wind overpowered his shout.

Sam struggled to turn his head against the pounding updrafts. Eventually, he saw his friends moving slowly along the ceiling in front of him. With an ear pressed against the stone ceiling, Sam sensed vibrations. *That's odd,* he thought. *Is there another level in this cavern world?* He turned his head again and peered into the abyss. He suffered a sharp pain on his face—then another.

Rock pellets burst from the abyss at great speeds, slashing the travelers and their clothing.

To shield their faces, they rotated themselves, placed their faces against the ceiling, and pressed the tips of their boots on the rock to advance along the ceiling.

Cindy stopped.

Dan crawled alongside her. "Move!" he shouted in her ear. "We don't know how long the updraft will last. We have to clear the abyss!"

"I can't go on!" she screamed.

"Keep moving!" he yelled.

Sam arrived at the feet of the teenagers. He raised his hands over his head and nudged their boots. "Move!" he shouted.

Dan squeezed Cindy's arm and urged her forward.

Quite unexpectedly, screams emerged from the abyss and quickly rose to a pitch that conquered the roar of the mighty winds. The shrieks were eerie and unending.

Whoever or whatever is confined in the abyss is obviously in great pain, thought Dan. Like Cindy, he was slowly surrendering to hopelessness.

Suddenly, the vibrations of the collapsing floor ended.

With great effort, Dan jerked his head and looked ahead. The falling ground had stopped at a large rock formation which extended the width of the tunnel. "The edge of the abyss is just ahead!" he shouted. "Let's go!"

Cindy drew on reserved strengths and made a surprisingly fast pace along the ceiling.

Sam also spotted the solid ground ahead. He raced toward the sanctuary.

THE SMELL OF EVIL

Though bombarded by slashing rock shards and beset with piercing screams from the abyss, the travelers pressed forward.

Cindy was the first to reach the solid ground. The upward current of air ended abruptly. She dropped twenty feet to the rock floor. Luckily, she landed on her feet and rolled. Sam did likewise. But Dan landed on his back. The wind was knocked out of him.

Cindy raced to his side and began mouth-to-mouth resuscitation. "Come on, breathe!" she yelled between breaths.

Sam pressed on Dan's chest to draw a response.

With the third lifesaving attempt, Dan coughed and opened his eyes. "Quite a landing," he mumbled.

"Dan, you scared us half to death!" yelled Cindy.

"Sorry." He gasped for air. "But it wasn't on purpose." After several more deep coughs, he tried to rise to a seated position.

Sam was quick to push his shoulders to the ground. "You need to rest for a while," he ordered.

A creak was heard from behind.

Though the darkness obscured the travelers' vision, all felt the dreadful rumblings.

The collapsing floor had moved beyond the retaining rock formation.

Sam yanked Dan to his feet. "You can rest later—run!"

Cindy and Sam supported Dan. The three dashed up the tunnel until they came across six large boulders—each extending the width of the cavern. In a matter of seconds, the explorers were standing on the opposite side of the rocks. They were hopeful they had bought themselves some time.

"Do you think we're protected?" asked Cindy.

Sam looked to the opposite side of the boulders. "It's hard to say for sure. But yeah, I think we're safe for the time being." He leaned Dan against a wall. "How are you feeling?" he asked.

"A little out of breath, but I'll be fine."

"Nevertheless, we'll not take any unnecessary chances." He looked to the far side of the boulders again to confirm the ground was not breaking up. "We'll rest here for a few moments and then continue our fast pace."

Cindy was uneasy with Sam's suggestion. "But what if the floor—"

"Cindy!" snapped Sam. "The boulders are acting like a retaining wall. We'll be okay."

Dan's labored breathing had not subsided; Cindy helped him to the ground.

"I'll be right back," said Sam.

Cindy jumped to her feet. "Where are you going?"

Sam pointed to a glowing torch in the distance. "I'll be only a few minutes. Stay here and keep an eye on Dan."

Cindy rested on her knees beside her teenage friend. "You never seem to get a break, do you?"

"I'll be fine. I only got the wind knocked out of me."

"Speaking of wind, what was the deal with the wind and screams back there?"

Dan looked in the direction of the abyss. "I guess the wind was a natural updraft." He took a moment to catch his breath. "I remember reading somewhere that the velocity of updrafts from a chasm is related to the depth of the abyss. And considering none of us have ever experienced ferocious winds like those—even when we left the parallel world—I'd imagine the depth of the abyss is limitless."

"Honestly Dan, you need to read something besides scientific journals."

He ignored her sarcasm. "And as far as the screams, it's hard to say who or what was screaming and for how long."

"What do you mean how long?"

"Unlike wind, the speed of sound is relatively fixed—somewhere around seven hundred miles per hour. Anyway, if the abyss is infinite, or at least unbelievably deep, then there's the possibility that the screams we just heard were voiced eons ago, even though they're only now reaching our ears."

Cindy displayed a puzzled look. "Are you saying that the screams we heard could have been set in motion thousands of years ago, but we're only now hearing them?"

Dan nodded. "And considering we're probably in some bizarre world, there's also the real possibility that the screams were not simply mouthed eons ago, but that the beings or creatures were screaming incessantly at one point in time. After all, the screams were not simply heard once and then followed by silence. They were constant."

Cindy stood and leaned against a tunnel wall. "But there was something different about the screams."

"What do you mean?"

"I'm not sure how to explain it. I've never heard screams like those before. It's as if the beings or creatures were screaming from some unthinkable horror." She lowered her gaze to Dan. "I know it sounds crazy, but I actually smelled evil above the chasm."

The teenagers switched their sights to movement ahead.

Sam was returning with the torch.

As he drew closer, Cindy blurted, "Sam, your face is bleeding."

He extended the flame nearer the teenagers and noticed that they too had sustained cuts on their faces, necks, and hands—bloody souvenirs of their encounter with flying rock above the abyss. Even their clothes sported rips and slashes. Sam squatted. "Dan, do you have any severe pain in your back, arms, or legs?"

"Well yeah. As a matter of fact, I've got a horrible backache. But if you're asking if I've broken any bones—no."

"I know your landing was unavoidable but...well...you can't take for granted that you'll be as lucky in the future," cautioned Sam. "You need to watch your every step."

Though Cindy was grateful that Dan was recovering, she was still greatly concerned with the safety factor. "Sam, do you still think the ground is stable enough to support our weight?"

"Yeah, I think so." He rose to his feet and jumped on the ground.

"Sam—don't!" she shouted. "You'll start another collapse!"

Dan braced himself against the cavern wall and rose to his feet.

Sam immediately had his arm around his friend's waist. "I know you're impatient to move on, but I still think you should rest a bit."

"I'm fine," assured Dan. "Besides, we need to find the others and put as much distance between us and the crumbling floor."

A morbid thought crossed Cindy's mind. "Sam, what if the floor collapses throughout the entire tunnel and there's no way of escape?"

"I guess we could go up."

"Up?" she blurted. "Up where?"

THE SINISTER REALM

"Didn't you feel it?"

"Feel what?" asked Dan.

"When we were crawling on the ceiling, I pressed my ear against the stone and felt vibrations," explained Sam.

"What kind of vibrations?" asked Cindy.

"I'm not sure. But there was definite movement."

Cindy was eager to get as far away from the disintegrating floor as possible. "If there's a safer level above us, how do we get there?"

"That's a good question," replied Sam. "Unfortunately, I haven't seen any rock formations or passageways leading upward. Have you, Dan?"

"No—nothing. After I left my cave—but before entering yours—I crossed paths with the king crab and the water spider. I constantly scanned the cavern walls, but I never saw a stone staircase or anything leading up."

Sam saw despair in Cindy's eyes. "Then we'll just keep looking. I'm sure we'll find something."

The group had hiked only a short distance up the tunnel with Sam bearing the torch when he asked, "Dan, for as long as we've been exploring this cavern, is it my imagination or do you think the tunnel veers slightly to the left?"

"I never really noticed. Actually, it's hard to tell in the poor light."

Sam extended the torch to arm's length. "It's probably nothing, but I wonder if this cavern is oval or if it runs straight and ends up—who knows where."

"I suppose anything's possible," admitted Dan. "But if it's oval, then eventually we'll reach the cave where I was confined."

Cindy's eyes lit up. "So, if it's oval—and since we haven't come across Dan's cave yet—then there's still a chance that an entry to an upper level could be somewhere up ahead—presuming there is an upper level."

Sam discerned enthusiasm in her voice and decided against dampening her spirits. He refused to disclose that an oval-shaped cavern was merely a hunch. "Let's keep an eye out for an upward passageway," he advised.

During the next one-hour hike, the travelers continually scanned

THE SMELL OF EVIL

the cavern walls for any upward exit. They knew they had to discover an upper passageway soon, lest the collapsing floor catch them off guard again.

With no luck finding a side cave or a vertical exit, their hope of escape slowly waned. To make matters worse, they noticed that the ceiling made a steep descent several yards ahead. Another crawlspace awaited them. As they approached the rock shaft, the light of the torch reflected off water within the narrow passageway.

"What's with this place?" complained Sam.

Cindy's frustrations were growing. "Where do we go now?"

The men remained silent.

"If we go back, we'll run into the abyss again," she reminded.

Dan grabbed Sam's torch and entered the tight passageway. His co-explorers trailed with Sam dragging the bag of weapons at his side.

After what seemed an eternity of crawling through stagnant water, the overhead rock wall slowly receded. The group found themselves splashing through the water in a stooped position.

"Look!" exclaimed Dan.

Twenty feet ahead lay dry land and another glowing torch in the cavern wall.

I wonder who or what reignites the torches? Dan thought.

Sam sensed he was being watched; everything was too still. He looked behind and spotted an enormous water spider closing the distance between itself and its next meal. "Run!" he yelled.

Without questioning or looking back, the teenagers dashed to the water's edge.

On the shore, the three travelers stood motionless, watching the spider creep closer.

Sam raised his weapon.

"My gosh, is that a human face?" whispered Cindy.

"Yeah, I met one of its kind earlier," replied Dan.

The spider placed its forelegs on the dry land. Thanks to the glow of Dan's torch and another one on a nearby wall, the spider noticed a resemblance in its prey to its own species. It withdrew into the shallow waters.

"This definitely is not the parallel world," declared Cindy.

As Sam watched the human-faced spider vanish in the darkness, he agreed. "Yeah, I don't think it is either."

Believing that the spider might return—and knowing that dangers certainly awaited them ahead—Sam opened the backpack and armed Cindy. "Oh, I almost forgot," he said while rummaging through the bag.

"Forgot what?" asked Dan.

"The snacks your Mom packed for me before I headed to the church." He pulled the bag from his backpack.

Dan held the care package and wondered how his parents were handling his disappearance.

"Sorry Dan, but it looks like the saturated food isn't salvageable," said Sam. "Even the juice cartons were damaged by the flying rocks."

"That's okay," he replied. "I still don't have an appetite."

Cindy grabbed a breakfast bar that had fallen from the bag. "You know, for as long and as hard as we've hiked, I still can't believe we're not hungry." In a near trance state, she scanned the water's surface. "Where the heck are we?" she asked.

"I haven't a clue," said Sam. He waved his wet revolver to dry the moisture.

Dan submerged the care package in the water under a rock. He knew that no evidence should be left behind for whomever or whatever tended the torches. With a torch in hand, he raced to the cavern wall to claim the second torch.

Sam and Cindy were on his heels.

CHAPTER SEVEN

The Messenger of Ill Tidings

IN THE TRAVELERS' HOME WORLD, JEFF CLAY WAS LIFTING the phone when he heard a knock at the back door. He looked through the kitchen window and saw Tom and Marie standing on the porch. He hung up the phone and invited them inside. "Tom, Marie, that's weird."

"What's that?" asked Tom.

"I was just getting ready to call you."

Nancy—who was still recovering on the living room sofa from Officer Moore's key discovery—heard voices around the corner. She grabbed another tissue, blew her nose, and stepped into the kitchen. "Tom, Marie," she greeted in a somber tone.

"Good afternoon, Nancy," said Marie.

"Marie and I saw the officer leaving your house just now and…um…we were curious about her second visit," said Tom. "Have the police discovered something?"

"Actually, the police found something concerning Dan and William. But there weren't any leads on Jimmy or Cindy," said Jeff.

"What did they find?" asked Marie.

"Officer Moore found Dan's house key in the church," informed Jeff. "Now we know that Dan and William were in the church before they disappeared."

"Did the officer have any clues where your sons or Jimmy might be now?" pressed Marie.

"No," Jeff replied.

Nancy sat at the kitchen table. "There's more," she whispered.

The Parkers couldn't help but notice her worried look and watery eyes. They and Jeff joined her at the table.

Nancy supported her chin on her folded hands. "We promised we'd share any new information with each other and the police," she reminded.

"Yes," affirmed Marie.

"Even though what was discovered has nothing to do with Jimmy or the others, I still think you should know," said Nancy.

Marie pulled her chair closer to Nancy's. "We're here for you. Whatever it is, we'll help you through it."

"It's not so much that Dan's house key was discovered in the church, as much as—" She fell silent.

Marie placed her arm around Nancy. "Please go on."

"There was blood on the key," said Nancy.

The Parkers were stunned.

Knowing that no words existed to comfort a heartbroken mother who had only recently lost her two sons, Tom reached across the table and squeezed Nancy's arm in a display of comfort and support. "Maybe it wasn't Dan's or William's blood," he posed. "I don't think we should jump to conclusions."

"Tom's right," said Jeff. "These are just speculations."

"But I just don't get it," said Nancy.

"What do you mean?" asked Marie.

Nancy stepped from the table and leaned against the kitchen sink. "Ever since their disappearance, I've had a hunch they entered the tree, though I can't prove it." She grabbed a napkin from the counter and dabbed her eyes. "As it stands right now, Jeff and I know they were in the church—and there's the real possibility they were injured as the blood would suggest. But the fact that Father James also is missing raises questions as to what really happened that night or early morning. I mean, either there was a burglary—as Officer Moore suspects—and the boys and Father James were injured and then abducted or there was a burglary and the boys and Father James were injured but escaped through the tree."

A momentary silence filled the room.

Nancy continued. "Despite the fact that Dan and William broke

THE MESSENGER OF ILL TIDINGS

their promise to Jeff and me about not nearing the tree, part of me hopes they entered the oak. At least that way, they are free of the burglars and hopefully in a peaceful world." She neared the table, stood behind her husband, and rested her hands on his shoulders. "I pray that the world is peaceful." She looked at Marie. "I wish we had some news about Jimmy, but the police don't have any evidence that he was in the church."

"I know," she replied. "He was at the movie theater with Cindy."

"But there's the possibility that he and Cindy met up with your sons after the movie," proposed Tom.

Jeff eyed the distraught faces around the kitchen table. "Look, these speculations aren't helping us. If our kids entered the church and were kidnapped, then it's a good thing that Officer Moore doesn't believe our story about the oak. This way, she and the entire police department will continue searching Lawton and the nearby towns for any signs of foul play. But if they escaped the burglars through the tree, then they're probably in a peaceful world and will return next month."

"You're probably right," remarked Tom after helping his wife from her chair.

"But there's one thing that bothers me," stated Marie.

"What's that?" asked Nancy.

"If Jimmy and Cindy joined your sons in the church—and if your boys were injured—who's to say that Jimmy and Cindy weren't injured also?"

Jeff warned the group again about jumping to conclusions. "With no proof of our children's whereabouts, everything at this point is mere conjecture. We'll just keep hoping and praying for everyone's safe return."

The Parkers left the house visibly shaken.

Shortly after their guests' departure, Nancy phoned and updated Sara on the latest finding. The Clays spent the remainder of the afternoon in the living room trying to piece together the elaborate puzzle of their sons' unexplained disappearance.

It seemed as though only an hour had passed when the clock in the hallway chimed five times.

"Wow, where did the afternoon go?" exclaimed Jeff. "We should probably think about dinner."

Nancy shook her head. "I'm not hungry. I'd rather take a walk to clear my head."

Given her condition, Jeff accompanied her.

The evening air was curiously still as the couple stepped onto the front porch. They had walked only a few blocks in the direction of Main Street when the church steeples came into view.

It came as no surprise to Jeff when Nancy insisted on visiting the church.

Before long, they were standing on the church steps.

Jeff had just opened the door when Nancy jumped to the sidewalk and dashed to the oak.

He raced to her side and grabbed her arm. "Honey, it's not a good idea."

Only feet from the oak, she wept. "I just want to touch the tree. It's probably the last thing our boys touched."

Jeff suspected the oak was safe since there wasn't a full moon. But on the other hand, he wasn't taking any chances. With caution, he stepped forward and extended his hand to its surface. "It's solid." He looked back at his wife and perceived a trace of guilt. "What's wrong?" he asked.

She placed her back to her husband and the tree. "There's something I didn't tell you the morning when we learned our boys disappeared."

"What?"

She turned and faced Jeff. "When I was walking Sara to our car that morning, a strong wind caused one of these branches to hit me on the back. When I looked at the tree, I saw a demonic face at its base."

Jeff stared at the tree trunk. "Maybe it was just a knot on the oak; it's pretty gnarled. Or maybe it—"

"No Jeff. Trust me, I know what I saw." She took a step closer to her husband. "I pray constantly that if our boys stepped into the tree that they're in a peaceful place and not in one inhabited by what I saw."

"Why didn't you tell me this earlier?"

"I don't know. I wanted to but—I don't know." After a few moments examining the tree's base for the fiendish image, she raised her eyes to Jeff. "And I purposely didn't tell Sara or the Parkers about the face on the tree because we don't know for sure their kids are with Dan and William. I didn't want to needlessly alarm them."

Jeff decided against pursuing the issue. *After all, it was probably just as I suspected—a raised tree knot,* he thought.

Nancy placed her hands on the oak, closed her eyes, and whispered a prayer.

Jeff rested his hands on hers.

She ended her prayer and opened her eyes. As she stepped from the tree, her attention was drawn to a reflection on the ground. She knelt on the lawn.

"Honey, what are you doing?" he asked.

She was too busy brushing over blades of grass to answer. To her astonishment, she unearthed a medal and chain. "Dan's medal!" she exclaimed. She jumped to her feet.

A skeptical Jeff inspected the medal in the palm of her hand. "Nancy, this could be anyone's. Let's face it, we're on church grounds. Besides, if it's—"

"I know it's Dan's." She raised the medal to Jeff's face and pointed out the scratch mark that Dan had made when replacing the chain.

As much as Jeff wanted to remain objective, even he remembered his son showing him the nick several months earlier.

Nancy bit her lower lip and displayed a puzzled look.

"What's wrong?" he asked.

"But it doesn't make sense."

"What doesn't make sense?" he prodded.

"With Dan's deep faith life, why on earth would he remove it before entering the tree," she posed. "Why?"

Jeff shrugged his shoulders. "If—and I mean if—he and William got into a clash with burglars, then maybe it fell from his neck during the struggle."

Nancy dropped to her knees again and searched the ground for more evidence of her sons' recent presence.

"That's enough," implored a concerned husband. "There's nothing more here."

"There's got to be; there just has to be!"

He clasped her wrists. "Let's go inside," he suggested.

Nancy recalled the indescribable comfort she felt in the past when praying in the church. She dropped the clumps of grass from her hands and walked with her husband to the church steps. She glanced back at the oak. "I'm sorry," she said.

He opened the church door a second time. "There's no need to apologize. I understand."

Nancy had just stepped over the threshold when she asserted, "Well, we know at least two things."

"What's that?"

"We know that our boys were in the church, as the key would suggest. We also know that they were near the oak, thanks to the medal." She refused to accept her husband's theory that Dan and William may have clashed with burglars near the oak. It was too painful for her to envision. She subconsciously blocked the thought. "I just don't understand why Dan would leave his medal behind and why there was blood in the church and on the key."

The door closed behind the couple.

•

On Beacon Lane, the Parkers were finishing their dinner.

Marie took a sip of tea and set the cup on a saucer. "Tom, do you think that Jimmy and Cindy met up with the Clay boys and entered the oak?"

Taken by surprise—since the entire meal up to that point had been consumed in complete silence—Tom wiped his mouth. "I can't imagine where else they would have gone after the movie since it was so late." He rose from the table and stared out the window to the Clays' house. "I'm glad that Jeff and Nancy are finally getting some answers about their boys, though I have to admit that the blood on the key has me stumped."

Marie joined her husband at the window. "If the blood on the house key was Dan's or William's—and if Jimmy and Cindy also entered the church—"

"Marie, don't torture yourself," he insisted.

"Who's to say that Jimmy and Cindy weren't injured too?" she concluded.

"Honey, you're jumping to conclusions again. Besides, I have every confidence that our son can defend himself."

Marie returned to the table. "Tom, there's something I've been meaning to discuss with you, but I'm not sure that now is the best time."

"What's that?"

She took a few moments to gather her thoughts. "If Jimmy stepped into the oak, and if there's the possibility that he and the others were injured—" She couldn't bring herself to ask the unthinkable.

"Yes—go on," he urged.

"I'm sorry, Tom. I was going to ask if you and Jeff would enter the oak to search for the kids, just in case they're hurt and can't make it back."

Tom joined her at the table. "I know you're worried about Jimmy's safety. I also know that you wouldn't ask me to take the trip unless you thought it was absolutely necessary. But in all honesty, I've considered stepping into the oak ever since I learned about the bloodstained key."

The potential dangers that her husband would likely encounter suddenly filled Marie with terror. "No," she reconsidered. "It was wrong of me to ask. I couldn't bear having you and Jeff in harm's way." She lowered her head and stared into her teacup. "I'm sorry I even suggested it. I don't know what I was thinking."

"I do. You were thinking about Jimmy's safety. And there's nothing wrong with that."

"I know, but I never should have even considered asking you to make such a sacrifice."

"Honey, I don't want you worrying about me and the trip. Let's not forget that there's still plenty of time before the next full moon. Who knows, maybe the kids will return from wherever they are before the next full moon rises. Remember, we don't know for sure that the oak is the cause of their disappearance."

"I hope you're right. I hope they return soon," she replied.

"Come on," he encouraged, "give the kids a little more credit for their resourcefulness."

"I suppose you're right. They were pretty amazing when battling the creatures during the homecoming meal."

"See, I told you. They're clever kids." He gathered the empty dishes from the table. "Why don't you wash and I'll dry," he proposed.

She stepped to the kitchen sink.

•

Father Andreas returned to the rectory after an exhaustive day of services—one wedding, three baptisms, and a sick call visit at the hospital. Parish responsibilities had consumed so much of his time since his arrival that he was only now getting around to opening the mail that had been piling up.

"Bill, bill, bill," he mumbled while flipping through the mound of letters. Midway through the stack, he noticed an odd-size envelope that was simply addressed to the priest in residence. Even more peculiar was the 'Saint Augustine of Canterbury Church' return address label. *That's odd*, he thought. He dropped the pile of letters to the desk and opened the one in question. He immediately turned over the letter to see who it was from. He dropped to his chair. The letter was from Father James Roberts.

> Dear Father,
>
> I apologize for the vague salutation, but as I write this letter I'm not sure who will replace me at the parish. If you're reading this letter, you've obviously been temporarily assigned to Saint Augustine Church and I've obviously been reported missing.
>
> You're probably wondering why I mailed this letter instead of placing it somewhere in the rectory. To be honest, I couldn't take the chance of it falling into the hands of a staff member. It's vitally important that only you be made aware of a potentially dire situation.
>
> Where should I begin?
>
> On July 30, I made a late night hospital call on a parishioner, Alice Schaeffer, who was near death. After administering the last rites, she told me about a dream she had earlier that evening which had greatly upset her. In her dream, I was praying in the church when I suddenly was yanked from the Communion rail. She

also mentioned seeing blood near the railing and the backs of two people who were also praying in the church. They were jerked from a pew.

In her dream, she looked around the church and saw several broken stained glass windows and a large tree on the church's lawn that was visible through the window openings. I found this troubling since Alice had been in the hospital for nearly a week and I had seen the tree for the first time only minutes before visiting her. Actually, my many glances at the tree in my rearview mirror during my drive to the hospital almost caused a collision with another car. This close call, by the way, also was recalled by Alice as part of her dream. Finally, just before she shut her eyes forever, she stared at me from her hospital bed and screamed, "Brad Blaze!"

By now, Father, you've probably heard the story from parish staff about a missing parishioner, Brad Blaze. What you haven't heard is that another parishioner, Sam White, will travel in search of Brad tonight, August 30.

Very early this morning, unable to shake Alice's dream and what may befall me, I wrote this letter. I'll admit that I'm not sure what to make of the situation, but I knew it would be best to put my thoughts and concerns in writing in case something unforeseeable happens. If, however, nothing does, then I'll receive this letter in the mail and shred it.

There are many stories I could tell you about the children of the Clays, the Parkers, and Sara Somer, but it would be inappropriate for me to share them without their permission.

However, I must insist that the oak on the church lawn remain. Without going into greater detail, the tree may be crucial to the safe return of Brad and Sam. Under no circumstances should the tree be removed.

In closing, please keep Brad and Sam in your prayers. As for me and the two unidentified church visitors, I don't know what's forthcoming—at least not at the time of writing this letter—but we could use your prayers as well.

Your brother in Christ,
Reverend James Roberts

Father Andreas inspected the postmark date—August 30. *Maybe the two unknown visitors were—* He tried to dismiss the thought, but failed. *The stories the families told me about their kids possibly stepping through the oak tree on the church's lawn to a parallel world and— That's impossible. It just can't be.* He took another look at the postmark date.

THE SINISTER REALM

●

The next day was dreary. Torrential rains had settled upon Lawton during the early morning hours and refused to leave.

While opening the car door for his wife beneath the protection of their shared umbrella, Jeff watched the Parkers pull out of their driveway. After a wave, he jumped into the driver's seat. "I suppose it'll rain all day."

Nancy disregarded her husband's prediction while collapsing the umbrella. "Maybe we should have called Sara earlier this morning to see if she wanted to ride with us. I don't like her being alone during this stressful time."

"Should I call her now?"

"That's all right. She's probably already on her way to the church."

The drive to Saint Augustine's took longer than normal, thanks to the steady downpour. As Jeff pulled into the parking lot, Nancy pointed. "There's Sara's car," she exclaimed.

Jeff bolted out of the car, raced to the passenger's side, and helped his wife who was trying to steady the umbrella against the driving winds. He huddled with her under the umbrella's protection.

"Good morning!" greeted Tom from three parking spaces away.

A clap of thunder startled the churchgoers.

Marie bolted from the car. "We're running late," she informed. "Let's get inside or we'll all be soaked in no time."

Protected by only two umbrellas, the couples raced to the church doors.

Sara was in such a profound state of prayer below the statue of Saint Michael the Archangel that she failed to hear the squeaky approach of the drenched shoes.

"Good morning, Sara," said Marie.

"Good morning," she replied.

Before Nancy had a chance to greet Sara, a bell chimed. Mass had begun.

"Sara, come sit with us," whispered Nancy.

With a silent nod, the offer was accepted.

THE MESSENGER OF ILL TIDINGS

Once seated in the fifth pew, the families offered the Mass for the safe return of their children, Sam, Brad, and Father James from wherever they were.

At the conclusion of the worship service, the parents left the pew and returned to the angelic statue which stood squarely between two boarded window openings.

The families were barely two minutes into their silent prayers when Marie leaned toward Nancy, asking, "What's keeping Father Andreas? Do you think that after hearing the story of our children and the oak he's decided not to join us?"

Nancy looked to the sanctuary. "Maybe he's being delayed by a parishioner."

Father Andreas was not with a parishioner. Instead, he was pacing the sacristy floor debating whether or not to tell the parents about the letter he received from Father James. He didn't want to add to the families' mounting worries. But at the same time, he knew they had the right to be informed of any developments. He left the sacristy and approached the marble statue.

"Good morning, Father," said Nancy when he was within earshot.

"Morning everyone." The priest remained standing behind the kneeling parents.

"Is something wrong, Father?" asked Sara.

"Before we begin our prayers, I'd like to share something with you," he advised. He pointed to a nearby pew. "Let's make ourselves comfortable." Once the families were seated, he began, "Something came to my attention last night."

"What?" blurted Marie.

"Actually, I'm not sure how or where to begin."

Nancy had a hunch that the strange tales the families had shared with him in confidence were the cause of his hesitation. "Father, if it's about the stories we told you concerning the oak and our children, you have to believe us. We were telling you the truth."

The priest refused to respond. Even after reading Father James's letter, he still harbored doubts about the families' claims. He found their stories too unbelievable. He also found it odd that the letter never mentioned specifics about the oak's supposed qualities. He grabbed an envelope from his shirt pocket. "Last night when I was sorting through the mail, I came upon something unusual." He ripped the letter from the envelope. "It's a message from Father James."

"Father James?" shouted Nancy.

"Shh," warned the priest. He glanced to the pews for worshipers. "Apparently, Father James wrote this letter and mailed it to the future priest in residence shortly before—" He ended his comment. An elderly woman had entered the church.

The group remained silent until the visitor was kneeling near the sanctuary.

"When did you say your children disappeared?" asked Father Andreas.

"Friday night, August thirtieth," said Nancy. "Why?"

"This letter was written the morning of the thirtieth and postmarked the same day."

Nancy snatched the letter from his hand while asking, "What does it say?"

Seeing that the lone worshiper was still in prayerful thought a great distance away, Marie asked Nancy to read the letter out loud.

At its conclusion, the parents were speechless.

"Since Dan's house key was found in the church, I'd imagine that the two unknown people in Alice Schaeffer's dream were Dan and William," said Marie.

"What key in the church?" asked Father Andreas.

Once the priest was updated on the police officer's discovery, Nancy returned the letter to him. "There's something Jeff and I need to share with the group also."

Father Andreas raised an eyebrow. "What's that?" he asked.

"Since I wasn't hungry for dinner last night, Jeff and I took a walk. Before we knew it, we were standing on the church grounds. I don't know what came over me, but I had the uncontrollable urge to touch the tree. Anyway, when I was standing beside it, I saw something shiny on the ground near its trunk." She pulled the medal from her purse. "This is what I found—Dan's medal."

All eyes were glued to the religious object.

"But how do you know it's Dan's?" asked Sara.

"Because of this scratch mark." Nancy pointed to the nick. "I remember Dan scratching it some time ago."

Tom held the medal in his hand. "So it would appear that Dan and William were not only in the church—as the discovery of your house key indicates—but also near the tree as this medal suggests."

Nancy accepted the medal from Tom. "That's the same conclusion I came to."

Jeff detected both fear and despair on the faces of Sara and Marie. "I'm sorry we haven't found anything to confirm Jimmy's or Cindy's whereabouts. But it doesn't look like they entered the church or checked out the oak after the movie."

Tom was desperate for answers. "Or maybe Cindy and Jimmy stayed outside the church," he suggested. "That would certainly explain why Alice Schaeffer never saw them in her dream."

Marie shook her head. "I don't know what to believe or hope for anymore. Part of me wishes Jimmy stepped into the tree and is in a peaceful world. But at the same time, I hope he didn't step into the oak, in case the person or persons who burglarized the church followed him into the tree."

Sara voiced the same mixed concerns.

Father Andreas introduced a dose of reality. "At this point in time, no one knows for sure where anyone is—including Dan and William. I suppose that the house key and the medal could point to the possibility that they were in the church and also near the tree. But even so, there are many inconsistencies and just as many unanswered questions." He stepped from the pew. "I think it's best that we resume our prayers for their safety."

Sara also rose from the pew. "You're probably right, Father." She followed him to the statue.

Within moments, the six adults were deep in prayer beneath the gaze of the heavenly messenger.

The families had just begun the fourth decade of the rosary when Nancy could have sworn she noticed something peculiar about the statue. She looked again, but the oddity was gone.

At the conclusion of their prayers, Father Andreas thanked the families for their attendance at Mass and for their ongoing prayers for their loved ones. The families, in turn, expressed their gratitude for his spiritual direction.

The priest crossed the church floor and headed to the sacristy.

"Nancy, I feel guilty," admitted Marie as the ladies walked to the church doors. "During the entire rosary I kept thinking about Father James's letter."

"I hate to admit it, but I also was distracted."

"Do you think Father Andreas believes us now?" asked Marie.

Nancy dipped a finger into the holy water font. "I think he's coming around."

Marie also blessed herself with the holy water. She looked across the church to the boarded window openings. "I wonder if Father James escaped through the tree or was abducted by whoever broke the windows and vandalized the church."

"It's hard to say," replied Nancy. "But as Father Andreas just mentioned, it's impossible to know for sure where anyone is." The ladies stepped into the rain.

The husbands caught up with their wives beneath the umbrellas and headed to their respective cars.

Sara ran to Nancy and Jeff. "Was it just my imagination or did something happen to the statue when we were praying?" she blurted.

Only three parking spaces away, Marie overheard Sara's comment. She slammed her car door and approached Sara.

Tom dashed through the rain to his wife's side.

"You noticed something too?" asked Nancy. "I thought it was just me."

"You mean the cuts on the statue's face?" questioned Sara.

"Uh-huh. I saw them for a brief moment before they disappeared," revealed Nancy.

"I didn't see any marks on the face," blurted Marie.

"Nor did I," seconded Tom.

"My gosh!" exclaimed Nancy. "There were so many. How could you miss them? Then the statue's face seemed—"

"Enraged!" blurted Jeff.

"Yeah, enraged," agreed Nancy.

"I didn't notice a look of anger on the statue's face," admitted Marie, "but for a split second, I could almost swear I saw a cord hanging from its mouth. But it all happened so fast. And since the lighting in the church isn't the greatest—especially below the boarded windows—I didn't say anything since no one else seemed to notice it."

"I saw it too!" exclaimed Tom.

"You did?" questioned his wife.

"Yeah."

"I never saw a cord dangling from its mouth," admitted Jeff, "but I—"

"And what about the blemish on its face?" interrupted Sara.

"What blemish?" asked Nancy.

Sara touched the area below her right eye. "Like a blotch on the face," she described.

"No. I didn't see a blotch below the statue's right eye," replied Nancy. She leaned against the car. "But come to think of it, I thought I saw marks on the calves and ankles of the statue. I'll admit that it sounds absurd that I don't know for sure, but for a fleeting moment I could almost swear—"

"Yeah, I also thought I saw something on the legs," interrupted Jeff. "But I assumed that my eyes were playing tricks on me in the poor lighting."

As the families discussed the supposed imperfections of the marble statue, a disturbing thought entered Nancy's mind. "Do you think our children have been harmed and that the statue is showing us the injuries they're suffering?" she proposed.

Everyone suspected that Nancy was onto something.

Jeff, however, tried to reassure his wife, his friends, and even himself that their children were not in danger. "Look, I'm sure there's a reasonable explanation why each of us noticed certain defects in the statue," he said.

There was no mistaking the looks of skepticism around him.

"Oh come on," he exclaimed. "You said it yourselves that everything happened in a split second and in poor lighting. For all we know, the flaws simply could have been optical illusions."

Unlike Nancy's assumption, everyone verbally rejected Jeff's theory.

"All right, I'll admit that I thought I saw something too," disclosed Jeff. "But I don't think we should torture ourselves by jumping to conclusions again. I suggest that we put the incident out of our minds and continue meeting here every morning until our kids return home."

The Parkers and Sara returned to their cars in complete silence.

Nancy buckled herself in the family car. "No offense, Jeff, but I don't believe your story about the optical illusion." She stared through the windshield at the rain. "Do you think there's a connection between the statue and our boys?" she posed.

Jeff ignored her question and glanced to the back seat. "Where's my prayer book?" he mumbled.

Nancy's stare at the rain remained unchanged.

"Maybe I left it in church," he said. "I'll be right back." He darted through the rain to the front doors.

After years of marriage, Nancy knew when her husband was troubled. And this was definitely one of those times. She also knew that the mere thought of their boys being harmed was unbearable for him. She raced from the car, stepped inside the church, and found her husband kneeling below the statue. He was clutching his recovered prayer book. As she made a hushed approach to the kneeler, she and Jeff witnessed a gash materialize on the statue's forehead. Blood dripped to the archangel's marble sandal.

Nancy collapsed.

Jeff spun and saw his wife gripping a pew and laboring to her feet. He raced to her side.

Supported by her husband and a pew, the grief-stricken mother declared, "Our boys are in danger."

Since no one knew the location of the missing persons, Jeff had no choice but to endure the mental anguish. He wanted nothing more than to rescue his sons.

Sadly, the sealed portal robbed him of his paternal instinct to safeguard his sons.

The couple knelt and resumed their prayers for the group's safety.

CHAPTER EIGHT
A Walk Through Time

SECONDS EARLIER IN THE UNKNOWN WORLD, DAN WAS CARRYING the sole torch and running to the cavern wall to snatch a second torch when he tripped over a stone and gashed his forehead on the rock ground. As he staggered to his feet, blood dripped to his boot.

"Are you all right!" yelled Cindy while dashing to his side.

Dan made light of the pain. "I'm fine." He touched his bleeding brow. "I guess I was so focused on the torch that I—"

"Now look, Dan," reprimanded Sam as he approached the teenagers, "I know perfectly well what you were thinking about."

"I wasn't thinking about anything except grabbing that torch." He pointed to the cavern wall.

"I know that you and Cindy have your parents on your minds. And that would be fine if we weren't in a deadly—" He cleared his throat and rephrased, "What I'm trying to say is that excessive thoughts about your folks while we're in this strange world could easily distract you and cause another accident. What good would it do your parents if both of you got yourselves killed?"

"But Sam," stressed Dan, "just because—"

"All I'm saying is that we have to be on the lookout for anything and everything on our walk through these tunnels and watch one another's backs like we used to. If we don't, I can promise you that none of us will make it out of this place alive."

Cindy lowered her head. "I know you're right, Sam, but I can't stop thinking about my Mom. When we returned from the parallel world, I learned how frantic she was during my disappearance. Actually, frantic is an understatement. And for all I know, she probably thinks I intentionally stepped into the tree again."

"That's exactly what I mean," said Sam. "We have to force ourselves to clear our minds about home and stay alert while we're in this rock world or someone is going to get seriously injured or worse."

Dan also knew that Sam had a valid concern. "All right, I'll try to stay focused," he agreed. With the torch still in hand, he peered up the tunnel. "But I think we should keep moving, especially since we don't know how much time we have until the next full moon." He took several steps closer to the cavern wall, yanked the second torch, and handed it to Sam.

The explorers advanced further into the unknown in search of their friends, answers, and the portal home.

"Sam, don't you think it's weird that we still don't have an appetite and we haven't had to use the bathroom?" asked Cindy.

He rubbed his clean-shaven face. "Yeah, it's weird. But remember, we're not sure this is the parallel world."

"But Sam, if our bodily functions have been suspended, then why are our wounds healing?" posed Dan. He touched the back of his head. "Even the cut on my head from the church pew isn't bleeding any more. And the nicks on our faces also have stopped bleeding."

"I wish I had an answer," replied Sam. He stepped alongside Dan, stopped in his tracks, and stared up the tunnel.

"What's wrong?" asked Dan.

Sam remained silent. Again, he sensed that something wasn't right.

"Sam, what do you see?" demanded Cindy.

"It's nothing," he assured.

She wasn't buying it. "What's wrong?" she demanded.

"It's nothing," he said again. Powerless to shake the feeling of danger in the tunnel ahead, Sam volunteered to take the lead.

"Be my guest," said Dan.

With each traveler clutching a weapon, Sam guided his friends while gripping one of the two torches.

The teenagers were overly watchful. Both knew that Sam suspected something awaited them up the cavern.

A WALK THROUGH TIME

"I've got a bad feeling about this tunnel," whispered Cindy.

"Just keep your eyes open," ordered Sam.

"Maybe it's nothing," said Dan. "For all we know—"

A vine shot through a cavern wall, wrapped around Sam's leg, and knocked him to the ground.

Cindy and Dan scrambled to his side.

A pod-like structure near the end of the vine swelled until it was larger than the captured traveler. It opened and swallowed up Sam.

Dan sank his lance into the vine whereas Cindy stabbed the pod. They made no headway.

The creeping vine began its slow retreat to the cavern wall, dragging the pod and its human contents along.

Dan had a hunch that the plant life would not be satisfied with just one warm meal. His thoughts were soon confirmed. Another vine exploded from the wall and coiled around his wrist.

While watching the tragedy unfold, Cindy knew that Dan needed her help. But she also knew that Sam was in a worse predicament since he was imprisoned inside the pod.

Dan was pulled closer to the wall.

He wildly slashed the vine until it was severed from his wrist. To his amazement, the man-eating plant made no further attempt to capture him. It vanished inside the wall. Dan raced to Cindy's side and hacked at the vine. Cindy altered her rescue strategy from stabbing the pod to prying her lance into its tight seal.

"Dan help!" she yelled.

He ignored her plea. Dan knew from personal experience that the key to Sam's release was a severed vine—a break in the pod's lifeline. He continued slashing. With the eighth stab, the pod opened, released Sam, and sought refuge inside the rock wall.

Cindy was sickened by the coat of green slime that covered Sam from head to toe. Knowing they were still in harm's way, the teenagers attempted to drag their unconscious co-traveler to a safe area. The slime, however, made a firm grip impossible. They grabbed Sam's belt and pulled him behind a boulder.

Cindy dropped to her knees and tapped Sam on the face. "Wake up!"

Dan remained standing with a close eye on the walls for more exploding vines.

"Dan, what do we do?" she shouted. "Should we carry him up the cavern?" She looked at the cracks in the rock wall that were created by the blasting vines. "I don't feel safe here anymore."

Sam shook.

"Wake up!" she yelled.

He opened his eyes.

Dan dropped to his knees and wiped slime from Sam's shirt. He rubbed the slippery substance between his fingers. "What the heck is this stuff?" he asked.

"Probably a digestive secretion from the plant," guessed Cindy. Fearing another pod episode, she offered no resistance when Sam rose to a seated position.

Dan gazed up the tunnel. "Look!" he exclaimed.

"What now?" grumbled Cindy. She glanced over his shoulder.

"Another side cave! And more torches!" shouted Dan.

The teenagers returned their attention to Sam and lifted him to the boulder.

Sam stared at the new side cave opening. "Let's check it out."

"Sam, you need to rest," urged Dan. "We don't know what inhabits that cave. And let's face it—it's not like our visits to side caves in the past have been uneventful. You need to catch your breath."

"I can rest inside the cave—once we're away from those creepy vines," he insisted.

"Yeah," agreed Cindy. "And who knows. For a change, maybe that side cave is safe."

Dan gave in. "All right, we'll rest inside the cave. But first we need to reach it without another vine incident."

"I couldn't agree with you more," said Sam.

Dan strapped the bag to his back and grabbed a torch; Cindy carried the three lances and the second burning torch.

Once Sam's arms were extended across their shoulders, the three raced up the cavern to the side cave, but not before narrowly missing four more vine eruptions.

Outside the cave's entrance, Cindy turned and watched the shoots retreat into the walls. "I hope we never run into them again."

"Yeah," said Dan. "Let's just hope they're not in another—"

Sam slipped from the grip of his friends and fell to his knees.

"Whoa!" exclaimed Dan. "This stuff is really slimy."

Only now imagining that the vines might have the uncanny ability of moving within the rock walls, Cindy demanded that they enter the side cave immediately.

Since Sam was already on his knees, he crawled inside first.

The young travelers were immediately behind.

Inside the cave, the explorers stood upon rocky ground. But the stone surface extended only several yards ahead. A narrow abyss lay at the far edge of the rock floor. Beyond the abyss was an isle of land that the group presumed was solid ground. It was simply a guess, however, since the inner realm was shrouded by driving snow and wind. The armed rescuers had entered an inner ice world.

During the group's exploration of the cave's perimeter, they discovered that the outer solid rock ground encircled the abyss and its isolated snowy region.

To Cindy, the area reminded her of three concentric circles with the ice world in the center, an abyss outside that, and a rock floor beyond that.

Dan suspected that the solid floor around the cave's perimeter allowed the light keeper to reignite the torches on the walls when the flames died.

Though the travelers easily heard excessive gales within the frozen world—on the far side of the abyss—the area where they stood was alarmingly calm. Even the torch flames that adorned the cave walls were unaffected by the ferocious winds only a short distance away.

"What's that?" Cindy pointed to movement within the frozen chamber.

Sam looked into the blowing snow and got a blurry view of the inner ice chamber. "It looks like—like people."

"People in the snowstorm?" questioned Dan.

Sam's sights remained fixed on the snowy region. "It's hard to say for sure. But yeah, that's what it looks like."

A crash was heard.

The travelers jumped.

A snow dweller had escaped the confines of the blizzard by jumping into the abyss. Similar to what the explorers had experienced firsthand over a different abyss, the male inhabitant had been smashed against the stone ceiling.

Cindy took two steps back. "He's crawling in our direction!"

"We'll be fine," assured Sam after aiming his weapon at the human target.

Quite unexpectedly, a white appendage descended from above the swirling snowstorm, coiled around the escapee's leg, and hurled him back into the frozen arena.

The appendage quickly concealed itself in the whiteout.

"What the heck was that?" exclaimed Cindy.

"I haven't a clue," said Sam.

The blizzard conditions prevented the travelers from seeing the outcome of the apprehended inhabitant or what lay at the end of the white appendage.

"I wonder what the story is with this cave and these dwellers?" asked Dan.

"I'm sure I don't know," said Sam. "But I'll let you know when I find out."

"What?" shouted Cindy. "You're not actually thinking about going into that storm? And don't kid yourself, Sam, there's something attached to the end of that feeler."

Sam turned and faced Cindy. "Look, there may be four other people who need our help. I don't want to find an entrance to an upper level—or better yet, stumble upon the portal—only to learn then that we're short a person or two." He took a tighter grip on his lance. "Once we leave this fourth cave, there's no way I'm returning to rescue someone. We have to search every cave we come upon."

Sam's sluggish movements—the result of his encounter with the creeping plant—didn't go unnoticed by Dan. "Sam," he said, "I'll check out the ice chamber while you take a breather."

"Absolutely not!" he shouted.

"Why not?" posed Dan. "It's my brother who could be in there. Besides, you're in no condition to battle whatever creature oversees these inhabitants. You need to rest from your run-in with the vine."

"I don't need to rest; I need to find the others. You stay here with Cindy, just in case the vines break through the cave's entrance."

A WALK THROUGH TIME

Cindy spun and eyed the entry. "I'll be fine," she asserted.

"Sam, my brother's safety is my responsibility, not yours," claimed Dan.

"Look Dan, it's great that you feel responsible for William's safety, but it was my decision to enter the tree to rescue Brad," reminded Sam. "So I'll go, since Brad may be in there."

After a losing battle, Dan unwillingly agreed to remain behind with Cindy. "So what's your plan?" asked Dan.

"It's pretty simple." Sam took a few steps closer to the abyss. "Obviously, some kind of creature refuses to let inhabitants flee the ice world. That would explain the abyss around its perimeter and the updrafts that smash prisoners against the ceiling for the creature's easy plucking. Once I leap into the chasm and I'm slammed against the ceiling, I'm sure the creature—whatever it is—will throw me into the snowstorm."

"But what about your escape?" asked Dan.

Sam hadn't thought that far ahead. He remained silent, staring at the ice chamber.

"Sam, what about your escape?" yelled Dan.

Sam pulled his revolver from the backpack that Dan was lugging and handed it to the young man. "Since you've got a good aim, I'll leave you to shoot the creature's appendage if it grabs me when I leave," instructed Sam.

Although the spot where the explorers stood was still, the powerful winds within the chasm concerned Dan. "But what if the updrafts cause the bullet to stray and it hits something or someone else?"

Sam displayed a worried look. "Just make sure you aim at a part of the creature that's far away from me."

Dan tossed him the backpack. "Wear this," he insisted. "When you're knocked against the ceiling, try landing on your back."

"Not a bad idea," Sam complimented.

With a lance in hand and the backpack secured, Sam looked at his friends. "Wish me luck." Within seconds, he crashed into the ceiling. As he had hoped, the backpack lessened the impact. He remained motionless on the ceiling, waiting for the arrival of the white appendage. Nothing approached. Knowing that time was crucial to their escape from the mysterious world, he began his crawl across the ceiling.

A white feeler with stiff hairs lunged at Sam and tried to wrap around his waist. After two failed attempts, the limb disappeared above the snowy chamber.

That's odd, Sam thought while continuing his crawl over the abyss. *Maybe since the creature saw that I was entering the ice chamber and not leaving, it backed off.*

Sam inched his way beyond the roaring winds of the abyss and fell into the snowstorm.

From the cave's entrance, Dan and Cindy watched their friend plummet from the ceiling and then lost sight of him behind the blizzard curtain.

Face down on the snow-packed ground, Sam shuddered at the fierce winds and bitter cold. The temperature was easily below freezing, though the roaring arctic winds made it feel subzero. He had no sooner risen to all fours when he was trampled to the ground by a crowd of inhabitants. He squinted into the blowing snow and saw a second throng of cave dwellers approaching. The beings appeared to be in a dazed state. As the frostbitten group drew nearer, he was shocked that a layer of ice covered their skin and clothing. Most were barefoot. The lucky residents—or possibly the latest arrivals—wore frayed foot coverings.

Sam was pinched.

"What the—" He jumped to his feet. The strong winds nearly blew him over.

After steadying himself against the gales, he brushed a patch of snow with his boot and unearthed four ant lion larvae. In a flashback to his childhood years, he recalled searching hillsides with his friends for the rare insects. While the bugs seldom grew longer than two inches, the numbing pain delivered by their oversize anterior pincers to humans and the death they wreaked to ants and larger insects made them a formidable land dweller.

Sam imagined that in the snow chamber, anyone sitting on the ground for even a brief moment was prodded and pinched to their feet by the larvae. He brushed another patch of snow and discovered six more ant lions. *This place must be crawling with these pests,* he thought.

Though the wind was constant, occasionally a stronger than normal gust swept through the frigid confines. The latest gale sent Sam tumbling. Preferring not to suffer another nip from the insects, he jumped to his feet.

He held out as long as he could with his face pressed against the lashing wind. But it was hopeless. Within seconds, the gusts proved too powerful an adversary. He turned and placed his back to the wind. Its unearthly force pushed him along at a fast pace. He realized then that the inhabitants could do nothing but surrender to the powerful force of nature.

Eventually, he found himself walking shoulder to shoulder with other cave dwellers. To his right was a man he imagined to be in his early fifties. Like the majority of the snow people, a layer of ice covered his face and his windswept clothing. He was barefoot.

In search of answers, Sam decided to speak with him. He had barely opened his mouth when he realized that carrying on a conversation would be next to impossible against the roaring winds.

He looked to the left and saw another man who appeared to be in his late thirties. He drew his face closer to the man's uniform. Sam revisited another childhood memory. As a high school student, he had tremendous respect for his history teacher, Joseph Walla, whose passion and interest in the Civil War era captivated a young Sam and nurtured his love of antiquities.

Sam took a step nearer to the man and inspected his unusual coat. *This can't be,* he thought. *Granted, it's ragged and torn—almost beyond recognition—but I swear that's a frock coat worn by generals in the American Civil War.* The dingy jacket with its braid trim and gold buttons—though just a handful remained—nearly confirmed his suspicions. He next noticed the man's bronze belt buckle with the initials CSA. *This can't be—the Confederate States of America,* he thought. *Has he been marching in this wretched storm since the 1860's?* Uneasy with what he may uncover, he refocused his sights from the Confederate general to a group of inhabitants ten feet ahead.

As he continued walking along the outer edge of the ice chamber, he watched a frosty inhabitant leap into the abyss. As he expected, the woman was thrown against the ceiling. She was only feet into her crawl to freedom when a white appendage wrapped around her leg and hurled her back into the snowstorm.

Sam looked overhead to see what he'd eventually be up against. But all he saw was the whiteout. Nevertheless, he sensed that he was being watched closely by something attached to the rock ceiling.

The woman hit the frozen ground and remained motionless.

As Sam drew closer, hidden larvae forced her to her feet and the high winds shoved her forward. He watched five ant lions burrow themselves below the icy covering when he walked past the flattened snow patch.

Between the insects nudging you off the ground and the relentless winds driving you forward, there isn't any rest for these people, he thought. *And their faces—covered with ice—it must be unbearable.*

He touched his face. *That's it,* he thought. *Like me, maybe the newest arrivals don't have a coating of ice yet.* He increased his pace—even faster than his fellow frozen prisoners—and studied the faces and clothing of each inhabitant. Unfortunately, the blizzard conditions forced him to place his face within inches of each hiker.

Given the large number of inhabitants and the enormous size of the wintry chamber, he knew his search efforts would be exhaustive and time consuming. But he also knew that now—more than ever—he'd never return to the cave. He had never been so cold in his life.

•

At the cave's entrance, Dan and Cindy kept a close eye above the abyss for Sam's reappearance.

"How long do you think he's been gone?" she asked.

"I'm not sure." His sights remained glued to the ceiling. "But I'd guess probably an hour or so."

She glanced back at the cave's entrance for shooting vines. "I don't like this waiting around and not knowing what to expect. At least in the parallel world we could see the forest creatures and knew what we were up against."

"I'm sure he won't be much longer," assured Dan.

Cindy jumped.

Dan spun. "What's wrong?" he shouted.

She brushed a daddy longlegs from her knee to the cave floor.

"It's just a daddy longlegs," he said. "It's completely harmless."

"Yeah, that's what I thought too. But it just bit me."

"Bit you? What do you mean it bit you? Daddy longlegs don't bite. Maybe you just—"

"It bit me, Dan!" She watched it scurry to safety under a rock. "So I wonder what creature inhabits the frozen world."

"Beats me. But whatever it is, we'll survive," promised Dan.

"Dan, I know this will probably sound weird or maybe even heartless but—" She paused and eyed the cave's entrance again.

"But what?" he asked.

She redirected her sights to the ceiling above the abyss. "But what if Sam—you know—has been attacked by something and—"

"Sam's fine!" he shouted. "He just needs more time."

She knew that Dan feared for Sam's safety as much as she did. She took a few moments to rephrase her concern. "What I'm trying to say is if something's happened to Sam, how will we know? We can't see inside the ice chamber. And if—heaven forbid—he's been injured and unable to come back, how long do we wait before going in after him?"

Though he never voiced it, he admitted to himself that Cindy had a valid concern. "Let's wait a little longer," he suggested. "If there's still no sign of him, I'll jump into the abyss."

"No Dan. Sam wanted us to stick together. We'll both enter the frozen world."

"All right; but not yet." He scanned the expanse of the ice chamber. "I mean, look at the size of that place. Sam will need a lot of time to cover every inch of it."

⬤

Within the frozen region, Sam blew on his hands. His fingers were going numb. "I have to keep focused," he mumbled to himself. He continued searching the area for familiar faces and clothing that wasn't coated with ice.

At last, the driving snow lifted. Sam spotted the back of a cave dweller who was free of ice. He increased his stride and was soon standing alongside the man. To his disappointment, he didn't recognize the middle-aged inhabitant. The rescue mission resumed.

Another cave dweller made the leap to freedom.

Although Sam had experienced the bitter cold for only a short time, he understood why the inhabitants—probably all of whom had endured the elements longer than he—wanted nothing more than to end their lives by jumping into the abyss. He suspected that the cave detainees hoped that by some freak of nature the updrafts would permit them to plunge to their deaths.

As expected, the inhabitant hit the ceiling, was captured, and pitched into the blizzard.

It's strange that these men and women are doomed to trudge for the rest of their lives, he thought. *They're not even permitted to end their miseries by jumping into the abyss.* He felt a profound sadness for his cave mates.

His thoughts were cut short by another person making the leap. Knowing the inevitable outcome, Sam was returning his attention to the search at hand when he noticed that the suicidal person's clothing wasn't encrusted with ice.

The cave dweller was quickly tossed into the snowy world. He landed at Sam's feet and jumped from the ground to avoid the annoying bites.

"Father James!" shouted Sam.

The priest—wearing his black priestly attire—was fortunate to have only a dusting of snow on him.

"Sam!" he yelled to be heard over the roaring gusts.

The gales pushed the men forward.

"Are you alone?" asked Father James.

"No! Cindy and Dan are at the cave's entrance."

"I thought I saw an exit through the storm when the blowing snow let up earlier," said the priest. "But I couldn't tell for sure. The storm's awfully wicked."

"The exit to this cave is on the other side of the abyss," said Sam.

"But how did you—" Father James recalled Sam's earlier comment. "What do you mean Cindy's here?"

"It's a long story. I'll explain later."

The men continued their wind-driven march.

"Have you seen Brad, William, or Jimmy in this storm?" yelled Sam in the priest's ear.

A look of disbelief emerged on Father James's face. "Jimmy's here too?" he yelled.

Sam ignored his question. "Have you seen anyone?"

"No! I was looking for you and Brad, and possibly Dan and William. I didn't know Cindy and Jimmy were here."

The men witnessed another wishful escapee hit the icy ground.

Sam focused on the situation at hand. "If any of the others arrived when you did, I doubt they'd be covered with ice."

"I've been searching this blizzard ever since I got here," informed the priest. "Since I didn't recognize anyone, I only recently decided to break away and search for the others somewhere else. I thought I'd try my luck crawling across the ceiling. Obviously, I wasn't that lucky."

Sam looked beyond the abyss and strained to spot Cindy and Dan.

"What are you looking for?" asked Father James.

"Dan and Cindy should be near the cave's exit. When we see them, that's where we'll make our leap into the abyss." He glimpsed a flicker of light beyond the blowing snow and across the chasm. But he also recalled that many torches graced the cave's rock wall.

Without warning, the winds picked up and the snow blew horizontally.

Sam decided that exiting anywhere would have to do. To endure the extreme temperatures any longer was unthinkable. *Wherever we end up in the cave will be better than freezing here,* he thought. He grabbed the priest's arm. "Here's where we'll make our jump!"

The priest nodded.

"As soon as we hit the ceiling, we need to crawl over the abyss as fast as we can," reminded Sam. "Otherwise, we'll be caught by the creature and thrown back in here."

"Yeah, I know."

"Put your arms around me," ordered Sam.

"What? Why?"

"If we hit the ceiling together, my backpack will soften the blow," explained Sam.

With his recent smash against the ceiling and its painful consequences still fresh in his memory, the priest put his arms around Sam.

The men stood on the edge of the abyss.

"One, two, three!" yelled Sam.

They plunged ten feet into the chasm before shooting to the overhead rock. The backpack made contact with the stone surface.

"Move!" shouted Sam.

They had just begun their crawl when a white appendage coiled around Sam's waist. To his surprise, it couldn't maintain its hold. A second attempt met the same fate. *The slime on my clothes,* he thought. *It can't get a grip.*

Unfortunately, the outcome was not the same for the priest.

The appendage abandoned Sam and wrapped around Father James's ankle.

"Sam!" yelled the priest who was being pulled nearer the frozen chamber.

Sam grabbed the priest's belt. Both men were being drawn toward the ice world.

A shot was fired.

The creature released its hold on the priest and disappeared above the snowstorm.

A puff of smoke rose from the barrel of the revolver. Dan's aim was flawless.

A second appendage combed the ceiling for the men.

"Fire again!" shouted Cindy.

Dan pulled the trigger.

At a fast pace, Sam and Father James made it beyond the abyss where they crashed to solid ground.

Dan tucked the revolver between his waist and jeans before dashing to the men. Cindy followed.

Dan stretched the priest's arm across his shoulders; Cindy did likewise with Sam. The four darted to the safety at the cave's entrance.

My gosh, he's colder than ice, thought Dan.

Cindy glanced backwards and screamed.

Enraged that two prisoners had escaped their eternal watch, two massive albino daddy longlegs were racing across the ceiling in the group's direction.

"Run!" yelled Sam.

The creatures scampered across the overhead rock and down the wall at the cave's exit. But they were too late. The explorers had reached shelter in the open cavern.

Cindy released Sam from her grasp. "That was way too close. That had to be the worst—" She screamed again.

A white leg—easily eight feet long—had invaded the deceptive safety of the cavern and coiled around Cindy's thigh.

Dan dropped the priest to the floor, snatched a torch from the cavern wall, and extinguished the flame against the creature's bristly leg.

A high-pitched squeal echoed within the side cave.

The wounded creature released its hold on Cindy and pulled its leg inside the cave.

As they turned to resume their escape, a second leg exploded into the tunnel, grabbed Dan, and dragged him toward the entrance. Before his friends could reach him, he pulled the revolver from his side and fired another shot. The leg sought shelter in the safety of the ice chamber. "Run!" yelled Dan.

Only a short distance up the tunnel, the travelers spun and were overcome with fear. A daddy longlegs was ramming its head against the cave's exit. Though its body was too large to break through the opening, the sight instilled unforgettable terror.

"Let's get out of here!" ordered Cindy. She yanked another torch from the cavern wall.

The teenagers dashed up the tunnel, assisting their freezing companions.

CHAPTER NINE
The Unimaginable

THROUGHOUT THEIR SPRINT, SAM FREQUENTLY GLANCED behind to confirm that the daddy longlegs had not penetrated the opening of the side cave. He needed to know it wasn't in pursuit.

Cindy scanned the cavern walls with the torch for exploding vines.

The priest's wobbly stride led Dan to suspect he was in pain. Dan slowed his pace to a brisk walk. "Father, are you all right?"

"Yeah, I'm fine."

Only now noticing the bloody shirt in the glow of the torch, Dan came to a complete stop. "That happened in the church?"

"Yeah." Father James looked at his waist. "But it's not as bad as it looks."

Nevertheless, Dan helped him to the ground and leaned him against the wall.

Sam rested on his knees and ordered the priest to expose his injury.

Father James lifted his black shirt.

Sam saw the deep gash and the reopened wound. He removed his own shirt and tied his tee shirt around Father James's side. "It's not the best, but it should reduce the flow of blood."

Cindy stepped nearer the men. "Sam, I don't think he should be resting against the wall."

Calling to mind what he suffered inside the pod, Sam helped the priest to his feet. "Father, I'll explain later, but there's something living inside these walls."

"What could possibly be living in the rock walls?" he exclaimed.

"Man-eating plants," blurted Cindy. She extended the torch and gazed up the tunnel for carnivorous vines on the footpath.

Father James jumped further from the wall.

With no sign of the vines, the travelers were soon reducing the distance between themselves and home, but at a much slower pace. Sam feared that another sprint would drain the priest of more blood.

Father James opened a conversation. "I don't understand the oak."

"What do you mean?" asked Sam.

"You never told me it was so aggressive."

"Don't tell me it attacked you too," responded Sam in disbelief.

"Attacked is an understatement," replied the priest. "The limbs went wild. They crashed through the stained glass windows of the church and wrapped around me. I saw Dan and William—" He stopped in his tracks. "Where's William?"

The travelers remained expressionless.

"You haven't found him?" asked Father James.

"Not yet," answered Dan. "But I'm sure he's in this world somewhere. Cindy saw him pitched into the tree too."

"Yeah," growled Cindy. "And I saw it only because Jimmy insisted on checking out the tree to see if it was solid."

Sam displayed a puzzled look. "But I still don't understand why the oak wasn't hostile with me."

"Who knows," said Dan. "Maybe the oak became more violent as the hours passed and the darkness grew. I mean, you stepped into the tree around eight o'clock. We were captured closer to midnight."

Sam and Dan watched Father James tightening the homemade bandage.

"I'm fine," claimed the priest. Determined to switch the discussion from his injury, he remarked, "Sam said Jimmy's here too."

"Oh yeah," exclaimed Cindy. "He's here somewhere; I can feel it. Maybe we should leave him here since he was so anxious to check out the tree."

"Cindy, we're not leaving anyone behind," reprimanded Sam.

"There's no way Jimmy could have known that his curiosity would lead the two of you here. Besides, maybe he remembers something about his entry into this world that could guide us home."

"But I thought the tree was our way home," said the priest.

"It was in the parallel world," replied Dan. He glanced at the walls. "But as you've probably noticed, Father, there aren't any trees in this world."

Silence won out.

Sam detected hopelessness on the faces around him. He broke the troublesome stillness by ordering, "Come on, we need to keep moving. The answers may be up ahead."

After what seemed a fifteen-minute walk up the tunnel, they came upon a boulder in the center of the footpath. The men helped Father James to its cold surface.

Sam removed the bandage and examined the priest's wound. "Well it's still bleeding, though not as badly as before. The tee shirt's helping a little."

Cindy lowered herself and the torch to the priest's side. "Father, do you remember anything about your arrival into the ice cave?"

Father James closed his eyes and relived the night of his abduction. He eventually shook his head. "No, not really. About the only thing I remember was praying at the Communion rail when the windows exploded and oak limbs invaded the church." He attempted to rise from the boulder.

Sam pressed on his shoulders. "You need to rest."

He returned to the boulder. "The next thing I remember, I was being yanked across the floor while yelling at Dan and William to get out of the church." He extended a leg and reached into his pants pocket. "I was holding this." He displayed a small prayer book.

"Are you serious?" exclaimed Cindy. "You actually hung on to your prayer book as you were being dragged across the church?"

"Yes. And I'm glad I did."

"Why?" she asked.

"What better place to carry a prayer book than in this unholy place?" He made another attempt to rise from the boulder.

As Sam helped him off the rock, his shirt cuffs moved up his arms and exposed his wrists. Dan grabbed his arm. "You're wearing a watch!" he exclaimed.

"Of course. I always do."

Dan stared at the watch. "This can't be."

"What's wrong?" asked Father James.

Dan ignored the priest's question. "Maybe it's not accurate. Or maybe the cold in the ice cave affected its—"

"It keeps perfect time," corrected Father James. "This watch was an anniversary gift. I've taken it to the mountains on countless skiing trips. Trust me, the time and date are accurate."

"What's wrong, Dan?" asked Cindy.

Dan stepped away from the group and placed his back to his friends. "According to his watch, today's September fifteenth."

"What?" shouted the priest. He raised his wrist to his face. Since he hadn't looked at the watch during his imprisonment in the ice chamber, he was speechless.

Sam yanked the priest's arm for a closer look. "How can it be? There's no way we've been in this world for fifteen days."

Cindy also inspected the watch. "How on earth could I not have an appetite or not have to use the bathroom in over two weeks?"

The priest scanned the cavern walls. "Maybe this isn't the parallel world."

Worrisome expressions surrounded Sam. "Look, it's possible that the watch is keeping perfect time and that it's the fifteenth," he said. "But it's also possible that the freezing temperatures in the ice cave or the abnormalities of this world have altered it somehow." He took the torch from Cindy. "But that shouldn't change our objective. We still need to find our friends, the portal, and an upward passageway."

"There's an upper level?" asked Father James.

"Not too long ago the three of us were crawling on the ceiling over an abyss when I felt movement above," explained Sam. "There's no question."

Cindy was still deep in thought about the lost time factor. "Then that means we have just fifteen days to find William, Jimmy, Brad, and the portal."

Father James joined Sam in easing the teenagers' anxieties. "I suppose it's also possible that something in the watch was damaged when I was pulled across the church floor by the oak limbs."

"Yeah, that's probably what happened," voiced a hopeful Cindy.

"But I agree with Sam," continued the priest. "We should continue our search."

Sam's eyes met the priest's. Both believed that the watch was accurate and that time was rapidly running out for their exit from the unknown world. However, they kept their unconfirmed suspicions to themselves.

"Come on, we've got a lot of territory to cover in only fifteen days," urged Sam.

"Maybe we should walk at a faster pace," suggested Cindy.

Sam looked at Father James. He was almost certain that the priest was still in pain. "We'll be fine at our normal pace."

"But Sam," she pleaded.

"We'll be fine!" he shouted.

Father James knew that his injury would slow down the group. "You three move along at a faster pace. I won't let my injury keep you from covering as much ground as possible. I'll catch up."

"Absolutely not!" yelled Sam. "Heaven only knows what lurks in this stone world. We'll not leave anyone behind to fend for themselves."

Cindy recalled her ill-timed comment. She echoed Sam's concern. "Father, Sam's right. We'll be fine at our normal pace. No one will be left behind—well, except maybe Jimmy."

"Cindy!" scolded Sam.

"Actually Father, sticking together during our adventures in the parallel world was key to our survival," related Dan. "If we want to make it through this place alive and in one piece, we'll need to work as a team." He looked at Cindy. "No one will be left behind—not even Jimmy."

With a torch in hand, Sam ordered the group to advance.

During their trek through the tunnel, Father James observed that Cindy was meticulously surveying the cavern walls. He attempted to distract her by opening a conversation. "Is this what you and the others experienced in the parallel world?"

"Not really," she replied.

"What do you mean?"

"Well for one thing, the creatures in this world seem larger and more unearthly than the ones in the parallel world— if that's possible. At least in the parallel world—even though it was usually dark—more often than not, we knew what we were dealing with." She ended her stride to shake a stink cockroach from her arm. "But in this place, you never know what's going to burst through the cavern walls or drop from the ceiling."

"Or drop from a stalactite," added Dan.

Though Father James opened the conversation to alleviate Cindy's anxieties, her and Dan's comments heightened his curiosities about the group's encounters during the past fifteen days. "Dan, did you share a cave with Sam or Cindy?" asked the priest.

"Neither, I was by myself. Actually, all of us were in separate caves—just like you."

His comment troubled the priest who slowed his pace.

Sam feared a surge of renewed pain in the priest's side. "Father, how are you feeling?" he demanded.

"I'm fine." Aware that he was delaying the march, he resumed his fast walk. "How did all of you escape on your own?" he continued.

"Actually, that was Dan's ingenuity," replied Sam.

"What do you mean?" asked the priest.

"Trust me, Father, it was by accident," admitted Dan.

The priest was overly intrigued with the young man's escape. "Dan, what was your cave like?"

Dan suspected that recounting his story would take everybody's minds off their sore limbs. He began, "Just like you, Father, after I was hurled into the oak, I appeared in a cave. The next thing I remember, I was being stepped on."

"Stepped on?" he asked.

"Yeah, by beings who were semitransparent. But trust me, they had definite weight."

Cindy postponed her inspection of the walls and took an interest in Dan's personal odyssey. She realized only then that their adventures—the flight from her cave, the crawl above the abyss, and the attack of the flesh-eating plants—had totally consumed her thoughts. She knew only bits and pieces of what Dan and Sam had suffered.

"So what happened?" pressed the priest.

"I was charged by the cave dwellers—or so I thought—so I jumped out of their path and took cover behind a boulder."

"How many inhabitants were in your cave?" asked the priest.

"I couldn't say for sure, but easily thousands."

Sam—who bore the torch—interrupted Dan's story and alerted the group to standing water ahead.

"Now what?" complained Cindy. "Can't anything in this world—" She stared at the pool in the distance and recalled the waterfront in the parallel world and how she took charge and defeated the octopus-like creature. She realized that her preoccupation with her wrongful entry into the present world was clouding her judgment, feeding her anxieties, and ultimately putting her friends' lives in danger. *I'll deal with Jimmy later,* she thought. *I have to focus on our safety and our exit from this miserable place.*

"The water doesn't appear too deep," yelled Sam.

Cindy yanked the backpack from Sam. "We'll be fine," she said.

Sam held the torch close to her face and noticed a grin.

Since her rescue from her cave, Sam and Dan had secretly feared that her obsession with her undeserved banishment from earth to wherever they were would eventually lead to an accident.

Sam was pleased that the risk-taking Cindy he knew from the parallel world was back.

Dan also noticed the change in her disposition and mannerisms. He felt more confident of their eventual safe return home.

Cindy strapped the backpack to her shoulders. "Dan, tell us more about the inhabitants in your cave," she said.

"The semitransparent beings were chasing a golden chest that would appear at various spots in the cave and then disappear, only to reappear a few minutes later somewhere else." He recalled that they had already been in the cavern world for fifteen days. "Or at least what I thought was a few minutes later," he added.

"Did you ever chase the golden chest?" asked Father James.

Dan lowered his head in shame. He refused to answer.

"I'll take that as a yes," said the priest. "Go on. What happened?"

Dan ended his march and leaned against the cavern wall. He jumped when Cindy raised her lance.

THE UNIMAGINABLE

She wasn't convinced that the man-eating vines weren't stalking them. "Sorry, but it's best to be prepared—just in case," she said.

Dan continued his story. "I chased the chest around the cave. But whenever an inhabitant was within arm's reach, the chest vanished and then reappeared at another spot."

Father James was determined to develop a theory on their location and the purpose of the caves. "Why did you want the chest?" he asked.

Again, he dropped his gaze. "I'm not sure. I mean, part of me wanted to leave the cave, but I also wanted to steal the chest. I thought it might hold precious stones, money, or some other priceless object that would lead to a plush life for my family and me." He raised his head and looked at the priest. "I suppose it's wrong to be abundantly wealthy, but the desire for riches was overwhelming in my cave."

"Dan, there's nothing wrong with being wealthy, as long as what you've acquired you've done legitimately and honestly," corrected the priest. "Of course, people should always share their resources with the less fortunate."

"Yeah, like me," teased Cindy.

A splash was heard. Sam had stepped into the frigid water.

The reflection of the teenagers on the water's surface—illuminated by Sam's torch—prompted Father James to ask about the cuts on their faces.

"After the ground collapsed behind us on our way to your cave, the updrafts from the new abyss smashed us against the ceiling," explained Cindy. "We were bombarded by flying rock pellets from the chasm. But that's a whole other story. I'd like to hear more about the golden chest."

"There's not much more to tell," said Dan.

"Did you give up on the chest?" asked Father James.

"Yeah, eventually."

"Why?" asked the priest.

"I remember thinking about William, Sam, you, and Brad." He glanced at Cindy. "At the time, I didn't know that you and Jimmy were in this world." He stared at his image on the water. "Hey Cindy, you're not mesmerized with your reflection!"

She looked at the water's surface. "That's odd. But you're right; I don't feel any attraction."

From the front of the line, Sam suggested, "Maybe the fact that you're outside your cave has everything to do with it."

"I suppose anything's possible," she admitted. Eager to change the unpleasant subject of her former fascination with her physique, she asked, "So Dan, what happened after you thought of the others in your cave?"

"I had a hunch that William and everyone else were in similar situations and could use some help."

"Hmm," muttered the priest while scratching his chin. "So it was your unselfish thoughts about your family and friends that set you free from your obsession."

"Yeah, I guess. Anyway, I may have been free from my obsession with the chest, but I wasn't free of the cave. Every time I tried to leave, the exit—just like the golden chest—disappeared and then reappeared somewhere else in the cave."

Unsure if any life forms inhabited the water, Cindy opened the backpack and armed Father James.

"Thanks," said the priest while accepting a lance. He directed his attention back to Dan. "If the exit kept moving, then how did you escape?"

"My cave had guardians—like yours—that refused to let anyone flee. Hundred-foot-long anacondas patrolled my rock world. Since I accidentally drew the attention of the snakes, I was desperate to escape. But like I said, whenever I tried to step through the exit, it relocated. At one point, I tripped over a corpse near the cave's entrance. I madly crawled backwards to avoid one of the snakes. In my panic, I never once removed my stare from the approaching anaconda. Before I knew what had happened, I had cleared the exit. In hindsight, I guess you could say that blind faith led me to safety."

"And it will lead you to safety in the open tunnel too," promised the priest.

As the explorers stepped from the water, Father James was the first to spot rare spiny cave worms stuck to his pants and those of his co-travelers.

Sam grazed the flame to the worms until all were removed.

THE UNIMAGINABLE

Dan was pleasantly surprised that the parasites were attached only to their clothing and not their legs. "I can't believe it," he exclaimed. "Maybe our luck is finally changing. With everything we've—"

Overhead movement drowned out his comment. The vibrations were so pronounced that the cavern walls shook.

"I told you there was an upper level," declared Sam. "Now do you believe me?"

No one answered.

The travelers stared at the rock ceiling until the falling dust blurred their vision.

"But how do we reach the second level?" asked Cindy.

"I wish I knew," said Sam. "I guess we'll keep looking for an upward passageway."

The rumblings ended.

Excited to leave the level known for its flesh-eating plant life, Cindy snatched the torch from Sam. "Come on, we need to keep moving."

"She's right," said Dan. He relieved her of the backpack.

The teenagers led the way.

At the rear of the line, Father James and Sam struck up a conversation.

"And your cave, Sam?" asked the priest.

"My cave was kind of like Dan's. It also had guardians. I was overly fixated with something inside."

"Go on," prodded Father James.

"There was a ladder that extended from the floor through a hole in the ceiling. The cave was enormous with thousands of beings who kept shoving one another to reach the ladder. Like Dan, I also was obsessed—not with stealing a golden chest—but with climbing into the ceiling's opening. And it's a good thing I never made it through the ceiling."

"Why's that?"

"The ladder turned out to be two giant walking sticks with deadly appetites."

"Walking sticks?" asked an unconvinced priest.

"Yeah. But I didn't know the ladder was alive when I was trying to climb it."

"Do you have any idea why you were set on reaching the opening?" asked Father James.

"You're going to think this is crazy, but I knew that once I climbed the ladder, I'd finally receive the recognition that I thought was stolen from me years ago. As you probably know, Father, for years Lawtonians have looked down on me because of my stories about the parallel world. I was sure that standing on the top ladder rung would be my chance to finally look down on others."

Sam took the torch from Cindy and placed it near the priest's side. "It looks like the bleeding has stopped." He returned the torch to Cindy.

"Hey wait a minute," blurted Dan. "I just thought of something."

"What's that?" asked Sam.

"We've apparently been in this world for over two weeks and we haven't been hungry, we haven't had to go to the bathroom, and we haven't had to shave. It's as if our bodily functions have been suspended."

"Yeah, we already discussed that," reminded Sam. "What are you getting at?"

"If our bodily functions have stopped for the time being, then why haven't our healing processes also stopped? It's almost like we're allowed to heal so we can suffer again."

Father James lost his balance.

Luckily, Sam's quick reflexes prevented the priest from hitting the ground. "What's wrong?" demanded Sam.

"It's nothing," assured the priest. "Just a little lightheaded, I guess."

"Maybe we should rest for a while," suggested Sam.

"No. I'll be fine," insisted Father James. "We need to keep moving."

Sam had a hunch that Dan's comment caught Father James by surprise. He mentally replayed Dan's theory about continually suffering. He remained at a loss, however, for the priest's unexpected reaction.

Although fearful of what he may ultimately uncover, Father James continued searching for clues. "Cindy, tell me about your cave."

"I don't recall much about it, except for what Dan and Sam told me after I was rescued. I only remember staring at my reflection in a pool and—this is really embarrassing—admiring my upper arms and physique. But like Dan and Sam, I couldn't pull myself away from my obsession. It was weird. I wanted to leave, but something inside wouldn't let me step away from the water."

"Actually, all the inhabitants in her cave were on their hands and knees, gawking at their reflections in the pools until a huge frilled lizard showed up," said Dan.

"A frilled lizard?" questioned the priest.

"Yeah," said Sam. "And it stood probably twenty feet and was nearly sixty feet long."

"What happened when the lizard appeared?" asked Father James.

"Its movements created ripples in the pools that practically erased the inhabitants' reflections," informed Dan. "Since they couldn't admire themselves in the water, they fought with the person next to them."

The priest wanted more information. "But how did you escape the frilled lizard?"

"That again was Dan's resourcefulness," said Sam. "When the creature was standing below a stalactite, he aimed the revolver at the hanging rock. It pierced the lizard's skull."

Father James displayed an unquestionable trace of fear.

"Don't worry, Father, it's dead," promised Sam.

The priest was fearful. But it wasn't a fear of the lizard. It was a fear of the group's likely location.

Dan was curious about the priest's cave of confinement. "What about your cave, Father?"

"Well as you probably know, it was an ice cave that was buffeted with hurricane-force winds that kept pushing the inhabitants forward. When I was in—"

"And if you sat on the ground to rest, ant lion larvae pinched you to your feet," interrupted Sam.

"When I was in the ice chamber," continued Father James, "I remember being so cold and tired that I wanted nothing more than to sit on the ground for only a second or two. But as Sam just pointed out—and as I experienced on a few occasions—every time I sat on the snow, the insects poked me to my feet. And the winds pushed me along. From the moment I entered the blizzard, I trudged in an endless circle with no possibility of rest. I also remember feeling trapped. A few inhabitants tried to escape the frozen arena by leaping into the abyss. I also made an attempt. But as soon as we made the jump, the updrafts within the abyss slammed us against the ceiling where the creature grabbed us and tossed us back into the ice chamber."

"And you're sure you didn't see William, Jimmy, or Brad in the snowstorm," asked Dan.

Father James rested his hand on his friend's shoulder. "I'm sorry. But I'm sure your brother is in this maze of caves somewhere. We'll find him." He looked at Sam and Cindy. "I searched everywhere for familiar faces for the longest time. But I have to admit that it didn't seem like fifteen days."

"I even saw a Confederate general in the blizzard," interrupted Sam again. "I remember wondering if he had been walking in the whiteout since the 1860's. After I saw another inhabitant make the leap, I got a morbid thought."

"What was that?" pressed Dan.

"Maybe the inhabitants were destined to spend the rest of their lives in the ice cave. I mean, every time they jumped into the abyss—whether for freedom or death—they were thrown back into the snowstorm. It's like they weren't permitted to end their lives."

The priest reached for the stone wall to avert a fall.

Dan dashed to his side and lowered the priest to the ground. "He's as white as a ghost!" exclaimed Dan. He touched the priest's bloody shirt. "Are you in pain?"

Father James made no response. His thoughts were lost in the darkness ahead.

Sam's comments about the Confederate general and the inability of the inhabitants to take their own lives had nearly confirmed the priest's worst suspicions.

"Father!" shouted Cindy.

The priest shook.

"What's wrong with him?" asked Dan.

"I don't know," said Sam. "Maybe his injury is worse than I suspected." He examined his wound.

"It's not that," whispered Father James.

"What then?" demanded Sam.

Again, the priest fell silent. He remained staring ahead.

"He's freaking me out," exclaimed Cindy.

Father James chose not to reveal his ghastly belief. He slowly drew his gaze from the distant darkness and made eye contact with Cindy. "Sorry, I don't know what came over me."

Sam helped him to his feet. "Father, are you sure you're not in any pain?" he asked.

"I'm sure," he replied. "Thanks." He surveyed the walls, the ceiling, and the tunnel behind.

The explorers knew that his reactions were most unusual and that something was terrifying him, especially since he had never scrutinized his surroundings so carefully.

Sam grabbed his arm and insisted on knowing what was troubling him.

"It's nothing. Just a—nothing."

"Just a what?" ordered Sam.

The priest pulled his arm from Sam's grip, raised a hand to his brow, but remained silent.

"Look Father, something's obviously bothering you," said Sam. "But we don't keep anything from anyone in this group. We're in this together; there are no secrets. Anything kept bottled up could ultimately lead to our demise." Sam reminded him of the daring rescue from the ice cave. "Don't forget that we risked our lives to save yours."

He knew Sam was right. But he still debated on whether or not to divulge his suspicions.

"Spill the beans," ordered Sam.

Father James stepped several feet from the group and hid himself in the darkness. He then turned to face his friends who were illuminated by the torch. "What I suspect is simply a gut feeling. I don't have any evidence to prove or disprove my theory."

"You know where we are, don't you?" asked Cindy.

"No. I don't know for sure."

"Then enlighten us as to where you think we might be," pressed Sam.

"Some theologians believe that most people have a predominant sin," began Father James.

"A predominant sin?" asked Cindy. "What's that?"

"Essentially, many people have a particular vice that he or she finds harder to resist than temptations toward other vices," explained the priest. "For example, someone may be more susceptible to lie, whereas another person may find it harder to resist the urge to steal." He stepped from the darkness and into the light. "Basically, all sins can be classified into one of seven groups which the Catholic Church labels as the capital sins. These sins are pride, avarice, envy, wrath, lust, gluttony, and sloth."

Cindy took a step closer to the priest. "But what does that have to do with us?"

"I think I know where he's going with this," interrupted Dan. "He thinks we were placed in a particular cave that corresponds to our predominant sin or fault."

"I told you it was only a hunch," reminded the priest. He looked at Sam. "Your cave was inhabited with people prone to envy. You said it yourself that you felt compelled to climb the ladder so you could look down on the other dwellers. You were envious of the other climbers and of their achievements. In short, you were craving their respect and recognition."

"I hate to admit it, Sam, but you were pretty stubborn about leaving the cave since you had to lower yourself and crawl on your hands and knees," recalled Dan.

"Well yeah. But I wasn't myself. I didn't have control over my faculties."

Dan got the priest's attention. "And you think my cave is reserved for avaricious or greedy people because I was tempted to excessive wealth."

"I can't say for sure. But yes, it's entirely possible," remarked the priest.

"And what about my cave?" challenged Cindy. "You think it was what—pride?"

"Perhaps."

"But I've never had excessive pride with anything or anyone."

"I believe you," said Father James. "But what about vanity? That's precisely what vanity is—excessive pride in oneself, whether it's beauty, clothes, accomplishments, or even one's physique."

There was no denying the fact that the priest's speculation seemed logical.

After noticing the expressions of disbelief around him, Father James revealed that his predominant vice was sloth. "Not initially of course, but a couple years after my ordination to the priesthood, my daily routine of celebrating the Mass, hearing confessions, visiting the sick, and leading parish meetings became just that—routine. Don't get me wrong, it's not that I disliked my priestly calling. As a matter of fact, I still enjoy it immensely. But in time, I found myself skipping a parish meeting here and there to relax. Granted, there's nothing wrong with taking a break, but my occasional breaks rapidly became a habit. In time, my pastoral duties suffered." In a near-dazed state, he stared into the darkness again. "If we make it out of here alive, I'll never neglect my responsibilities as a priest again."

Cindy extended the torch nearer his face. "But you still haven't told us where you think we are."

Sam was fairly confident of the priest's forthcoming response. "Go ahead, Father. Tell us where you think we are."

"Sam's earlier comment about seeing a Confederate general, his speculation that the inhabitants can't end their lives, and Dan's theory that our bodies heal so we can suffer again led me to suspect the worst."

"Father!" pleaded Cindy. "Where are we?"

The priest looked directly at her. "I think we're in hell."

"Hell?" she shouted. "What do you mean hell? You mean *the* hell?"

"I know it's difficult to grasp, but don't you think it's odd that time is askew, that Sam walked alongside a general who should have been dead more than a hundred years ago, that the cave dwellers apparently can't take their own lives, and that we haven't eaten, slept, or shaved in more than two weeks?"

"Wait a minute, Father," challenged Dan. "In my cave, I saw dwellers killed by the anacondas. And in Sam's cave, inhabitants were flayed alive by flesh-eating spiders."

"And I saw the shreds of a man's shirt dangling from a walking stick's mouth in my cave," recalled Sam.

"I believe you," assured the priest. "But did you also see them come back to life?"

"What?" blurted Cindy.

"Believe me, I really hope I'm wrong," stressed the priest. "I hope the cave dwellers died and stayed dead. But I've got a bad feeling that once inhabitants arrive in this world they can't end their lives—at least not permanently. It's as if their eternal punishment is to die and come back to life so they can suffer the pain and agony of death again and again for all eternity." He glanced from face to face for a reaction. "As a matter of fact, I wouldn't be surprised if the inhabitants who died in front of you also rose from the dead after you left your caves."

"Okay Father, for argument's sake, let's say you're right and this is hell," posed Dan. "Then where are William, Jimmy, and Brad?"

"Probably in the other caves."

"What other caves?" asked Cindy.

"If I'm correct, there may be three more side caves in the tunnel ahead—one for gluttony, one for wrath, and the other for lust."

"And you believe that William, Jimmy, and Brad are in those caves?" asked Dan.

"Either that or all of them could be in one. Again, it depends on their predominant sin."

"So where do we look for Jimmy?" asked Sam.

"Gluttony," shouted Dan and Cindy.

"All right you two," he rebuked. "You don't know for sure Jimmy's—" He grabbed the torch from Cindy. "Oh who am I kidding? Of course he's in the gluttony cave."

As the rescuers resumed their hike up the cavern, Cindy stepped alongside Sam. "If there are three more side caves in the tunnel ahead, then what's overhead?"

Father James overheard her comment. "I wouldn't even venture to guess what's above us. I suggest that we stay on this level if at all possible."

With Sam clutching the torch, the travelers inched up the darkened cavern.

CHAPTER TEN

The Ripped Pages

"So now we're not looking for an upper passageway?" asked Cindy.

"I guess not," said Sam.

"But what if the floor collapses or if the portal is on the level above?"

Sam bounced on the ground to test its stability. "It seems solid for now. And as far as the portal, I suppose we'll have to wait and see." He moved the torch alongside her face. "Besides, maybe Father James is right. Perhaps there are three more side caves in the tunnel ahead."

"Remember, I said there may be," stressed Father James.

"What do you mean there may be?" questioned Cindy.

"I would presume—" He paused to rub his nose that was irritated by the falling dust in the tunnel. "I would presume that the seven side caves would be in close proximity to each other," he continued.

"What makes you say that?" inquired Dan.

"It's merely a guess on my part, but it seems logical that the caves of the seven capital sins would be clustered together," proposed the priest. He glanced at the ceiling and cautioned a second time, "I wouldn't recommend exploring the upper region unless it's absolutely necessary."

"But what if the portal is above us?" asked Cindy again.

Sam tried to relieve her worries. "Let's be on the lookout for an upper passageway, in case we don't find the three caves or the portal on this level."

The flame died. The march stopped.

"Oh great," complained Cindy.

"It's all right," assured Sam. He dropped the torch to the ground, opened the backpack that Dan was lugging, and grabbed the flashlight.

The area was soon bathed in artificial light.

"You guys thought of everything," complimented Father James.

"Not really," corrected Sam. "The first-aid kit would have come in handy when bandaging your side."

"I'm fine, really."

Sam aimed the flashlight's beam ahead. The distance between the cavern walls gradually widened and the ceiling was adorned with many stalactites of various shapes and sizes.

Certain that engaging in any conversation would take her mind off the likelihood of finding the portal in time, Cindy asked, "Sam, do you agree with Father?"

"About what?"

"What do you mean about what?" she asked in disbelief. "About this being hell."

"There's no way anyone can know for sure. But he did raise some convincing theories."

As Sam and Cindy led the group, she glanced back at the priest. "Father, what else do you know about hell?"

"Very little, I'm afraid."

"But I thought that men studying for the priesthood took courses on God, heaven, Satan, and hell in the seminary."

"We did. But our studies in demonology dealt mainly with sin, the powers of demons, and the effects of the fallen angels on humankind."

"Fallen angels?" asked Cindy. "What do you mean?"

"The throng of fallen angels consists of those spirits who attempted to overthrow God and assume his heavenly throne. For their failed mutiny, they fell from the sky and were banished forever from paradise. The leader of the rebellion—"

"Wait a minute—a throng?" she asked. "You mean there could be hundreds of these fallen angels in this place—presuming this is hell."

"I wish," whispered Father James.

"What do you mean you wish?" she asked.

"It's nothing. We'll be fine," he promised.

"Father James wishes there were only hundreds," clarified Dan. "In reality, there could be thousands or perhaps millions of these evil spirits."

Cindy spun and stared at the priest. "Could there be thousands or millions like Dan said?"

"We'll be fine," reassured the priest.

Sam tugged on Cindy's arm. "Come on. We need to keep moving."

She resumed her pace. "Father, why isn't more known about hell? If we knew more about its qualities and entrapments, then maybe we'd know how to battle the demons and escape this place."

"Very little is known about the underworld," admitted Father James. "To be perfectly honest, no human has ever visited the realm and returned to earth to tell about it."

"Cindy, wasn't there mention of hell or Hades in your mythology course?" asked Dan.

"Of course, but that's mythology—you know—made-up stories that were told and retold from generation to generation by the Greeks and Romans. But two things I do remember about Hades from my mythology class are that the souls were ferried across the River Styx and that the abode was guarded by a three-headed dog named Cerberus."

Sam raised the flashlight to her face. "We've waded through a couple water holes. Maybe we should keep an eye out for a dog," he joked.

She knocked the flashlight from her face. "I'm just making conversation to pass the time." She looked in the direction of the flashlight's beam. "Hey, another cave!"

The group dashed to its entrance.

"You three wait here. I'll check it out," ordered Sam.

"I'm going with you," insisted Cindy.

"Sam, I think it would be safer if we came along," suggested Father James. "As Dan mentioned earlier, sticking together was key to your safe return from the parallel world. Or was that just a story?"

Dan remained uncharacteristically quiet.

"Dan, don't you agree? Shouldn't we stick together?" asked Cindy.

The teenager remained fixated on the cave's entrance.

"Dan!" she shouted.

Sam stepped nearer the opening.

Dan lunged and knocked him to the ground.

Sam jerked to a seated position. "What's got into you, Dan?" he shouted.

The cave's interior was suddenly illuminated.

"That's my cave," alerted Dan.

A golden chest appeared on a boulder, just inside the entrance.

Cindy stared at the chest. "Are you sure?"

"Positive," he replied.

Sam reached for the flashlight beside him and jumped to his feet. "I don't get it. How did we miss the other three caves?"

"Oh no," whispered Cindy.

"What?" questioned Sam.

"Do you think we've wasted our time hiking in a large circle and ended up back at the first cave?"

Sam switched his sights to Dan. "Are you absolutely sure this is your cave? Maybe it's one that just looks like yours."

Cindy screamed.

The explorers stumbled backwards as an oversize anaconda tried to escape its confinement.

The opening vanished.

"Yeah, that's my cave," confirmed Dan.

Sam helped Cindy to her feet. "I don't get it," he said. "How could we have missed not one, but three caves in our—"

"I don't know!" shouted Dan. "But they've got to be around here somewhere. It's not like a cave can get up and—"

Tremors were heard above.

"—and walk away," finished Dan.

All eyes gazed upward.

"I have an awful feeling about the upper region," admitted Sam.

"What's that noise?" asked Cindy.

"Shh," ordered the priest.

The sounds and vibrations ended.

"It sounded like chains rattling," whispered Sam.

"Yeah, it did sound like chains," agreed Dan. "Should we check it out?"

Cindy lowered her sights from the ceiling. "But Father said we should avoid the upper level if at all possible."

"I know what he said," replied Dan. "But there aren't any new caves on this level. We don't have a choice."

The priest eventually nodded. Though he suspected that William, Jimmy, and Brad needed rescuing, he also feared for the safety of his traveling companions.

"So how do we get up there?" asked Cindy.

"I'm sure we'll find something," said Sam. "I promise."

"Hey Sam, what about the opening in your cave's ceiling?" blurted Dan.

"Hmm," he mumbled.

"Actually Sam, that's not a bad idea," seconded Cindy.

Sam scratched his scalp as he called to mind his cave of imprisonment. "I suppose it's a good idea, but it won't work."

"Why not?" asked Cindy.

"The hole is easily twenty feet above the ground. We don't have a rope and the walking sticks are dead—not that I'd suggest climbing on them even if they were alive."

"But what about standing on someone's shoulders?" she proposed.

"I'm afraid not," said Sam. "Even if you stood on my shoulders, your reach would still fall way below the opening." He glanced at the priest. "Besides, I don't think the stretch would do Father James's injury any good."

"My side is fine. I can do it."

"I appreciate it, Father, but like I said, it's beyond our reach. What's more, I'm sure the rowdy inhabitants would stampede us."

"Then what about the waterfall in Cindy's cave?" said Dan.

"What about it?" asked Sam.

"We could scale the rock wall behind the waterfall. And we'd have plenty of time to help Father James climb since the frilled lizard is dead."

"Would you stop worrying about my side!" protested the priest.

Even though Sam wasn't thrilled with the idea of Father James climbing the wall, he couldn't deny the fact that time was passing quickly and they needed to find their friends before the next full moon.

Father James grabbed Sam's arm. "I'll be fine." He exposed his wound. "Look, the bleeding has stopped."

"Sam, the entrance to my cave has vanished," said Dan. "And there's no longer a living ladder in yours. So the rock wall is our only way up." He glanced at the spot where his cave's entrance previously existed. "And even if the entrance hadn't disappeared, there wasn't an upward passageway in my cave."

Overhead vibrations rumbled again.

"Besides Sam, I've walked this entire level," reminded Dan. "Trust me, there's nothing left for us here. If we continue hiking on this path we'll run into the same creatures, never find our friends, end up back in this spot, and lose valuable time in the process."

The noise above their heads ended.

"Our friends and answers are a level up," concluded Dan.

"I guess there's no other way," yielded Sam. "But based on the sounds overhead, we'll need to be extra cautious." He directed the flashlight ahead and led the group up the tunnel. Cindy's cave was their destination.

Nearly two miles up the footpath, Sam spotted a flicker of light in the distance. Energized, the group raced to four glowing torches wedged in the wall.

Dan stared at the torches.

"What's wrong?" asked Sam.

The teenager maintained his distant look.

"Dan!" shouted Sam.

The teenager escaped his daze. "Sam, when I made my first trip up this tunnel to your side cave there weren't four burning torches on the wall."

"Are you sure?" asked Sam.

"Of course I'm sure. I'd remember a set of four glowing torches."

"Well there's got to be a rational explanation," said Sam.

"The light keeper!" Dan shouted.

"The what?" asked Sam.

THE RIPPED PAGES

"Didn't I mention the light keeper to you before?"

Sam shook his head. "Not that I remember."

"When I came across a torch after I escaped my cave, I wondered who or what lit the torches in this world when they burned out."

"I don't think we should focus on that now," advised the priest. "Maybe we'll get lucky and avoid the so-called light keeper once we're on the next level."

"He's right," agreed Sam. "We should forget about the light keeper and concentrate on the waterfall."

With each traveler gripping a lance and a torch, the hike resumed.

"I have to admit that I feel uncomfortable carrying a weapon," confessed the priest.

"Father, it's for your protection and the group's," reminded Dan. "We're not trying to harm anything deliberately, but we have to use them in self-defense. Remember, these aren't earthly creatures we're dealing with."

"I suppose you're right. I just wish it wasn't necessary."

Dan stopped and rested his hand on the rock wall.

"What are you doing?" asked Cindy.

"Just checking."

"For what?" she prodded.

"Dan, is this where you met the king crab?" questioned Sam.

"I think so. I know that every area of this tunnel looks virtually the same, but it chased me when I was hiking to your cave." He removed his hand from the wall. "I don't feel any tremors." He extended his torch and saw its flame reflecting on the water. "There's the pool!"

"The pool?" asked Cindy.

"Shh," whispered Dan. "I don't think we should make any noise."

"Is that where you met the giant water spider?" whispered Sam without his stare leaving the pool.

"Yeah," replied Dan. "And even though I don't think it wanted to harm me, I still don't think we should announce our presence."

"No problem," promised Cindy.

Dan took the silent lead and was soon wading in the water. He waved his torch from side to side, searching for the arachnid. He turned to his friends and cautioned, "There are a lot of rocks on the floor. Be careful."

The three explorers simply nodded.

They were waist deep in water when something dropped into the pool.

Dan froze, but only momentarily. He suspected it was the residential spider. He turned to the group. "I think we should pick up the pace," he whispered.

Father James, Sam, and Cindy waved their torches in search of the predator.

At the rear of the party line, Sam turned. Though half expecting it, he still gasped when seeing the four-foot-long spider standing atop the water and inching in the group's direction. "Let's move faster," he quietly warned.

His co-travelers spun and spotted the spider.

Father James dropped his lance in fright.

They continued their hushed escape across the pool—but in a backward direction—keeping a watchful eye on the arachnid with three weapons aimed at the creature.

"What is it?" whispered Father James. "It has a human—" He stumbled on a rock and fell below the water's surface.

To the group's surprise, the spider made no charge on its supposed helpless prey. The creature coughed.

Dan mimicked its cough.

The spider, thinking it was dealing with its own species, retreated and masked itself behind a boulder to await its next trespasser.

Convinced now more than ever that their weapons were priceless in the cavernous world, Father James retraced his steps and snatched his lance. His quenched torch, however, was left floating on the water.

With the arachnid concealed behind the boulder and not posing an immediate threat, Dan and Cindy turned and resumed their escape while scanning the area ahead for more arachnids. Father James and Sam maintained their backward stride with a close eye on the boulder where the spider was lurking.

The explorers stepped from the water and dashed ahead.

THE RIPPED PAGES

Sam offered periodic backward glances until the pool was lost in the darkness.

"I've never seen anything like that in my life—not even in my worst dreams," admitted the priest.

"I wonder if that was the same spider we saw earlier," said Cindy.

"I was thinking the same thing," replied Sam.

Father James turned and looked in the pool's direction. "Did spiders that size exist in the parallel world?"

"Yeah," said Dan. "There were huge spiders in the parallel world too. But they didn't have human faces."

The priest realized that he lacked the fearlessness of his companions. "Sorry I freaked out and dropped my lance back there."

"Father, there's no need to apologize," said Sam. "The three of us encountered that particular species earlier. I reacted the same way when I first saw it."

"You're just being kind," replied Father James. He pulled his prayer book from his pants pocket.

"Father, he's telling the truth," said Dan. "I also freaked out when I saw the spider for the first time in that very pool." He watched the priest inspect the drenched pages of his prayer book. "Sorry about your book."

"That's okay. It'll dry," said the priest.

"Hand it to me," insisted Dan.

"Why?" asked the priest.

Dan grabbed the book, held it near his torch, and fanned its pages to dry some of the moisture.

"Dan, that'll take forever," criticized Cindy.

"I suppose. But it's a start."

Father James cringed.

Sam suspected that his tumble in the pool may have reopened his wound. "Are you all right, Father?"

"Oh sure, I'm fine," he claimed.

"Be that as it may, let's have another look at your side," Sam insisted.

"Sam, there's no need to mother me. I'll be fine."

Sam wasn't dissuaded. He and Cindy removed the priest's shirt and bloody tee shirt while Dan continued fanning the pages of the prayer book.

"Well, you've opened the wound again," alerted Sam.

"But I hardly feel any pain."

"Obviously, you're in no condition to climb the wall behind the waterfall," declared Sam.

"Knock it off, Sam! I can handle the wall!" screamed Father James.

The priest's unexpected outburst startled Dan who fumbled the prayer book. In his effort to catch the book before it hit the ground, he accidentally ripped three pages. Realizing that then was not the best time to mention the mishap to Father James, he stuffed the pages in his pants pocket.

"Father," warned Sam, "if it continues bleeding—"

"Sam!" he yelled again. "Enough!"

A momentary silence filled the tunnel.

"Sorry Sam," expressed a remorseful priest. "But I refuse to be the cause of you three not finding your friends or your way home."

"What are you talking about?" asked Cindy.

"Look," explained the priest, "we all know that we're in a race against time." He glanced at his watch. "It's already September nineteenth which means we have to find the others and the portal in eleven days. Either I march with the three of you at our normal pace or I stay behind."

"Are you out of your mind? We're not leaving anyone behind!" shouted Sam.

"That's the deal. Either you leave me here—in this very spot—or I walk with you at our normal pace to the waterfall. If we miss the portal because my injury slowed us down … well … I just won't let that happen."

Sam looked at Cindy and Dan. Both nodded.

"Okay Father," agreed a reluctant Sam. "We'll do it your way. We'll march at our normal pace."

"Thanks Sam."

"But Father, there's no shame in sustaining an injury," said Sam. "If you knew the injuries we suffered on our way to your cave, you'd—" He looked at Dan. "How are your calves and ankles?"

"They're fine," he replied while fanning the book—minus three pages.

"Let's have a look," ordered Sam.

Dan stepped to the group and raised his pant legs.

"They still look pretty bad," informed Sam.

"How'd that happen?" asked Father James.

"I ran into some white mist in the tunnel ahead. But my legs really don't hurt." He returned the damaged prayer book to the priest.

"Dan, where was the white mist?" questioned Cindy.

"That's not important. We'll be fine."

"So it's before my cave," she deduced.

"Cindy, don't worry," Dan reiterated. Uncomfortable being the center of attention, he lowered his pant legs and changed the subject. "I think we should move on. We've got a lot of ground to cover before the waterfall."

"Father, are you sure it's September nineteenth?" questioned Cindy.

"Well, at least according to my watch."

"Sam, do you think we'll still have enough time to find the others and the portal before the thirtieth?" she asked.

"I hope so. The way I figure it, we've discovered four caves in nineteen days which leaves us with eleven days to find the last three."

"And the portal?" she added.

"Yeah, I think it's possible," said Sam.

"Sam, since I've explored this part of the tunnel before, maybe I should take the lead," proposed Dan. "I know what I'm looking for."

"And I'll join him," volunteered Cindy.

"That's fine," agreed Sam. "Father James and I will follow." Though Sam didn't like the idea of the teenagers being the first to encounter potential dangers, he felt he should remain at the priest's side in case he needed support.

The march continued.

To Sam's surprise, Father James matched the pace of the teenagers with little to no discomfort. The priest tripped only twice. Luckily, Sam prevented him from hitting the ground.

"So Dan, what do you think the odds are of us finding the side caves and the portal in time?" asked Cindy. "And I want the truth—no sugarcoating."

"It's hard to say."

"What do you mean?"

"Well, if the three caves and the portal are overhead, then I think our chances are pretty good. But if they're not above, then our chances are pretty slim."

"But Dan, you've already scouted this entire level and didn't find the other caves or the portal. So they have to be up above. Where else could they be? We both know that nothing's below us except a giant abyss."

"The last three caves could be anywhere," said Dan. "For all we know, they may have the ability of relocating—like the exit in my cave."

"Hey, are you two talking or surveying?" yelled Sam from behind.

"Both!" shouted Cindy.

"You know Sam, you're pretty lucky," said Father James.

"How so?"

"Cindy, Dan, William, and Jimmy have a lot of respect for you."

"Yeah, I guess I am pretty lucky. Actually, it's the kids who brought some meaning back into my life. I wouldn't trade our adventures in the parallel world for anything. But at the same time, it's strange."

"What's strange?" asked Father James.

"As much as I hate being in this miserable world, I'm sort of glad at the same time," answered Sam.

"You've got to be kidding."

"Don't get me wrong. It's not that we didn't enjoy our times together and our outings on earth—we did. But in this place, it's different. Here, we must rely on one another for our very lives and also be prepared to offer our lives for each other." He slowed his pace. "It's weird, but here—if this is hell—it's selfless for us."

"I'd say that sounds more like heaven. But we both know that's not where we are. Maybe this is our bit of heaven in hell—if that's possible."

"Speaking of offering our lives for each other, if this is hell, what do you think would happen—I mean our souls—if one of us died in this place?" asked Sam.

THE RIPPED PAGES

"Wow! I never thought about that," admitted Father James.

To the men's astonishment, Cindy and Dan had overheard Sam's thought-provoking question.

The hike halted.

"Yeah Father, what would happen to us?" asked Dan.

"I honestly don't know. An adventure like ours has never happened in the history of mankind. As all of you know, I suspect this is hell. But at the same time, I haven't any conclusive proof. There's a chance I could be wrong."

Dan persisted. "What would be conclusive proof—an encounter with Lucifer?"

The priest avoided Dan's troublesome question by stressing caution. "Until we know for sure where we are, let's do our best not to get killed."

"That was my plan," replied Cindy.

"But Father, deep down, do you really think we're in hell?" pressed Dan.

The priest looked overhead to prevent his friends from detecting fear in his eyes. "Yes Dan, deep down, I believe this is the sinister realm."

Cindy took a loud gulp.

"Come on, let's move," ordered Sam. "We're losing travel time."

His diversion worked. The party was soon marching, though in complete silence.

A short distance up the tunnel, Sam couldn't shake the feeling that the teenagers' thoughts had reverted to the likelihood of their presence in hell. "Cindy, Dan, we have to remain focused on our hike. Dwelling too much on our probable location could cause distractions and possibly our destruction. We must stay alert."

Dan knew that Cindy was apprehensive. "He's right, Cindy. We've got this far, we'll finish the journey."

She made a desperate attempt to grin, but failed miserably.

"Sam look, another cave!" exclaimed Dan.

Father James and Sam quickly stepped alongside the teenagers.

"Are you sure that's an entrance to a cave?" asked Father James.

"Trust me. I'd never forget that entrance," swore Dan. "It's the smallest one on this level. Sam and I had to crawl through it."

Sam dropped to his knees to look inside.

Father James pushed him from the entrance. "Sorry Sam, but if you were obsessed with the inner workings of this cave earlier, then you can't look inside now."

Sam rose to his feet. "I suppose you're right. But you didn't have to knock me to the ground."

He disregarded Sam's comment and told the teenagers that they shouldn't look inside either.

"Why not?" asked Dan. "I was in there before. Besides, I'm not an envious person."

"Perhaps not," said the priest. "However, I know for a fact that some people fluctuate between a predominant vice and another less overpowering one. It's entirely possible that any of us could be captivated with what's inside. In the end, we'd lose more travel time."

In shame, Dan admitted to himself that he had a growing interest to revisit the cave. He refused, however, to tell the priest of his temptation.

Cindy also was curious. She fell to her knees.

Father James yanked her to her feet. "Cindy, we already know this is the second cave. None of our friends are inside. We must move on."

Reluctantly, she and the others agreed, though each wanted to peek inside.

As their walk continued, Father James remarked, "I hope you understand why none of us should have entered Sam's cave."

"Not really," admitted Cindy.

"Cindy, why welcome temptations that will lead to sin and unhappiness?" posed the priest. "In the confessional, I've witnessed hundreds of men and women ruin their lives and endanger their immortal souls simply because they gave into temptations or were curious. What we did back there was avoid the near occasion of sin." He sensed that she was disappointed by not being allowed entry into the side cave. "Trust me; you'll be glad you didn't crawl inside once you're home." He looked at Sam. "I'm proud of you. Heaven only knows what would have happened to us if you had entered your cave."

"Thanks. But it was tough."

The priest pulled his prayer book from his pocket and waved the

THE RIPPED PAGES

damp pages in the air. He began reading Scripture by the light of Sam's torch.

"What are you reading?" asked Cindy.

"Each page contains a Gospel passage and thoughts for reflection."

"What's today's reading?" questioned Dan.

"The Parable of the Lost Son," he replied.

"I never understood that parable," admitted Cindy.

"Essentially, our Lord is ready to forgive us of our sins once we admit repentance with the desire to sin no more," explained Father James. "In this parable, for example, the younger son has squandered his wealth on depraved living. When he is down and out, he finally comes to his senses and returns to his father's house."

"Yeah, I understand that. But what about the older son?" asked Cindy. "Is he meant to represent—"

"Sam, the dirt mounds are ahead," shouted Dan.

Father James returned the prayer book to his pocket. "What mounds?" he asked.

"The clods ahead aren't what they seem," cautioned Sam.

"Then what are they?" asked Cindy.

"When Dan and I made this trip earlier, I was grabbed by skeletal arms that burst from the mounds. But unlike our first pass, now we have plenty of light. So it should be easier to sidestep the clods." Since Father James was without a torch, Sam suggested that Dan take the lead since he was familiar with the area.

Dan agreed.

Cindy offered to follow him.

"Father, I think you should walk behind Cindy and her torch," suggested Sam. "I'll bring up the rear with mine. This should give you plenty of light."

"Sam, maybe we should warn Cindy and Father James that our lances are useless against the skeletal arms in case one explodes from a mound," alerted Dan.

"If our lances are useless, then how'd you escape the skeletal arms before?" asked Cindy.

"Dan pulled me free," said Sam.

"Apparently, the skeletal arms are fearful of heat—at least they were the last time," explained Dan.

"So let's watch our step," stressed Sam.

Dan guided the group. He rested each foot on a level plot of ground, taking every precaution to avoid contact with the clods. "Sam, is it my imagination or are there more mounds than before?"

"Keep focused!" shouted Sam.

"I am! It just seems—" His comment trailed off. In front of him lay six rows of mounds. Each row stretched the width of the tunnel. Advancing any further would be next to impossible without disturbing the clods. "Sam, look at this!"

Sam stepped alongside Father James and Cindy. He looked over Dan's shoulder. "I don't remember those rows before."

"That's what I've been trying to tell you." Dan took a closer look at their precarious situation. "But I'll bet we can jump over them. They extend only several feet."

"I suppose it's possible," said Sam. An alarming thought crossed his mind. *Could Father James make the leap with his injury?* He examined the area for a safer escape route. "There's got to be a way around these mounds—there just has to be."

"Sam, I think Dan's right," seconded Cindy. "We can jump it."

Sam neared the priest. "But I doubt Father James will make it with his injury."

"Oh," mumbled a mortified Cindy.

"Sam, it's not that far. I'm sure I can make it," predicted the priest.

Aware that there was no way around the deadly mounds, Sam was left with no alternatives. "All right, but I'll make the jump first. If I'm successful, then the rest of you can make the leap. But I want someone to stay behind with Father James."

Dan offered to remain with the priest for the time being.

"Okay then, wish me luck," said Sam. He took several steps back and dashed to the mounds with his lance and torch in hand.

The travelers held their breaths the moment he became airborne.

On witnessing his safe but rough landing on the opposite side, all exhaled sharply.

THE RIPPED PAGES

"Great job, Sam!" yelled Cindy. After a nerve-racking jump, she was standing at his side.

"Father, are you ready?" directed Sam from beyond the mounds.

"Yeah, I think so."

"Take a deep breath and make your dash," instructed Dan.

The priest bolted and had successfully soared over five rows of mounds. He fell short of his target and was immediately grabbed around his legs and waist by nine skeletal arms.

Sam and Cindy crashed to their knees and pressed their torches to the skeletons. Fortunately, the ceaseless tugging of one skeletal arm against another prevented the priest from sinking below the surface.

Dan remained several feet away. As much as he wanted to make the leap and help, the commotion prevented a clear jump.

Cindy witnessed four skeletal arms release their hold on their victim and sink below the soil. "Pull him!" she screamed.

Sam dropped his torch and grasped the priest with both arms.

Cindy snatched his grounded torch and touched both flames against the five lingering bony creatures.

Sensing eventual defeat, the arms sought refuge beneath the surface.

Sam pulled Father James to safety.

"Thank you," said a short-winded priest. He took several deep breaths. "Where did those things come from?" he asked.

Sam helped him to his feet. "I don't know, but we're not sticking around long enough to find out."

"Sam, are you ready?" yelled Dan.

The party of three stepped from the mounds to give him a clear path.

"Go ahead!" shouted Sam.

After a mighty launch, he was standing alongside his friends.

"All right, we're not through this yet," reminded Sam. "We still have a long hike ahead of us. Let's just hope and pray we don't discover any new groupings of clods."

"I've already been praying," assured Father James.

"Great. Don't stop now," said Sam.

Precise footing and vigilance had their eventual reward. After what seemed a forty-minute hike, they escaped the mound-riddled tunnel.

All breathed a pronounced sigh of relief when they stepped from the narrow tunnel and into a lit open cavern with walls nearly a hundred feet apart and the ceiling soaring almost fifty feet.

"We made it," exclaimed Father James.

"Thanks to your prayers," replied Sam.

At Sam's suggestion, the group relaxed to recuperate and regain their composure. A burning torch that was wedged in the cavern wall illuminated the rest area. The priest gladly accepted the torch from Sam.

The homeward trek resumed.

It seemed as though the explorers had barely opened a conversation when they were standing alongside the entrance to the crawlspace where Dan had encountered the white mist.

"Dan, is this where you got your leg burns?" asked Father James.

"Yeah."

"Is there any defense against the mist?" asked Cindy.

"Not that I'm aware of," replied Sam. He squatted and extended his torch inside the shaft. "I don't see the mist, so I suggest we enter now and move fast."

Within seconds, Dan, Cindy, and Father James were squirming on their stomachs in the crawlspace, lugging their lances and torches. Sam insisted on dragging the backpack and bringing up the rear.

Much like the water snakes that Sam and Dan had encountered earlier, the travelers' slithering movements brought them closer to their destination. Throughout their backbreaking crossing, Sam continually looked to the rear entrance. Thankfully, the burning mist never invaded the area.

The group was overjoyed on crawling from the passageway and standing in another open cavern. Cindy's side cave was spotted ahead.

"Let's go!" ordered Sam. He wasn't convinced that the mist wasn't waiting nearby.

He and his companions darted to the side cave.

CHAPTER ELEVEN

Haunting Visions

"WILLIAM!" SCREAMED NANCY. THE ALARM CLOCK STIRRED her from her sleep. She rolled onto her side to wake her husband. He wasn't there. She threw on her bathrobe, ran from the bedroom, and bolted down the staircase. She was puzzled seeing Jeff asleep on the living room sofa. She knelt beside him. "Honey," she whispered. With no response, she squeezed his arm.

He slowly opened his eyes.

"Good morning," she said.

"Morning."

She pulled the afghan over his chest. "Why'd you sleep down here last night?"

After a prolonged yawn, he explained, "I was reading a little before watching the local news." He looked to the television set that was still on. "I guess I dozed off."

She reached for the remote on a side table and switched off the television. "Was there anything on the news about the kids?"

"I'm afraid not."

She rose from the floor. "I'll fix some breakfast before church."

Jeff jumped from the couch, insisting, "I'll give you a hand."

"I'm fine. Get dressed."

He tossed the afghan over the back of the sofa and headed upstairs.

Though the loss of her boys weighed heavily and constantly on her mind, Nancy battled internally to suppress her agonizing thoughts so she could remain strong for her husband and the other families. But that morning was different. In a dazed state, she sat at the kitchen table and recalled her dream.

Jeff entered the room. He was shaved, showered, and dressed.

His unexpected entrance drew Nancy from her thoughts. She glanced at the wall clock and realized that she had been revisiting her dream for nearly twenty minutes.

Jeff joined her at the table. "Are you okay?"

Caught off guard, she rose from her chair, replying, "I'm fine." She opened the refrigerator door.

After many years of marriage, Jeff knew when something was bothering her. He was certain that she was thinking about their boys. "They'll be okay," he promised. "We can't give up hope."

She reached for a carton of eggs. "Like I said, I'm fine. I was just thinking about—" She decided against sharing her dream. She closed the refrigerator door and admitted, "I guess I didn't sleep too well last night."

"Neither did I," he said.

"Well, it's no wonder. It's almost impossible to sleep on that sofa," she remarked.

"You're probably right. And I'm sure my back will pay for it all day. The last time—"

Nancy dropped the carton of eggs and supported herself against the counter.

Jeff raced to her side. "What's wrong?"

"I'm sorry. It's just that last night—" She paused and tried to regain her composure. "Last night—"

"What about last night?" Jeff demanded. He rested his hand upon hers on the counter. "My gosh! You're shaking like a leaf." He helped her to the table. "What happened last night?"

Nancy looked at the clock again. "We better hold off on breakfast until after Mass."

"Breakfast is the least of my concerns. What about last night?"

The last thing she wanted to do was burden her husband. But she couldn't bear it alone anymore. While staring at the broken eggs on the kitchen floor she questioned whether or not to unload her fears. Eventually she divulged, "I had another dream about the boys."

"Go on." He pulled his chair closer to hers.

She grabbed a napkin from a stack on the table. "Dan was helping Father James out of a cave and Cindy was helping Sam. In the background—in my dream—I saw a snowstorm whirling about; just looking at it made me shiver." She blew her nose. "Then almost immediately, I saw something crawl down a cave wall and chase them. When the creatures came into focus, I saw two—"

"Huge daddy longlegs," finished Jeff.

"Yes," exclaimed a bewildered Nancy. "How on earth did you know?"

"And then, one of the creatures wrapped its leg around Cindy and then Dan," he continued.

Nancy clasped her husband's hand. "You had the same dream?"

"Apparently so."

"But how is that possible?" she asked.

Jeff was equally confused. "I remember wanting nothing more than to do something—anything," he admitted. "But there was nothing I could do, except watch in horror as the beast wrapped itself around the kids." He stood from the table, approached the kitchen window, and looked into the backyard.

Nancy knew that his helplessness to rescue their sons troubled him greatly. She joined him at the window. "There was nothing you could do. It was just a dream."

"Was it?" he posed.

Nancy kept her unconfirmed suspicions to herself.

Jeff remained staring out the window. "Then I saw Dan, Cindy, Sam, and Father James wading through a pool of water," he related. "I remember the look of terror on Father James's face when an enormous spider walked on the water in their direction. Other than the abnormal size of the spider, what was really disturbing was—"

"Its face," she interrupted. "It had a human face."

He redirected his sights from the backyard to his wife. "Yeah, how'd you know?"

"And Father James stumbled on a rock and fell into the pool," she added.

Jeff was completely baffled. He leaned against the counter. "You had the same dream?"

THE SINISTER REALM

"Apparently so. What do you think it means?"

He returned to the table. "Obviously, there's no denying the fact that the boys have been on our minds constantly."

Nancy—who also had seated herself at the table—simply nodded.

"So it stands to reason that we'd dream about them," he continued.

"I agree, but the two of us having identical dreams?" she asked. "That's weird." As they exchanged glances, Nancy revealed what she had suspected since waking from her dream. "Do you think that someone or something is showing us what our boys and the others are going through? I mean, first the markings on the statue and now our dreams."

"I don't know. I guess it's possible that our boys—" His comment faded.

"What about the boys?" she demanded.

"You said you saw Cindy, Sam, Father James, and Dan in your dream."

"Yes, yes," replied an impatient Nancy. "What about the boys?"

"William, did you see him?" he asked.

She closed her eyes before replying. "Near the end of my dream I saw William yelling. I don't know how to explain what I felt during the dream, but I sensed that he was furious with someone or something."

"Then what happened?" he pressed.

"The alarm clock rang." She grabbed another napkin. "Did you see William?"

"Yeah, but like you, I only saw him yelling. That's the last thing I remember before you woke me." He rose from the table again and suggested that she get dressed for church while he cleaned the mess on the kitchen floor.

"All right." She paused at the kitchen entryway and turned. "Maybe Father Andreas will have some insight into this phenomenon."

"Maybe." He reached for a rag below the kitchen sink.

During their drive to church, the shared dream conversation resumed.

"Honey, from the moment we first learned of the boys' disappearance, I've had conflicting emotions about whether they entered the tree or if they were the innocent victims of a robbery and kidnapping like Officer Moore believes," said Nancy. "But ever since we found Dan's medal at the base of the oak, I've felt almost certain that they stepped into the tree."

The car turned onto Main Street.

"But I have a nagging feeling that the parallel world is no longer peaceful," she continued. "The dream still terrifies me."

The car pulled into the church parking lot.

"I can't stop thinking about last night's dream either," admitted Jeff. He removed the key from the ignition. "It infuriates me that our boys might be in danger and there's nothing I can do but sit and watch."

She dabbed her eyes. "We can pray for them."

"I know, but I wish there was something more I could do."

"For now, there's nothing else."

As they stepped from the car, each clearly detected the smell of autumn in the air. They neared the church steps and spotted the Parkers' and Sara's cars.

Jeff looked at his watch and commented that they were already several minutes late for Mass. As the couple entered the church, they saw Father Andreas standing at the pulpit proclaiming the Gospel passage about Herod's attempt to locate the Christ child.

Nancy lost her balance on her approach to the fifth pew when Father Andreas read that the angel of the Lord appeared to Joseph in a dream and told him to take the child and his mother and flee to Egypt.

Luckily, Jeff was at her side to prevent her from nose-diving into the aisle. The commotion, however, drew the attention of nearby worshipers.

"This story keeps getting more bizarre," she whispered.

Jeff nodded.

Thirty minutes later, the Clays, the Parkers, Sara, and Father Andreas were kneeling below the marble statue imploring safety for their children and friends—just as they had done every morning since learning the tragic news.

During their drive to the church, the Clays had decided to hold off on mentioning their shared dream and the possibility that the message was heaven sent until after the prayer session. They felt it would be prudent to recount their dream to Father Andreas in private. Unfortunately, the conversation would not wait until the three were alone.

At the conclusion of the rosary, Marie wept.

Nancy placed her arm around her in a display of comfort. "Jimmy will be fine," she promised.

"I've been praying constantly—morning, noon, and night," she disclosed. "But I'm losing hope of ever seeing Jimmy again."

"Marie, I can't begin to imagine what you're going through, but we must keep our hopes alive," counseled Father Andreas. "Our prayerful efforts will be rewarded."

"I hope you're right, Father. But I miss Jimmy so much that he's now entered my dreams. They're complete hell."

"What?" exclaimed her husband. "You never told me you had dreams about Jimmy."

"I'm sorry, but I didn't think it was important—until last night."

"What happened last night?" Tom asked.

She looked at the marble statue towering above. "During the past couple weeks I've had many dreams about Jimmy. But they were always about the pranks he played as a child—like the time he hid a kitten in the bathroom cabinet. But last night's dream was different."

"How do you mean?" asked Nancy.

"Last night I saw Jimmy standing in a cave with something hanging from his mouth." She looked overhead again. "It was just like the cord I saw dangling from this statue's mouth during an earlier prayer session."

Tom raised an eyebrow. "What else do you remember?"

"It was the strangest thing. After noticing the string hanging from his mouth, I glanced at the ground where I saw something squirming below the surface. I never saw what it was, but something was definitely moving."

"Do you remember anything else?" questioned Nancy.

"Yes. I looked next to Jimmy and saw—"

"An obese, middle-aged woman with something twisting in her stomach," interrupted Tom.

Marie stared at her husband in disbelief. "You saw it too?"

"That's the dream I had last night."

Marie shook her head. "But isn't that odd?"

"Not really," said Nancy.

"What do you mean?" asked a curious priest.

"Jeff and I had the same dream last night—down to the smallest detail."

"Really?" doubted Marie. "You had a dream about Jimmy?"

"Not exactly." Nancy rose from the kneeler. "In our dream, Jeff and I saw Dan, Cindy, Sam, and Father James being chased by what appeared to be two oversize daddy longlegs."

"Daddy longlegs?" exclaimed Marie.

"Incredible, I know," replied Nancy. "Then an enormous spider—with a human face—was hunting them. The next thing we saw was Father James—"

"Tripping on a rock and falling into the water," said Sara.

"What'd you say?" blurted Nancy.

"That's what I dreamed last night," informed Sara.

Skeptical of Sara's dream, Jeff stepped from the kneeler and stood alongside his wife. "And how did they escape the spider?"

"The human-faced spider coughed," related Sara. "So Dan mimicked its cough. In my dream, I sensed that the spider recognized its own species so it hid behind a boulder."

Nancy and Jeff were astounded.

"Is that what you two dreamed?" asked Sara.

"Yeah," replied Nancy. "That's what happened."

Five sets of eyes were glued to the priest.

"Any explanation?" urged Nancy.

Father Andreas also was stunned. In his years of spiritual guidance and psychological counseling, he had never experienced such an oddity. "I'm not sure what to make of it," he replied. "On the one hand, it's perfectly normal—actually expected—that you would dream of your children since they're constantly in your thoughts. But on the other hand, it is peculiar that each spouse would have the same dream."

Nancy sensed that he was withholding something. "What else?"

"There's nothing else," he replied.

"Father, if we want to get to the bottom of this, you can't hold anything back. What aren't you telling us?" demanded Nancy.

He also rose from the kneeler and sat in a nearby pew. "I also had a dream last night about the group. But it wasn't like any of yours."

Overly intrigued, the parents joined him in the pew.

"Father, tell us—please," implored Sara.

He straightened a hymnal in the pew before beginning. "I saw Sam and Cindy leaping over clods of dirt in a darkened cavern. I was confused why they were jumping over the mounds. It didn't make any sense. Seconds later, I saw my brother priest, Father James, fall short of his leap. Skeletal arms exploded from the clods and grabbed his legs and waist. Fortunately, Cindy and Sam were able to free him by pressing torch flames against the bony arms. Dan made the final jump over the mounds."

"Was Jimmy in your dream?" asked Marie.

"No, sorry," answered the priest.

"I don't get it," declared Nancy. "Why are some of us sharing identical dreams while others are having completely different visions?"

"Hey wait a minute!" exclaimed Jeff. He leaned forward in the pew. "Maybe Tom and Marie had a different dream because Jimmy isn't with the others."

"If you're trying to make Marie and me feel better, it's not working," said Tom.

"Sorry," said Jeff. "But suppose that wherever our kids are, they're not together. For argument's sake, let's say that everyone stepped into the oak, but Dan and William entered at a different time than Cindy and Jimmy. Then they could be in different locations."

"Then why was Cindy seen with Dan in the dreams if they entered the tree at different times?" asked Sara.

"Oh yeah," mumbled Jeff. "But there's got to be a reasonable explanation."

"And if William and Dan entered the tree at the same time, then why wasn't William with Dan in your dream?" posed Tom. "You never mentioned William."

"I wish I knew," confessed Jeff. He rubbed his forehead.

"So William wasn't in your dream?" asked Sara.

"He was in our shared dream, but for only a moment," disclosed Nancy. "But he wasn't with the others."

"What'd you see?" questioned Sara.

"Jeff and I saw him yelling, but then we woke up," explained Nancy.

The six adults remained deep in thought, trying to unearth answers to perplexing questions.

"Father, do you think someone from above is telling us what's happening to our kids?" proposed Nancy.

"I suppose it's possible, but not too likely."

"What do you mean?" she snapped. "We just heard in today's Gospel how an angel appeared to Joseph in a dream."

"Like I said, it's possible, but not too likely." He pulled the white clerical collar tab from his shirt and unbuttoned the top button. "I wonder why none of you shared the dream I had last night."

No one offered a plausible explanation.

"I still think that someone is showing us what our family members are enduring," maintained Nancy.

"Then how do you explain my dreams?" asked Father Andreas. "I have no family member missing."

"Father, you just said that Father James is your brother priest," she reminded.

Father Andreas fell silent. He couldn't refute her comment.

Certain that the group would not arrive at any immediate answers, Father Andreas suggested that they resume their normal routine and asked them to return the next day for Mass and prayers. He escorted the families to the church doors.

"Thank you for your time, Father," expressed Nancy.

"It was my pleasure." He opened the door and followed the group onto the church steps. "I'll see you tomorrow morning." After the parents drove away—but before re-entering the church—he glanced at the oak. Consumed with a growing curiosity, he stepped nearer the tree. As he was inspecting it, his thoughts were cut short.

"Morning Father," shouted Officer Moore from the street curb. She approached the priest.

"Good morning. Can I help you?" asked the priest.

"Since the department is still at a dead end on the group's disappearance, I thought I'd search the parish grounds and inside the church once more—with your permission of course."

"Absolutely. Anything to bring this unusual case to a close." As the two approached the church steps, Father Andreas reconfirmed, "So there are no clues to their whereabouts?"

She shook her head. "It's a grueling case."

Father Andreas looked back at the oak's base, specifically to the raised ground. "I wish we also could solve the mystery of those destructive moles. It seems that each time the maintenance crew traps one rodent, another mound appears. It's an endless battle." He tilted his head. "It reminds me of a dream I had last night."

The officer stood on the top step and displayed a troubled look. "You had a dream about moles?"

"Not exactly." The priest grabbed the doorknob. "You probably wouldn't believe me or understand its possible significance, but I dreamed that Father James and three other members of the missing party were jumping over mounds like those by the tree."

Officer Moore looked at a mound several feet away. "I understand—probably more than you think. If their jump was unsuccessful, they were grabbed by skeletal arms."

The priest let go of the doorknob. "What'd you say?" he blurted.

"It's a dream I had last night—a dream that I can't shake, no matter how hard I try," explained the policewoman. "In fact, that's the reason why I'm here now."

"I don't understand."

"In addition to the mounds, I also had a dream about the alleged abduction."

Father Andreas grasped the officer's arm and insisted they step inside. Once seated in the last pew, the priest and the policewoman exchanged details about their dreams.

Officer Moore looked at the boarded window openings. "Isn't it odd that we had the same dream?"

"Yes and no."

"Come on, Father, don't talk in circles. It's either yes or no."

"Just a few minutes ago, I learned that Nancy, Jeff, and Sara all had the same dream last night—a dream that was identical in every detail. Marie and Tom also had a shared dream about their son. And now I find out that you and I had the same dream about the mounds." He replaced his white clerical collar tab. "But I didn't dream about the group's abduction like you did. Would you mind sharing?"

The policewoman refused to be dragged into a discussion about the paranormal. She bolted into the aisle and headed to the church doors.

"Officer—please!" shouted the priest.

She stomped back to the pew. "Look, I've heard and read about weird things happening during full moons, but this story keeps getting more bizarre. It's simply beyond the realm of possibility!"

"What was bizarre about your dream?"

"The limbs of the oak—outside this very church—came to life," she recounted. "I saw them smash through the stained glass windows and grab Father James!" She took a moment to collect herself before continuing, "It was eerie. It was like I was watching the events unfold from above the turmoil."

"Go on," pleaded Father Andreas.

"I saw Father James grab a Communion rail post which snapped from the railing. Blood flowed from a gash on his side. Then I saw him thrown into the oak."

"That would certainly account for the vertical post found in a pool of blood and Father James's mysterious disappearance," reminded the priest.

"I also saw the Clay brothers taken hostage by the limbs. It was pretty violent. Dan was thrown about and bashed his head against a pew. I guess that would explain his house key on the church floor and the trace of blood on it. Within seconds, both brothers were tossed into the oak."

"Do you remember anything else?" asked the priest.

"Father, this is insane!"

"What's insane?"

"This whole story!" she exclaimed. "For years, I've been instructed and trained on using my mental faculties and rock-solid evidence to solve crimes. And now you're asking me to explain the mystery of the group's disappearance by an enchanted tree. Do you know how ridiculous that sounds?"

"I know. I'll admit it sounds absurd. In fact, a part of me still struggles to accept that the stories are—" He switched his tone. "For the sake of the families, do you remember anything else about your dream?"

She unwillingly divulged more details. "I remember Cindy and Jimmy dashing to the church. It all happened so fast. Within seconds, a limb fell from the sky and threw Jimmy into the oak."

"And Cindy?" posed the priest.

"The limbs went really wild. They were whipping in all directions, but there was no wind. I remember Cindy racing across the church lawn—to escape the violent branches, I imagine—when a limb crashed into the church building, grabbed her, and—"

Officer Moore ran out the door.

The priest tried to keep pace. "What's wrong?" he shouted. Moments later, he was standing beside the policewoman on the church grounds. He watched her inspect a corner of the church building.

A brick was jutting out from the wall with mortar resting on the ground.

"Have you ever noticed this before?" asked the officer.

"No, never."

"This can't be. It just can't be. It's impossible," she maintained. She removed a twig that was stuck behind the loose brick. On a closer examination, she noticed that the twig was ripped—not snipped—and that an autumn-colored oak leaf clung to it. She placed the potential evidence in her pocket and headed to the street.

"Officer—wait!" The priest trailed her. "You must tell the families about your dream and what you discovered."

The two reached the curb and stood alongside the patrol car.

"Sorry Father, but there's got to be a logical explanation for my dream and this twig."

"Look, I'll admit that I have some doubts too," confessed the priest. "But as things stand right now, we have five adults who are emotionally spent with the loss of their children. It's your responsibility to tell them what you found. They have the right to know."

"Tell them what? I don't have any concrete evidence where their kids are. All I have are a dream and a twig."

The priest placed his hands on the hood of the patrol car. "Let the families judge the evidence. You owe it to them." He sensed that he was slowly winning her over. "They'll be here tomorrow morning for Mass. We'll see you then." He stepped onto the sidewalk and entered the church.

Father Andreas spent the remainder of the day in prayer, while Officer Moore sat alone in her office replaying the dream in her head.

•

With the onset of evening, the Clays, the Parkers, and Sara retired earlier than normal. Each looked forward to dreaming up vital clues.

Nancy rose early the next morning, faced her husband in bed, and asked if he dreamed about the boys.

"No. Come to think of it, I can't remember what I dreamed." He sat up in bed. "Did you?"

"I wish I had, but no." She grabbed a pen from the nightstand, jumped from the bed, and placed another check mark on the wall calendar. "Only nine more days until the boys return."

Though each parent strongly suspected that their sons had entered the tree, Jeff had a haunting feeling that something or someone could prevent them from returning through the oak. His wife's earlier comment that the parallel world was no longer peaceful greatly disturbed him. But the last thing he wanted to do was dash his wife's hopes. "Yeah, just nine more days," he replied.

Once in the church, the Clays, the Parkers, and Sara knelt in the fifth pew. Like clockwork, they headed to the marble statue immediately after Mass. Within minutes, Father Andreas was on his knees beside them.

"Morning," he whispered.

"Good morning, Father," they greeted.

"Did anyone have unusual dreams last night?"

One by one, the five shook their heads.

"Well, let's remember that time is still on our side." He raised his eyes heavenward and began, "In the name of the Father, and of the Son, and of the Holy Spirit."

"Amen," responded the parents.

During the final decade of the rosary, footsteps were heard from behind. Father Andreas glanced over his shoulder and spotted Officer Moore sitting in a nearby pew. At the conclusion of their prayers, the priest told the parents that the policewoman had something she wanted to share with them.

"Did you find something, officer?" shouted Sara from the kneeler.

"Not exactly," she replied.

Father Andreas led the parents to the pew where the officer was sitting. "Let's have a seat," he said.

"Have there been any developments in the case, officer?" asked Marie.

"Please, let's give the policewoman a few moments to speak," ordered Father Andreas.

All eyes focused on the officer.

"Actually, I'm not sure how to begin," she admitted.

Witnessing her hesitation in opening the conversation, Father Andreas decided to help her along. "Yesterday, Officer Moore paid me a visit. During our discussion, it was brought to light that she and I shared the same dream about the group jumping over the mounds in a cavern."

"But I don't understand," said Nancy. "Why would Officer Moore—"

"Nancy, let me finish," insisted the priest. "I also discovered that parts of her dream were different from mine. She dreamed of the group's abduction."

Complete silence befell the group.

During the next several minutes, the officer disclosed every detail of her dream. At the priest's prodding, she also informed the parents of her discovery behind the loose brick on the church building.

Nancy looked at Jeff. "So our boys didn't intentionally enter the tree."

"And the children weren't kidnapped by burglars," added a thankful Sara. "They vanished through the oak."

"Maybe," said the policewoman.

"What do you mean maybe?" shouted Sara.

"Look, I came here this morning to tell you about my dream because Father Andreas thought it would be helpful to you," explained an annoyed officer. "Personally, I don't believe in solving crimes through dreams or any other paranormal means. The Lawton Police Department has never solved a case with dreams—and it never will."

"Father, as I started to ask earlier, why would Officer Moore have a dream about the group if we suspect the visions are showing us what our families are suffering?" asked Nancy.

"I'm not sure. But maybe the group's original assumption of only family members having dreams was flawed."

"Or maybe the officer is destined to play a key role in the rescue of our kids," proposed Jeff.

"Not very likely," snapped the officer. She stood and stepped into the aisle.

Father Andreas joined her in the aisle and thanked her for sharing her dream with the families.

Before taking her leave, Officer Moore leaned into the pew. "The police department will continue using all available resources in our search for your missing children—not through dreams—but in the traditional way with evidence and solid proof."

"But isn't the oak twig evidence?" challenged Nancy.

The officer disregarded her question. "Good day." She stormed out of the church.

The door slammed.

For the first time in weeks, the parents experienced a glimmer of hope.

"Well then, shall we meet again tomorrow morning?" asked Father Andreas.

"Absolutely," replied Sara, "one day closer to their return."

CHAPTER TWELVE
The Resurrection

THE TRAVELERS STOOD ONLY FEET OUTSIDE CINDY'S CAVE. No one was excited about entering the hollow world of the ponds. But they knew they had no choice if they wanted to reach the upper level.

Father James was nearly certain that Cindy would fall victim to the allurements again. "Cindy," he warned, "since this is the cave where you experienced—how shall I say it—an unhealthy attraction to yourself, I think you should cover your eyes."

"Thanks Father, but I'll be fine."

"Actually, that's not a bad idea," seconded Sam. He pulled a handkerchief from his pocket. "Cover your eyes with this. We'll lead you to the waterfall."

"But Sam, I'm not the least bit tempted. Besides, I want to see the giant frilled lizard that you and Dan killed."

"Trust me, Cindy, the handkerchief is for your own safety—and ours," stressed Sam.

After her eyes were covered, Sam and Dan grasped her arms and led her closer to the cave's entrance.

"Wait!" shouted Father James.

The men stopped.

The blindfolded Cindy also remained at a standstill between Dan and Sam.

"Even though only Cindy was conquered by the attractions in this cave not too long ago," reminded Father James, "there's still the real possibility that any of us could fall victim to its enticements."

"What are you saying, Father?" asked Dan.

"I'm saying that just because you and Sam resisted the cave's powers during your previous visit doesn't necessarily make you immune this time. Remember what I said before? Some people fluctuate between a predominant vice and another less overpowering one."

"But Father, how do you expect us to reach the waterfall with our eyes covered?" posed Dan.

"I'm not suggesting we cover our eyes. I'm just saying that we should avoid glimpsing the ponds if at all possible."

"I guess that makes sense," said Sam. "It's better to be safe than sorry. Dan and I will focus on the waterfall and not the ponds."

"But what about the waterfall?" asked Dan.

"What about it?" said Sam.

"It might have hypnotic qualities like the water in the ponds."

"I never thought about that," said Sam. "But when we were here before and searched near the waterfall, I don't remember being entranced by its water. Do you?"

"Well no, but—"

"I'm sure it's safe!" yelled Cindy. She lifted a corner of the blindfold from her face. "Unless of course, you want me climbing the wall wearing this stupid handkerchief."

"Cindy, cover your eyes!" shouted Sam.

"But even if the waterfall is mesmerizing, we don't have a choice if we want to reach the upper level," reminded Dan.

"All right then, let's move," ordered the priest.

"Father, help Dan lead Cindy to the waterfall," suggested Sam.

"Why?"

"I've been here before," said Sam. "I know how hostile the inhabitants can be. I'd rather take the lead."

"Sam, I appreciate your concern, but I'm sure I can guide the group to the waterfall," remarked the priest.

Throughout their journeys in the parallel world and in the present realm, Dan had grown to anticipate and appreciate Sam's logic and paternal protection. If a pond gazer attacked the group, he suspected that Sam wanted to have his hands free to protect his friends. "Father, let Sam lead the way," insisted Dan.

"Would you guys make up your minds," grumbled Cindy. "This handkerchief reeks."

The priest unwillingly agreed.

Sam—bearing a torch, a weapon, and the backpack—stepped to the front of the line. Although cumbersome at best, Father James and Dan also carried a torch and a lance in one hand, while grasping Cindy's arms with the other. The blindfolded Cindy held a lance and torch. For safety concerns, however, her torch was extinguished. Though the group never had any luck reigniting a dead flame, they hoped their luck would change on the upper level.

The travelers stepped into the cave and climbed the slope near its entrance.

"Wow!" exclaimed the priest from atop the incline. "This place is beautiful!"

"Don't get too attached to it, Father," warned Sam. "It can be painful—even deadly."

"Let me see!" shouted Cindy. She broke free from the priest's grip and grabbed her facial covering.

Sam knocked her hand from her face. "Cindy, don't make this any harder for us than it already is."

After Father James grasped her arm again, Dan tried to ease her curiosity. "Actually Cindy, it's pretty boring."

A creak was heard in the distance. A stalactite plunged to the cave floor. The travelers—minus Cindy—witnessed the seldom-seen event.

"Whoa!" exclaimed Dan. "Did you see that? Awesome!"

"Yeah, it sounds pretty boring," replied Cindy in a sarcastic voice. She slapped Dan across the chest.

"What was that for?" he snapped.

"Pretty boring, huh?"

"All right, all right; I guess I had it coming," said Dan. "The falling rock caught me by surprise."

"Sam, did the teenagers bicker like this in the parallel world?" asked Father James.

"These two are tolerable. Wait until we find Jimmy."

THE RESURRECTION

Sam, Dan, and Father James set their sights on the imposing waterfall in the distance.

"How high is the rock wall behind the waterfall?" asked the priest.

"About forty to fifty feet," estimated Sam.

"I'm almost embarrassed to ask only now, but is it climbable? I mean, is it steep or is the wall at an angle?"

"Sorry Father, we never inspected it that closely before," replied Sam. "But I'm sure we'll manage." He directed his attention to the base of the incline. "Let's go."

With added caution, Father James and Dan led Cindy down the bumpy slope. Sam tripped and rolled to its base.

At the bottom of the hill, Dan put a death grip on Cindy's arm while Father James helped Sam to his feet.

"I'm okay, Father," remarked a mortified Sam.

The men stared at a nearby pond. Its beauty was breathtaking.

Dozens of individuals surrounded the pond. The men's burning torches provided sufficient light for them to observe the physical features of the pond gazers. As expected, their actual appearances were nothing like those reflected on the water. Their true features were so appalling that even Dan's and Sam's previous trip to the cave of pride failed to prepare them for what they were looking at now—even with one eye shut and their heads cocked.

Father James retched at the sight of their decomposing legs and the leaky pustules on their faces and necks. "My God, these poor souls," he whispered.

"What's that foul odor?" exclaimed Cindy.

"Nothing!" shouted Sam. "Keep your eyes covered!"

"I want to see!" she demanded.

"Cindy, just hang on a little longer," urged Dan.

With an uncontrollable desire to view her surroundings, Cindy wrestled to free herself from Dan and the priest.

"Cindy!" shouted Dan. "Relax!"

The escalating commotion got Sam's attention. He backtracked to the group to subdue Cindy's unruly behavior. During his dash, he unintentionally kicked a rock into a pond.

Cindy had been successful. The handkerchief—along with her lance and unlit torch—fell to the ground.

"Let me go!" she shouted. She kicked, bit, and squirmed to escape the men's hold. Her determination and resourcefulness paid off. Within seconds of punching Dan in the ribs, she dropped to her knees and scrambled to the closest pond.

To her disappointment, her reflection was distorted. The ripples—created by Sam knocking a rock into the water moments earlier—had reached the outer limits of the pool.

The wavelike motion on the water's surface caused savage brawls among the pond gazers.

"Heaven help us," whispered Father James while watching a woman dislocate the arm of her neighbor.

As Dan and Sam crashed to their knees to free Cindy from a skirmish, the priest remained standing in near shock at what was unfolding before him. Never before had he witnessed such violence and disregard for human dignity and decency.

A female inhabitant spotted the priestly attire and crawled to Father James's feet.

The priest jumped back.

She wrapped her decaying arms around his injured side. "Father, forgive me for I have sinned. Deliver me from this hellhole."

The priest trembled. He broke free from her grip and madly shook his arm. A pond skater dropped from his sleeve.

"Please Father!" she bewailed with folded hands. "I need your absolution!" Her boisterous plea for spiritual release captured the attention of her neighboring pond mates who were still engaged in mortal combat.

Three more inhabitants crawled on their hands and knees to the priest's feet, clutched his legs, and begged forgiveness.

"Sam—Dan!" he yelled.

Although the men were preoccupied pulling Cindy's hands from the throat of a young man, each offered a glimpse at the priest and his unusual predicament.

"Dan!" yelled Sam. "Can you handle Cindy?"

"No! But I'll try."

Sam jumped to his feet and raced to Father James.

The pond's surface was gradually returning to normal. Sam dragged a woman from the priest's feet to the pool's edge. On seeing her deceptively attractive reflection, she remained at the water's side. Her frantic attempt to seek forgiveness from the priest was now ancient history.

Once freed of the remaining begging inhabitants, Father James and Sam rushed to Dan's aid.

With the ripples erased from the pond's surface, Dan was now fighting to pull Cindy from her hypnotic stare at her reflection.

"Dan, we have to do it again," said Sam.

"I know."

"Do what?" questioned Father James.

Sam was convinced that the priest would condemn their actions. "Father, turn your head."

"What are you going to do?" demanded the priest.

Sam ignored his question, squatted beside Dan, and shouted, "One, two, three!"

Dan dragged Cindy from the pond.

During her heated rage, Sam delivered a perfect jab.

She was out cold.

Father James dropped to her side. "What were you thinking? There had to be another way!"

"Sorry Father, but we've been down this road before," defended Sam. "There was no other way."

"Besides, now it'll be safer moving her to the waterfall," said Dan.

"What do you mean safer?" asked Father James.

"With her unconscious, she won't be vulnerable to the allurements of the ponds," explained Dan. "Granted, we'll have to carry her, but in the long run, we'll save time—something we don't have a lot of."

Though the priest didn't approve of their actions, he couldn't argue with Dan's logic.

Sam was eager to change the unpleasant subject. "Father James, what was the deal with the pond gazers at your feet?"

The priest knew that the men would be disbelieving—not to mention uneasy—with his answer. He remained silent while holding Cindy's hand.

"Yeah Father, what did they want?" pressed Dan.

Again, he failed to respond. He had growing suspicions that his initial hunch of their present location was correct.

"Father James, what did the dwellers want with you?" shouted Sam.

"I suppose they thought that if I forgave them of their sins, then they'd be transported from this place."

Sam found it difficult accepting the priest's response. "So you still think we're in—"

"Hell!" Father James shouted. "Yes, I believe we're in hell."

"But if these people want to escape this place, then why do they stay at the ponds?" asked Dan.

Father James shook his head. "I don't know. Maybe when the waters calmed, their desire to look upon themselves overpowered their desire to flee this cave." He handed the discarded handkerchief to Sam. "But I couldn't forgive them of their sins. They've already been judged by the Almighty."

"Huh, imagine that, a person in hell trying to go to confession," said Dan.

"For Cindy's safety, we need to get out of this cave before she wakes up," ordered the priest.

"Yeah. And the sooner the better," stressed Sam.

Father James and Sam lifted Cindy and supported her between their shoulders. The men abandoned their torches, wagering they'd discover some on the upper level. They grabbed their lances—and Dan the backpack—and continued their hike to the waterfall.

They were amazed that Cindy never stirred, even at their fast pace.

A warm breeze was felt. The men halted.

"Sam, that wind brings back some bad memories," whispered Dan.

"I know. But it can't be."

The men stared at the waterfall. For a split second, they glimpsed what appeared to be a jaw behind the cascading water.

"Our eyes must be playing tricks on us," declared Sam. "It can't be."

Dan looked to the left and dropped the backpack in disbelief.

THE RESURRECTION

"Shh," whispered Sam.

"Bad news, Sam," warned Dan.

"What now?"

"To the left—you know—where the stalactite fell on the lizard earlier—"

"Yeah."

"There's nothing there."

"What? That's impossible." Sam turned and saw only stalactite fragments on the barren ground. "Maybe the cave dwellers moved the dead lizard somewhere else."

"Sam, I doubt seriously that they moved it," said Dan.

"Father, you mentioned earlier the possibility of the inhabitants coming back to life," reminded Sam. "Do you also think the creatures can rise from the dead?"

"In this world, I dare say that anything's possible."

Though still uncertain of the creature's identity—since it was masked behind the falling water—Sam suggested that they not take any chances. "Let's sit on the ground and blend in with the other inhabitants around the pond."

The enormous beast lunged from beside the cascade. It was careful to avoid contact with the water.

"Whoa!" shouted the priest.

"Quiet," ordered Sam.

The frilled lizard bared its teeth and hissed.

Maybe that's a different lizard, thought Dan.

As Sam and Dan expected, the movements of the colossal creature produced ripples in the ponds which ushered in brutal clashes. Within seconds, thousands of inhabitants were at one another's throats.

Sam looked down at Cindy and was grateful that she was still unconscious.

The beast stepped away from the waterfall and stomped from pool to pool in search of the four trespassers.

Now's the perfect time to escape behind the waterfall, thought Sam.

But to reach the rock wall undetected, the men needed a diversion that would lure the creature further away from the waterfall.

"Dan, do you have any ideas for a distraction so we can reach the waterfall unnoticed?" whispered Sam.

"Your revolver."

"I don't think so," replied Sam.

"Why not?"

"Because it would give away our location." He looked down at Cindy. "And with her out cold, she'd be an easy meal for the lizard. Besides, I doubt we'd be as lucky a second time with a stalactite."

Even amid the violent clashes of the inhabitants, the men never removed their sights from the frilled lizard that was now nearing the cave's center.

Cindy jerked briefly, drawing the attention of Sam and Dan.

With the two men focused on their teenage friend, Father James sprang to his feet and ran to the rear of the cave, yelling madly to capture the beast's attention.

Sam jumped to his feet. "Father—freeze!"

The frilled lizard hissed even louder, flared its folds of skin around its head, and charged the priest.

It was too late for Sam to reach Father James and knock him to the ground. Sam was desperate. He spotted a darkened area at the back of the cave. "Hide in the dark!" he yelled. "Hide in the dark!"

The creature halted its dash on Father James and set its deadly gaze on Sam.

"Great," mumbled Sam who quickly dropped to all fours. "Dan, can you get Cindy to the waterfall?" he asked.

"I think so. What are you going to do?"

Sam glanced to the darkness where the priest had fled. "Someone's got to help him."

"Sam, I can run faster and—"

"Forget it," snapped Sam. "I need you to get Cindy to the waterfall as fast as you can. Once you're behind it, do whatever it takes to climb the wall—even if Father James and I aren't there. Let's hope the pouring water from the fall won't have an effect on her."

The men stared at the back of the cave. Neither spotted Father James in the shadows.

The creature remained at a standstill, switching its deadly stare between the rear darkness and the area where the three travelers were camouflaged among the pond gazers.

THE RESURRECTION

"If it weren't for the commotion of the inhabitants around us, I'm afraid we'd all be dead by now," whispered Sam.

"But how are you going to rescue Father James and avoid the lizard?" asked Dan.

"I'm thinking." He looked at Cindy. "That's it!" screamed Sam.

"That's what?"

"As soon as I run, get yourselves and the backpack to the waterfall," ordered Sam. "Do you understand?"

"But Sam."

"Just do it. Trust me." With his lance in hand, Sam sprinted between the feuding inhabitants. His constant screaming—as he had hoped—was heard easily over the noisy cave combatants.

The frilled lizard resumed its charge, but this time toward Sam.

Dan strapped the backpack to his back, grabbed the weapons, and placed his arm around Cindy. With great effort, he stepped toward the majestic waterfall.

In the shadows, Father James sought refuge behind a boulder.

Sam, however, took the opposite approach and made himself as conspicuous as possible by running in a zigzag motion among the cave dwellers. The quarreling inhabitants and his erratic movements confused the beast. It failed to process the growing number of disturbances. Sam set a course for one of the larger ponds.

In its rush toward Sam, the creature thoughtlessly flattened sixteen cave dwellers.

"Come on!" screamed Sam to the lizard.

To his disappointment, the beast sidestepped the large pond and reduced the distance between itself and its prey. With no options available, Sam raced to the relative safety at the back of the cave. "Father," he whispered in the darkness.

There was no response.

Sam gathered his courage and stepped into the light.

The towering monster stood only a short distance away.

The hunt resumed.

Sam spotted another large pond. With skillful maneuvering, he placed the water between himself and the stalking creature. The frilled lizard and the human stared each other down. Sam took several backward steps, but without losing eye contact with the flesh-eater. Each step brought him closer to the shadows.

The beast made another charge at its target.

As Sam stepped into the darkness, the frilled lizard stepped into the water. Six self-worshipers were crushed.

Sam's prayer was answered when the reptile escaped the pool. Its skin peeled from its legs.

Sam emerged from the shadows again. His focus was drawn to the creature's exposed muscular structure.

With each painful step, the frilled lizard neared death's door.

But Sam refused to leave the area until he was convinced the creature was dead. He would not permit his friends to climb the rock wall with a bloodthirsty reptile on the loose. He took a wide view of the cave and saw a stalagmite projecting upward from the rock floor. *I wonder,* he thought. With utmost caution, he positioned himself several feet behind the cone-shaped rock.

The creature continued its agonizing but single-minded approach to its victim. It made a final charge.

Sam took careful aim, hurled his weapon, and pierced the lizard's side.

The creature's flayed legs gave way. It fell forward and impaled its neck on the four-foot-high stalagmite. The beast closed its eyes.

Sam bent over and rested his hands on his knees to catch his breath. *Father,* he thought. He returned to the darkness, yelling for the priest. He searched and eventually spotted something on the ground alongside a boulder at the edge of the shadows. He neared the rock. In the dim light, he discovered that Father James was unconscious with a gash to his forehead. "Father!" He shook his friend.

●

As Sam was trying to revive Father James, Dan was struggling to revive Cindy. He had been successful in dragging her and the equipment to the waterfall's base.

She opened her eyes. "What happened? Why are we—?"

"Cindy, does this water make you feel—you know—different?" he asked.

She stared at the waterfall. "No. Why?"

As Dan had hoped, the rushing water was incapable of sustaining her reflection. Certain that she was safe, he explained their situation and how they arrived at the fall.

"Are Father James and Sam all right?" she asked.

"I'm not sure. But we need to climb the wall." He looked up. "At least the rock face isn't straight up and down. That should make our climb a little easier." He helped her to her feet.

She extended her arms and searched for overhead crevices to place her hands for the climb. "But what about Sam and Father James?" she asked.

"I'm sure they'll be here soon," he predicted.

The climb went more smoothly than either of the teenagers had expected.

Almost halfway up the fifty-foot-high wall, the climbers came across an opening in the rock face. They sat inside the large hole and waited for their friends.

Dan inspected their new surroundings. Behind him—within the opening—was a flat area of rock and a narrow tunnel at its far side. "Huh, I wonder if that tunnel leads to the second level."

Cindy looked to the darkened tunnel. "But what if it doesn't?"

"Well it's got to lead somewhere. Besides, it's definitely above the first level. Let's wait and see what Sam thinks." He dropped the backpack to the rock ledge. "So how are you feeling?'

"I'll be fine."

"Since we're not going anywhere until Sam and Father James arrive, maybe you should take a breather," he suggested.

"I guess it wouldn't hurt." She rested her head on the backpack. "Just don't let me fall asleep."

"I'll let you know the moment I see or hear Sam and Father James."

•

In the shadows at the back of the cave, the priest stirred.

"Father!" yelled Sam.

The priest touched his bleeding forehead. "I guess I tripped."

"Yeah, it would seem." He helped the priest to a seated position and leaned him against the boulder. "Why on earth did you run off? You could have placed the group in a far worse situation."

He touched his head wound again. "You said you needed a distraction."

"I did, but not a human distraction." He assisted the priest to his feet. "Look Father, I know you were trying to save the others with your heroic act, but this group works together and no one takes unnecessary chances. Heroism is fine on earth, but I wouldn't recommend it in hell—if that's where we are. You could end up here forever."

Uncomfortable with the criticism, Father James was eager to change the subject. "Where's the frilled lizard?"

"It's dead—see." Sam pointed to the lifeless creature a short distance away. He supported the priest during their walk to the carcass. "But Father, if your theory is correct about the inhabitants—and possibly the creatures in this world—coming back to life, then we don't know how long the lizard will stay dead." He pulled the lance from the lizard's side. "If it will rise, all the more reason to get to the waterfall as soon as possible or our efforts in killing it were meaningless. We bought ourselves some time, so let's take advantage of it. I'd rather not witness its resurrection firsthand."

"You're right. Let's go."

During their hike, Sam continually glanced behind at the dead lizard. He needed the reassurance that it wasn't rising from the dead.

"So how did you kill it?"

Sam remained silent. He was busy scanning the cave that was now peaceful.

Minutes earlier, with the collapse of the beast and its cave-rocking effects, fights had erupted. But the waters were now tranquil. The conflicts had ended.

"Sam, how did you kill it?" the priest asked again.

"Before I left Dan and Cindy in search of you, I saw the blemish below Cindy's right eye. It was then when I remembered Dan saying that he saw a stream of water burst from a pond and spray her face that caused the blemish. I got to thinking. If a squirt of water caused the mark on her face, then what would happen if the lizard stepped into the water?"

"So you tricked the lizard into a pond?"

Sam nodded.

"Pretty clever," praised the priest.

"But the idea never would have come to me if it hadn't been for Cindy. She's always—"

"What's wrong?" asked the priest. He scanned the area.

Sam glanced from pond to pond. "They're not here. I hope they made it to the waterfall." He pulled on the priest's arm. "Come on; hurry."

The men were soon short-winded, but standing at the cascade's base.

"Dan—Cindy!" yelled Sam.

Dan leaned through the opening. "Up here!"

To Sam's and the priest's delight, Cindy's head also emerged overhead.

"The climb's not that bad, just a little slippery," yelled Dan. "Be careful."

"We intend to," replied Sam. He searched for a fissure in the wall. "Father, let's take our time since it's awfully wet. Feel around for large cracks in the rock to put your hands. Then—"

"Sam, I've been rock climbing for years."

"Really?" asked a disbelieving Sam.

"Yeah, during my trips to the mountains."

"Then what are we waiting for? Let's go."

The men located more than enough cracks along their upward journey. Cindy and Dan pulled the men to the safety of the ledge.

"Cindy, how are you feeling?" demanded Sam.

"A little disoriented, but I'll be fine," she replied.

Even in the poor light, Dan saw blood dripping down the priest's forehead. "Father, what happened to you?"

He touched his injury again. "I tripped. But it's not serious."

Since the torches were abandoned below, Sam grabbed his flashlight from the backpack that Dan had replaced to his back after Cindy's rest. He pointed the beam behind the group. "A tunnel—I wonder where it leads."

"I'm sure it ends up somewhere on the second level," declared Dan.

Sam stepped several feet inside the rock opening and examined the tunnel. "What the heck is that?"

The light beam revealed countless dirt tubes—each nearly a foot in diameter—that extended the width of the tunnel. While most of the cylinders were horizontal, some ran diagonally.

As Sam inspected the network of crisscross tubes, he immediately called to mind the child's game of cat's cradle. To Father James, the cylinders reminded him of lattice. The group estimated that there were thousands of tubes which seemed to go on forever.

"What do you think they are?" asked Dan who stepped within inches of the tunnel's entrance for a closer look.

"I'm sure I don't know," admitted Sam.

Dan spun and faced the waterfall. He sensed movement from behind. As he turned, the backpack shattered a dirt tube. Brown dust spewed from the ruptured tube.

"Be careful, Dan," reprimanded Sam.

"I thought I heard something behind us."

Sam looked toward the waterfall. "There's nothing there. Come on, we need to be careful. We can't afford to get jittery."

The travelers turned and focused their attentions on the dust cloud. Brown particles had settled to the ground and on adjacent tubes.

With the light's beam directed at the smashed cylinder, Sam speculated that it was composed of hardened mud. He rubbed particles of the tube between his fingers. "It's just dust."

Everyone's anxieties were eased.

"But Sam," cautioned Cindy, "for all we know, that dust could—"

A gust of air swirled from behind.

The group spun again and saw a frilled lizard's head at eye level with the rock opening.

As it arched its head, Sam gasped. A pointed rock stuck through its neck.

Dan cringed when he spotted the remnant of a second rock wedged in its skull—the cause of its first death. *That can't be the same frilled lizard,* he thought.

Fortunately, the group was nearly twenty-five feet above the cave floor and deep within the opening.

THE RESURRECTION

The beast whipped its elongated tongue in their direction.

The travelers jumped backwards. They were trapped between the dirt tubes and the creature's tongue which fell a few feet short of the pinned group.

"We're fine for now," assured Sam. "We're out of its reach." He looked over his shoulder. "But if we want to get out of here alive, the tunnel behind is the answer."

"But Sam, what if that brown stuff in the tunnel isn't just dust?" warned Cindy.

"Cindy, he's right," said Dan. "The tunnel is our only way out. Trust me, the lizard's not going away. We have to get out of here now. Besides, you're overreacting. Like Sam said, it's just dust."

"But what if—"

"Cindy, if it'll make you feel better, we'll step over and under the tubes so we don't break any more," compromised Sam.

The tongue recoiled from the ledge.

"Maybe we don't have to enter the tunnel after all," she remarked. "The tongue's already—"

Without warning, a tail rammed inside the opening, wrapped around Dan's leg, and dragged him forward.

Before Cindy or Father James could react to the lizard's latest invasion, Sam dropped the flashlight and pierced the tail with his lance. After several stabs, it released its hold.

Sam yanked Dan and the flashlight from the ground. "Let's go!" he yelled.

With Dan still in Sam's grip, the two men ran at top speed, carelessly smashing every tube in their path and clearing the way for Cindy and Father James.

After racing nearly a hundred feet up the tunnel, Sam slowed his sprint to a fast walk and aimed the light's beam ahead. Dozens of tubes still obstructed their path. With the destruction of countless cylinders behind, the tunnel was shrouded in a thick haze.

Sam turned and informed his friends that they were well out of the tail's reach.

"Sam look!" shouted Dan. He pointed up the tunnel.

"Light!" exclaimed Sam. "Hopefully it's a torch."

"Let's go!" demanded Cindy.

Dan stepped through another dirt tube.

"Dan," she rebuked, "Sam said we're out of the creature's reach. We don't need to destroy any more tubes."

"But we've already demolished hundreds," said Dan. "What's the difference?"

"Cindy relax, it's just dust," reiterated Sam.

"Fine," she snapped. "But I'm telling you, I've got a bad feeling about this so-called dust."

"We'll be fine," promised Sam. "Trust me."

A stone's throw up the tunnel, the group stepped into an open cavern.

"So this must be the second level," presumed Dan. He dusted himself off.

"I hope so," said Sam. "I also hope it has fewer creatures than the first level."

Though there wasn't a great deal of light, there was enough for Cindy to spot purple blotches on the faces, hands, and arms of her co-travelers. She brought it to her friends' attention.

"There probably was an allergen in the dust particles," proposed Sam.

Cindy inspected her hands closely. "I hope you're right. I hope that's all it is."

"We'll be fine," assured Sam.

Trusting he was right, she changed the conversation. "Sam, I thought you and Dan killed that lizard."

"We did," said Sam.

"So that was what—a distant relative?" she remarked in a derisive tone.

"Not exactly," said Dan.

"Then what?" she demanded.

"Cindy, if Father James's theory is correct that this is hell, then there's no way of killing these creatures—at least not forever," explained Sam.

She looked at the priest. "Father, you can't be serious that these beasts come back to life again and again."

"Yes, I am. And I think we have our proof."

"That's absurd!" she maintained.

THE RESURRECTION

"Hey wait a minute!" blurted Dan.

"Now what?" asked Sam.

"Sam, do you remember stabbing the walking stick outside your cave's entrance when it was trying to take a bite out of me?"

"Sure. How could I forget?"

"Then you probably also remember that when we passed your cave a little while back there wasn't a dead creature outside the entrance."

All eyes came to rest upon the priest who remained curiously silent.

Sam removed his stare from Father James and surveyed their new surroundings. "I think this cavern is different from the one below."

"What makes you say that?" asked Cindy.

"On the first level, we could see a greater distance ahead since the tunnel's curve was barely noticeable to the naked eye. But here, we can't see nearly as far. The bend on this level is more pronounced."

"Sam, in plain English," she implored.

"If this were the first level, we'd see not only the light ahead, but also the torch."

She scratched her hand. "So should we head to the left—you know—to the light?"

"Absolutely, we need the torch."

Just watching Cindy scratch her hand caused Father James and Dan to do likewise.

"Sam, why am I so itchy all of a sudden?" asked Cindy.

Sam held the flashlight next to her hand. Ticks surfaced from the purple blotches that she had scratched open. He pulled her hand nearer his face and guessed that the ticks had voracious appetites since they had a bloodsucking head at each end of their bodies.

Cindy glared at Sam and Dan. "Just dust!" She scraped her fingernails against her cheek.

Within seconds, everyone was scratching exposed skin and releasing hundreds of hungry ticks. Suddenly, the itching frenzy ended. There was a commotion to the right—just beyond the cavern's bend.

"I wonder what—," began Dan.

"Shh," whispered Sam.

Growling echoed up the tunnel. A swarm of bats flew in their direction.

"Something or someone flushed them this way," exclaimed Sam. "Run!"

They had dashed only several yards when the flying mammals swooped from the cavern heights and landed on them.

The explorers were covered—from head to toe—with bats feasting on the newly-hatched ticks. The sensation of bats' tongues on their faces, hands, and arms was excruciating.

Amazingly, the travelers remained silent throughout their hair-raising ordeal for fear of alerting their presence to the being or creature beyond the tunnel's curve. They fell to the ground and rolled in a fruitless attempt to free themselves from the bats.

Once the flock of bats had consumed every parasitic morsel, they soared to the overhead shadows.

Sam sat up. "I've never seen bats act so aggressively before."

"Shh," warned Dan. "Whatever or whoever sent the bats in this direction is heading this way. We have to get out of here now." He squatted alongside Cindy. The moment she rolled onto her back, he pressed his hand over her mouth. He expected a scream. He lowered his face to hers. "We have to be quiet. Something or someone is coming this way. Let's move."

She simply nodded. As she staggered to her feet, she sarcastically mumbled, "Just dust."

The rescuers quickly but quietly darted up the cavern with the flashlight switched off.

CHAPTER THIRTEEN
Bodily Invasion

THE TRAVELERS RACED UP THE TUNNEL TO PUT AS MUCH DIStance as possible between themselves and their unseen pursuer beyond the bend of the cavern wall.

"Sam, for the record, I never believed that was just dust," whispered Cindy.

"So I was wrong about that. But I'm not wrong about something behind us."

She persisted. "And those bats were totally disgusting. If I'm ever licked on the face again by a swarm of—"

The group stopped in their tracks and turned in the direction of the noise echoing up the tunnel.

"What is it?" asked Father James.

"I don't know," whispered Sam. "Let's keep moving and pray we're not discovered."

The spine-tingling noises were heard again, though much louder.

Cindy trembled.

"That sounded like growling again," said Dan. "Like we just—"

Rattling noises drowned out his comment and filled the tunnel.

The clatter quickly ended.

"And that sounded like chains—just like we heard earlier on the lower level," added Cindy.

The travelers faced the oncoming disturbances. Suddenly, an explosion of light beyond the bend brightened the cavern and cast shadows of a four-legged creature and a tall figure upon the wall. A torch beyond the tunnel's curve had been lit.

In complete silence, the travelers turned and resumed their sprint.

"Sam, what if they spot us?" asked Cindy.

"I don't think we have to worry about that as long as we keep moving."

"What do you mean don't worry?" she demanded.

Sam stole a backward glance. "Whatever is back there is obviously beyond the cavern's curve. If we can't see them, then they can't see us. We should count our blessings that the burst of light came when it did so we could see their shadows before they spotted us."

"Sam, don't you think it's strange that for as long as we hiked on the first level we didn't run into a cave dweller in the open tunnel—like now?" posed Dan.

"Kind of, I suppose. What are you getting at?"

"It's just that—"

"Shh," ordered Father James. "This talking isn't helping our situation."

"He's right," agreed Sam who looked at the shadows again. "I think they're gaining on us."

Without disrupting their stride, the travelers looked back.

"Cerby—slow down!" was heard from beyond the tunnel's bend.

"Faster!" ordered the priest.

With the growling and rattling sounds growing louder and the threatening shadows growing larger, hopelessness consumed the travelers.

Fearful that they would eventually be spotted, Sam ordered everyone to look for a place to hide.

"But Sam, there's nothing ahead except tunnel," alerted Cindy. "And there aren't any boulders to hide behind."

"Cerby!" was shouted up the tunnel again.

The explorers wrenched their necks.

"Sam, what do we do?" pleaded Cindy. "There's nowhere to hide."

"Our Father, who art in heaven, hallowed be thy name," prayed the priest.

"Look!" shouted Sam. He pointed his lance ahead.

On the right wall was the answer to the priest's prayer—another side cave.

As the group continued their mad dash to the opening, their hopelessness was replaced with apprehension with the unknown that awaited them inside. A thunderous growl that shook the cavern walls convinced them to take their chances in the unexplored cave.

Sam stood watch at the entrance, switching his gaze from his friends to the looming shadows until all were inside. He was the last to enter.

Cindy immediately covered her nose. "Phew, what's that awful smell?" she exclaimed.

"Who cares?" replied Sam. "At least we're safe." He glanced about the new surroundings. "It's not very bright in here."

A lone torch near the cave's entrance struggled to illuminate the subterranean world.

Overwhelmed with curiosity, Cindy took refuge behind a boulder near the entrance.

"Cindy!" shouted Sam. He covered his nose to block the offensive odor. "What are you doing? We have to search for William, Jimmy, and Brad."

She poked her head from behind the rock. "Sam, aren't you the least bit curious with what's been trailing us?"

He stepped alongside the boulder. "Of course I am. But our friends are more important."

"Sam, what if whatever's been following us enters this cave?" she asked. "Don't you think we should wait to see if it passes beyond the entrance or enters this place?"

He knew she had a point. "I suppose you're right." He looked at Dan and Father James—who were also covering their noses—and ordered them to hide behind the rock.

With everyone grasping a weapon, they silently awaited the appearance of the unknown creatures.

They stared at the empty entrance for what seemed five minutes.

"Come on, Sam. We need to find the others," said an impatient Dan. "William could be here." He looked at the cave's entrance. "Besides, we haven't heard the slightest—"

His comment was overpowered by a bloodcurdling growl.

Two shadows moved beyond the cave's opening.

Seconds later, a lanky being dressed in a floor-length, black hooded cloak stopped at the entrance. At its side stood a three-headed dog that was restrained by a metal chain. As one head sniffed the entrance, the other two snarled. The hound leaped into the opening but was pulled back by a yank on the chain.

The four travelers watched in horror at what stood at the cave's entrance.

A dying flame that was wedged in the tunnel wall outside the entrance afforded the travelers a poor vision of the beings.

The dog made another lunge at the opening. It was jerked away.

Luckily, the boulder prevented the explorers from being spotted by the tall being or its three-headed companion.

From the rock's side, the group watched the being grab an unlit torch from the bag it was lugging and ram it into the tunnel wall. Sam and Dan were equally amazed at the ease with which the being anchored it into solid rock.

The being spit on the lifeless torch. A spark and then a blaze were born from its saliva.

"The light keeper," whispered Dan.

"Shh," warned Sam.

The newborn flame presented a clearer vision of the creatures.

The tall being turned from the torch and squarely faced the cave's entrance.

Father James gasped.

Though it slightly resembled a human, it was covered with scales.

The dog's features were also clearly visible. Each head was marred with overhanging upper fangs and a drooling mouth. Its eyes were dark as night.

The hound was determined. It made another attempt to enter the cave.

The being yanked the chain again. "Come on, Cerby. You mangled an inhabitant earlier. There'll be more residents to play with later." The light keeper stared at the newly lit torch and recalled the ones missing on the lower level. "I suspect that an inhabitant has broken free from its rock prison and has been taking torches," the being openly declared. "Let's go. The master above needs to know about this escapee."

"The master above?" whispered Dan.

Sam placed a finger over his lips demanding silence.

"That's the three-headed dog, Cerberus, from mythology," said Cindy under her breath.

Sam motioned for silence again.

A piercing scream beyond the entrance toppled Cindy from a squat position to the ground.

The light keeper was bashing its body against the tunnel wall while shouting profanities. It fell to the ground in torment.

As the hound witnessed its caretaker's display of pain, its earlier craving to track the foreign scent in the side cave waned. It whimpered at the light keeper's side before nipping its master's face.

On its back, the being raised its hands to its face, gripped its scales around its mouth, and pulled.

Cindy gagged as the light keeper peeled its scaly covering.

"Look, it's shedding its skin," whispered Dan.

Four sets of eyes were glued to the being.

Once its outer layer of facial scales was stripped away, it pulled its chest scales down to its abdomen. The being squirmed and slipped from its hooded cloak.

Cerberus tugged on the strips of scales resting on the ground at the being's side.

Given the brief time and ease with which the hound tore its master's outer layer, Dan imagined that it had performed this essential task on a regular basis. The three heads engaged in a bloody battle to devour the body wrap.

In great pain, the being labored to its feet and replaced its cloak.

The brawl intensified between the three heads for the appetizing scales.

The light keeper offered a fleeting look at the battling heads before snatching its bag and restraining chain from the ground. With a mighty pull on the chain, the heads yelped.

The being remained outside the cave's entrance. Its new scales glistened in the light of the blazing torch.

The group—still concealed behind the boulder—was sickened watching the three heads gnaw and swallow their snack. The hound was dragged away.

Sam rose slowly from the rock and peered beyond the cave's entrance to confirm that the being and Cerberus were out of sight. "Well at least the light keeper's dilemma drew the hound's attention away from us," he remarked.

"Yeah," agreed Dan. "I think the dog smelled us—even over the foul odor of this cave. The shedding couldn't have come at a better time."

"That was gross," complained a queasy Cindy.

Sam noticed the priest's unusual silence and suspected he was still horrified by the ordeal. "Father, are you okay?"

He nodded. "Yeah, I'm fine."

Dan rose to his feet and looked at Cindy. "What did you say the dog's name was?"

"Cerberus." She continued staring at the entrance; she wasn't taking any chances. Eventually, she gave Dan her complete attention. "In Greek and Roman mythology, Cerberus was the three-headed dog that guarded the entrance of—" She refused to finish her explanation.

"Guarded the entrance of Hades," completed the priest. "I think the Greeks and the Romans were on to something."

"Father, I don't mean any disrespect, but why are you so convinced that this is hell?" she asked.

"Like I said before, I don't have any tangible proof," he reminded. "It's simply a hunch—but a strong one."

"And what about the light keeper covered with scales?" recalled Dan. "You can't deny that it shed its skin just like serpents do on earth."

"So you think this is hell too?" she posed.

"I'm not sure. But you have to admit there are a few convincing similarities—like the three-headed dog, the shedding serpent, or even the fact that the creatures in this world don't stay dead forever."

"I guess it's not so much that I don't believe Father James, as much as I hope he's wrong," she admitted.

"Cindy, you've all told me that if we want to escape, we must be open and honest with each other," reminded the priest. "We can't hold anything back. What I've speculated is simply that—a speculation." He rested his hand on her shoulder. "What are you holding back?"

"It's just that—"

"Just what?" he urged.

"I was taught in Sunday school that when a person's in hell there's no escape." She lowered her eyes. "I suppose that's what I'm most fearful of—not so much where we are, but that there's no way out."

Father James realized now why she refused to consider his theory. He was quick to stress that their situation was completely different.

"What do you mean?" she asked.

"Your Sunday school teachers were right. When someone's in hell, there is no escape. But our circumstance is entirely different. When a person dies on earth and is condemned to hell, they stay there forever. But remember, we didn't die on earth before entering this realm."

"So what will happen if we die here?" blurted Dan. "Will we be here forever?"

The priest removed his hand from Cindy's shoulder and covered his nose to block the wretched odor. He shook his head. "I don't know. Like I said before, let's all try to stay alive."

"Speaking of all," reminded Sam, "I wonder if our friends are in this cave." He reached for the burning torch on the cave wall.

Just when the group's sense of smell was adjusting to the stench, a sudden breeze reminded them of their atrocious surroundings.

"What's that awful smell?" asked Cindy.

Dan believed he knew the cause of the odor but decided to keep it to himself.

Sam stepped away from the cave's entrance and held the torch at arm's length. He and his co-travelers surveyed their new rock world.

As Dan inspected the twenty-foot-high ceiling for daddy longlegs, Cindy was quick to point out the moist ground. Row after row of inhabitants soon fell under the torch's glow.

"What are they doing?" asked Cindy. She stared at several cave dwellers who were wildly whipping their arms.

"I don't know," said Sam. "But we can't worry about that now. We're on a tight schedule."

The travelers invaded the masses, though careful to avoid the inhabitants' upper body movements.

Sam observed that all the cave dwellers were facing forward. "It looks like they're fixated with something up ahead."

"I wonder what's up ahead," said Dan.

Sam held the torch aloft. "I can't tell from here. But I'm sure we'll find out."

Dan stepped between two cave dwellers and was knocked off his feet by their violent arm movements. He had the advantage of a ground-level perspective. "Hey, these people are stuck!" he shouted.

"What do you mean stuck?" asked the priest.

"Their feet and ankles are buried beneath the soil," informed Dan. "I don't think they could move even if they wanted to." He studied their upper body motions and the occasional tug of their legs. "If I didn't know better, I'd say they're waving their arms and jerking their legs to break free from the soggy soil and walk."

"Walk where?" asked Cindy.

"Probably to whatever's up ahead," answered Sam.

"Good heavens, these helpless souls," exclaimed the priest.

Cindy jumped. From the corner of her eye, she saw something drop from a male inhabitant.

Dan saw her jump. "Sam, hand me the torch!"

Dan lowered the flame to the male inhabitant's feet and saw something vanish beneath the soil.

"I've got a bad feeling about this," said Cindy.

Aware that a moving target would be harder to attack than a stationary one, Sam insisted they keep searching. "Remember, we're looking for William, Jimmy, and Brad."

"But I don't know what Brad Blaze looks like," said Cindy.

"That's all right," said Father James. "You search for Jimmy and William. I'll keep an eye out for Brad."

"Gross!" shouted Dan. He saw firsthand what he and Cindy failed to spot moments earlier at the feet of the male inhabitant.

"What's wrong?" yelled Sam.

"Look at this!" exclaimed Dan.

The travelers stepped alongside Dan. In near shock, all eyed the end of a tapeworm dangling from the mouth of an inhabitant.

"I think I'm going to be sick," forewarned Cindy.

"I'm sure it wouldn't be the first time in this place," mumbled Dan.

Although a part of her dreaded the answer, her curiosity won out. "What do you mean?"

"Judging from the horrible stench and the mushy ground, I can guarantee that you won't be the first or the last to vomit in this cave," replied Dan.

She looked down. "You mean we're standing in sickness?"

Dan suspected that she'd probably add to the pile if he answered directly. "It's not that bad," he played down. "It could be worse."

"I doubt it. I'm sure this entire—" She screamed.

A tapeworm reared its head from the loose soil and slithered inside Cindy's pant leg.

"Get it off!" she yelled. "Get it off!" She tried to grab the parasite through her jeans.

Sam and Dan were positioned and ready.

The head of the four-foot-long tapeworm emerged from her neckline and arched forward. It was determined to take up residence in her intestines.

Dan quickly pressed his hand over her mouth to thwart the tapeworm's sole purpose of existence.

The tapeworm sprang at Dan's hand and sank its hooks and suckers in his wrist.

Dan refused to leave Cindy's mouth an easy target. He endured the pain.

Though her mouth was protected, nearly the entire length of the parasite was still squirming beneath her clothing.

Sam carefully gripped the tapeworm, released its hold on Dan's wrist, and slowly pulled its lower body from Cindy's neckline.

"Sam!" she screamed through Dan's hand. "Yank!"

"Cindy, I have to be gentle!" warned Sam. "If I pull too hard, it'll snap in two and grow a new head. And in this world, I'd guess right away. Trust me, you don't want that."

The parasite was safely removed from Cindy's clothes. It slipped from Sam's hands and dropped to the warm soil. Before Sam could target it with his lance, it disappeared below the sickness.

Cindy took a few moments to catch her breath. "You were right, Dan. It's worse."

"Sam," warned Father James. "I don't want to alarm you, but something's climbing inside my—"

Before he could finish his comment, Dan had the torch lowered to his feet and saw the end of another tapeworm disappear up his pant leg.

"Keep your mouth closed!" ordered Sam. Without removing his stare from the priest's neck, he instructed Dan to raise the torch to his face.

Nothing emerged from the priest's neckline.

Cindy noticed Sam's puzzled look in the glow of the torch. "What's wrong?" she asked.

"I'm not sure, but something's not right," said Sam. "It should be at the top of his shirt by now."

"Maybe it's slower than the other one," suggested Cindy.

"I don't think so. It's not like tapeworms to—" Sam lowered his eyes to the priest's waist. "Father, I need to open your shirt."

"Why?" asked the priest.

Sam refused to answer. He reached for the priest's top button.

Within seconds, the shirt fell to his side.

Cindy gasped.

The head of the tapeworm was buried beneath the bloodstained tee shirt. Once the homemade bandage was removed, Sam's worse fear was confirmed. The parasite had secured its hooks and suckers within the priest's wound and was enjoying a warm meal.

Father James lowered his sights to view the invasion of his body. He became dizzy and nearly collapsed.

Cindy supported him.

Sam reached for the flat invader.

Dan quickly grabbed Sam's arm and warned, "This isn't like Cindy's tapeworm that had a hold on my wrist. This one's head is already attached deep inside Father James's wound. It'll take a powerful yank to release it. You might end up snapping its head from its body. We can't have the head lodged permanently in his side."

Sam returned his hands to his side. "There's got to be a way to remove it without breaking it in two." He looked at Cindy and Dan for suggestions. None were forthcoming.

Lost in his thoughts on how to release the tapeworm intact, Dan unknowingly lowered the torch and grazed the priest's exposed shoulder.

"Dan!" yelled Sam. He knocked the torch away.

"Sorry Father," apologized Dan.

"Hey wait a minute," exclaimed Sam. He took the torch from Dan. "Father, I think we can remove the tapeworm if we place the flame next to the wound."

The priest took a noisy gulp. "I understand. Go ahead."

"But Father, I may have to put the blaze pretty close."

"How close?" he asked with a hint of fear in his voice.

"Actually, I may have to touch the flame to the skin."

The priest took another look at his reopened injury and the twitching tapeworm. He raised his eyes to Sam's. "All right, I'm ready."

Sam squatted and steadied the torch alongside the wound. He neared the flame to the tapeworm.

"Wait," said Dan.

"What?" shouted Sam. He pulled the torch away from Father James's side.

Dan raised the wooden shaft of his lance to the priest's face. "Bite down on this."

"Is it necessary?" asked Father James.

"Trust me. It's a trick we learned in the parallel world," related Dan.

The priest pressed his teeth into the handle.

Sam moved the flame to the injury.

With the torch stabilized about an inch from the tapeworm, Dan saw that Father James's eyes were closed and his fists were clenched.

"It's not working," whispered Sam. Though he knew that burning his friend's side would be better in the long run than letting the tapeworm steal more blood, he still couldn't bring himself to touch the flame to his flesh.

"Sam, you have to do it," urged Dan.

"I know, I know," he snapped.

"Sam!" yelled Cindy.

Another tapeworm poked its head from the soil at Sam's heels.

Sam jumped to his feet and inadvertently touched the burning flame to the priest's injury.

Even with his teeth buried in the wooden shaft, Father James's moans echoed throughout the cave.

The bloodsucker dropped—head and all—to the ground and vanished beneath the soil.

The lance fell from the priest's mouth. He dropped to his knees, bringing Cindy down with him.

"Father!" she cried.

"I'm okay," he mumbled. The priest slowly opened his eyes.

Cindy and Dan helped him to his feet.

"Father, I don't mean to sound heartless, but in the future you need to be more careful," cautioned Sam. "If you're lightheaded, you have to let us know. This isn't the place to pass out. The tapeworms would have a field day on an unresponsive body."

"I'll try to remember," he promised.

Sam took a closer look at the bleeding wound. "I'll have to reapply the tee shirt to reduce the flow of blood. I'm sure it'll hurt but there's—"

"I understand," interrupted Father James.

Sam handed the torch to Dan.

In the short time it took Sam to reattach the makeshift bandage and replace the priest's shirt, the group was the target of four underground attacks. Each was driven back by the flame of the torch.

After watching the fourth parasite try to slip inside Dan's pant leg, Cindy suggested that everyone pull their socks over their pant legs. "Then if the tapeworms climb, they'll have to do it outside our clothes," she explained. "They'll be easy to spot."

"I suppose that's not a bad idea," said Sam. He squatted and pulled his socks over his pant legs.

Everyone did likewise.

"So Father, I guess it's safe to say that this is the cave of gluttony," posed Dan.

The priest took a wide view of the cave. "Judging from the foul odor, the vomit on the ground, and the tapeworms, yeah, I'd say it's pretty likely this is gluttony."

"Then that means we're looking for Jimmy," asserted Cindy.

"Cindy!" shouted Sam. "Just because Jimmy likes to eat doesn't make him—" Deep down, he also thought the odds were pretty good that Jimmy was imprisoned in the cave of gluttony. "Sorry Cindy," he apologized. "What was he wearing the night of the movie?"

"Jeans and a polo shirt."

"What color was the shirt?" he asked.

"Purple."

"Are you absolutely certain?"

"Oh yeah, Sam. I told him a couple times that the shirt was too tight." She shook her head in disgust before adding, "He said that's what women like."

"All right then, let's all be on the lookout for a purple shirt," ordered Sam.

The group continued their trek through the rows of inhabitants.

Cindy was slammed to the ground by the unbridled movements of an obese woman. Before Cindy placed her hands in the sickness to stand, Dan was squatting beside her. With the torch in hand, he was ready to dissuade any daring parasites. To their surprise, nothing surfaced from the regurgitated matter.

Throughout their zigzag search between the cave dwellers, only two tapeworms tried to slither up the outside of Dan's jeans. The torch sent them nose-diving to the ground.

After what seemed a thirty-minute walk, they reached the first row of inhabitants.

Father James's sights were drawn to a long, flat rock that was resting on two boulders. Each boulder was several feet distant from the other. "What's that?" he asked.

Sam ordered Dan to give him the torch. Sam neared the object in question. "It looks like a table of some sort."

"A table? For what?" asked Dan.

"It's loaded with fruits and vegetables!" shouted Cindy.

"This is definitely the cave of gluttony," affirmed Father James.

"But if the food is in front of them, then why aren't they eating it?" asked Cindy.

Father James stared at the inhabitants. "This is just a guess on my part, but I'd presume that since these people continually gave into the temptation of gluttony throughout their earthly lives, then their eternal punishment probably is to gaze upon food without being able to approach the table—much less eat the food. I'd also imagine that the food in front of them is meant to torment them. If this is hell—as I suspect—they're not permitted to eat the food in front of them. They're not even permitted to—"

"Wait a minute," interrupted Cindy. "If they're not permitted to eat, then where did all the sickness on the ground come from?"

"Again, it's only a theory," forewarned the priest. "But I'd guess that the unbearable smell causes the newly arrived overeaters to disgorge what's in their stomachs. What's under our feet probably has been accumulating for ages."

Cindy nearly gagged in disgust.

"But what's holding them below the soil?" asked Dan.

Cindy watched Sam open his mouth. She rolled her eyes before remarking, "Let me guess—I'm sure we'll find out."

"Actually, I was going to say—" His comment trailed off. He noticed a green apple stir on the rock table. "That's odd." With great care, he approached the table with his lance raised.

"What's wrong?" asked Dan.

"Stay where you are," ordered Sam. "Don't move." He continued his advance to the forbidden fruit. Two feet from the table, he extended his lance and lowered it to the apple. He jumped.

The apple unraveled, revealing a thirty-foot-long green tapeworm that was rolled to mimic fruit. It slithered from the tabletop, fell to the soggy ground, and buried itself from sight.

Sam held his lance over other tantalizing fruits and vegetables. The results were the same. Red tapeworms were rolled tightly to mimic tomatoes, yellow tapeworms were masked as squash, and dark purple tapeworms copied mouthwatering beets. The entire tabletop was crawling with life.

"This place gives me the creeps," exclaimed Cindy. She stared at the ground. "There are tapeworms everywhere."

On his return to the group, Sam accidentally booted the green tapeworm that had poked its head from the sickness and assumed its previous deceptive appearance.

The green apple rolled to the first row of inhabitants.

"Cindy, as soon as we find Jimmy we'll be out of here," promised Sam.

The rescuers focused on a disturbance at the front of the line—more specifically, on a middle-aged woman who was anchored to the ground. Though the cave residents couldn't walk, they could bend. She stooped, grabbed the fake apple, and swallowed it whole.

"Father, it looks like you were wrong about the cave dwellers not being permitted to eat the food," challenged Dan.

"Not really," he replied. "That wasn't food she just devoured. It's probably a trick of the tapeworms to invade the shells of these humans."

"I can't take much more of this," exclaimed Cindy. "Let's find that purple shirt and get the heck out of here."

"I'm with her," seconded Sam.

With each explorer clutching a weapon, Dan the backpack, and Sam the only torch, they continued their search among the rows of inhabitants for any familiar faces.

CHAPTER FOURTEEN
The Unseeing Adversary

SAM WAS SEARCHING AMID THE CAVE DWELLERS OF THE THIRD row when he spotted a purple shirt on the sixth inhabitant to his right. "Jimmy!" he shouted.

Dan, Cindy, and Father James were immediately at his side.

As the light of the torch enveloped Jimmy, the travelers were repulsed with a tapeworm dangling from his mouth.

"Oh Jimmy," mumbled the priest.

The parasite slipped down his throat.

Jimmy remained expressionless and motionless during the oral invasion with his sights set on the rock table ahead.

"What do we do?" exclaimed Cindy.

Her companions remained gawking at Jimmy in shock.

"Sam, what do we do?" she shouted again.

"I'm thinking!" he snapped.

"We have to draw out the tapeworm," ordered Dan. "But how?"

"Maybe we could lure it out with food," suggested the priest.

Cindy looked to the rock table. "I doubt those tomatoes or squash will do the trick."

"Wait a minute," exclaimed Sam. He handed the torch to Cindy, snatched the backpack from Dan, and rummaged through its contents.

"What are you looking for?" asked Cindy.

"We had some snacks earlier," reminded Sam.

"Yeah, but I submerged them in the water a long time ago, remember?" said Dan.

"I was hoping—" Sam cut his remark short and continued searching. "Here we go." He pulled a crushed breakfast bar from the backpack. "I guess we didn't submerge everything."

"Sam, what are you going to do?" questioned Cindy.

"I don't know if it'll work, but I've seen it done in old educational films. I think this is what Father James was suggesting."

The priest nodded.

Sam grabbed two rocks from the ground and faced Jimmy. "Dan, help me," he ordered.

The men opened Jimmy's mouth and wedged a rock on either side, between his upper and lower jaws.

With his mouth pried open, Sam ordered Dan to rip open the breakfast bar and hold it near Jimmy's mouth.

"Then what?" asked Dan.

"Then if it goes as I hope, the tapeworm will slither up Jimmy's esophagus and fix itself to the breakfast bar. When it does—if it does—I'll pull it slowly from his gut."

"Sam, do you think it'll work?" asked Cindy.

"Let's keep our fingers crossed."

Cindy jumped back. "There's something moving under Jimmy's feet."

"Of course there is—more tapeworms," said Dan. "But we'll be fine." He struggled to tear the wrapper on the snack.

"Dan, hurry up," ordered Sam.

He finally ripped the packaging and raised the edible lure to Jimmy's lips. Dan was caught off guard by movement at his own feet and dropped the breakfast bar. As he was bending over to recover the snack, he noticed something twisting in the stomach of an obese, middle-aged woman standing beside Jimmy. The travelers were gaping at her condition when a green tapeworm fell from her mouth and buried itself in the sickness. With the parasite's departure, the woman was freed from the ground's hold. She collapsed to the ground.

"The bar—grab it!" yelled Sam.

Dan snatched the breakfast bar before it was pulled below the surface.

As the priest had done countless times at the deathbeds of his former parishioners, he knelt at the woman's side, folded her hands, and rested them on her stomach. "My gosh, it's empty," he declared.

"What's empty?" asked Sam.

"Her stomach. Here Sam, feel."

Sam dropped to his knees alongside the deceased and felt her stomach. "My gosh, you're right." He moved his hand over her entire midsection. "It's nothing but a huge cavity. The tapeworm must have devoured her from the inside out."

"From the inside out?" exclaimed the priest. "You can't be serious!"

"That would be my guess," said Sam, "which is all the more reason to get the killer out of Jimmy."

"Come on Sam, we have to act fast," urged Dan.

The priest and Sam returned to Jimmy's side.

Dan and Sam had just resumed their former positions when the recently departed middle-aged woman sank below the sickness. Seconds later, she fell from the ceiling. To the explorers, it appeared as though nothing had changed since her death. But there was a change. The woman labored to breathe, stood, and took one step nearer the rock table in a dazed state. She took her second step, wobbled, and then paused to regain her balance. Not having used her lower limbs in centuries, she tried to coordinate her movements and relearn the art of walking.

The priest took advantage of her standstill and her unresponsive condition. He rested his hand on her stomach. "It doesn't feel hollow anymore."

"Father, I guess you probably were right," admitted Cindy.

"About what?"

"About no one staying dead in this world forever," she clarified.

The priest shook his head at what he suspected eternity held for this woman.

Cindy observed the troubled look on his face. "Father, what's wrong?"

"Since her midsection doesn't feel empty anymore, she probably will suffer the pain of being eaten from the inside out again and again."

Cindy refused to engage in the topic.

"We have to make sure that what happened to her doesn't happen to Jimmy," declared Sam. He turned to Dan. "Are you ready?"

Instinctively, all eyes were drawn to movement below the ground at their feet. A large tapeworm crawled up the formerly deceased woman's leg and slipped into her mouth.

The priest's efforts to prevent the parasite from entering her were useless.

The woman yanked her legs to resume her approach to the rock table. But it was a losing battle. Her feet and ankles were once again anchored in the ground.

Dan focused on the present plight and held the breakfast bar close to Jimmy's mouth.

Sam rubbed his hands on his pants to dry his sweaty palms for a firm grip on the parasite. Without warning, a tapeworm sprang from Jimmy's throat and sank its hooks and suckers into the breakfast treat.

"Sam!" yelled Cindy. She grabbed the head of the six-foot-long tapeworm with her free hand and pulled the parasite from Jimmy's insides. Her single-handed grasp on the slippery intruder was so firm and exact that it released its grip on the breakfast bar.

Dan was left holding the bait.

She dropped the tapeworm to the ground where it instantly vanished.

Sam, Dan, and the priest stared at the torch-bearing Cindy in disbelief.

"What?" she exclaimed. "Someone had to do something!"

"Great job," complimented Sam. He looked at Dan to congratulate him on his valiant efforts when he saw something resting on Jimmy's tongue. "Not another one!"

"Are you serious?" asked Dan in disbelief. He looked inside Jimmy's mouth.

"Raise the bait!" ordered Sam.

Within moments, it and a third tapeworm shot from Jimmy's mouth. The two belly-dwelling worms met the same fate as the first—one at the hand of Cindy and the other at Sam's.

"How many more do you think are in him?" asked Cindy.

"There's no way of knowing," said Sam. "We'll keep luring them out until there are no more."

After six more tapeworms were removed, Jimmy closed his eyes and fell to the ground.

"His feet!" yelled Cindy. "They're free of the soil!" She and Dan dropped to their knees and pulled Jimmy's socks over his pant legs.

"I wonder how he was released from the ground," posed Dan.

"It's hard to explain anything in this world," admitted Father James. "But there's obviously a connection between being fixed in the ground and hosting one or more tapeworms—like the woman next to us. Maybe once the tapeworms were pulled from Jimmy, he was released from his excessive desire for food and from the mental grasp of this cave's curse of gluttony. And it's also possible that once he was freed from the mental hold, he was also freed from the physical hold of this place."

"Father, I'm not following," admitted Cindy.

"It's purely speculation on my part," he admitted, "but think about it. People on earth who consume enormous amounts of food and drink often find it difficult—if not impossible—to separate themselves from their eating addictions." He looked at the spellbound cave dwellers around him. "Before their earthly deaths, these inhabitants most likely were unable to step away from the table. But after their earthly deaths, they're unable to approach the rock table. I suppose that's their eternal punishment."

Jimmy licked his lips.

"He's coming to!" shouted Cindy.

Jimmy opened his eyes. He immediately spotted the purple blotches on Cindy's and Dan's faces—the physical scars of the embedded ticks. "Nice complexions," he mumbled.

Cindy lowered her face next to his. "It was your stupid obsession with the oak that landed me here and ultimately gave me these marks."

"Cindy, he's been through a lot. Go easy on him," advised Sam.

She recalled the promise she made to herself about not being overly judgmental of Jimmy. She kept her remaining criticisms to herself.

Jimmy, however, refused to drop the issue. He stared at the blemish below Cindy's right eye. "What happened to your face?"

"Shut up, Jimmy," she snapped.

Dan also looked at Cindy's face that was bathed in the torchlight. "Hey Sam, the cuts on our faces and hands from our crawl on the ceiling are almost healed."

"I hadn't noticed it. But now that you mention it, you're right."

"I wonder why," posed Cindy. She examined her hands closely. "Do you think our—"

"I'd suspect that the accelerated time in this world has everything to do with it," interjected Sam.

"Of course; that makes perfect sense," agreed Dan.

Only now, Jimmy noticed the priest. "Father James, what are you doing here? I don't remember seeing you thrown into the oak."

"It's a long story. I'll fill you in later."

Sam and Father James helped Jimmy to his feet.

"Are you strong enough to walk?" asked Sam.

"Yeah, I think so."

"Let's give it a shot," urged Sam.

Jimmy took a step and staggered.

Sam immediately grabbed him around the waist.

Jimmy broke free from his grip. "Thanks Sam, but I can manage."

"Nevertheless, I'll keep a close eye on you," warned Sam.

Dan stepped nearer to Jimmy. "I guess it's pointless asking if you've seen William or Brad Blaze in this place."

Jimmy spit a foul taste from his mouth. "Sorry, I don't remember much." He looked at the shifting ground with a puzzled look. "Come to think of it, I don't remember anything after being thrown into the oak. I guess I've been out of it."

"That's okay. Hardly anyone remembers anything," said Dan.

Jimmy sensed his friend's frustration. "But your brother's got to be here somewhere since he was tossed into the oak like us."

Dan made no response.

"Jimmy, are you hungry?" asked Cindy.

He placed his hand on his stomach. "That's funny. No, not at all."

"I don't mean to sound impatient or uncaring, but considering we're on a tight schedule, I wonder if we'd be wasting valuable time searching for William and Brad in this cave," posed Father James.

Sam took the torch from Cindy. "What's the date now?"

Father James lifted his sleeve. "The twenty-third," he announced.

"The twenty-third!" shouted Jimmy. "That's impossible. I haven't been here that long."

"I know it's hard to believe," stated Sam. "But trust me, it's September twenty-third."

"But how?" asked a visibly shaken teenager. "I just got here."

"Jimmy, we'll explain everything later," promised Sam. "But in the meantime, I think Father James raises a good point." He looked at Dan. "Do you think your brother was a glutton for food or drink?"

"I'm not sure."

"Think Dan," urged Sam. "We can't waste our time looking for him among all these gluttons if he—"

"Hey wait a minute!" shouted Jimmy. "Are you saying I'm a glutton?"

"If the shoe fits," replied Cindy.

Jimmy shot a snide look at her.

"Jimmy, Cindy, shh," ordered Sam. He glanced at Dan again. "Do you think William was prone to gluttony?"

"It's hard to say. Remember, he's been away most of my life. But since our return from the parallel world, I haven't seen him eating or drinking excessively."

"That's good enough for me," replied Sam. He posed the same question to Father James concerning his parishioner Brad Blaze.

"I'm not sure, since I spoke with him only briefly on Sundays after Mass. But Sam, you have to remember that not all obese people are gluttons. For many, it's a medical condition. Still, if I had to guess—and it's only a guess—I'd say that Brad didn't overindulge in food or drink."

Sam tightened the backpack on his shoulders. "Then I suggest we leave this place and search the other two caves."

"Hey wait!" shouted Jimmy. "How do you know there are more caves? It's entirely possible that—" His comment ended abruptly. At last, the inattentive teenager spun and took in his mysterious surroundings. "I don't remember a cave in the parallel world. And what's with this soggy ground?"

"Jimmy, like Sam said, we'll explain everything later," stressed the priest.

"Sam, I doubt that William is in this cave," declared Dan. He pulled his glasses from his face and blew cave dust from the lenses. "So I guess that means he's either in the cave of anger or lust." He looked at the cave's exit. "And as much as I hate to admit it, we've never had an easy way out from any of the side caves. And to make matters worse, we haven't seen the guardian of this one yet."

"Maybe the tapeworms are the guardians," suggested an optimistic priest.

"That would be a welcome change," expressed Sam. "But considering the unnatural size guardians we've met in the past, I doubt it." He pulled a lance from the backpack and armed Jimmy.

"What's a guardian?" asked Jimmy.

"Jimmy, I said we'll explain everything later," said Sam. He ordered his co-travelers to follow him.

With each bearing a weapon, the explorers trailed Sam and his glowing torch.

Barely several yards into their escape, Cindy and Dan spotted an abnormally large tapeworm arch its head from the moist ground at Cindy's heels. The teenagers jumped back.

Dan discouraged its advance by stomping his boot near its head.

Once it buried itself in the sickness, Cindy took advantage of their standstill and pulled her sagging socks over her pant legs. "You can't be too careful," she warned.

A few steps further, Cindy stopped and took a sweeping view of the cave. "What was that?" she whispered.

"What was what?" asked Dan.

"There it is again," she alerted.

Dan also felt the weak tremor.

The breeze in the hollow world gradually increased to a roaring wind.

Cindy turned to face the back of the cave where she sensed the quake had originated. "What's happening?" she shouted.

The ground shook again, but with greater force.

"I don't know," exclaimed Dan who also spun and peered to the rear of the cave.

Chunks of moist sickness exploded into the air.

Even though their surroundings were poorly lit, there was no mistaking what Cindy and Dan witnessed in the recesses of the cave. They froze. The ground was upturning rapidly in their direction.

Sam, Jimmy, and Father James—who unknowingly had advanced a great distance ahead of the stragglers—also turned when the ground quaked.

Sam spotted Cindy and Dan lagging behind. "Come on! Hurry!"

The unseen guardian increased its burrowing speed, swaying the anchored cave dwellers along its path. The width of the approaching furrow was nearly five feet.

Sam also witnessed the tragedy developing behind Dan and Cindy. "Run!" he screamed.

Dan grabbed Cindy's arm, placed their backs toward the intruder, and dashed to the men.

The raging gusts that had loosened eons-old dust particles and dirt from the cave walls and ceiling created a formidable dust storm. The winds and dust obscured the men from Cindy's and Dan's vision.

"Sam!" yelled Cindy into the wind's fury.

As Sam watched his friends vanish in the thick haze, the roaring winds extinguished his torch. He ripped open the backpack and grabbed the flashlight. Unfortunately, the storm was so fierce that even the flashlight's beam failed to penetrate the flying particles. "Dan! Cindy!" he yelled. "Run for the entrance!"

No response was heard.

Dear God, I hope they can find us, thought Sam.

Although the teenagers failed to hear Sam's scream over the winds, they immediately set on placing as much distance between themselves and their unknown assailant.

"Where are the others?" shouted Cindy.

Despite the fact that Dan was standing beside her, the gusts overpowered her question.

Nearer the cave's exit, Sam ordered Jimmy and Father James to get to the safety of the open tunnel. "I'll wait for the others," he explained.

THE UNSEEING ADVERSARY

"No! We'll all wait for them!" screamed Father James.

Sam disregarded his demand and continued scanning the expanse with the flashlight.

Disoriented in the dust storm, Cindy and Dan veered off course and were racing toward an area of the cave that was populated with cave dwellers.

Sadly, they didn't realize their faulty heading until Dan bumped into an inhabitant and fell to the ground. He jumped to his feet and placed his face next to Cindy's ear. "We're off track! Run to the right!"

Their race to the open tunnel resumed.

The burrowing creature, however, detected the vibrations of Dan's collision with the ground. It altered its path of destruction and tunneled toward the fleeing teenagers.

Only a short distance from the cave's exit, Jimmy and Father James remained motionless behind Sam who continually waved the flashlight's beam in all directions. He trusted that something would reflect the light.

Sam suspected that he, Jimmy, and Father James were safe from the creature as long as they didn't make any detectable movements. He hoped that Dan or Cindy knew likewise.

Though the racing teenagers couldn't hear the approach of the creature over the winds, they clearly felt its tremors on the ground. Dan imagined it was nearby.

Within the storm's darkness, the sprinters ran into a cave wall and were knocked to the ground.

Face down, Dan frantically felt the area for Cindy.

The tremors stopped.

Dan realized then that his and Cindy's hurried movements had been announcing their location to the creature. *How stupid of me,* he thought.

The winds continued to roar.

Dan resumed his desperate but silent search for Cindy in the darkness. Just when hopelessness was settling in, he felt her shoulder. She had suffered a head-on collision with the rock wall and was out cold.

Since he knew he didn't have the luxury of waiting for her to wake—and knowing that any sudden movement would disclose their location—he lifted her into his arms, grazed a foot against the base of the cave wall, and silently traced its perimeter.

The unidentified creature, meanwhile, remained motionless several feet from the wall of impact. Its head was elevated above the cave floor, ready to lunge at the first sign of perceptible movement.

The dust storm prevented Dan from eyeing certain death only yards away. With great effort, he carried Cindy to the cave's exit without alerting the creature. Once inside the tunnel, he placed her on her back against the far wall. He looked up and down the cavern for his friends. Dust particles caused him to cough uncontrollably. *Don't tell me they're still in the cave,* he thought. After coughing to the point of nearly gagging, he filled his lungs with air and re-entered the cave of gluttony. He had hoped that the violent winds would have calmed and the dust would have settled so he could spot his friends. But that was not the case. Convinced that hasty movements would draw the creature to himself and ultimately his friends, he crept in the darkness.

Sam—who was still waving the flashlight in search of his co-travelers—turned to Jimmy. "Get Father James to the tunnel. I'll go in search of the others."

Though Jimmy wanted to help Sam rescue their friends, he unwillingly agreed to lead the priest through the storm to the exit. He grabbed Father James's arm.

"No! We have to find the others!" shouted the priest.

"Sam's orders!" screamed Jimmy.

Jimmy had guided the priest only several steps closer to the exit when he bumped into Dan. "Dan!" he shouted.

"Cindy's in the tunnel!" yelled Dan.

Jimmy retraced his steps to Sam and slapped him on the back.

Sam nearly jumped out of his skin with the strike of Jimmy's open hand. He dropped the flashlight.

"They're behind us!" shouted Jimmy.

"What?" screamed Sam.

"They're behind us!" he yelled again.

Sam snatched the flashlight from the ground and joined the men in their trek to the opening in the cave wall.

The flashlight hitting the ground, however, provided ample vibration to reveal the group's location.

The creature plunged into the sickness and tunneled in the direction of the recent impact.

The four men were not oblivious to the growing tremors.

"Faster!" yelled Sam who was bringing up the rear.

Several agonizing steps later, a dim light was seen through the storm. The cave's exit was within sight.

Jimmy was the first to dart through the opening. His friends were on his heels.

Sam was the last to escape the cave of gluttony. He was shocked at seeing the men slow their pace inside the tunnel. "Run! It's not stopping!" he shouted.

Jimmy and Father James continued their dash up the open cavern. Sam nearly outran them.

Unknown to the men, Dan had darted to the far cavern wall and fell to the ground alongside a motionless Cindy.

A massive white tapeworm rammed its head through the cave's opening.

The impact knocked Father James, Sam, and Jimmy to their stomachs.

The creature's forceful arrival blasted the entry to double its original size. The enormous length of the predator allowed its lower body segments to remain hidden within the cave's storm.

Sam glared at the priest and Jimmy. "Remain perfectly still," he whispered. Only then he realized that Cindy and Dan weren't around. He turned his head and saw his friends twenty feet nearer the cave's entrance.

They were on their backs and completely motionless.

Knowing that shouting to Dan would endanger the two teenagers, Sam kept quiet. He hoped his silence would be contagious.

Since the overgrown parasite was sightless, it pressed its upper body against a tunnel wall seeking out vibrations. Sensing nothing, it ran its head down the rock wall and stopped only feet above Dan and Cindy where it remained for a few moments. It eventually retreated inside the stormy cave.

Though the dust storm blocked his vision, Dan suspected that the creature was lingering just inside the entrance for a surprise attack. He looked at Sam and placed a finger over his lips.

Sam remained silent.

Cindy, however, did not. She stirred and knocked her foot against the cavern wall.

Dan immediately placed his hand over her mouth.

Rocks hurled into the open cavern. The beast had thrust itself into the tunnel again. But unlike before, it smashed its head through a solid rock wall. A second entrance was created to the cave of gluttony.

Cindy opened her eyes to the creature ten feet overhead.

With his hand still covering her mouth, Dan also remained perfectly still.

The parasite placed its body against the stone wall again in search of movement. Detecting nothing, it withdrew slowly into the cave.

Unsure whether or not the tapeworm remained just inside the entrance, the group kept silent for what seemed twenty minutes. Eventually, Dan and Cindy quietly rose to all fours and crawled to their co-escapees.

"Let's go, but without making a sound," whispered Sam.

The explorers simply nodded.

A couple hundred feet up the tunnel, Sam dropped the flashlight into the backpack and yanked a burning torch from the wall. "It's probably safe to talk now."

"What was that thing?" blurted Jimmy.

Dan glanced back in the direction of the cave. "That, Jimmy, was a guardian."

CHAPTER FIFTEEN

The Stonehearted Sisters

THE FARTHER THE GROUP HIKED UP THE CAVERN, THE MORE dependent they became on Sam's fading torch.

Cindy watched him turn it upside down to revitalize the flame. "Hey Sam," she blurted, "maybe the light keeper planted a few more torches in the walls ahead."

"I hope so. I'd rather save the flashlight for emergencies."

"Emergencies?" snapped Jimmy. "Isn't not knowing where you're walking in almost total darkness and unsure what creatures await you considered an emergency?"

"Jimmy, other than the light keeper, we really haven't run into any creatures in the open cavern," said Sam.

"What about the shooting pods?" asked Cindy.

"Oh yeah, the pods," recalled Sam. "How could I forget?"

"And the huge human-faced spider," added Father James.

"There also were the dirt mounds," reminded Dan.

"All right, all right!" shouted Sam. "So we've encountered a few species in the open cavern."

Jimmy leaped over a boulder in his pathway. "What are shooting pods and—" He looked at Cindy. "What'd you call it—a light keeper?"

Sam placed the torch flame close to Jimmy's face. "The light keeper is a being that roams this world relighting the torches when they burn out. And as far as the shooting pods, well...let's just hope we never cross their paths again."

"And what about the dirt mounds and the human-faced spider?" asked Jimmy.

"The dirt mounds concealed skeletal arms," explained Sam. "And the giant spider was just as Father James said. It had a human face. But I wouldn't be too concerned since they were on a different level."

"I don't remember shooting pods or dirt mounds when we visited the parallel world the last time," admitted Jimmy.

No one commented on his observation.

"And like I said earlier," Jimmy continued, "I don't remember a cave in the parallel world, except for the centaur's cave."

"Jimmy, our hikes in the parallel world were a walk in the park compared to this gloomy place," warned Dan. "Here, even the dead don't stay dead."

"But I thought this was the parallel world," he said.

A cold breeze swept through the tunnel.

Jimmy looked from face to face. "Then where are we?" he asked.

A prolonged silence followed.

As much as Father James's assumption of the group's possible location terrified Cindy, she was slowly coming to accept his theory. "Jimmy, we think this may be hell," she stated.

"Hell?" he chuckled in a disbelieving voice. "What do you mean hell?"

"Didn't you take religion classes at your grade school?" she asked.

"Of course, but what does that have to do with this place?"

"Jimmy, we have reason to believe that we're stuck in hell," asserted Father James.

The travelers halted.

"Oh I get it, you're trying to scare me to keep me on my toes," accused Jimmy. He tightened the grip on his weapon and promised, "I'll stay alert."

"I wish we were just trying to scare you," said Father James. "But this trip is turning into one hellish nightmare."

As Jimmy looked into the priest's eyes, goose bumps surfaced on his arms. He knew that Father James wasn't joking. "But how can this be hell?"

Father James looked at Dan. "Tell him about your adventures since you were the first to escape your cave."

"After I was thrown into the oak," Dan began, "I ended up in a side cave that was crowded with greedy people."

Nearly a mile up the tunnel, Sam was relating the atrocities of his cave of confinement and explaining the rapid passage of time to Jimmy.

Once Cindy and Father James shared their strange imprisonments, Dan explained how the group hid from the light keeper in the cave of gluttony and how they freed Jimmy from his cave's spell.

"So you see, Jimmy, that's why we think this is hell," concluded the priest.

"Are you sure these creatures keep coming back to life?" asked an unconvinced teenager.

"Oh yeah," promised Dan. "We figured it out when the frilled lizard attacked us after we already killed it two times earlier."

Though Jimmy knew that he and his friends had embarked on another ghastly journey, he remained unconvinced that they were I hell. Believing that he was partially responsible for Cindy's presence in the dark world, he pulled her aside. "Sorry about luring you to the tree after the movie," he apologized.

She detected genuine remorse in his voice. "I suppose it wasn't totally your fault. Obviously, the oak has a supernatural quality that—" She ended her comment and blurted, "Jimmy, do you remember anything about your entry into the tree?"

The men overheard her question and spun to face the young travelers.

As Jimmy replayed the night of his abduction in his head, Cindy stressed the importance of any detail, even those which he considered trivial.

In the end, he shook his head. "No. I can't remember a thing. It all happened so fast."

The march resumed.

Cindy persisted. "But Jimmy, there has to be something you remember. Anything could prove crucial to our escape."

"Crucial? Why is it crucial to our escape? Let's just find the oak and get out of here."

She slapped him across the chest. "Fine Jimmy, then you lead us to the oak."

He glanced up and down the tunnel. "Oh, I see your point."

Sam stumbled, but reached for the cavern wall to prevent a fall.

Dan grabbed the straps on the backpack. "I'll carry it for a while," he insisted. To his surprise, Sam didn't object. Dan swung the bag onto his back before prompting, "Jimmy, as we already explained, we're quickly running out of time. Like Cindy said, anything you can remember about your trip could help."

Jimmy revisited his memories again. "Well, I saw you and William thrown into the oak. Then I was grabbed by a limb and hurled into the tree. That's it. That's all I remember."

"Don't worry, Jimmy," comforted the priest. "Nobody seems to remember much more."

"Wait!" he shouted. "There is something."

The travelers stopped in their tracks.

"What?" demanded Sam. "What do you remember?"

"It's kind of vague," he forewarned.

"What Jimmy?" prodded Cindy. "What's vague?"

Jimmy stepped closer to a cavern wall. "When I was crossing over, I saw a piece of wood—a flat piece of wood."

"Go on," urged Father James. "What else do you remember?"

He leaned against the rock wall. "I'm afraid that's it." He pushed from the wall and was nearing his friends when he halted. "No wait, there is something else."

"What?" shouted Dan.

"There was a carving on the wood."

"A carving?" questioned Dan.

"Yeah—you know—like a reptile or something," suggested Jimmy.

"You mean like a lizard or a snake or a—"

"A snake!" Jimmy shouted. "I'm sure of it now." He rubbed his forehead. "But there was something odd about the carving," he recalled.

"What do you mean?" asked the priest.

"There was just one serpent, but six heads," he revealed.

"Six heads?" questioned Sam. "Are you sure?"

"I told you it was odd. But I'm sure that's what I saw."

"But how come none of us saw a wooden carving?" asked Father James.

"That's a good question," admitted Sam. He looked at his co-travelers and asked if anyone remembered seeing a carving.

No one supported Jimmy's story.

"Well, maybe we'll find a carving up ahead," said Sam. "But in the meantime, we need to keep hiking. Remember, we don't have a lot of time until the next full moon."

The group took another step closer to home.

"I wonder what was so different about Jimmy's entrance into this world that allowed him to see something that no one else saw," posed Dan.

"It's hard to say," replied Sam. "Maybe the moonbeams reflected off an object which caused him to see something he thought was—"

"Sam!" called Cindy.

Sam spun, expecting to battle an unknown creature. Instead, he saw Cindy deep in thought. "What's wrong?" he demanded.

"Jimmy may be right about what he saw," she replied.

"What do you mean?" questioned Sam.

She blinked from her daze and recounted, "Like Jimmy, I also saw Dan and William tossed into the tree. But I also saw Jimmy hurled in."

"Cindy hurry, we're running out of time," pleaded Dan.

She pointed at Jimmy. "But he was the only one thrown backwards into the oak."

"So how does that matter?" asked Father James.

"Don't you get it?" she exclaimed. "Unlike all of us who entered the tree face first, he may have seen the portal in this world since he entered the oak backwards. Remember, since he was being drawn into this place backwards, he was facing this world's portal."

Doubt draped the priest's face.

Cindy looked at Sam. "When you stepped inside the oak, you entered face first, right?"

"Of course. Why would I—"

Dan interrupted, saying, "And I saw Father James pitched into the tree also face first."

"Well yeah," admitted the priest. "But I don't think—"

"And I also entered face first," said Cindy.

A short-lived silence was followed by cheers of elation.

Sam smacked Jimmy on the back. "Great job! I knew we brought you along for some reason," he teased.

The torch died.

"Great," complained Cindy. "Just when we had some light shed on our situation, we're left standing in the dark."

Sam stepped alongside Dan and pulled his flashlight from the backpack. "It's all right. At least now we know what we're looking for—a wooden carving."

"I suppose," said Father James. "But we don't know where to look."

"True," agreed Sam. "But we know more now than when we left Jimmy's cave." He directed the beam ahead. "Let's move," he ordered.

"Oh no," said Cindy.

Sam aimed the beam at her face. "Now what?"

She raised her hand to block the light. "This means we're putting our escape and our lives in Jimmy's hands. I've got a bad feeling about this."

"Very funny," mumbled Jimmy.

"But actually, it's probably only fitting," she declared.

"Why's that?" asked Jimmy.

"Since you tricked me into this world, it's only right that you get me out—but in one piece," she stressed.

"Quit bickering, you two," said Sam. "We've got two more caves to find."

With the flashlight's beam pointed ahead, the group pressed on with Sam and Cindy taking the lead.

"Jimmy, is there anything else you remember about the carving?" asked Father James.

"No, not really. It came and went in a flash."

Sam overheard Jimmy's response and assured him that he had helped the group more than he knew.

"Hey Sam, I don't know if you noticed, but we passed a torch on the wall that wasn't lit," alerted Dan.

"Yeah, I know."

"But if the light keeper is ahead of us somewhere, then why didn't he light the torch?" asked Cindy.

"That thought crossed my mind too," divulged Sam. "But I'd imagine that the light keeper skipped his duties and reported to the master above."

"There's another level to this place?" asked Jimmy.

"Sorry, I guess we left out that part of the story," apologized Dan.

"So there's no need to panic," reasoned Sam. "As long as the torches aren't lit, then the light keeper's probably up above and we're safe."

No sooner had Sam voiced his prediction when Cindy murmured, "Um…Sam."

"Yeah, I see it."

Light radiated beyond the cavern's curve.

"But what about the light keeper?" asked an edgy Cindy. "Do you think he's close by?"

Sam switched off the flashlight. "I don't know, but I suggest we make a silent approach to the area."

After what seemed a ten-minute walk up the tunnel, the explorers were bathed in light. They scanned the area. To their relief, they were alone.

Sam yanked five torches from the wall. "Let's be on the lookout. And remember, keep our voices down." He dropped the flashlight into the backpack.

Dan scanned the area. "This part of the tunnel is different."

"Yeah," agreed Cindy. "There are lots of boulders scattered around."

"No, I mean something feels different," he corrected. "It's weird—like we're being watched."

"Dan, they're just boulders—that's all," stressed Sam. "Nothing's watching us. Let's not read something into nothing." He took another visual sweep of the area. "We've got enough real problems to deal with. We don't need to create imaginary ones."

"I suppose," yielded Dan. "I guess I need to keep telling myself that nothing in this world is like anything on earth."

Cindy gazed up the lit tunnel. "So how far ahead, do you suppose, is the next cave?"

"It's impossible to say," replied Sam. "But I'm sure we'll find it and the other cave in plenty of time—presuming we keep walking."

Father James, while bearing his torch and lance in one hand, pulled his prayer book from his pocket. "I think I'll take advantage of the light. It's been days since I've read any Scripture."

Dan recalled the three missing pages. He placed his back to the group, shoved his hand into his pocket, and removed the pages. Considering they were once submerged in water, he was surprised that they were completely dry.

"Can you believe it?" asked the priest.

Dan suspected that the priest had discovered the torn pages. He spun. "What?"

"My book! It's totally dry," he exclaimed. "I thought my plunge in the pool would have ruined it."

Dan secretly returned the pages to his pocket.

At Sam's insistence, the group picked up their pace amid the strewn boulders.

The priest began reading to himself.

"Why don't you read out loud, Father?" suggested Cindy. "It might take our minds off this miserable place."

"I don't know. Sam, what do you think?"

"Sure, just not too loudly."

He began reading a reflection on Saint Mark's account of "The Greatest Commandment."

As the priest read, the explorers listened intently, but without disrupting their panoramic scan of their surroundings.

"Father, sorry to interrupt," said Cindy.

"That's okay."

She looked at Sam. "Since the light keeper mentioned an upper level, shouldn't we be searching for an upper passageway, in addition to the wooden carving?"

Dan stepped alongside Cindy. "But we need to find William and Brad."

"I know," she said. "But what if the last two caves are above? Trust me, I don't have any plans on leaving this world until everyone is found. I'm just wondering if we're looking on the wrong level."

Dan couldn't argue, since he knew that the last two caves could be anywhere, including the area above.

"Father, I believe your theory that there are two more undiscovered caves," said Sam. "But what are your thoughts about them being on this level or above?"

He returned the prayer book to his pocket. "It was merely a speculation that the caves would be in proximity to each other. They could be overhead; anything's possible. I'd suggest we look for an upper passageway, while also keeping our eyes peeled for the side caves and the carving. If we find an entry to the third level before we spot a side cave or the carving, we'll determine then what to do. But for now, we're wasting time deciding what to pursue when we haven't found an upper passageway or a—"

"That's what I was going to suggest," interjected Jimmy. He plopped himself on the ground.

"Jimmy, what are you doing?" demanded a disgruntled Sam.

"I've got a rock or something in my boot."

"Come on," complained Sam. "Can't you do that later? We've got to keep moving."

With reluctance, Jimmy rose to his feet.

Three miles up the tunnel, the group reached an area where the walls were lined with burning torches as far as the eye could see.

"What's that?" blurted Dan. He pointed ahead to objects that were resting against the left cavern wall.

"I don't know," said Sam. "Let's check it out. But let's be careful."

The travelers hiked until they were standing at the base of three towering figures.

"They're just stones," played down Jimmy.

"Few things in this world are as they seem," cautioned Sam.

"Huh, they're stone statues," mumbled Cindy.

"Who are they supposed to be?" asked Dan.

Cindy took a step closer.

Sam grabbed her shoulder. "Not too close," he warned.

"I'm fine." She squirmed from his hold. "As Jimmy so scientifically observed, they're just stones." She analyzed the twelve-foot-high rock statues depicting three women. "Well, the one in the middle is obviously Medusa."

"Medusa? Who's that?" asked Jimmy.

Without removing her stare from the stone artwork, she ridiculed, "Jimmy, didn't you take a mythology class your senior year? You can tell it's Medusa by her snake hair."

"And the other two?" questioned Sam.

"I'm not sure," she replied. "I know Medusa was one of three Gorgon sisters, but I don't remember the other names off the top of my head."

Sam extended his torch closer to the statues. "So what's the story of the sisters?"

"Zeus—the chief god in Greek mythology—found the three sisters enticing," she explained. "In jealousy and rage, Hera, his wife, disfigured the legendary beauty of the three Gorgon sisters into unforgettable repulsiveness so her husband—and all mortal men, for that matter—would find them hideous."

Jimmy gazed at their unsightly features. "I'd say her plan worked."

Cindy ignored his rude interruption. "Anyway, Medusa's hair was transformed into deadly serpents and her blue eyes were changed to the color of stone. Consequently, any person or object she looked upon was turned into stone." She took a step closer. "Stheno and Euryale," she recalled, "those were the names of the other sisters. As you can tell from these stone sculptures, Euryale was cursed with no arms whereas Stheno was disfigured with four arms—her own and Euryale's."

"And if I remember from the mythology course, Perseus killed Medusa," added Dan. He stepped alongside Cindy.

Cindy glanced at Jimmy. "At least someone went to class."

"What about the other two sisters?" asked Sam. "Could their stares turn things into stone?"

"Some myths say no, but others say yes. In any event, their touch was equally effective in turning things into stone."

"But if that's mythology—you know—make-believe, then why are the statues here in the underworld?" posed Sam.

All heads turned to the priest.

"Mythology is not my area of expertise," admitted Father James.

THE STONEHEARTED SISTERS

"Though I must admit I find it interesting that the mythological hound Cerberus and these Greek sisters are portrayed in hell."

"But Cerberus was real. We saw it," remarked Dan. He looked at the rock women. "But these statues are—" He stepped closer to the Gorgon sisters. "They're just stone," he said.

Sam grabbed Cindy and Dan by the shoulders and yanked them back.

"Sam, what are you doing?" snapped Cindy.

"I don't want you two taking any chances."

"But Sam, they're not going to hurt us," she insisted. "They're not even alive."

Sam maintained his hold. "Look Cindy, you just said it yourself that anything or anyone Medusa looked upon was turned into stone."

"So?"

"So," he challenged, "who's to say that these statues weren't roaming this tunnel eons ago—long before Medusa turned her sisters and everything else into stone?"

"That's ridiculous," replied Cindy. She struggled to free herself from Sam's grip. "Besides Sam, if that's true, then how did Medusa turn into stone?"

"I haven't the foggiest idea. Maybe she saw her reflection or maybe one of her sisters touched her. At any rate, I don't have any intention of finding out." He took a wide view of their new surroundings. "Look at this place. It's all stone. For all we know, this original world may have been something entirely different than what we see now. Maybe Medusa's glare transformed this entire realm. I mean, it's all rock—the ceiling, the walls, the ground."

"If that's what you believe—that these statues once roamed this world—then why weren't the inhabitants in the side caves turned into stone?" proposed Cindy.

Sam looked at the towering statues again. "Maybe they couldn't enter the side caves because of their abnormally large sizes."

"That's absurd," exclaimed Cindy. "You actually think these statues were living humans in the past?"

"I didn't say anything about them being human," he corrected. "Look Cindy, I just don't want anyone taking unnecessary risks."

As Sam and Cindy debated the likelihood of the stone figures being alive in a distant time, Father James neared the cavern wall opposite the statues. "What's this?" He bent down and inspected footprints in a layer of dust that blanketed the stone ground.

His co-explorers approached.

Jimmy moaned as he placed his weight on his left foot. "That's it. I can't take it anymore," he mumbled. He retraced his steps to the wall, sat on the ground, and kicked off his boot.

At the distant wall, his companions analyzed the footprints.

"Well those are dog tracks," said Dan while pointing to the smaller of two sets of prints.

Sam dropped to his knees for a closer inspection. "And the larger ones must be the light keeper's."

"But I thought the light keeper was going to the upper level," said Cindy.

Sam stood and looked around. "Maybe this tunnel is the way to the upper level."

"I told you we were being watched," insisted Dan.

"There's no one here," maintained Sam.

As his friends discussed their latest discovery, Jimmy flicked a bothersome pebble from the bottom of his sock and replaced his boot. He rose too quickly and stumbled.

His misstep did not go unnoticed by his co-travelers.

Jimmy grabbed an arm of Stheno to regain his balance. His hand was stuck. A spine-chilling cold penetrated to his core. The contact had initiated a cellular transformation. The physical suffering was beyond human comprehension. Jimmy was powerless even to scream. Sadly, throughout the transmutation process he was completely conscious. He watched his hand turn into stone while witnessing one of Stheno's four arms take on the appearance of human flesh. Once his hand and arm were petrified, the metamorphosis invaded his upper chest. From there, the change spread throughout the length of his body. As his eyes were slowly being altered to stone, he watched his friends darting in his direction.

Absolute terror consumed the group.

The teenager's hearing was the last sense to fail him. "Jimmy!" was the last word he heard screamed from Dan's mouth.

The teenager was a lifeless stone statue.

The Gorgon sister, on the other hand, was transformed into an unrivaled, hostile being that was set on revenge for her centuries-long stone captivity—revenge on anything or anyone that crossed her path.

The four potential rescuers ended their dash to Jimmy when Stheno pushed herself from the rock wall.

"Don't let her touch you!" shouted Cindy.

The explorers dropped their torches and assumed defensive postures.

Dan aimed his lance and pierced Stheno's shoulder.

A high-pitched shriek came from the creature. She pulled the lance and dropped it to the ground. The colossal Gorgon sister took a step—the first in millennia—toward the group. The ground quaked. Fortunately for the travelers, the sluggish flow of coagulated blood through her body prevented her from making a rush on the trespassers.

Sam hurled his lance at her chest.

The Gorgon sister wailed loudly. She yanked the weapon and threw it to her side.

"Our lances are useless!" yelled Sam.

Dan walked backwards up the tunnel, while keeping a watchful eye on the Gorgon. He was reaching into the backpack for another lance when he felt the revolver. He pulled it from the bag, aimed, and fired.

Another shrill screech echoed throughout the cavern. The bullet had lodged in the beast's neck. Stheno tried to pull it from her throat but failed. A green puslike substance dripped from her wound to the ground.

"Fire again!" yelled Sam.

Dan pulled the trigger a second time, but nothing happened.

Father James tossed his weapon to Sam.

"Sam! Where are the bullets?" screamed Dan.

The four-armed beast took a step closer to Sam.

Sam was too preoccupied with the advancing Gorgon to answer. Sam aimed, hurled the priest's lance, and pierced one of the Gorgon's four wrists.

Cindy targeted the creature's chest.

Dan continued rummaging through the backpack for bullets.

"Dan, another lance!" yelled Sam.

Within seconds of tossing a spear in Sam's direction, Dan found the box of bullets.

Another shriek reverberated up and down the open cavern. Sam had sunk a lance into Stheno's thigh. Like the other weapons, it was pulled and dropped to the ground.

The group's constant backward movements to escape the creature had left the stone Jimmy a great distance away and leaning against a rock wall. To make matters worse, the injuries inflicted on the Gorgon had only temporary effects. The age-old beast was slowly recovering her renowned strength and speed. With her arms whipping wildly, Stheno effortlessly crushed large boulders in her path. Rocks flew in all directions.

Father James was hit on the forehead by a large stone and fell to the ground.

Before Sam, Cindy, or Dan could race to his aid, the Gorgon was standing over him. She offered a look of victory to the three distant travelers. As she was lowering a hand to the priest, she fell to her back and closed her eyes.

Dan had pulled the trigger. The bullet lodged in Stheno's heart.

"Great shot!" shouted Sam.

Seeing Jimmy beyond the motionless Gorgon, Sam and Dan sidestepped the pus-stained ground and raced to their friend.

"Don't!" yelled Cindy as she dashed to the unconscious priest.

The men stopped in their tracks.

"You can't touch him!" she warned.

"Why not?" screamed Sam.

"If you touch him, you'll probably turn into stone."

"What do you mean probably?" demanded Dan. "Don't you know for sure?"

"Of course I can't say for sure. But I do know that you can't take the chance."

"Then what are we supposed to do? Just leave him here?" asked Sam.

"Give me a minute," she snapped. "He's not going anywhere. We'll think of—"

The priest stirred.

"Father!" Cindy shouted.

"How's Jimmy?" mumbled the priest. He struggled to a seated position and saw his stone parishioner leaning against a far wall. "We have to do something!"

Cindy helped him to his feet.

"That's what Cindy and I were just debating," said Sam.

Father James and Cindy stepped alongside the men.

"Sam, I think there's a pretty good chance that whatever was transferred from the Gorgon to Jimmy also will be transferred to anyone who touches him," she warned.

"I'm willing to take the chance," volunteered Sam.

"Sam, I think she's right," seconded Father James. "There's got to be another way. Besides, if something happens to you—well, we need your help getting the rest of the group home."

Sam knew that the priest and Cindy had valid concerns. In frustration, he kicked a rock which bounced off the cavern wall and nicked Jimmy's stone hand.

"Sam, be careful!" shouted Cindy. "We can't damage him."

"What if we touched Jimmy to the Gorgon?" proposed Dan.

"What do you mean?" asked Cindy.

"If the stone qualities were shifted from the Gorgon to Jimmy on contact, then what would happen if we reversed the process and touched Jimmy to the Gorgon?"

"But we can't touch Jimmy or the Gorgon," reminded Cindy.

"I know, I know," replied an annoyed Dan. "But for argument's sake, do you think that touching one to the other would reverse the change?"

"Probably not," she replied.

"Why not?" asked Dan.

"Because Stheno's dead," said Cindy. She stared at the expired Gorgon.

"But if she's like the other creatures in this world, she won't be dead for long," reminded Dan.

"He's right," agreed Sam. "I think we should give it a try. It's not like we have anything to lose."

"But what if the creature doesn't arise?" asked Cindy.

"I think it's a pretty safe bet that she will," maintained Sam.

The men stepped closer to Jimmy.

"Wait!" yelled Cindy.

They stopped and turned.

"What now?" Sam shouted.

"We haven't figured out how to move Jimmy without touching him."

"Cindy, you just said you weren't sure we'd turn into stone if we touched him," said Sam.

"There's got to be something," she insisted. "And remember, Sam, you keep telling us that we shouldn't take unnecessary risks." She lowered her gaze to the ground and spotted her untied bootlace. "Our socks!" she blurted.

"What about our socks?" asked Dan.

"Put your socks over your hands before you carry Jimmy to the Gorgon."

Dan turned his back to Cindy and faced Sam and Father James. "Actually, that's not a bad idea," he whispered.

"Of course it's not," she said after overhearing his hushed compliment.

The men removed their boots and socks.

Cindy spotted holes in the heels of Dan's socks. "Dan, that won't work." She removed her own socks and handed them to him.

In exchange, Dan gave her the revolver. "If the creature rises from the dead before we get there with Jimmy, shoot it."

With their hands protected, the men took their final steps to Jimmy.

Father James stared in disbelief at the statue. "Poor Jimmy, he always seems to end up in impossible situations."

Cindy, Dan, and Father James nervously watched Sam touch Jimmy.

Thankfully, Sam felt no change in his body chemistry. He exhaled slowly. "I think we'll be okay."

Once the men were in position, Cindy offered one final warning. "Be careful not to break him. If your plan works, I wouldn't want him returning to life missing an arm or a leg." She neared the lifeless Gorgon.

At Sam's suggestion, the men stretched their socks over their forearms.

Sam had just pulled the cumbersome statue away from the wall and was lowering it into Dan's and Father James's waiting hands when a shot was fired. The men fumbled and nearly dropped Jimmy to the rock ground.

"Hurry!" screamed Cindy. "She's coming back to life."

The Gorgon closed her eyes with another bullet through the heart.

With a firm grip on Jimmy, the men lugged him to Cindy's patrol spot where they lowered him to the ground alongside the twice-deceased Stheno.

Jimmy's outstretched rock arm came to rest on the creature's waist.

Sam looked at Cindy holding the smoking revolver. "Are you all right?"

"I think so," she replied in a trembling voice. "The Gorgon opened her eyes so fast that I—yeah, I'm all right."

Sam threw his socks to the ground and took the revolver from Cindy. "You did fine," he praised. He looked at the beast. "At least we know it's capable of rising from the dead."

With the trap set, the travelers snatched their lances from the cavern floor and stepped a safe distance away. They raised their weapons.

Father James whispered a brief prayer.

The explorers were barely twenty feet from the Gorgon when her lower right arm twitched.

Sam steadied his finger on the trigger. His companions aimed their lances in the event the transformation failed and the creature charged them.

"Come on, rise!" shouted Sam.

Before the Gorgon opened her eyes, she opened her mouth and screeched. The cry was deafening. Dan, Cindy, and Father James dropped their lances and covered their ears. Sam, on the other hand, endured the death shrieks with the revolver's aim unchanged.

At once, the color and texture of Stheno's skin on her waist changed. The petrifying process slowly invaded her entire body. In her misery, she tried to break free from Jimmy but her efforts were useless. The irreversible cellular alteration had begun.

As Stheno returned to stone, the statue of Jimmy gradually took on a flesh tone.

The shrill cries of the Gorgon ended.

Jimmy's living arm dropped to his side. Though appearing human, he remained motionless with his eyes closed.

Before stepping nearer their friend, the explorers carefully eyed the Gorgon for subtle movements. Thankfully, there were none.

Stheno was again imprisoned in solid rock.

The group advanced.

Sam dropped to his knees and was extending his bare hand to Jimmy when Dan kicked his arm away. "Sam, are you sure it's safe to touch him now?" he asked.

"Let's hope so." Sam dragged Jimmy several paces from the Gorgon's reach—just in case she came back to life.

To everyone's delight, Sam was unscathed.

Cindy knelt at Jimmy's side and placed a hand on his forehead. "Come on Jimmy, pull through."

"I'm sure he'll be fine," comforted Sam.

"What good is it yelling at him for touching the statue if he can't hear me?" she asked.

"He'll be fine," restated Sam.

Jimmy coughed.

"Jimmy!" she yelled.

The dazed teenager opened his eyes. "What—" He paused to lick his dry lips. "What happened?"

"You touched the statue of Stheno," informed Sam.

With great difficulty, he raised his hands to his chest. "Oh yeah, I remember. I stumbled and grabbed the statue." He glanced at his sore hand. "What the heck?" he blurted. His thumbnail was missing, though no blood dripped from his hand.

"Sorry. I guess I did that," apologized Sam.

"What? Why?" he asked.

"I think I knocked it off when I kicked a rock earlier," he explained.

As much as Cindy wanted to rebuke Jimmy for his carelessness, she knew he had suffered enough. After all, she remembered vividly the harrowing experience of her transformation to a Jezebel plant in the parallel world.

Sam knew that Jimmy needed to rest. But he also was aware of their tight schedule. He helped Jimmy to his feet. "Can you—you know—walk?"

"Yeah, I think so."

"You can lean against me," offered the priest.

"Thanks Father, but I'll be okay once the tingly feeling leaves my legs. It feels like my feet are asleep."

"Maybe the walk will speed up the circulation," proposed Dan. Thinking that his ill-timed comment could easily have been misinterpreted, he quickly added, "But maybe you should rest until you feel comfortable walking."

Jimmy stared at the stone Gorgon. "What a cold woman." He switched his sights to Cindy, taunting, "I think I see a resemblance."

Up to that moment, Cindy withheld her criticisms. His latest jest, however, provoked her. "Jimmy, I'm really glad you're okay. But how is it that Dan, Sam, and Father James can walk past the statue of a woman without touching it and you can't?"

"I was just teasing. Besides, my run-in with the woman was an accident."

"What is it with you and women?" she continued. "First you were enamored with Ceremonia in the parallel world and now you can't keep your hands off a female statue in this world."

"Cindy, can't you wait until he's recovered before lashing out at him?" pleaded Sam.

"That's okay Sam," said Jimmy. He directed his sights to Cindy. "Look, I'm sorry I got all of us in this mess...really...but I'll try to be more careful from now on."

Sam stepped behind the priest to grab an overlooked lance from the ground. "See Father, I told you it would be more interesting once we found Jimmy."

"So I see," he replied.

Once the travelers replaced their socks and boots, each pulled a burning torch from the wall.

Sam helped Jimmy up the tunnel while an armed priest, Dan, and Cindy trailed.

Shortly into their hike, Jimmy ran his hand along the cavern wall.

Cindy witnessed his childlike behavior. "Jimmy, don't touch anything," she teased. "That's what got you in trouble with the statue."

Jimmy shook his head. "We need to get out of this place—fast."

CHAPTER SIXTEEN
Self-Inflicted Punishment

DAN WAS CONSISTENTLY PLAGUED WITH THOUGHTS ON THE location of the portal and tormented with growing worries on whether they'd reach it in time. He grabbed Father James's wrist. "What's the date now?"

"The twenty-fifth," announced the priest.

"What?" exclaimed Jimmy. "It can't be the twenty-fifth already!"

"Trust me, Jimmy, it is," assured Father James.

"But that's impossible," said Jimmy. "Just a short time ago in my cave you said it was the twenty-third."

Sam called to mind his own skepticism when he first learned of the time discrepancy ten days prior. "Jimmy, let's say the watch is wrong and that we've been in this world for just a few days," proposed Sam. He came to a complete stop and held his torch next to Jimmy's face. "Do you want to take the chance that we've been here only a short time, slow our pace, and miss the portal's next opening?"

As was most uncharacteristic, Jimmy remained silent.

In awkward stillness, the hike resumed.

The silence was broken eventually by Jimmy. "I guess it's better to presume that the watch is correct and keep hiking."

"Besides Jimmy, even if we've been here only a short time, I'd rather arrive at the portal before it opens and wait instead of missing it all together," remarked Cindy.

"Speaking of the portal, Jimmy, do you think you'll recognize the wooden carving when you see it?" asked Dan.

"Pretty sure. It's the only thing I remember about my entry."

Sam slowed his pace.

Cindy bumped into him. "What's wrong?" she shouted.

Sam pointed ahead. "Number six," he said.

Cindy stepped to his side. "Another side cave!"

With his torch and lance in hand, Dan raced up the tunnel with the backpack strapped to his shoulders.

"Dan, wait for the group!" yelled Sam. "We don't know what's in the cave."

Sam and the others darted up the cavern.

"Dan stop!" shouted Sam again.

Against his will, Dan slowed his sprint to a brisk walk. "But William's in there!" he claimed.

The group caught up with him.

"How do you know he's in this cave?" asked Sam.

"It's just a hunch," claimed Dan, "but a strong one."

"Dan, if your brother's in there, we'll find him," promised Father James. "But Sam's right. The group needs to stick together. If we get separated, then there's—"

"What the heck?" blurted Jimmy.

The priest's remark and Jimmy's interruption were drowned out by voices.

"It's coming from the side cave," alerted Sam.

The closer the group neared the entry, the louder the noises became.

"It sounds like screaming," said Cindy.

Dan squatted at the cave's entrance and looked inside.

His co-explorers were immediately on their knees and staring through the cave's opening.

"What are they doing?" asked Cindy.

In front of the group lay an inner rock world that was partially aglow. Throngs of inhabitants were engaged in combat, though all remained conspicuously distant from the cave's opening.

"I guess there's no question about the identity of this cave," remarked the priest.

"Wrath," said Cindy.

"Yes, wrath," confirmed Father James.

SELF-INFLICTED PUNISHMENT

"Wrath?" asked Jimmy with a perplexed look.

"It's the same as anger," snapped Cindy. "Honestly Jimmy, didn't you learn anything in high school?"

Jimmy returned his attention to the skirmishes.

Sam scrutinized the area ahead. His gaze was immediately drawn to a rock pillar—roughly a hundred feet inside the cave's opening—that reached from the ground to the unknown darkness above. The stone column was easily twenty feet in girth if not more. He peered deeper inside the cave. "That's strange. I wonder why the inhabitants are fighting on the far side of the pillar and not closer to the entrance."

Father James crawled next to Dan and also took note of the unoccupied area directly ahead of them. "Do you think the cave dwellers are afraid of something near the entrance?" he posed.

"Anything's possible," replied Sam. "Maybe something's waiting around the corner and out of sight."

Dan tried to scramble through the opening but was yanked back by Sam and the priest.

"Dan, if William's here, we'll find him!" shouted Sam. "But for the safety of the group, we need to check out the area before darting inside."

"Come on Sam, there's nothing different about this entry than any of the others," he claimed.

"Nevertheless, we're not rushing in recklessly." Sam extended his burning torch beyond the entrance.

"Sam!" shouted the priest.

Sam's arm and torch had vanished the moment they passed beyond the cave's entrance.

Although Sam felt no pain, the shock caused him to jerk his arm back through the opening.

After examining himself and finding no injuries or visual distortions, Sam glared at Dan. "So there's nothing different about this entry?"

Dan shunned Sam and looked inside the cave again.

"I've never read or even heard of an anomaly like this," admitted the priest.

"But remember, Father, this isn't earth—or even the parallel world for that matter," reminded Sam.

"I know," he acknowledged. "But even though the differences between earth and this lower realm are beyond belief, I still thought there might be—"

"Dan!" screamed Sam.

The teenager had extended his arm and torch through the opening. With strength and determination, he held his arm beyond the entrance, despite the efforts of Sam and the priest to pull it back inside the tunnel.

The moment Dan's arm penetrated the entry, it and the torch disappeared from the opening and reappeared sticking out of the stone pillar.

"Sam look!" shouted Dan.

At his outburst, everyone gazed inside the cave.

Astonishment seized everyone. Dan's arm—from his elbow down—and his torch were jutting out from the rock column nearly a hundred feet away.

Cindy inched closer to the entrance on her knees and accidentally knocked Dan.

Startled, Dan dropped the torch alongside the stone pillar. From the cave's entrance—more than thirty yards away—he felt the ground alongside the rock column for the lost torch. To everyone's amazement, he grabbed it and raised it from the rock floor. "Cool," he exclaimed while waving the torch next to the pillar.

Equally fascinated, Jimmy stuck his leg through the entrance. It instantly vanished and then poked through the rock column.

"Jimmy! Dan!" yelled Sam. "This isn't a joke." He demanded they pull their arm and leg inside.

As expected, the moment Dan drew his arm to his side and Jimmy pulled his leg from the opening, their extremities disappeared from the rock column.

"Give me your arm!" demanded Sam.

"I'm fine," insisted Dan. "It didn't hurt at all."

"Let me see it!" shouted Sam.

After a thorough inspection under the glow of the torches, Dan's

SELF-INFLICTED PUNISHMENT

arm—like Sam's earlier—bore nothing unusual. Sam ordered Jimmy to pull up his pant leg. Again, nothing out of the ordinary was detected.

"All right, everybody move away from the entrance," ordered Sam.

"But Sam," implored Dan, "there's nothing—"

"Now!" Sam shouted.

The young men withdrew a few feet.

Sam meticulously surveyed the cave's opening. Though there was nothing peculiar, he wasn't taking any chances. "There's got to be another way in," he asserted.

"Dan's right," said Jimmy. "It didn't hurt at all."

With no second entrance to the cave, Sam looked at Father James. "What do you think?"

Quite certain that William or Brad was trapped inside—not to mention the fact that the group was losing hiking time debating the issue—the priest grabbed Dan's arm. "We don't want to endanger anyone in this group. Are you absolutely certain you didn't feel any pain?" he asked.

"I'm positive," he replied, "not even a weird sensation like I felt when passing through the oak."

"It might be best Father, if you and the others wait here where it's safe," suggested Sam. "I'll check it out."

"Sam, if William's in there, then I should enter—not you," challenged Dan.

"But this is my responsibility," said Sam.

"Your responsibility? How do you figure it's yours?" demanded Dan.

"When I learned that you and the others were in this world, I made a promise to myself that I'd do whatever it took to get everyone home safely. If you enter this cave and don't come out, then I've failed." He paused to rub cave dust from his eyelashes. "Besides, I'm sure that separating a limb—even if for only a second or two—can't be good for the body. You stay here with the others. I won't be long."

"But Sam, if you're saying that temporarily losing an arm or a leg could cause physical abnormalities later in life, then Dan and I should go since we've already separated a limb," suggested Jimmy.

"So did I," Sam reminded.

"Then maybe the three of us should go," proposed Jimmy.

"Um... Sam, Jimmy's already abnormal," teased Cindy. "Let him go."

"Very funny," Jimmy snidely remarked.

Sam was not persuaded. He looked at Father James and Cindy. "You two stay here with Dan and Jimmy."

"Sam!" screamed the three teenagers simultaneously.

"Enough!" Sam shouted. "There's no reason for all of us to risk our health and our lives."

"Sam, we appreciate your concern. But it'll be safer if we stay together," said Cindy. "After all, you're always telling us that we need to look out for one another."

"But this is different," he said.

"How?" she asked.

"Well for starters—" Sam paused to come up with a convincing reason to separate the group. His thoughts were cut short by growling echoing up the tunnel.

The group spun in fright.

"The light keeper and Cerberus," whispered Dan.

"How did we pass them in the cavern without running into them?" asked Cindy.

"Shh!" ordered Sam.

"Maybe they were on the upper level with the master while we were hiking to this cave," whispered Dan.

A disturbing idea invaded Father James's thoughts. "Or maybe more than one hound and one light keeper patrol the cavern. I mean, the tunnel's enormous."

"I doubt it, since only one three-headed dog is mentioned in mythology," said Cindy under her breath.

"Quiet!" urged Sam again.

The barks grew louder.

"Cerby, slow down!" was heard from beyond the tunnel's curve.

"Well, I guess we got our answer," remarked Cindy.

"What answer?" asked Sam.

"We're all entering the cave," she replied. "There's no way I'm waiting out here to be ripped to pieces by that hound or to watch the light keeper shed its disgusting skin again."

SELF-INFLICTED PUNISHMENT

Father James looked at Sam and nodded. "I think it's wise that we all step inside," he advised.

Sam hated the idea of endangering his friends' lives in the uncharted cave. But at the same time, he knew that if the group skipped the sixth cave and raced up the tunnel, the two beings would be in pursuit in no time—not to mention the fact that William or Brad could be left behind in the cave. "All right," he halfheartedly agreed. "But I'll go first in case something's waiting inside for an ambush." He took another glance down the tunnel.

Although the cavern's bend prevented Sam from spotting the beings, their large shadows cast upon the wall and the intensifying growls confirmed their inevitable arrival. "Wish me luck." He stepped into the cave of wrath.

The instant he cleared the opening, he stepped from the stone pillar. Certain that yelling would alert the stalking beings to their presence, he gave a thumbs-up to his friends at the entrance.

At Dan's and Jimmy's insistence, Father James and Cindy walked through the cave's opening. In a split second, they were standing at Sam's side—one hundred feet away—thanks to the translocation qualities of the cave's entrance.

After a quick look down the tunnel, Dan and Jimmy placed a foot inside the entry. Their second step landed them beside the column.

"Move!" ordered Sam.

"Why?" asked Cindy. "We're a good hundred feet away."

"If the light keeper decides to relight the torches in this cave, he'll end up right where we're standing." He scanned the area and spotted a waist-high boulder only feet away. "Everyone to the rock—now!"

Behind the boulder, the explorers rested on their heels and covertly watched the light keeper and Cerberus linger at the cave's entrance. The hound sniffed the opening and detected a foreign presence. It rammed half its body through the entrance. Its three heads jutted out of the rock pillar. This time—unlike the encounter in the cave of gluttony—the hound spotted the fugitives.

Cerberus snarled and snapped its drooling jaws at the group. It lunged.

In fear, Father James and Cindy fell to the ground.

Behind the boulder, Sam, Dan, and Jimmy aimed their weapons.

The light keeper's firm yank on the chain foiled the dog's next meal.

But Cerberus persisted. It made another attempt to leap through the cave's entry.

Just when the travelers sensed certain discovery, the light keeper delivered a mighty tug on the chain at the cave's entrance. The hound's heads were pulled from the rock column to its caretaker's side. The beings resumed their patrol up the cavern.

Terrified to move a muscle, the travelers remained motionless for what seemed several minutes. Their sights were fixed on the entrance in the event the creatures returned.

"Are they gone?" whispered Father James.

"Yeah, I think so," answered Sam.

"That was too close," said Cindy. She rose to her feet with her sights still focused on the entry. Her companions stepped from the boulder.

Sam examined the walls, the ceiling, and the residents of their new rock cell. "That's interesting," he mumbled.

"What's that?" asked Jimmy.

"That," said Sam. He pointed to a group of nearby inhabitants.

During Cerberus's partial emergence through the stone pillar, a handful of residents had unknowingly strayed in front of the rock column—an area that was previously free of cave dwellers. The remaining multitudes clashed in the expanse behind the pillar. Each cave dweller was still screaming at his or her adversary. Obviously, they didn't notice the hound's heads sticking through the column.

Cindy was baffled with a two-man skirmish nearby. "Something's not right," she declared.

"Yeah," said Dan. "One guy seems real, but the other one looks—" He paused to study the man in question.

Father James stepped nearer the scuffle. "You can almost see through one man—like he's an image or something," he declared. "If I didn't know better, I'd say that the condemned residents of this rock world are the ones who look real and are inciting the fights, whereas those who appear almost transparent are illusions."

"They sort of remind me of the people in my cave, but not quite," compared Dan.

SELF-INFLICTED PUNISHMENT

"What do you mean?" asked Sam.

"Like I said earlier," Dan reminded, "even though the inhabitants in my cave were semitransparent, they had definite dimensions and obvious weight. If you bumped into them, you knew it. But here—" He made a sweeping pass of his lance through an illusionary being. "But here, they have no mass. I mean, you could walk right through them."

"Yeah, they look almost—I don't know—shadowy," stated Cindy.

Jimmy threw a punch at an image. His fist passed through the being without the slightest resistance. "It's like hitting air," he exclaimed.

Sam looked at the priest for a possible explanation. "Father, I agree with you. I also think this is the cave of wrath. But do you have any idea why these people are tormented by make-believe enemies?"

The priest took a wider glance at their surroundings. "Obviously, I can't say for sure," he admitted, "but if you're asking me to guess, I'd say that since these inhabitants wasted the majority of their earthly lives provoking fights and taking pleasure in conflicts—"

"Whoa! Did you see that?" shouted Jimmy.

"That was weird," exclaimed Dan.

Barely four feet from the group, a middle-aged man—in the midst of screaming profanities—delivered a jab at his illusionary enemy. The moment his fist invaded the spatial boundaries of his ghostly opponent, his own head was knocked back. He had sustained a broken lip. He raised his hand to his mouth and became even more enraged when he discovered blood. He delivered another blow. Unfortunately, the outcome was the same.

"My gosh!" cried Cindy. "It's like he's punching himself senseless."

The man delivered a third jab at his rival. Again, the pain was inflicted on the attacker.

"I wonder why my punch at the image didn't come back at me," posed Jimmy.

"Probably because it wasn't your assigned enemy," guessed Sam.

Dan attempted to distract the near-hypnotic stares of his companions, shouting, "Come on, we need to find William and Brad!"

"Sorry," said the priest who slowly turned from the bleeding cave dweller. He quickly spun again to view the assault.

"Father, hurry!" shouted Dan.

"You're right; you're right," he acknowledged. "We need to find the others."

Before the other travelers snapped from their spellbound gazes at the self-inflicted punishment of the cave dweller, Sam, Cindy, and Jimmy watched him try to bite the arm of his illusionary adversary. Immediately, blood dripped from his own forearm. Infuriated, he released another blow. On grazing the image, the instigator was knocked to the ground.

"Cool!" exclaimed Jimmy.

"Come on," ordered Father James. "We're wasting time."

"Sorry Father," apologized Sam. "It's just that I've never seen anything so bizarre."

"Hey, what would happen if he spit in the guy's face?" blurted Jimmy.

"Jimmy, don't even go there," admonished Sam. He dragged his young friend from the cave dweller's side.

"Why don't we split up into two groups," suggested Cindy. "It'll save time."

"I don't think that's a good idea," advised Sam. He stared at the darkness that shrouded the ceiling. "I'm sure this cave has its guardian like all the others." A puzzled look surfaced. "That's odd."

"What's odd?" asked Father James. He also looked overhead.

"I hadn't noticed it before," said Sam.

"Noticed what?" urged the priest.

"The ceiling between the cave's entrance and the stone column is completely black," alerted Sam. "But the ceiling behind the rock pillar is free of the darkness." He stepped to the far side of the column. "Here, you can actually see the rock ceiling. It must soar fifty feet."

"So what do you think the darkness is?" asked Father James.

Sam lowered his sights. "I haven't the foggiest. But let's hope we don't find out."

"Sam, if we break up into two search parties, we'll cover the area in half the time," restated Cindy.

SELF-INFLICTED PUNISHMENT

Unsure whether or not something was watching their every move, he denied her request.

"But Sam, there's nothing going on here except bickering and an occasional scuffle," she reminded.

"That may be true, but I'm sure there's a guardian in this place too." He took another unlimited view of the cave. *But where?* he thought.

"For our safety, Cindy, I suggest we stick together and be on the lookout for our friends and any creature that may be watching over this place," suggested Father James.

"All right," she grumbled. "But I still say we'd cover more ground in less time if we split up."

Sam placed his hand on her shoulder and assured, "We'll still reach the portal in time."

The group left the middle-aged male inhabitant who was gasping for air from a botched stranglehold on his archenemy. The travelers entered deeper into the battleground beyond the stone pillar.

Below the unobstructed ceiling, Father James watched an elderly woman smack the face of a partially transparent man and then massage her own cheek to relieve the pain. "It certainly puts a new twist on the golden rule," he said.

"The what?" asked Jimmy with a confused look.

"You know, do unto others as you would have them do unto you."

"Oh, yeah," he mumbled.

Cindy was slammed to the ground by an unruly cave dweller who had unintentionally elbowed her in the ribs. She glared up at the old man and was surprised that he never offered her even a passing glance. He was determined to slay or at least harm the make-believe figure before him.

Dan helped her to her feet. "Cindy, we have to watch our steps," he cautioned.

She darted to the priest's side. "Father, why don't these people stop their endless fighting?"

"Probably because they can't."

"Why not?" she asked.

The priest effortlessly waved his lance through the image of a young woman. "Like I started to say earlier, since these people probably spent most of their earthly lives causing fights and arguing with others, then any other way of life would be foreign to them. Actually, it wouldn't surprise me if the cave dwellers' worst enemies in life were represented in the shadowy figures before them." He glanced at a resident beside him. "They'll most likely live out their eternities among the dead doing what they did best while among the living—fighting."

The explorers sidestepped the violent clashes in search of William and Brad.

CHAPTER SEVENTEEN

The Image and Likeness of God

WHAT SEEMED NEARLY AN HOUR INTO THEIR SEARCH—THOUGH in reality it was almost eight—Dan spotted light shining on the rear wall of the cave. "Hey Sam, look!" he shouted. He pointed his lance to the lit area.

Sam scanned the rear wall in the distance, but failed to spot a torch. "That's odd. I wonder where the light's coming from," he said.

"Come on Sam, let's check it out," insisted Dan.

The teenager had taken only two steps when he was yanked by the backpack straps. "Let's be careful," warned Sam.

"I will. But we have to hurry." Dan broke free from Sam's hold.

After seeing the men change their course, the other travelers were soon on their heels.

Nearer the wall, Dan noticed that the beam of light was originating from a flashlight on the ground. In a flashback, he recalled that he and William each had grabbed a flashlight from their bedroom before dashing to the church. He raced the remaining distance, carefully dodging the quarrelsome inhabitants.

"Dan, wait up!" yelled Sam.

"Where's he going?" asked Father James.

"He's checking out a light at the back of the cave," replied Sam.

The explorers reduced the distance between themselves and the rear wall.

"Look!" exclaimed Cindy. She slowed her pace. "It's William!"

"You had no right to steal thirteen years of my life," screamed an enraged William. "You have no right to exist. You're—" His shouts of revenge were cut short. He released an uppercut at his make-believe rival.

Father James stared at William's deformed enemy. "What is it?"

"That's a Reclaimer, Father," answered Cindy.

"My gosh, it's hideous," exclaimed the priest.

As expected, William's act of violence against the Reclaimer was inflicted on himself. He fell to the ground.

Dan dropped to his brother's side. "William!"

His brother gave no response. In William's mind, he and the Reclaimer were alone in the cave.

The Reclaimer's appearances were sickening. Father James looked away from the imaginary being. "So this is what you battled in the parallel world?" he asked.

"Not exactly," informed Cindy. "Ours were real."

Though he had envisioned what the Reclaimers might look like from the travelers' detailed descriptions, even their accounts paled in comparison to what stood only feet away.

William grabbed a rock, jumped to his feet, and hurled the stone at his opponent. The moment it passed through the unreal Reclaimer, a gash appeared across the length of William's forehead. Blood dripped.

Determined to prevent further injuries, Dan sprang to his feet and tackled his brother. Both men hit the ground.

William threw him off, scrambled to his knees, and was prepared to attack his half-serpent enemy when Sam and Jimmy charged him and pinned him to the ground.

In shock, Dan stared at his restrained brother. William's eyes were filled with an intense hatred.

William glared at the Reclaimer. "You'll die! If it's the last thing I do, you'll never terrorize another human being!" He fought to free himself from his friendly captors. His constant squirming and will power to assault the vision paid off. He escaped Sam and Jimmy's hold and rushed the Reclaimer. He hadn't even grazed the image when he fell backwards. The intended attack was wreaked upon him.

Sam, Jimmy, and Dan pounced on him.

"How do we keep him down?" yelled Jimmy.

"Hold his legs!" shouted Sam. "Don't let him—"

William jabbed Sam in the ribs. Another punch was delivered. Sam lost his grip.

Father James crashed to William's side. "Hold him still!"

"We're trying!" they shouted.

The priest ripped open his shirt, yanked the bloody tee shirt from his side, and covered William's eyes.

Immediately, William's profanities and struggles ceased. The Reclaimer had been stolen from his vision.

The explorers were astonished. The imaginary half-man and half-serpent creature had also vanished from their sights.

"Where did it go?" shouted Cindy. She spun, expecting the Reclaimer to be hiding in the shadows.

"What just happened?" asked Jimmy.

"I wouldn't be surprised if William's hatred of the Reclaimers was so intense that his mind projected the creature into a visible image that he and everyone else could see," speculated Father James. "Once his eyes were covered and he was robbed of his sight, the ghostly figure vanished into thin air. For all we know, his eyesight was sustaining the image. Perhaps that's the power of this particular cave."

"But Father, you need the tee shirt around your waist," insisted Sam.

He stood and exposed his injury. "I'm fine. It's nearly healed."

Sam looked down at the blindfolded William. "I guess his hatred of the Reclaimers was more intense than any of us suspected." He glanced back at the priest standing over him. "But Father, we can't risk reopening your wound. Take the tee shirt back and I'll cover William's eyes with my handkerchief."

"I appreciate it, Sam, but William needs a thick covering over his face."

"But my handkerchief would—"

"Sam, for his safety, we can't take the chance of him looking at anything in this cave," warned the priest. "I'm sure he could see through your handkerchief. For his protection he has to stay blindfolded."

Sam unwillingly agreed.

"Father, if all of us saw the image of the Reclaimer, then why didn't we react like William?" asked Cindy.

"I suppose that since thirteen years of his life were stolen by the snake creatures—not to mention the physical and mental torment he must have endured at their hands—he developed an intense loathing of them." He looked at William. "While all of you despised the Reclaimers, I'm sure it was nothing compared to William's feelings toward them."

Throughout their conversation, William remained motionless.

Becoming concerned, Dan shook his brother.

Understandably exhausted, disoriented, and dazed from his twenty-five-day skirmish with the Reclaimer, William was slow to stir.

"William, say something," implored Dan.

"Dan?" he whispered.

"Yeah, it's me."

William raised his hands to the blindfold.

Dan grabbed his wrists.

"What are you doing?" shouted William. "What's going on? What's all the screaming?"

"Look William, I'm not sure where to begin," said Dan, "but we're in a cave and—"

"A cave?"

"Yeah," confirmed Dan. "Anyway, when we found you…well… you were fighting a Reclaimer."

"What do you mean I was fighting a Reclaimer? What are you talking about? I was just now thrown into the oak."

Father James knelt alongside the brothers. "William, for the safety of the group, you need to keep the tee shirt over your eyes until we're out of this cave."

William recognized the voice. "Father James?" he asked.

"Yeah."

"You ended up in the tree too?" asked William.

"I'm afraid so."

"But where are we?" questioned William. "And why can't I take off this covering?"

"We're in hell," divulged Jimmy. "And you can't take that tee shirt off until we're in the open tunnel."

Again, William recognized the voice. "Jimmy, you're here too?"

"Yeah, so is Cindy."

"But I don't understand," admitted William. "You weren't in the church the night—" Only now recalling his previous comment, he blurted, "What do you mean hell?"

"We'll fill you in later," promised Father James.

Dan and Sam helped the blindfolded William to his feet and assisted him to a nearby wall.

"What do you mean we're in hell?" he asked again.

The men lowered him to the ground and leaned him against the cave wall. As he recuperated, Cindy pointed out the time irregularity between the two worlds while Sam and Father James explained in great detail how they arrived at their theory that they were in hell.

"But that's impossible. This has to be the parallel world," exclaimed William.

"I wish," said Sam under his breath.

Father James looked at his watch. "Sam, again, I don't mean to sound uncaring, but we really should move."

"William, like we just explained, we're in a race against time," reminded Sam. "We need to find the other cave. Are you strong enough to walk?"

"Yeah, I think so."

After William's flashlight was recovered, Sam and Dan guided the sightless William among the fighting inhabitants toward the cave's exit. Along the way, the hikers further updated him on their encounters in the unholy realm.

Cindy had just begun describing the tapeworm that was disguised as a green apple on the rock table in the cave of gluttony when Dan spotted the rock column ahead.

Dan interrupted her story. "William, we'll be through the cave's exit in a few minutes. Once we're in the tunnel, then you can pull off the tee shirt."

The group was several feet in front of the stone pillar when Sam stopped in his tracks.

"What's wrong?" asked Dan.

"This isn't right," he said.

"What's not right?" said Dan.

"Escaping—it can't be this easy."

Cindy overheard their supposed dilemma. "Maybe—just maybe—this is one cave that doesn't have a guardian," she proposed.

"That would be nice, but we have to be realistic," replied Sam.

"Does every cave have a guardian?" asked William.

"Apparently so," said Dan. "Each cave that we've searched has had a guardian whose purpose—we think—is to make sure the inhabitants don't escape. Sometimes the guardians conceal themselves against the ceiling. And other times, they've hidden behind a waterfall or buried themselves in the ground."

As Dan was describing the previous hiding places, the travelers scanned the walls, the ground, and the ceiling for a guardian.

"I can't even see the ceiling," declared Cindy. "It's covered in darkness."

"That's what bothers me," revealed Sam. "How do we know that something isn't masked in the darkness and watching our every move?"

"Sam, it's probably just what you said—darkness," said Dan. "Remember when we were in the tunnel heading to the Gorgon statues and I could have sworn that we were being watched?"

"Yeah."

"Then you probably also remember telling me that I was overreacting and not to read something into nothing since we had enough real problems to deal with." Dan stared at the overhead darkness. "It's entirely possible that we're worrying about something that isn't a threat." He switched his sights to the cave's opening. "The exit is less than a hundred feet away. Come on, we need to move. We're running out of time."

"Dan's right," agreed Father James. "Standing here idle won't help us reach the exit—or the portal for that matter. I suggest we walk, but keep our eyes peeled for any movements between here and the opening."

"All right," yielded Sam. "It's just that I don't like the idea that it's been this easy."

THE IMAGE AND LIKENESS OF GOD

With William's arms stretched across Sam's and Dan's shoulders, they resumed their hike to the opening.

The moment the travelers reached the cave's exit, Sam turned to Cindy. "For the record, I wasn't complaining that it was too easy—just surprised, that's all."

The explorers walked through the exit.

"What the heck!" shouted Sam.

He and his friends had stepped from the rock pillar and remained standing in the cave of wrath.

Dan looked over his shoulder at the stone column. "Walking through the exit from inside the cave landed us back here, just like when we stepped through the entrance from the open tunnel."

"But it doesn't make any sense," said Cindy.

"Wait a minute," said Father James. He stuck his arm through the column and watched it materialize at the exit—but on the inside. "It's like a mini-portal between the cave's opening and this pillar," he deduced.

"Cool!" exclaimed Jimmy. He jumped into the column and reappeared two feet inside the cave's opening.

"Jimmy!" yelled an irate Sam from a hundred feet away.

"You mean there's no way out?" asked Cindy.

"We'll find an exit," assured Sam. "I promise."

Enraged with their mind-boggling predicament, Cindy thrust her arm into the pillar at Jimmy's point of entry. Her tightened fist burst from the cave opening and knocked Jimmy on the back of the head.

"Hey, watch it!" he shouted from the exit.

Sam and Dan set William on the ground.

Sam knew that Jimmy wouldn't hear him over the screams of the twelve inhabitants who were battling their personal illusions near the cave's opening. "Wait here. I'll be right back," Sam directed. He recalled that Jimmy had entered the pillar facing forward and reappeared a couple feet inside the cave's opening. *Maybe if I walk backwards into the column, I'll appear on the opposite side of the exit—inside the tunnel*, he thought. With his back facing the pillar, he took several steps back, disappeared, and then reappeared a hundred feet away. Unfortunately, he remained inside the cave. *There's got to be a way out of this place,* he thought. He was distracted by movement from the corner of his eye.

Jimmy was kicking his leg into the cave's exit to repay Cindy for her recent punch.

"Jimmy!" yelled Sam. "This isn't a game. We need to find a way out. Every second lost is a second we may need at the portal."

"I was just—you know—checking it out."

Sam yanked his teenage friend by the arm and attempted to escape the cave by walking through its exit. As before, they ended up stepping from the column.

"Sam, I don't get it," said Cindy.

"What's that?"

"When we first stepped through the entrance—from the open tunnel—we landed at this pillar." She pointed to the column behind.

"Yeah," said Sam.

"And then when you and Jimmy stepped through this same pillar you both ended up back at the entrance, but inside this cave. That's what doesn't make any sense. You'd think the reverse—walking into the pillar—would transport us back into the open tunnel. But now that we're trapped inside this cave, it doesn't matter if we step into the exit or into the pillar. Either way we're stuck here."

"I'll admit it sounds hopeless," replied Sam, "but I'm sure we'll find a way out."

"But why didn't Jimmy and I—I mean our entire bodies—materialize at the pillar when we shoved our arm and leg through the entrance from inside the tunnel?" asked Dan.

"Maybe the fact that you stuck only part of your bodies through the entry had something to do with it," guessed Father James.

"Like I said, it doesn't make any difference if we step into the cave's exit or into the pillar," restated Cindy. "Either way, we never reach the open tunnel." She looked at the overhead darkness. "Maybe we're not meant to leave this place."

Sam spun in her direction and rebuked, "We can't think that way, much less talk that way. It's precisely that bleak outlook that will prevent us from reaching the tunnel."

"Fine," she snapped. "Then how do you propose we break free from here?"

"I'm working on it."

"But time's running out!" she cried.

Sam scratched his chin. "Maybe we should think about this logically."

"Logically?" she challenged. "There's nothing logical about this cave. Nothing is as it appears."

"That's exactly what I mean." Sam stepped away from the rock column. "Obviously, certain things in this cave are illusions—like the make-believe inhabitants and possibly the darkness above."

"If you're suggesting that the real exit is an illusion, then we'd see it—or at least an outline of it—just like we see the outline of the inhabitants' imaginary enemies," posed Dan.

"Possibly," said Sam. "But what if the cave's exit is camouflaged? For all we know, it could be staring us in the face."

"So you're saying the exit is through one of these walls?" asked Cindy.

"It's only a guess," admitted Sam. "But yes, I think it's entirely possible." He took note of Jimmy's dubious look. "Of course, I'd gladly entertain other ideas," he sarcastically added.

"Actually, I think your idea makes sense," said Father James.

"You do?" asked Jimmy.

"Yeah. Like Cindy just said, nothing is as it appears. A cloaked exit would certainly prevent the inhabitants from fleeing. The way things stand right now, if cave dwellers try to leave through the visible opening, they're instantly transported back to the pillar." Father James watched a struggling torch flame surge in brightness before dying. "That's it!" he shouted.

"That's what?" asked Sam.

"The torch!" exclaimed the priest. "If the light keeper enters this cave to light the torches, he must leave somehow."

"So what do we do?" asked Cindy. "Search the walls for an exit?"

Sam shook his head. "That would take too long, especially considering the size of this cave. We don't have a lot of time as it is."

"As long as we're on the subject of logic," said Dan, "I'd think that if the exit is hidden on one of these walls, then it's probably on the one where we entered."

"Why's that?" asked Cindy.

"Because the exit would have to lead to the tunnel so the light keeper could continue his rounds."

Sam looked at the priest, seeking a gesture of approval or rejection of Dan's theory.

The priest nodded.

Sam stepped closer to the column. "Okay then, everyone wait here while I check out the wall at the exit."

"I'm going with you," insisted Dan.

"No!" shouted Sam. "Look Dan, we still haven't seen the guardian of this cave. If it makes its appearance, you need to help protect the group."

"But Sam, what if the guardian is at the exit?" he challenged. "Who'll defend you?"

As Sam tried to concoct a convincing response, Father James seconded Dan's suggestion. "Sam, he's right. It's too dangerous to do it alone."

"All right," yielded Sam. "Dan can come along." He demanded, however, that Father James, Cindy, Jimmy, and William—whose eyes were still covered—stay put and be on the watch for a possible guardian. Thinking he may have offended William, he squatted alongside the young man and advised him to keep his ears open.

"Sure," he replied.

Sam and Dan left their torches behind, gripped their lances, and jumped into the stone pillar. The moment they reappeared two feet inside the cave's opening, they dropped their weapons and ran their hands along the wall in search of a secret opening.

From a hundred feet away, Father James, Cindy, and Jimmy watched for a sign of discovery from their friends.

"William!" yelled Father James. The priest lunged at him and grabbed his hands, foiling his attempt to pull the tee shirt from his face. "It's not safe to remove it—not yet."

"But Father, I want to see what's going on."

Cindy dropped to William's side. "We'll be out of here in a few minutes. Then you can take it off." She squeezed his arm. "Promise me you won't remove it until we're free from this cave."

He remained silent.

"William, promise me!" she shouted.

"Okay, okay," he agreed, "as long as it's just a few more minutes."

Alongside the cave wall, Sam and Dan felt the rock with growing anxiety. Both knew that the group's escape from the sinister realm depended on finding the cave's disguised opening in record time.

"Sam, this is taking longer than I thought," said Dan. "Maybe we should get the others to help."

"Absolutely not! That's exactly what I don't want."

"Why not?"

"With everyone busy trying to find a hole in the wall, it would be far too easy for William to yank the tee shirt from his face," warned Sam. "I want your brother resting on the ground with at least two sets of eyes watching over him at all times. If he rips the covering from his face, it'll take two or more people to restrain him. And given his vulnerable condition, I want the others close by in case a guardian makes its appearance. Besides, the breather will do the others some good."

"I guess that makes sense," voiced Dan.

"And remember, we've been pretty lucky exiting caves in the past," reminded Sam. "Hopefully, we'll get lucky again and avoid the—"

"Hey Sam, look at this!" Dan knelt alongside a set of footprints.

Sam stepped nearer, asking, "Are you thinking what I'm thinking?"

Dan eyed a burning torch only yards away. "Yeah, they're similar to the tracks of the hound and the light keeper near the Gorgon statues."

They followed the footprints until the markings vanished at the base of the wall.

Sam placed his hands on the rock where the trail ended. His forearms fell through the wall.

After a brief moment of exhilaration, Dan saw a worried look surface on Sam's face. "What's wrong?" he asked.

Sam pulled his arms from the rock. "I just got a horrible thought. If we suspect this cave is riddled with illusions, then what if this exit leads somewhere other than the tunnel?"

Though Dan felt fairly certain that the opening was a path to the tunnel, a part of him shared Sam's apprehension. "If it leads somewhere other than the tunnel, then both of us should step into the wall.

If we find ourselves in another part of hell, we'll need each other's help."

Sam refused to endanger his friend. "Wait here. I'll be fine."

"Sam, either I walk in with you or I'll step in after you. Either way, we're both going through the wall."

Sam agreed, but with great hesitancy. "Grab the lances at the fake exit."

"Why?"

Sam stuck his arms through the rock again. "I'll show you. Get the weapons."

Before Sam pulled his arms from the wall, Dan was standing at his side with the lances in hand.

Sam took the weapons, traced the border of the opening, and placed the lances on the ground—one on either side of the exit. "This way," he explained, "if it leads to the tunnel, then the others will know the point of entry." With the weapons marking the eight-foot-wide hole, he ordered, "Let's go."

Dan and Sam stepped into the rock.

"They found a way out!" shouted Cindy.

Their joy, however, was short-lived.

Cindy, Jimmy, and the priest fell to the ground.

A tremor had rocked their cave world.

Father James, Jimmy, and Cindy rose unsteadily to their feet. William, although baffled with the sudden quake, kept his promise to Cindy. He remained blindfolded and seated on the ground.

"What the heck was that?" exclaimed Jimmy.

"I don't know," admitted the priest.

Hundreds of inhabitants—both near and far—labored to stand in the midst of ongoing aftershocks.

The travelers took an extensive view of their rock confinement.

Cindy stared overhead. "It's probably nothing, but I've got a bad feeling about the darkness. It's just not right."

"What do you mean?" asked Father James.

"In the other caves we could see large sections of the ceiling. But in this cave—at least in this particular spot—the ceiling is hidden in shadows. I mean, it's so dark that the light from the torches can't break through the barrier."

"I'm sure it's nothing to worry about," played down Father James. "All the caves have their own peculiarities. For all we know, the darkness may be another illusion like Sam suspects."

Cindy redirected her attention from the ceiling to the cave wall, asking, "Do you think they made it into the tunnel?"

Before anyone could voice their opinion, Sam and Dan stood in the open cavern—on the opposite side of the cave's fake exit.

A round of applause echoed throughout the cave.

The men walked through the opening and stepped from the rock pillar alongside their friends.

"You found the exit!" congratulated Cindy.

The nearby inhabitants who were making great efforts to stand did not go unnoticed. "What happened to them?" asked Sam.

"It was the weirdest thing," recounted Father James. "Just seconds after you and Dan walked through the wall, the cave shook violently. All of us, including many of the cave dwellers, fell to the ground."

As the priest was detailing the quake and its subsequent aftershocks, Dan was guiding William to the column for a short cut to the cave wall.

Sam grabbed Dan's arm.

"What?" shouted Dan.

"We're not taking any chances," ordered Sam. "We'll walk to the new exit."

"But Sam, walking to the exit will put us awfully close to the rowdy inhabitants," reminded Cindy. "Besides, stepping into the pillar will buy us some lost time. Remember, we need every minute we can get."

Sam looked at the overhead darkness and posed, "Don't you think it's odd that during the entire time we've spent in this cave not a single tremor was felt until Dan and I stepped through the wall? For all we know, our breach may have announced our presence to something or someone."

"Sam, I'm sure the mini-portal is safe," maintained Jimmy.

"Maybe, but maybe not." He looked from face to face. "Look, we've come too far on our journey to be careless or to start taking chances now."

"I'm inclined to agree with Sam," said Father James. "It's just a hundred feet or so. We can walk it in a few minutes."

"All right," agreed Dan. "But we need to move fast. Remember, there's always the possibility that the exit could relocate—like the one in my cave."

"Good point," said Sam. "Let's move."

Dan and Sam guided the blindfolded William among the warlike cave dwellers.

Another tremor rocked the cave. Like before, its magnitude dropped the escapees and many cave dwellers to the ground.

"Is that what you felt earlier?" asked Sam.

"Yeah!" shouted Cindy to be heard over the vulgar language nearby. "Didn't you feel it in the tunnel?"

"No!" He and Dan helped William to his feet. Sam looked up and froze.

The darkness was descending.

Not wanting to alarm his co-explorers, Sam refocused his attention on the exit and shouted, "Move!"

Cindy sensed fear in his voice and looked up. "The ceiling is falling!" she screamed.

"We'll be fine!" yelled Sam. "Keep moving!"

With all chins pointed upward, they were terror-stricken. The darkness dropped with each step to freedom.

Fascinated with the phenomenon, Father James raised his lance as high as he could and pierced the darkness. A shrill cry was heard from the overhead shadows. After several tugs, he released his weapon from the sticky barrier. He gasped. The tip of the lance had been obliterated.

"What the—" exclaimed Cindy who witnessed the event. "It melted the metal point!"

Even Sam was stunned. "Don't panic! Keep moving!" he shouted.

Given the alarming rate at which the shadows were falling, the group was forced to race to the exit in a stooped position.

"William, stay in a hunched position!" shouted Dan.

"Why?"

"Just do it!" yelled Sam before pushing William's head down.

Another tremor dropped the travelers to the ground.

THE IMAGE AND LIKENESS OF GOD

Screams echoed throughout the cave.

On their hands and knees, the travelers looked behind in the direction of the shrieks. They watched in horror as the darkness came to rest on the heads of several close by inhabitants.

Engrossed with slaughtering their imaginary adversaries, the cave dwellers were unaware of their inescapable doom. The moment the boiling tarlike substance dripped over their eyes, their opponents vanished. The inhabitants, however, were powerless to escape the sticky grasp of the foreign darkness despite numerous attempts. The merciless hold of the shadows prevented them from even collapsing to the ground. Unlike drowning in rising water, they were being drowned in descending darkness.

The explorers remained motionless on all fours, gawking at the sight before them. Another tremor rocked the cave.

As William was rising from the ground, the tee shirt fell from his face. In his crouched posture, he looked ahead and spotted a make-believe Reclaimer. He released his bottled-up rage and rushed at the creature. Fortunately, his head never made contact with the plunging darkness. Unfortunately, the effect of the intended collision was returned to him. He fell backwards on the ground.

With the burning substance still descending and the exit still thirty feet away, Dan and Sam tried to cover William's eyes.

In the fierce struggle, William pushed, kicked, and punched until he was on his knees, ready for another charge.

On witnessing Sam's and Dan's failure in restraining William, Father James darted from behind—in a slouched position—and struck William on the back of his head with his lance. The older brother was knocked out cold. He hit the stone ground again.

"Father!" screamed Dan.

"Run!" yelled the priest. "We haven't got time."

Sam suspected that the tee shirt would come in handy before their journey's end. He snatched it from the ground and shoved it down his shirt.

The darkness had descended to such a depth that the travelers were crawling the remaining distance. With no options available, Sam and Dan dragged an unconscious William.

Suddenly, terrifying hisses were heard from behind.

Although reaching the exit was crucial to their escape and survival, the strange noises forced the group to look behind again.

The dark death had reached the necks of the drowned cave dwellers.

The hissing sounds grew louder. Dark winged creatures oozed headfirst from the burning substance.

Cindy watched the beings swirl dangerously close to the immobile cave dwellers. "What are they?"

"Princes of this kingdom!" yelled the priest. "Move!"

The mere touch of the demons' wings against the cave dwellers melted their exposed skin. Their flesh dripped to the cave floor.

Father James realized then that the death of the inhabitants wasn't enough for the demonic princes. Annihilation of their bodies—since they were made in the image and likeness of God—was their one and only purpose of existence.

Though shocked beyond words at the horrid mutilation taking place, Sam yelled, "Move! It's directly above!" With great pains, he and Dan pulled William closer to the exit.

Father James—who was bringing up the rear—offered another look behind. He froze momentarily in fear. He spotted a pair of red eyes on a winged demon that was hovering around the skeletal remains of an inhabitant.

As quickly as the eyes appeared, they disappeared.

Father James rolled onto his back and stared at the falling darkness. Four feet above, he saw another pair of red eyes glaring down at its next victim. The eyes vanished within the burning shadows. "Faster!" he shouted. He rolled onto his stomach. "Move!"

The explorers hastened their crawl.

Sam and Dan were the first to arrive at the lances which marked the exit's border. They pulled themselves and William through. Cindy, Jimmy, and Father James were just seconds behind.

Father James yanked his legs through the opening and grabbed the two weapons from the ground. Only the upper halves of the lances were spared. The lower portions were nonexistent.

Father James examined the worthless lances. "I'd say we made it in the nick of time!"

Sam wasn't convinced that the searing darkness wouldn't seep through the cave's opening. "Come on—move!" he ordered.

The travelers jumped to their feet and raced up the tunnel. Sam and Dan supported William.

A great distance into their escape, Sam slowed his pace. He and Dan lowered William to the ground.

Dan glared at the priest. "You didn't have to knock him unconscious!"

"I don't know what came over me," apologized Father James. He knelt at William's side. "In my entire life, I've never raised my hand in anger."

"Father that wasn't anger," corrected Sam. "You did what was necessary for William's safety—and ours."

"Are you sure it wasn't anger?" posed the priest.

"What do you mean?" asked Sam.

Father James stood and leaned against a tunnel wall. "I mentioned earlier that many people have a predominant sin or vice. I also pointed out that no one is completely immune to the temptations of every capital sin. Maybe I was more prone to wrath than I thought."

Dan realized that he had judged prematurely. "Sorry about blaming you, Father. Sam's right. You acted with our safety in mind." He glanced at his brother. "If you didn't react when you did, I suppose all of us would have been charred."

"Thanks Dan," said the priest.

William stirred.

"William!" shouted Dan.

He opened his eyes.

"Are you all right?" asked Dan.

"Yeah, I think so." He displayed a puzzled look. "What happened?"

"You tried to charge another Reclaimer," shouted Jimmy.

"What?"

"Yeah," seconded Cindy. "Don't you remember?"

"No, not really." He rubbed the back of his head.

"I'm afraid I gave you that bump," admitted Father James.

"You? But why would—"

"He had to," interrupted Dan, "to save your life."

"Thanks Father, I guess," said William.

"So William, you really don't remember the Reclaimer?" asked Jimmy.

"The last thing I remember," recounted William, "I was rising to a stooped position when the tee shirt fell off." He massaged the back of his head again before offering a grin to the priest. "Remind me never to pick a fight with you."

The priest returned the grin.

"Wait a minute, Sam," reminded Cindy. "What about Brad?"

Focused on fleeing the falling darkness with their lives, everyone had unintentionally forgotten about Brad.

Sam glanced down the tunnel. "I sure hope he wasn't in there—or at least not below the burning darkness."

Father James suspected that his friend was entertaining needless guilt. "Sam, I doubt that Brad was in the cave of wrath. But if he were—and if he were fighting with an illusion below the darkness—trust me, we would have spotted him."

"I hope you're right," mumbled Sam.

"Come on. Let's search for Brad in the last cave," suggested the priest.

"So Father, do you think Brad is a man of lust?" asked Jimmy.

"I can't believe what I'm about to say. But yeah, I hope so. I have no desire to revisit any of the previous caves."

After the tee shirt was tied around the priest's waist, the travelers pressed on.

With William fully recovered and able to walk on his own, Dan pulled the final three lances from the backpack—two to replace those destroyed by the scorching shadows and one to arm his weaponless brother.

Since the travelers had understandably left their torches behind during their scramble to the cave's exit, Sam reached for a glowing torch that was wedged in the cavern wall. He led the group up the tunnel in search of Brad Blaze—the original objective that launched their adventures into the sinister realm.

CHAPTER EIGHTEEN
The Neanderthals

As the explorers hiked up the tunnel, Cindy's thoughts reverted to the previous cave. "Father, why do you think the cave of wrath was cursed with burning darkness that concealed the fallen angels?"

"It's hard to say for sure," he replied, "but I suppose there could be a connection between the hot substance and the fact that the inhabitants were hot with rage for the better part of their earthly lives."

"That makes sense," said William.

"But William, since our return from the parallel world, I've never known you to have a hot temper or fly off the handle with rage," admitted Cindy.

William touched his bleeding forehead—the result of his attempt to hurl a rock at the imaginary Reclaimer in his cave. "I never told anyone, but the few times my personal Reclaimer, Daedalus, was off investigating a castle disturbance and my thoughts were my own, I developed an intense hatred of the snake-men and secretly swore revenge against them someday. Unfortunately, Daedalus's superior mental powers prevented me from retaliating. I remember sitting in the Great Tower as if it were only yesterday, plotting ways to defeat the Reclaimers and flee the castle." He looked back to the cave of wrath. "I guess something in the cave brought it all to the surface."

Jimmy sensed that William was uneasy revealing the hidden and dark years of his childhood and teenage years. He successfully changed the subject, saying, "I suppose we know now why most of the inhabitants in the last cave avoided the area at the entrance."

"Yeah," said Sam. "I'm sure that after previous deaths they knew that the darkness covered only the front area of the cave near the exit. It's probably safe to say that all the inhabitants—at one time or another—had experienced the burning effects of the darkness and avoided the exit at all costs."

"Except for the few who wandered into the forbidden zone during our visit," recalled Dan. "Maybe they were the newest arrivals who hadn't been melted by the darkness yet."

"And as we've experienced firsthand, I'm sure that the cave dwellers who died during our exit will rise to life and resume their unending skirmishes," predicted Father James.

Dan saw the priest glance at his watch. "What's the date now?"

"The twenty-seventh," he replied.

"If it's already the twenty-seventh, then that means we have only three days to find Brad and escape this place," alerted William.

"Speaking of our escape, William, do you remember anything after leaving earth?" questioned Cindy.

After a sneeze brought on by the plentiful cavern dust, he related, "I saw Father James and Dan grabbed by the limbs. But I never actually saw them thrown into the oak because of all the commotion in the church. Then I was tossed into the tree." He sneezed a second time.

"Then what?" prodded Cindy.

"The next thing I remember, I was trying to pull the tee shirt off my face."

"Hey Sam, I just thought of something," said Dan.

"What's that?"

"How come some of us remember details about our caves and others don't? I clearly recall the anacondas and the golden chest in my cave, for example, but William doesn't remember a thing."

Dan raised a baffling question. Sam glanced at Father James for a possible explanation.

The priest also was stumped. "Maybe, just maybe, the degree of recollection is related to the degree of obsession."

"What?" asked Jimmy.

"I mean," clarified the priest, "perhaps William was so consumed with wrath and revenge that he was oblivious to his surroundings, whereas our obsessions may have been less severe." He looked at William. "But I'm sure that I would have reacted the same way if I had suffered what you did at the castle for all those years."

William shrugged his shoulders. "Sorry, I don't remember anything."

"There's no need to apologize," said the priest.

William gazed up the tunnel and then to the cavern walls. "If this is hell like you claim—and since there's no oak tree—then where's the portal that will lead us home?"

"When Jimmy entered this realm, he remembered seeing a piece of wood with a serpent carving on it," explained Dan.

"I don't understand," said William.

"Apparently, since Jimmy was the only one who was thrown backwards into the tree, he claims he saw a wooden carving on his entry into this world," clarified Cindy.

"I didn't claim to see it—I saw it," corrected Jimmy.

"We believe you," said Sam.

"So our exit out of hell—if this is hell—is through a wooden carving?" posed William.

"Apparently," said Sam who remained in the lead, clutching his lance and the only torch.

"Hey guys!" shouted Dan.

Sam darted to the rear of the line, demanding, "What's wrong?"

"Look!" Dan pointed to the cavern wall.

Sam extended the torch and illuminated what appeared to be either an enormous crack in the tunnel wall or a very narrow entry to another side cave.

"What is it?" asked Jimmy.

"Shh," ordered Sam. He tried to make out the shouts beyond the opening.

"Sam, do you think it's another cave?" asked Cindy.

"I'm not sure." He placed the torch inside the tight opening. "From what little I can see, I'd say it's about five feet deep, but only a couple feet wide."

Cindy looked into the restricted entry and then at her larger co-traveler. "Maybe Jimmy should wait for us out here," she suggested.

"Very funny," snapped Jimmy. He rested his hand on his belly. "It'll be a piece of cake."

"Cake!" she blurted. "That's exactly what caused—"

"Quiet!" ordered Sam. He raised the torch alongside the priest's face. "Father, since I can't see beyond the opening, I can't tell if it's an entrance to another cave or simply a large crack. The only way to know for sure is to step inside—any thoughts?"

Even in the dim light, Father James detected restlessness on the faces of his traveling companions. He knew how eager everyone was to reach their final destination within three days. "We really don't have a choice," he replied. "We're running out of time."

"All right," said Sam. He faced the opening again. "But we'll have to enter in a single file."

Jimmy sucked in his gut; Cindy chuckled.

Sam took the backpack from Dan, strapped it to his back, and squeezed into the narrow entry with his lance and the burning torch at his side. Several side steps later, he emerged from the hole in the wall. He lowered the torch to the ground—inside the cave's tight opening—and brightened the path for his friends.

William and Father James also walked sideways through the gap, stepped over the torch, and waited alongside Sam.

Jimmy was not as lucky. Fortunately, his minor setback was quickly remedied when he inhaled and freed his belly from the tight passageway.

Cindy and Dan made a swift entry and exit.

Certain that Cindy had noticed his embarrassing jam in the crevice, Jimmy grabbed Sam's arm and raised the torch alongside Cindy's face. "Don't even start."

Cindy directed her smirk to the ground.

Sam moved the torch nearer to Dan. "I think you may have bought us some time."

The explorers stood within the largest cave yet. Though a handful of torches were stuck in the wall at the entrance, only one was aglow. Strangely, in the sinister realm, a newborn flame required the mysterious qualities of the light keeper's saliva. It was impossible to reignite a torch from an existing flame. The travelers had discovered this on many occasions.

Sam pulled the burning torch from the wall and handed it to the priest before taking a panoramic view of their newest rock prison. "Wow, look at the size of this place!" exclaimed Sam.

The number of inhabitants easily surpassed those of all the previous caves combined.

Sam had taken only one step when Father James pulled him back.

"What's wrong?" asked Sam.

"Nothing—not yet," replied the priest. "But all of us need to practice self-control." He saw Jimmy's blank look. "If this is the cave of lust, then we're all at risk. No one is immune to temptations of the flesh." He eyed the Clay brothers and then Jimmy. "It may even be more alluring to the young at heart. Let's be careful."

"Good advice," said Sam. "And let's stick together. If anyone sees someone giving into the temptations of this cave, I want—" He noticed Cindy staring at the ground only several paces away.

Father James stepped away from the group and lowered his torch. Six teenage corpses fell under its glow.

William approached the priest. "I wonder what drew them to the exit." He turned and faced the central part of the cave. "The throng of inhabitants is over there."

"Maybe they were trying to leave this place," suggested Dan. "I wouldn't blame them."

Father James left the dead bodies and assumed the lead. "Let's move, but with added caution."

Without warning, the six corpses sprang to their feet and dashed to the multitudes.

The priest took a few moments to calm his nerves from the shock. "Let's find Brad and get the heck out of here." The stench of carnal sins made him queasy. He retched. "The smell is horrible," he exclaimed.

"It's disgusting," seconded Sam.

Cindy covered her nose. "Where's it coming from?"

Jimmy took a prolonged whiff before claiming, "I don't smell anything."

William and Dan displayed bewildered looks. The brothers couldn't detect the odor either.

Father James's initial hunch that the young men could be more vulnerable than the others was confirmed. He stepped alongside the young men. "I think you guys should wait at the entrance."

"Why?" asked Dan.

Father James covered his nose. "Since you three can't smell the foul odor, then you're obviously more likely than the rest of us to fall victim to the cave's physical temptations."

"Father, that's ridiculous," insisted Jimmy.

"Is it?" he posed.

Fearful that the young men might easily surrender to one of the many enticements in the cave of lust, Sam reconsidered his original comment that the group stick together. "Maybe you three should head back and guard the exit."

"Guard it?" snapped Dan. "From what—corpses?"

"Besides, thanks to the police postings around town, I know what Brad Blaze looks like," reminded Jimmy. "If we're all searching for him, we'll find him that much sooner and be on our way home. Remember, we've got only three days."

"But we can't take the chance of you three becoming prisoners of this place," stressed Sam. "Lord knows we don't have extra time to free you from the powers of this cave if you fall prey."

"Sam, I also saw the police postings around Lawton," disclosed William. "I'm sure I can help. You've been telling me all along that the group has survived and made it this far because everyone worked together. Splitting us up now won't help our situation."

William had a point and Sam knew it. He also knew that extra eyes scouting for Brad would speed up the rescue mission. But he couldn't shake the safety factor. He was troubled with what lured the six teenagers to the exit and what killed them. As much as it pained him to admit it, he had a gut feeling that the three men would be safer with the group—presuming they could control their carnal desires.

After a heated discussion, William, Dan, and Jimmy were permitted to join the search party, but not before receiving a stern warning from Father James to keep their senses and their desires in check.

The march continued.

The inhabitants at the back of the masses were slowly engulfed in light as the travelers stepped nearer with the two torches. The group noted immediately that the cave dwellers were facing a distant wall. They entered the mob.

Screams were heard at the far wall, followed by unruly cheers within the mob.

Cindy placed her face next to Sam's ear. "What are they cheering at?"

"Probably something up ahead," he said.

The search for Brad resumed.

After a loss of precious travel time and after suffering an occasional elbow to the face from the disorderly cave dwellers, the explorers found themselves standing at the front of the crowd.

As they surveyed the area ahead, their sights were drawn to six niches roughly a hundred feet away that were hewn into the rock wall. Each dwelling—or domicile—was several feet wide. An attractive, indecently clothed woman occupied the first niche.

"Whoa!" shouted Jimmy. "She's hot!"

"Jimmy!" reprimanded Cindy. She punched him in the jaw, knocking his gaze from the alluring domicile dweller.

"Hey!" he exclaimed while rubbing his face. "I was just paying the redhead in the first hole a compliment."

"Jimmy, keep your eyes lowered!" ordered Sam.

"Redhead?" questioned Dan. "She's a blonde."

"Actually, she's more of a brunette," corrected William.

Certain that the young men were becoming enamored with the woman, Sam ordered all of them to stare at the ground.

Given the group's immediate fascination with the recesses in the wall, they had overlooked a pool of water that lay between them and the niches which was partially concealed by an embankment on their side.

At Sam's command to lower his sights, Jimmy noticed the pool which extended the width of the cave. "What's with the water?" he asked.

The travelers stepped forward and gazed into the pool.

"Maybe it's to prevent the mob behind us from storming the domiciles and reaching the woman," guessed Cindy.

Dan spotted six vines dangling halfway across the water. In the poor light, they seemed to vanish in the overhead shadows. "And what's with the vines?" he posed.

"I haven't a clue," replied the priest. "And why are they hanging over the water and not closer to our shoreline?" he added.

No one responded. All were busy scanning their peculiar surroundings.

Across the pool, five more domicile dwellers materialized inside the five empty niches.

"Wow!" exclaimed Jimmy. "The woman in the second hole is even more beautiful than—"

"Jimmy!" yelled the priest. He yanked his friend's arm and redirected his gaze. "Don't stare. She'll be your downfall."

Cindy stared at a shirtless young man in the fifth domicile. "Whoa!" she exclaimed.

Sam ordered her to look away.

Certain that the perfect bodies on display were quickly spellbinding his friends, Father James tried to snap them from their hypnotic-like stares. "Come on!" he ordered. "We need to find Brad!"

William disregarded the priest's directive and expressed his longing for the woman in the fourth domicile.

"Gawking at these supposedly perfect models before us will delay or possibly prevent our escape," warned the priest.

In a dazed state, the young men and Cindy stepped closer to the pool.

Several restless male inhabitants dashed from the throng to the water's edge, leveling the travelers in the process.

The men dived into the pool. Their carnal appetites were insatiable.

Haunting screams erupted from the water.

The six rescuers jumped to their feet and peered down the embankment. The priest shuddered at what was unfolding before him. Thousands of bloodworms shot from the water's depths, squirmed atop the pool, and sank their miniature teeth into the men. Though several bloodworms couldn't inflict serious injury, hundreds feasting upon an individual proved deadly. The cave men fought to reach the opposite side and crawl to safety. Their strength quickly waned as they were drained of their vital fluids.

Cindy closed her eyes and turned her head from the turbulent water. In the end, however, her curiosity won out. She faced the horrific aftermath. The bodies were transformed beyond recognition; their skin cleaved to their bones. The corpses sank below the surface.

Father James was determined to draw his friends' attention from the watery deaths. "Come on, we need to find Brad!" he shouted. "We don't want him to suffer the same fate."

"He's right," said Sam.

As the group turned from the bloody pool to face the multitudes, William noticed one of the vines twitch. He cocked his head. With the absence of even the slightest breeze in the cave, he questioned its strange behavior. As he was pointing out the anomaly to his co-travelers, the six vines moved to the shoreline.

No less than fifty men and ten women bolted from the mob and jumped for the vines.

The travelers narrowly escaped the stampede. They watched the inhabitants push and elbow one another for property rights to the vines. In the midst of punches, bites, and jabs, a handful of men and women fell to the ground. These were the lucky ones. As the clashes continued on the vines during the transport to the domiciles, the unlucky cave dwellers were knocked into the water. They met the same misfortune as the previous impulsive male inhabitants.

The waters churned. Shrieks rose from the pool.

In the end, only one inhabitant maintained a victorious grasp on each vine.

Although the group knew that finding Brad was critical, the interactions between the cave inhabitants and the domicile dwellers across the water intrigued them. The travelers inched closer to the pool.

Each of the four male and two female cave dwellers who were triumphant in battle over the waters raced to one of the six niches. After a passionate embrace with the domicile dwellers, the couples reclined in the secluded openings.

The female domicile dweller in the first niche jumped to her feet, turned sideways, and vanished.

"What the heck!" exclaimed Dan.

To the group's astonishment, the woman reappeared when she faced the throng of applauding inhabitants across the water.

"She's only two-dimensional!" shouted Dan.

"What do you mean?" asked Jimmy.

"She's got height and width, but no depth," explained Dan.

"Are you sure?" Jimmy stared into the first niche.

Again, the woman turned and vanished. On her reappearance, her lover jumped into her arms.

"What's happening?" asked Jimmy.

Sam was uneasy with the young men staring at the woman. He grabbed their attention by stating, "Look guys, like all the creatures in this realm, I'm sure there's a purpose for her unnatural abilities." He grabbed Jimmy and Dan by the arm and pulled them from the water's edge. "But we'll not be around long enough to find out," he concluded.

A grating sound was heard.

To Dan, the noise reminded him of stone rubbing against stone.

"What is that?" asked Cindy. She stared into the fifth niche where the grinding sound seemed to originate.

The male domicile dweller was standing and embracing a female cave dweller. The two-dimensional man stepped from the woman, turned to one side, and disappeared.

At once, the side walls of the niche slammed against the female cave dweller and crushed her. A shrill scream was heard—then silence.

In the first domicile, the woman released her embrace from the male cave dweller, turned sideways, and vanished. The same death ritual was played out. The stone walls flattened her male lover. His screams of unmatched agony echoed throughout the cave of lust.

"Heavens!" exclaimed the priest. "We've got to find Brad and get out of here—now!"

The travelers turned from the gruesome scene and neared the front lines.

"I hope Brad didn't cross the water before we got here," expressed Sam. "Let's pray to God he's still in the mob. If he's—"

His comment was drowned out by screams from the remaining domiciles. Four cave dwellers were crushed. Though their death screams were painfully loud, they were no match for the shouts of victory from the throng of inhabitants who interpreted the shrieks of the squashed cave dwellers as cries of delight.

The group spun and faced the uproar in the niches. When the walls of the first domicile separated, they watched the woman kick the male corpse into the pool. She was preparing for her next suitor. And from the looks on the cave dwellers' faces, every man was eager to jump at the opportunity.

The vines shifted from the domiciles to the shoreline.

"Focus!" ordered the priest. He turned and extended his torch to the crowds. "Brad has to be in there somewhere. Let's go!"

The group returned to the throng.

The woman in the first domicile beckoned the mad mob which caused another charge. The travelers were pushed to the front of the line.

More than sixty inhabitants were exchanging blows with their cave mates for possession of the six swaying vines.

"Come on!" yelled Sam. "Back to the mob. We need to find Brad!"

They stepped into the throng again—all except Father James.

Sam noticed the motionless priest from the corner of his eye and backtracked. "Father, what's wrong?" he asked.

The priest was focused on something at the shoreline. "I think that's Brad near the fourth vine."

Sam squinted. "It's hard to tell in this poor light."

Father James took several steps closer to the vine. "It is Brad!" he shouted. He sprinted to a gang of men who were jostling each other for the vine. "Brad!" he yelled.

The man in question refused to acknowledge the priest. He was busy wrestling with his co-inhabitants for control of the vine.

The group dashed after the priest.

Father James dropped his lance and torch and jumped on Brad's back to frustrate his quest for possession of the vine. Within seconds, four other rescuers were on Brad.

Knowing that the loss of a weapon could likely result in the loss of a life, Cindy snatched the lance and the burning torch from the ground.

Obsessed with reaching the woman in the fourth niche, Brad

burst with rage and fought to escape the rescuers' hold. But he was outnumbered.

As the five men struggled to pin him to the ground, Dan grazed the vine with his lance. The other liberators were too preoccupied restraining Brad to notice what Dan saw.

Two drops of green fluid dripped from the vine to Dan's hand. *What in the world?* he thought.

The injured vine began its journey across the shoreline, carrying one male victor along its predetermined path.

Brad refused to conquer his animal desires. He continued fighting his potential deliverers.

For Brad's safety—not to mention the time factor—Sam and Father James knew what they had to do. They tightened their fists and took advantage of their trapped friend.

After several jabs, Brad was out cold.

"Now what?" asked William.

"What do you mean?" asked Sam.

"Do we wait for him to wake up?"

"Not on your life," snapped Sam. "As soon as he wakes, he'll be mesmerized with this cave again."

The group followed Sam's gaze across the water.

Five cave dwellers dropped from five vines and dashed to the domiciles. The wounded vine coiled around its male inhabitant and pulled him beyond the overhead darkness.

"Where's the vine taking him?" asked Cindy.

"I don't think it's a vine," alerted Dan.

Father James took his torch and lance from Cindy, placed the flame under Dan's chin, and asked, "What do you mean it's not a vine?"

"When we were busy with Brad, I accidentally nicked the vine with my lance."

"And?" urged the priest.

Dan looked at his stained hand. "Green fluid dripped from the vine."

"Dan, all plant life has fluids," informed Cindy. "That's normal."

Screams were heard from the overhead darkness. Silence followed.

"But that's not normal!" shouted Dan.

In record time, Sam and Dan raised the unconscious Brad between their shoulders.

"Let's go!" yelled Sam.

Cindy strapped Sam's backpack over her shoulders and grabbed his torch. She raced with her companions into the horde of inhabitants. A short distance into the mob, she screamed for help.

Two middle-aged men had taken an interest in Cindy.

William, Jimmy, and Father James bolted to her side.

The lovesick cave dwellers were dragged from Cindy and thrown to the ground. The three travelers escorted Cindy through the maze of ill-mannered men and women.

Suddenly, rocks blasted from the ceiling above the niches and fell into the pool.

The explorers turned and witnessed a dark object dropping into the water.

"Run!" shouted Father James.

The group raced deeper into the crowd.

Death screams filled the air.

Cindy suspected that the victims were close by; Dan suspected that he had provoked the cave's guardian with his lance.

Only now thinking that the lit torches were announcing their location, Sam ordered Father James and Cindy to kill the flames. In near darkness, they blended in with the cave dwellers.

"Do you think it can smell us?" whispered Cindy.

"Shh," demanded the priest.

High-pitched screams reverberated throughout the rock world—two female cave dwellers had been crushed in the domiciles.

The unidentified creature crawled from the crowds and scaled a rock wall.

"What is it?" exclaimed Dan. He looked closely at the most unusual creature he had ever seen—including those in the parallel world.

In the faint light, Father James looked intently at the beast until it was hidden in the ceiling's shadows. "It can't be," he whispered. "It just can't be."

"What?" blurted Cindy.

"The creature," he said.

"Father, do you know what it is?" asked Sam.

"I'm not sure." The priest's stare never left the overhead darkness.

"Then what do you think it is?" pressed Sam.

Father James lowered his gaze before responding, "During a vacation several years ago at a skiing village in Austria, the townspeople told me about a reptile creature in Alpine folklore known as the tatzelwurm or the Swiss dragon. They described it as a serpent-like creature—nearly fifty feet long—with two clawed front paws directly behind its feline head and stubby neck."

"You mean a large snake with a tiger's head?" asked Cindy in disbelief.

"An oversize head to be exact," corrected the priest. "Its razor-sharp teeth, pointed ears, and exceptional night vision for stalking prey in the dark were widely known in the Alps. The entire length of its body—including its head—was covered with scales. Since it had no hind legs, it dragged its lengthy body with its front undersized legs. The claws would certainly explain why it climbed the cave wall with ease. And its armored skin obviously made the beast impenetrable to the bloodworms in the pool. I've been told that it used to hunt livestock in the Alps. Legends also speak of its ability to release a toxic odor that's fatal to humans."

"Father, what do you mean it used to hunt livestock in the Alps?" asked Dan.

"The last reported sighting of the tatzelwurm was in the late 1800's," recalled the priest, "though many Alpine residents refuse to accept its extinction. Regardless of whether or not it exists on earth, it's obviously alive and well in hell." He looked to the cave's exit before directing, "I think we should move."

"But quietly," stressed Sam. He and Dan lugged Brad closer to the cave's opening. Thankfully, the newest member of the group was out cold throughout the ordeal.

The travelers spotted a young man and woman in an embrace near the cave's exit.

"It would appear that some inhabitants are attracted to their cave mates," whispered the priest.

"Maybe since they were at the back of the crowd and figured their chances of reaching the domiciles were slim to none, they coupled with another co-inhabitant," suggested Cindy.

At a safe distance from the young lovers, they watched the couple end their embrace and walk sideways into the narrow exit.

The moment the woman stepped inside the crevice behind her partner, the walls of the opening—like those of the domiciles—crushed them instantly. They didn't even have time to scream.

"What's with the walls in this place?" asked Jimmy with a hint of fear in his voice.

"I don't know, but there's got to be some logical explanation," replied Sam.

The explorers stepped from the throng.

Father James glanced at his watch. "We better think of something fast. September twenty-seventh is almost history."

"There's got to be another way out," maintained Cindy. "Maybe there's a second opening to this cave."

"But we don't have time to look for another one," insisted Father James.

"Since the exit is just a short distance ahead, I say we check it out more closely," suggested Sam. He and Dan carried the unconscious Brad to the cave's opening and set him on the ground. In minimal light, Sam searched the area for a mechanism that would permit a crush-free release from their confinement.

"Sam, what about the rock wall by the domiciles?" asked William. "Maybe there's another exit there."

Sam was too absorbed examining the closed exit to respond.

A creak was heard. The crack in the wall gradually widened.

"Run to the mob!" ordered Sam.

"What? Why?" blurted Cindy.

"Just do it!" Sam demanded. He and Dan grabbed Brad's arms and dragged him from the exit. In record time, the seven were hidden within the hostile environment.

Light streamed through the expanding exit.

The explorers watched the deceased young lovers tumble to the ground. Moments later, a tall being came into view carrying a torch. It kicked the flattened corpses from its path.

"The light keeper," whispered Cindy.

"Shh," said Sam.

Next, Cerberus stepped from the opening in the wall.

Death screams were heard from the domiciles at the distant end of the cave. The light keeper grinned before spitting on the extinguished torches along the wall near the cave's exit. Within seconds, eight torches were burning. On two occasions, Cerberus snarled and tried to break free of its chain. Fortunately, the light keeper prevented its attempts at escape.

With several torches illuminating the cave's opening—and with his assigned chore completed—the light keeper and the hound departed through the passageway. Incredibly, the crevice remained open.

For several minutes, the travelers were completely silent until they presumed that the beings were a considerable distance up the tunnel.

"I think it's safe to move," announced Sam.

The group dashed to the exit again.

"So, how is it that the light keeper and Cerberus left this place unharmed, but the lovers were crushed?" posed Cindy.

"Maybe the light keeper released a lever or something at the opening which kept it from closing," proposed Jimmy. "I'm sure he's made the trip in and out of this cave millions of times to light the torches."

"The torch!" shouted Sam. He and Dan lowered Brad to the ground. Sam raced to the wall and yanked a glowing torch. He retraced his steps to the group. "Maybe the torch had something to do with it."

"What do you mean?" asked Cindy.

"Don't you remember?" he posed. "When I stepped into this crevice earlier, I was carrying a lit torch and I held it inside the cave's opening until everyone was through. The light keeper also had a torch when he entered and left this cave. But the young lovers weren't carrying a torch."

"But why did the walls stay closed on the lovers when they left, but remained open on the light keeper and Cerberus when they left?" asked Cindy.

"I'm not sure," admitted Sam. "But maybe the walls slam when they detect movement in the absence of light."

"Sam, I'll admit that anything's possible in this world, but do we want to risk our lives to prove your theory?" she asked.

"No, but I will," he replied.

"Sam, you can't be serious!" she exclaimed.

Jimmy jumped two feet.

The previously deceased lovers had sprung from the ground and raced to the mob.

He attempted to play down his overreaction. "Muscle spasm, I guess."

Cindy grinned and shook her head.

Sam stuck his torch and arm inside the cave's opening. "I don't hear any creaking."

"Sam, there's got to be another way out," pleaded Cindy.

He pulled his arm from the passageway. "There could be another way out, but we're running out of time." He looked at the men. "Jimmy, William, grab some torches. We're out of here."

"But Sam," implored Cindy, "what if—"

"Cindy, if we don't take this chance, I can promise you that we won't reach the portal in time," said Sam. "Then all our risks and adventures in this world were for nothing."

In her heart, she knew that Sam would never suggest a plan of escape if the odds of losing outweighed the odds of winning. Recalling the critical time factor, she decided to put her life on the line for her friends. "Sam, can you and Dan carry Brad through the opening?" she asked.

"We'll be fine." The men lifted Brad.

With the backpack strapped to her back, she snatched a torch from William. "Wish me luck!" she shouted.

"Cindy wait!" screamed Sam. He dropped Brad to the ground.

It was too late. Cindy had already crossed the threshold of the crevice.

Sam dashed to the exit, placed a torch between the rock walls, and saw her step into the open tunnel. "Don't you ever do that again!" he yelled.

"Why not?" she asked. "You thought it was safe. I trust you."

He turned from the entry, mumbling, "Teenagers."

With a torch and lance in one hand—and Brad in the middle—Sam and Dan stepped into the opening.

Cindy extended her torch through the opposite end for maximum brightness.

Within seconds, four explorers were standing in the cavern.

"Send the portly one through!" shouted Cindy.

"I think she means you, Jimmy," said William.

"It's muscle!" he yelled.

"Whatever," was heard through the hole in the wall.

Jimmy had placed only one foot inside the entryway when he was seized from above and lifted from the opening.

The tatzelwurm had returned.

The captured teenager dropped his torch and weapon in the struggle. His screams forced a handful of cave dwellers at the rear of the crowd to turn and take notice.

Father James also dropped his torch and lance and leaped for Jimmy. With a loose grip around Jimmy's legs, the priest fought to maintain his hold.

The snake creature smashed its coiled lower body against the cave wall to drop the priest. Though the tatzelwurm failed in releasing him, it was successful in knocking its initial victim unconscious. Jimmy's head had bashed into the rock wall.

William aimed his spear several feet above Jimmy. The weapon missed its moving target, bounced off the rock wall, and fell to the cave floor. In a mad scurry, William recovered his lance, as well as the other two grounded weapons. The two lifeless torches, however, were left behind.

Sam and Dan heard the screams and commotion from beyond the opening. They grabbed their torches and lances and bolted into the cave of lust.

The beast was targeted again. Sam's perfect aim pierced its lower body. It recoiled slightly. Jimmy was lowered a few feet.

"The torch!" yelled the priest. He caught Sam's torch and extinguished the flame against the tatzelwurm's serpent body.

Although the beast was covered with scales, the blaze got its attention. In response, it flung the priest and Jimmy a great distance from the cave's opening.

With the tatzelwurm's head and upper body still cloaked in darkness, Sam, William, and Dan dashed to their co-travelers. Father James was uninjured; Jimmy was still out cold. As the men tried to rouse the teenager, a cave-rocking thud was felt and heard. The rescuers collapsed to the ground.

The snake creature had dropped to the cave floor, landing between the exit and the men.

Father James continued shaking Jimmy. "Wake up!" he shouted.

Jimmy remained motionless.

The tatzelwurm, however, did not.

Dan and William hurled their weapons at the approaching creature. One nicked the beast's ear. The other grazed its feline head.

The reptile suspended its crawl in the direction of its prey, but only momentarily.

The distance between the hunter and the hunted was eventually reduced. The unearthly-size creature planted its two clawed front paws on the rock ground and advanced another five feet.

"Jimmy!" shouted the priest again.

There was no reaction.

With William still clutching Jimmy's and the priest's recovered lances, the men had two weapons in reserve. Regrettably, they knew that to inflict a deadly wound—or at least a temporary one until it rose from the dead—the creature had to crawl much closer. The wait was excruciating.

The tatzelwurm paused and analyzed the terrain and its potential victims.

Maybe this is the first time it's confronted armed escapees, thought Sam. *Maybe its injuries have forced it to think twice about advancing.*

Sam's assumption was flawed. The creature pulled its body five feet nearer the trapped men.

With two lances at the ready, William and Dan stood motionless. They waited for the opportune time to strike.

Cindy deserted the unconscious Brad, grabbed her lance and torch, and re-entered the cave.

"Cindy, get back!" yelled Sam.

The reptile detected backward movement. It rotated its head and saw another morsel. It slowly redirected its cold-blooded stare to its five-course meal ahead.

Cindy evaluated the situation before her—four trapped men, a motionless teenager, only two lances raised for release, and a deadly beast salivating between the men and the exit. *I wonder if I could use the allurements of this cave to our advantage,* she thought. *All I need—*

The tatzelwurm crashed its lower snakelike body at the cave's exit, narrowly missing Cindy.

Her close brush with certain death was exactly what she needed to set her plan of escape into motion. She slowly set her lance and torch at the cave's exit and raced behind the creature to the throng of cave dwellers.

"Cindy stop!" yelled Sam. "You can't—"

In addition to Sam's order going unheeded, it was also interrupted by Jimmy stirring on the ground.

The creature advanced another five feet.

Jimmy reeled to his feet which further incited the tatzelwurm.

Once the creature was within forty feet, the two lances were soaring through the air. William's impaled a front paw; Dan's sank into its stubby neck.

The creature roared and continued its attack, though at a slower and painful pace. Quite unpredictably, it stopped when it was no more than twenty feet from the weaponless men. Blood dripped from its neck to the ground.

From the masses, Cindy observed her friends' dismal situation. She gathered her courage and charmed a male inhabitant. Once several more men were enthralled with her fraudulent flirtations, she raced toward the tatzelwurm. During her sprint, she glanced back and was pleased that the eight male cave dwellers were still in pursuit. As she had hoped, the lustful cave men were more interested in satisfying their carnal desires than in avoiding the temporary end of their lives. The boisterous arrival of eight charging men did not go unnoticed by the wounded beast.

Cindy slowed her pace, allowing her suitors to reach her. The moment they were on her heels, she dropped face forward only yards from the tatzelwurm.

The cave dwellers stood over their defenseless prize.

Although bleeding from the neck, the creature couldn't resist a meal so close at hand. Immediately, it assumed a cobra-like posture and arched its upper body and feline head twenty feet overhead. It opened its mouth, dived, and pinned two cave dwellers to the cave floor with its clawed paws. Six terrified inhabitants fled to the safety of the mob.

With the tatzelwurm busy ripping flesh from the men, Cindy crept to her friends. "Let's go!" she ordered.

The explorers made the most of the beast's feeding frenzy and slipped to the exit with Dan and Sam helping Jimmy. They grabbed Cindy's lance and burning torch at the cave's exit. With three torches aglow—William's, Dan's, and Cindy's—they entered the crevice.

Sensing backward movement again, the tatzelwurm gulped the remains of the second inhabitant, jerked its head, and rushed toward the last traveler who was squeezing through the passageway. Its tongue wrapped around William's leg. The creature's craving for flesh was not satisfied.

William touched his torch against the tongue.

The beast released its hold and pulled its tongue from the hole in the wall. Seconds later, it was rammed into the exit again. Fortunately, William had escaped the passageway and was standing in the open tunnel.

With the absence of light in the opening, the tatzelwurm's tongue was crushed between the two walls. It roared in agony.

Exhausted, the rescuers fell to the ground.

Sam dropped alongside Brad. He was grateful that the most recent member of the team was still unconscious. Concerned with what could have been a fatal outcome, he looked at Cindy. "Don't get me wrong, I appreciate what you did for us in there. But you shouldn't have left Brad alone."

"He was still out cold while you five were in danger," explained Cindy.

"I know," acknowledged Sam.

"Then what?" she asked.

Sam stared at the closed crevice and stated, "I'm just glad that he never woke up and stepped into the opening. If he had, he would have been flattened since he didn't have a torch."

"Actually, I did think about that before I ran into the cave," she defended. "But when I saw the five of you in trouble—and saw that Brad was still motionless—I had to do something. I couldn't just sit back and watch."

"I guess I would have done the same thing," Sam ultimately admitted. He lessened the tension by teasing, "Don't ever let me catch you flirting with those Neanderthals again."

A couple feet away, Jimmy struggled to a seated position.

"How are you feeling?" asked Sam.

Jimmy rubbed the back of his head. "A wicked headache," he complained.

"Count your blessings that you're still in one piece," reminded Sam.

Dan looked at the sealed entrance. "Hey Sam, should we sneak inside and grab the lances? Remember, we don't have any more in the backpack."

"I'd rather not press our luck," said Sam. "We barely got out alive. Besides, Cindy still has her lance and we've got three torches. If we're lucky, we'll—"

"And the revolver," interrupted Cindy.

"And the revolver," confirmed Sam.

Brad squirmed, opened his eyes, and stared at the tunnel's ceiling. "What happened?" he muttered. He noticed the priest sitting beside him. "Father James, what are you doing here?" he asked. The newest traveler took a wide view of his surroundings before questioning, "Where are we?"

"It's a long story," replied the priest who helped him to his feet. "I'll explain as we walk up the tunnel."

After introductions were exchanged between the explorers and Brad, the group took another step closer to home.

As expected, Sam took the lead, bearing Cindy's lance and a torch.

The travelers had walked only a short distance when Sam came to a sudden stop.

"What's wrong?" asked William.

"Nothing." Sam turned and faced the group. "It's great seeing the seven of us together—relatively unharmed and ready to leave this miserable world. I probably shouldn't say it, but I had serious doubts we'd make it this far. I'd say we make a pretty good team."

"I had a hunch we'd make it this far," revealed Dan. He refused, however, to voice his growing concern that he and his friends hadn't experienced the worst yet.

"But we still have to find the wooden carving," reminded Cindy.

"Wooden carving?" asked Brad. "What's going on? Where are we?"

"Like I said, I'll explain later," reminded the priest. "But we need to keep moving."

"Father, what's the date now?" asked Sam.

"The twenty-eighth," he announced.

CHAPTER NINETEEN
The Rise to Pandemonium

THE TRANSWORLD EXPLORERS HAD HIKED NEARLY TWO MILES up the open cavern when Sam turned and looked at Brad and Jimmy. "How are you guys holding up?"

"We're fine," they replied.

"Sam, I don't get it," confessed Brad. "How did I get here?" He slowed his pace and took another view of the tunnel. "And where's here?"

Father James pulled on Brad's arm. "We need to keep moving. I'll explain our situation as we walk."

"But it doesn't make any sense," Brad continued. He came to a complete stop. "Just a second ago, I was—"

"Come on," demanded the priest. "Standing idle could make us an easy target."

"An easy target? For what?" demanded Brad.

"Later Brad, let's move!" ordered the priest.

Father James was true to his word. Along the way, he and the group updated Brad on their adventures in the side caves over the past twenty-eight days, including the cave of lust of which Brad remembered only bits and pieces. But since the travelers weren't sure if Brad had heard of the oak's unique qualities and had willingly stepped inside or was an innocent victim, they cleverly omitted the oak's portal.

At the conclusion of their sketchy story, Brad shouted, "Hell! What do you mean we're in hell?" He looked at each expressionless face. "Did it ever occur to you guys that somehow we stumbled on or fell into an undiscovered cavern in Lawton? This has to be Lawton. It can't be hell."

"All of us were skeptical at first," admitted Father James. "But the more enticements and anomalies we encountered in this world—like the inhabitants and creatures that keep coming back to life—the more I suspected that we were tossed into the lower regions of hell." He paused to cough dust particles from his throat. "Take your cave of lust for example."

"What do you mean?" he asked.

"Well before we found you," recalled the priest, "I thought it was strange that even though Dan, William, and Jimmy were staring at the same woman in the first domicile, they each saw different physical features."

"Hey, you're right," said Dan. "I never thought about it until now. That was strange."

"That doesn't happen on earth," reminded the priest. "And then there were the screams of the cave dwellers who reached the domiciles and the shouts of the inhabitants in the mob."

"What do you mean?" asked William.

"The screams of the cave dwellers who were being crushed were obviously those of pain but the throng of inhabitants interpreted them as shouts of delight. I'd imagine that's why they cheered them on. And as far as our young friends looking at the woman in the first domicile, each was seeing what he wanted to see. It wasn't reality."

"You've obviously given this a lot of thought, Father," said Jimmy.

"Not really. It's pretty basic in the study of human desires. With the temptation of lust, oftentimes the victim is allured to a person or situation that's only partially real. The individual soon discovers that the experienced pleasure fell far short of his or her expectations."

"But Father, why were the men and women in the domiciles only two-dimensional?" asked Cindy.

"That also is fairly easy to understand. Since the mob was focused exclusively on the outward appearances of the domicile dwellers—and not on their inner qualities—the supposed perfect models were only two-dimensional. The most unique and everlasting traits of the individuals were missing."

"I guess that makes sense," admitted Jimmy.

"Of course it does," said Cindy. She switched her gaze to Brad. "Do you remember anything about your arrival into this world?"

"I got an early morning phone call from the police, saying that a streetlight on the church's lawn was smashed," he related. "I refilled my coffee and drove to the sight. When I got there, I searched the grounds for a rock or something that may have been thrown at the light. Nine times out of ten, vandals are the culprits. But I didn't see anything out of the ordinary until I reached for my tools. With my back facing the church, I got a weird feeling—you know, the kind you get when you're being watched."

"Yeah, we know the feeling," said Dan.

"Anyway," Brad continued, "this is where it gets really bizarre."

The travelers ended their stride and gathered around the electrician.

"The streetlight across the road gave enough light for me to gather the tools from my truck. I had just grabbed my tool belt when—from the corner of my eye—I saw something hovering a few feet above the ground at my side. In a split second, a tree limb wrapped around my throat. I dropped the tools and tried to pull it from my neck. But it all happened so fast. Then I was thrown into the base of a tree and ended up at the back of a mob where everyone was shoving for the front of the line." He paused and observed the deadpan looks around him. "I know it sounds crazy, but you have to believe me. That's exactly what happened."

No one said a word.

Brad misread their silence as skepticism. "You've got to believe me. I couldn't make up a story like that."

Though everyone now knew that Brad was conscious during his abduction and an innocent victim, they debated internally on whether or not to disclose the complete history of the aggressive oak.

Since unforeseen circumstances had made Brad a member of the group—not to mention the fact that a future incident may require him to put his life on the line for the other travelers—Sam decided that their newest hell mate had the right to know the whole story. "Of course we believe you," he said.

"You do?" asked a relieved Brad.

Sam suddenly questioned if he had spoken too soon. He looked at his weary co-travelers. After five nods, he redirected his attention to Brad. "You see, that's how all of us ended up here—well except for me. I walked into the tree."

"What?" exclaimed Brad. He shook his head and admitted, "I can't believe we're even having this conversation. It doesn't make any sense."

"Actually, it makes perfect sense," interjected Dan.

Brad's look of relief was replaced by one of confusion.

"Come on, Brad, we need to keep moving," urged Father James. "We'll explain the rest of the story—including the parallel world—as we walk."

"The parallel world?" he blurted.

"Let's move," ordered Father James. "We've got only two days."

"Two days for what?"

"Move!" shouted the priest.

With Sam, William, and Dan each bearing a torch, the group resumed their exploration of the unknown world with renewed energy and enthusiasm. Each member sensed that home was now within reach.

"Sam, there's something I still don't get," said Cindy.

"What's that?"

"The oak on the church lawn," she said.

"What about it?"

"How come the tree on the church grounds put us in this realm, while the oak in the forest landed us in the parallel world?"

"I suppose that since the second oak was in a different spot, it transported us to a different place," he suggested.

"So you're saying that a different tree and a different location mean a different destination," she posed.

"Basically."

"And what about the cave dwellers who were devoured by the tatzelwurm in the last cave," asked Jimmy.

"What about them?" said Sam.

"If they were eaten alive, then how can they come back to life?"

Father James overheard Jimmy's question. "I'll admit it's hard to imagine," he interrupted, "but I have no doubt they'll rise from the dead. And since we barely escaped in one piece ourselves, I have no intention of revisiting the cave of lust to learn how they come back to life."

Cindy backtracked to Jimmy. "So what exactly does this wooden carving look like?"

"I told you. It was a six-headed serpent."

"Do you remember anything else?" she pressed. "How big was it?"

Jimmy ran his hand along the tunnel wall. "I don't know for sure, but I guess it was about—" He jerked his hand from the wall and came to an abrupt stop. "Wait a minute!"

"What's wrong?" yelled Cindy.

Her outcry forced Sam to Jimmy's side. "What?" Sam demanded.

A puzzled look surfaced on Jimmy's face.

"Oh no," pleaded Sam. "Don't tell us you're changing your story."

"No. It's not that," he assured.

"Then what?" shouted Cindy.

Jimmy closed his eyes and replayed his entry into hell. "The area was really bright."

"Brighter than any of the side caves?" asked Cindy.

"Oh yeah, a lot brighter."

"Do you remember anything else?" prodded Sam.

"No, sorry," he apologized. "I thought I did. I know it probably sounds unimportant, but like Brad said, it all happened so fast."

"Sam, now that all the missing persons have been found, shouldn't we be looking for an entrance to the third level?" asked Dan.

"There's another level?" questioned Brad.

"We think so," answered Dan. He took the backpack from Cindy. "We overheard the light keeper mentioning an upper level when we were hiding from him in Jimmy's cave."

"But Dan, the wooden carving is our way home," reminded Cindy.

"I know. But if the carving is on an upper level, then we're wasting our time here. And remember, we don't have a lot of time as it is."

"But what if we find the upper region, run into the master—whatever it is—and learn only then that the wooden carving is somewhere on this level?" asked Cindy.

Sam raised his hand motioning for silence. "If we keep talking at this volume we're sure to be discovered." He looked at Cindy and Dan, compromising, "Let's continue searching on this level for the wooden carving and an entrance to an upper region. Whatever we find first, that's the path we'll take."

Cindy and Dan remained silent.

"Agreed?" prodded Sam.

Cindy and Dan simply nodded.

The hike continued with Sam resuming the lead. Dan and his torch brought up the rear.

"Sam, can we pitch this bag since only the flashlights, the revolver, and a few bullets are inside?" asked Dan.

"Absolutely not!" shouted Sam. "We've been really good about not leaving any evidence of our passage in this world. The last thing we want is for someone or something to find our discarded bag. Then we'd really be hunted."

Dan tested the three flashlights—Sam's, William's, and his. "Hey Sam, William's flashlight is the only one that works," he informed.

"I noticed that before," replied Sam.

"But yours was working fine earlier in the trip," said Dan.

"I know. I guess the batteries have been losing juice," remarked Sam. "I don't need to remind you that in this world a few minutes are more like hours. That's why I insisted we use the torches as much as possible."

"But what about William's flashlight in his cave?" asked Cindy. "How could it have been shining on the wall for weeks?"

"I doubt it was shining for weeks," corrected Sam. "I'd guess that he or some other cave dweller turned it on just before we arrived."

Dan snatched the revolver from the bag. Trusting that Sam was right about not leaving any clues behind, he swung the backpack over his shoulders.

As seven sets of eyes scanned the walls for a wooden carving or an upper entrance, the travelers deliberately increased their speed. The quick passage of time weighed heavily on their minds. Sam maintained the lead while Dan defended the rear of the evacuation line with a tight grip on the revolver.

A noise from behind startled Dan. He spun.

Only steps ahead of him, Cindy heard the shuffling of feet. She turned and stepped alongside Dan. "What's wrong?" she asked.

"Nothing."

With the glow of his torch under his chin, she detected a hint of confusion. "Dan, don't tell me nothing's wrong. I know that look."

The other explorers—unaware that Cindy and Dan had come to a halt—put a greater distance between themselves and the straggling teenagers.

Dan extended his torch into the darkness and raised the revolver.

Cindy also stared into the poorly lit area.

The two teenagers scanned the nearby walls. They were alone.

"I told you it was nothing," he restated.

"What was nothing?"

"I thought I heard something behind me," he said.

Since she knew that Sam and Dan were the most observant members of the group, she looked into the darkness again. "What do you think it was?"

"It was probably just the breeze in this miserable tunnel."

She turned again and spotted Sam's and William's burning torches a great distance ahead. "Come on, let's catch up," she insisted.

They rushed ahead.

Hearing movement in the darkness behind, Jimmy spun in fright. "My gosh, you guys! You scared the heck—"

"Sorry," blurted Cindy. "Dan and I were checking out something."

"Like what?" he asked.

"It was nothing, just the breeze," she replied.

Father James had been reading his prayer book for the last couple miles by the glow of William's torch. On hearing Cindy's comment, he stopped in his tracks. "Speaking of breeze," he said.

"What's that, Father?" asked Sam who stepped alongside the priest.

"There it is again," alerted Father James. "Sam, did you see that?"

"Yeah."

A stronger than normal breeze flipped the page in his prayer book.

Sam raised his left hand. "If I didn't know better, I'd say the wind is coming from this wall." He took a step closer to the left wall.

"Be careful!" warned Cindy. "Remember, nothing in this world is as it seems."

"Thanks, but you don't need to remind me."

The group huddled around the priest, eager to see what Sam discovered. Quite by accident, William's torch flame touched Jimmy's bare arm.

Jimmy jumped from the blaze, tripped, and fell into the wall.

"Jimmy!" screamed Cindy.

His upper body had vanished inside a cloaked opening in the cavern wall.

Sam crashed to his knees and pulled his friend from the rock.

"Jimmy!" cried Cindy. "Are you all right?"

"Sam, I found our way up," Jimmy exclaimed.

Sam helped him to his feet. "What'd you see?" he demanded.

Jimmy continued breathing heavily. "A stone staircase on—" He paused to catch his breath. "Steps on the left wall."

"What?" asked Sam in disbelief. "Are you sure? You weren't in there that long."

Curiosity got the better of Dan. He took a step nearer the wall.

Fortunately, Father James had anticipated his move and prevented his entry.

Sam stuck his lance through the wall. "That's strange. We found a hidden opening on the wall in William's cave, but never one in the open tunnel."

"It's not any stranger than anything else we've seen in this place," reminded Cindy.

"This particular section of the wall must be an optical illusion," said Sam. He traced the opening with his lance and discovered that the invisible entry was roughly four feet wide and several feet high.

"Then I guess we're going upstairs," exclaimed Dan.

"Not so fast," cautioned Sam. "Before we step inside, I need to check it out."

"Sam, it's fine," declared Jimmy. "There's nothing dangerous or wicked in there—just a stone staircase, though it's pretty hot inside."

"Then you won't mind me checking it out," challenged Sam.

"Sam, why don't you wait here with the group," proposed Father James. "I'll investigate."

"If Jimmy's right, then I'll be fine," said Sam. "I'll be only a minute or two."

Sam had set only one foot inside the unseen opening when Jimmy grabbed his arm. "What?" shouted Sam.

"The first step is just a couple feet wide. Don't fall into the abyss," warned Jimmy.

"Abyss!" shouted Sam. He pulled his foot from the wall. "I thought you said it was fine."

"Well yeah, on the first step," he clarified.

Sam shook his head in disgust at Jimmy's inexcusable oversight. With greater caution than before, he disappeared through the wall with his lance and torch in hand.

"Jimmy, what's in the abyss?" asked Dan.

"I'm not sure. There wasn't a lot of light."

"Where did the steps lead?" asked Cindy.

"Up."

"I figured that," she snapped in a cynical tone. "What was at the top of the staircase?"

"I couldn't see that far." He brushed the dirt off his pants from his recent stumble.

Brad's sights had never left the wall since Sam's disappearance. "What's taking him so long?" he asked.

"Maybe he fell asleep," teased Jimmy. "Old guys—you know—need their naps."

"Jimmy!" yelled Sam from beyond the wall. "I can still hear you." He stepped into the open tunnel.

"What did you find?" asked an impatient Dan.

"Jimmy's right," Sam admitted. "There's a staircase to the left and an abyss below."

"How far does the staircase go?" asked Cindy.

"Quite a ways, I'm afraid. There's not a lot of light and it's awfully hot inside."

"Is there enough light to see where we're going so no one falls into the abyss?" questioned Father James.

"Yeah, I think so," replied Sam. "There are two torches wedged in the wall, though they're pretty far up the staircase."

"The light keeper!" exclaimed Dan. "That's probably how he and Cerberus reach the third level."

"I guess anything's possible," conceded Sam. He looked at the wall that held the masked opening. "But I'm not wild about using the staircase."

"Why not?" asked Cindy. "What's wrong with it?"

"I'm not sure how stable it is."

"Did you walk on it?" questioned Jimmy.

"Yeah, a few feet up," said Sam. "But it's weird. The steps aren't like any I've ever seen before."

"What do you mean?" asked Father James.

Sam took another glance at the penetrable rock wall. "They aren't joined together."

"Not joined?" asked Cindy. "What do you mean?"

"I mean, there's nothing holding the steps together," clarified Sam. "There aren't any risers between the steps."

"Then what are they attached to?" asked Dan.

"That's what's odd. Whoever built the staircase anchored the left side of each step inside the abyss wall."

"If the steps are secured in the rock wall, then they have to be sturdy," reasoned Dan.

"And the abyss?" posed Cindy.

"Yeah, there's an abyss."

"I know," she replied. "But what's in the abyss?"

"I got a glimpse when a streak of lightning lit up the area."

"Lightning!" exclaimed Brad.

"Unfortunately, it wasn't a good look. When the lightning flashed, I was checking out the staircase. By the time I looked into the abyss, the light had faded."

"So should we check it out?" asked William.

Sam was presented a dilemma. On the one hand, he was well aware that the time for the portal's opening was rapidly approaching. But on the other hand, he had serious concerns about the stability of the stone staircase. "I'm not sure," he said.

"But Sam, we have to," insisted William. "We're running out of time!"

"Trust me, I haven't forgotten the time factor. But I'm not wild about climbing a questionable staircase in poor light without knowing where it leads and an abyss at one misstep."

Father James knew the risk had to be taken. "Let me climb the steps to see—"

"No!" shouted Sam. He took a moment to regain his composure. In a civil tone, he reminded, "Father, you know I hate the idea of separating the group—especially above an abyss—even if it's for only a few minutes."

The priest looked at his watch. "But Sam, the twenty-eighth is almost over."

"Sam, we appreciate your concern for our safety," expressed Dan. "But if we don't take this risk, then there's no way we'll make it home and we'll be doomed in hell for eternity."

Sam couldn't argue with his logic. "All right. But remember, we don't know how reliable the staircase is. So let's tread lightly." He stared at Jimmy. "And let's keep our voices down."

"Sam, I'll bring up the rear," volunteered Dan as he displayed the revolver.

"There's no question about your aim. But are you up for it?"

"Yeah."

"Just make sure you watch your back," Sam cautioned.

"I'll be careful."

As expected, Sam was adamant about taking the lead with his torch and lance. In the event of an attack from behind, he insisted that Dan have both hands on the revolver. "Cindy," he directed, "take Dan's torch and climb the staircase near the middle of the group." He looked at William—the other torch bearer—and ordered, "Stay close to your brother at the back of the line."

Once everyone was in position, Sam entered the rock face and stood on the first step. Even though he had tested its stability only minutes earlier, he bounced lightly on it again. *If it gives way, the opening is still within reach,* he thought. The step seemed secure.

Sam was standing on the fifth step when Father James walked through the wall.

After Sam planted his feet on the tenth step and the priest on the fifth, Brad entered the sweltering chasm. Cindy, Jimmy, and William followed. Seconds later, Dan appeared through the wall with the revolver raised.

On reaching the fortieth step, Sam turned. He was pleased that his friends were climbing the staircase with surprising ease, though the heat was becoming unbearable. The explorers—each several steps from the other—hugged the left wall above the abyss. They knew that certain death was just feet to the right.

Father James raced to Sam's side on the fiftieth step where they tried to yank a burning torch from the wall. It was firmly embedded. Disappointed, they resumed their climb.

"Sam!" yelled Jimmy. "What's in the abyss?"

Sam turned to face his noisy companion twenty-eight steps below. "Quiet! We don't want to announce our presence," he reminded.

"Whatever," grumbled Jimmy. "I was just curious."

"Shh," reprimanded Cindy from six steps above.

Lightning lit up the abyss.

The travelers gazed into the illuminated chasm.

Cindy cringed. She spotted hundreds of flying creatures hovering a short distance below the staircase. "What are they?" she blurted.

"I don't know," replied Brad. "But let's hope they're more afraid of us than we are of them."

As expected, the discovery of the flying creatures forced the party to increase their pace.

Sam and Father James reached the seventy-fifth step where they made another attempt to pull the last burning torch from the wall. The results were the same as the first.

"Let's be grateful that we've got three of our own," reminded the priest.

Sam made no response. He climbed to the next step.

A grating sound echoed up the staircase.

Dan spun.

A grotesque imp—a small demon—was scraping its clawed feet on the first step. Its glare at Dan was replaced with a devilish grin. The four-foot-tall fiend was disfigured with a pair of black wings that were bordered with three-inch spikes. Its resourcefulness and tenacity compensated for its small stature. Only a fool or a lover of death would dare trivialize its ability to inflict torture before killing its prey.

That must be what I heard in the tunnel earlier, thought Dan.

A streak of lightning revealed the demon's remaining facial features. Its haunting red eyes sent shivers down Dan's spine. The imp's pointed ears and its horn above each temple were clearly visible in the light. During the extended explosion of light, the creature offered Dan a wider grin. Two rows of crooked fangs glistened in the glow. A dangling tail at the corner of its mouth suggested that it had recently engorged a cave rat. It slurped the tail down its throat and focused on its next meal.

Cursed with abnormally large feet, the demon tripped on the second step, but quickly regained its balance and dashed up the next five while rapidly flapping its wings. Within a matter of seconds, it was airborne and heading for Dan.

Any lingering concerns the teenager had about shooting the imp—in the unlikely event its intent was not malicious—vanished into thin air when Dan realized that its death would be only temporary.

Like all demons, however, the imp was cunning. Since it suspected that the other humans would risk their lives to save another, it carried out its aerial assault in silence and in the shadows. Nothing was left to chance. To avoid detection from the overhead climbers, it intentionally flew only inches above the staircase.

Twenty-one steps separated it from Dan.

Dan aimed the revolver and pulled the trigger. He missed the flying target.

The stray bullet lodged in a step several feet below.

The staircase rocked violently.

A scream was heard.

Jimmy had lost his balance during the tremor and was clinging to the edge of a step with his finger tips.

Though everyone heard the shot, the dim light and the imp's clever tactical flight path prevented them from seeing the creature.

William darted up six steps to Jimmy; Cindy raced down five.

In her struggle to maintain her balance on the wobbly staircase, Cindy lost her torch in the abyss.

Lightning strikes lit up the higher realm of the abyss.

During the display of natural light, William and Cindy were

alarmed with the approach of a winged serpent from the darkness below. In fright, they nearly lost their grip on Jimmy.

The flying snake—measuring easily ten feet in length and nearly a foot in diameter—wrapped its lower body around one of Jimmy's legs.

"Pull!" screamed Jimmy.

William and Cindy were too involved in their lifesaving efforts to respond.

The abyss darkened.

William's torch met the same fate as Cindy's.

"Help!" yelled Jimmy.

Another burst of lightning brightened the area.

Cindy noticed a pair of wings at the serpent's midsection and smaller versions behind its jaw and near the end of its body. Each set fluttered at an incredible speed, allowing the snake to hover at a fixed point in space above the abyss. It tugged on its human prey.

A second serpent swooped from above and coiled around Jimmy's other leg.

"Pull!" screamed William.

"I am!" shouted Cindy.

Another shot was fired fourteen steps below which sent the staircase shaking wildly.

One of the winged snakes released its hold and glided into the lower darkness.

Seeing its quick release and its surprising getaway, Cindy suspected that something was wrong. *What would frighten it?* she thought.

The first serpent, on the other hand, remained twisted around Jimmy's leg.

Steps below, Dan pressed himself against the left wall for balance. He glanced below and was thrilled that the second bullet had hit its target between the eyes.

The imp rolled off the step and plummeted into the abyss.

Dan was turning to climb the staircase when he spotted an orange fluid seeping from the step where the first bullet was embedded.

Sam, Father James, and Brad had reached Cindy and William.

Overpowered and outnumbered, the serpent relinquished its hold on Jimmy and nose-dived into the chasm.

THE SINISTER REALM

Jimmy was pulled to safety. As he recuperated on the staircase, William hugged the wall and descended the stairs to Dan.

Not even the approach of his brother drew Dan from his stare at the injured step. William also spotted the oddity. The orange fluid dripped into the abyss.

"My gosh, Dan, what are we walking on?" whispered William.

"I don't know. I think we should move faster, but without alarming the others."

William turned to face the group above. "Hey Sam, let's hurry!" he shouted.

"Why? What's wrong?"

William feared that the group might become overly agitated with the bleeding staircase and take a tumble. "Nothing," he replied, "just move faster!"

"All right then, let's go," ordered Sam.

With Jimmy's misstep fresh in their minds, the explorers resumed their ascent on the unsteady staircase with greater trepidation.

Nearly fifty steps later, Sam raised the torch and glimpsed the end of the staircase ahead. His climb continued. On reaching the top step, he tapped the wall with his lance. He hoped to find a secret opening like the one below that led to the staircase. *If there's no way out, we'll have to climb down the staircase to the lower tunnel,* he thought. He tapped again, but the wall was solid rock. He continued striking the wall as far as his lance would reach. Eventually, a concealed passageway was discovered, though it was three feet above the top step.

"Run!" screamed Dan.

Sam looked below.

The flight of stairs shook uncontrollably. The travelers pressed themselves against the left wall for stability.

Dan had a gut feeling that the staircase was a living creature and that the group's presence was unwelcome. "Run!" he yelled again.

With each tremor, it became more likely that the abyss would be the travelers' final destination.

Sam realized that a downward escape was no longer an option since most of his co-explorers were nearer the top of the staircase. He took careful aim before throwing his lance and torch inside the opening. With the point of entry clearly etched in his memory, he leaped for the hole. The wild movements of the staircase, however, made his jump less than successful. He was hanging from the bottom edge of the opening by his hands. The screams of his friends and the thought of their deaths in the abyss forced him to collect the courage and the strength he needed to pull himself to safety within the hidden passageway.

In unspeakable terror, the climbers fought to maintain their balances as they ascended the staircase.

Sam was on his hands and knees inside the wall's opening. Only his head and upper body were visible. His lower half remained hidden behind the deceptive rock wall.

Father James was closing in on the top step.

"Jump!" yelled Sam.

The priest took a precarious leap into Sam's waiting arms and was pulled inside the opening. Brad, Cindy, and Jimmy immediately followed. The chances of William and Dan making a successful jump to safety were rapidly deteriorating. The staircase was out of control.

"Run!" screamed Sam.

A flock of winged serpents rose from the chasm and floated alongside the staircase.

Sam noticed the flying reptiles and imagined they were fearful of direct contact with the staircase. But it was only a hunch.

William approached the top step.

"Jump!" yelled the priest who was squatting alongside Sam inside the hidden passageway.

As much as William hated leaving his brother behind, he knew that he'd be more helpful inside the opening, ready to catch Dan when he made his leap. William jumped.

Sam and the priest placed a firm grip on William's wrists and pulled him to solid ground.

Before even catching his breath, William spun and leaned through the opening. "Come on, Dan, jump!" he shouted.

Dan took a quick look into the abyss. With the erratic movements of the stairs and hundreds of floating serpents, he was almost certain that his time had run out. To him, the last five steps may well have been fifty.

"Jump!" yelled William again.

In Dan's wild dash over the remaining steps, the backpack and revolver fell into the abyss. He made his leap.

William leaned further through the opening—nearly to the point of plummeting himself—and grabbed Dan's left arm.

Sam scrambled deeper inside the passageway and wrapped his arms around William's waist to prevent the young man from falling into the abyss.

Dan remained hanging in midair.

Four flying serpents dived from above and coiled around his legs.

Sam jumped from William's side and jabbed the point of his lance at the snakes.

Although they released their hold on the seventh traveler, they refused to totally abandon their prize. They drifted beyond the reach of the lance.

With Sam's weapon extended as a deterrent, Father James reached below the confines of the opening and helped William support Dan.

Suddenly, rocks exploded from the wall and shot into the abyss.

A gigantic thermosaurus thrust its upper body from the wall—just feet from the unseen opening.

The serpents flew from harm's way.

The arrival of the creature produced various reactions from the travelers. Jimmy, Cindy, and Brad jumped deeper inside the opening; Father James and William momentarily relaxed their grip on the hanging teenager; and Sam nearly dropped his lance into the abyss.

Unknown to the explorers, the bullet that Dan had lodged in a step during his climb had roused a sleeping thermosaurus—a hundred-foot-long wormlike, scaled creature that lived within the cavern walls. Its ability to scavenge the interior regions of the rock world and devour vegetation roots prevented sprouting plants from reaching maturity. Its widespread excavations explained the sparse plant life in the rock world. The only exceptions were the shooting pods that had acquired the art of locomotion—in an evolutionary triumph—to safeguard its species from annihilation. Minutes earlier, the thermosaurus's bony horizontal plates that ran the length of its body—that the travelers perceived as steps—were jutting out of the abyss wall and absorbing life-sustaining heat. Its inclined position between the second and third levels mimicked a stone staircase.

The most unusual characteristic of the thermosaurus was a long twisted horn at the top of its head which allowed it to bore through the maze of caverns.

Though vegetarian by nature, the creature would defend itself and its territory if threatened.

Sam took a closer look at the armored reptile.

It lacked eyes.

Sam speculated that it—like many prehistoric dinosaurs with poor or no vision—defended itself from suicidal predators by motion. "Dan!" he yelled. "Don't move!"

William and Father James also remained motionless while supporting Dan.

In near shock, Dan hung lifeless above the abyss.

The creature also remained at rest. But its inactivity was fleeting.

A daring serpent rose from the darkness, wrapped around Dan's ankle, and yanked against Father James and William.

With its lower body buried deeply in the wall, the thermosaurus extended its head over the abyss and remained still. It zeroed in on the fluttering vibrations of the snake. With a quick lunge, the creature impaled the flying serpent with its horn. Dan narrowly escaped the one-sided assault. Fortunately for Dan, the stabbing was delivered with such force that the creature's horn was stuck in the rock. The thermosaurus jerked to free its horn from the wall.

Sam ordered Dan to take advantage of the creature's trapped predicament. "Dan—now! Step on the horn!"

Having just witnessed the goring death of the large snake at close range, Dan kept his eyes shut. He slipped from the hold of Father James and William.

"Step on the horn!" yelled William.

Dan opened his eyes. His attention was drawn to the rocking horn at his feet. He set one foot on the horn. Before his second foot was placed on the creature, Father James and William pulled him through the opening.

The rescuers dragged him until they were thirty feet up the new tunnel.

Thinking they were out of danger, Father James and William helped him to his feet.

"Are you all right," demanded Sam. "Are you hurt anywhere?"

The stunned teenager shook his head, but didn't say a word. Several deep breaths later, he whispered, "I'm fine; just dazed." He glanced back in the direction of the concealed opening. "I thought for sure I was a goner. I raced as fast as I could up the—" He paused.

"What's wrong?" asked Sam.

"I dropped the revolver and the backpack into the abyss," disclosed Dan.

"As long as you're safe, that's all that matters," replied Sam. "Besides, if we're as close to home as I think, maybe we won't need the revolver anymore."

William rested his hand on his brother's shoulder. "I dropped my torch in the abyss too."

"So did I," admitted Cindy.

Dan's encounter with the flying serpents and the thermosaurus was grueling. He would have hit the ground if it weren't for William's quick reflexes.

"What was that thing?" asked Cindy.

Sam helped William lower Dan to the ground.

"I'm not sure," said Sam. "But it's probably a primeval creature that lives in the walls of this world."

"But what made it so violent?" questioned Jimmy.

"That was my doing," confessed Dan.

"What do you mean?" asked Jimmy.

"When I was climbing the staircase, I heard noise behind." He looked at Cindy and reminded, "It was the same noise I heard earlier in the open tunnel." He redirected his attention to Sam. "When I turned, I saw a winged imp standing at the bottom of the staircase. It eventually flew at me. I was almost certain it stepped through the wall to hunt us down. So I fired, but I missed."

"I was wondering why you fired the revolver," said Sam.

"The bullet hit a step which I suppose caused the staircase to shake. Anyway, after I fired a second time and killed the imp, I saw orange fluid oozing from the step where the first bullet had lodged. But I didn't know the staircase was alive."

"There's no way you could have known the staircase was alive," said Sam. "Of course it was an accident. And knowing you, I'm sure you were trying to protect the group from the imp. But in the future, remember that your friends have the right to know what they're up against."

"Yeah, I know," he confessed.

"I also saw the bleeding step," said William. "But I didn't think it would affect our escape—at least not right away."

Convinced that it was pointless to dwell on the issue—not to mention the fact that time was rapidly ticking away—Sam urged everyone to resume their hike on the new level. He grabbed the sole lance and torch.

They marched on.

"Now can we search for the wooden carving?" pleaded Jimmy.

"Yeah," replied Sam with a chuckle in his voice. "Now we can search for the carving."

Dan outpaced his friends and stepped alongside Sam. "I just got a creepy thought," he said.

"What now?" asked Sam.

"What are the odds that the light keeper is intentionally leading us somewhere?"

Sam stopped in his tracks. "Dan, what makes you think we're being led somewhere?"

"Doesn't it seem strange to you that we've broken free from the side caves and made it this far into our journey while thousands—if not millions—of other inhabitants haven't escaped their caves?" asked Dan.

Father James overheard his observation. "Actually, that thought crossed my mind not too long ago," said the priest. He stepped closer to Sam and Dan. "I can't tell you if we're being led somewhere, but I can tell you that as far as our escape is concerned, we've made it this far because it's been a team effort."

The other travelers gathered around the priest.

"In order to escape a cave, a person must first perform a selfless act," explained the priest. "If it weren't for Dan's selfless act that permitted him to escape his cave, I doubt that any of us would be standing here right now."

"So can the other cave dwellers escape?" asked Jimmy.

"Probably," guessed the priest. "But they choose to stay."

"But Father, why would someone choose to stay in this place?" posed Cindy.

"Actually," corrected the priest, "it's probably not so much that they choose to stay, as much as they refuse to leave."

"I don't understand," said Cindy.

"If someone wants to leave a cave, he or she would have to do what Dan did—conquer his or her temptations by practicing self-denial," clarified Father James. "But for the inhabitants in this world, escaping a cave is not worth the sacrifice of even one act of self-denial."

"You mean we've made it this far because we've helped each other?" asked Jimmy.

"Yes," declared the priest.

Only now realizing that the group was at a standstill, Sam urged, "Come on, we're wasting time."

"And be on the lookout for a wooden carving," added Jimmy.

The group hiked up the tunnel.

After what seemed a thirty-minute walk, Cindy called Sam's attention to a lit area ahead.

"Yeah, I see it—torches on the walls," he said.

Jimmy stepped to the front of the line. "I'll grab a few before—"

Sam grabbed his arm.

"Sam, no one's going to miss a few torches," assured Jimmy. "There are hundreds."

"That's what bothers me." Almost certain that the path home lay beyond the collection of torches, Sam warned, "Let's move, but with extreme caution—and no talking." He resumed the lead.

Closer to the lit area, Sam raised his torch overhead.

Throughout their journey, the explorers had come to learn that this gesture was Sam's signal to halt.

Voices were heard up the tunnel.

Sam quenched the flame.

The travelers pressed their backs against a cavern wall. They hoped—and Father James prayed—that the distant conversation would fade.

The voices grew louder.

Father James took advantage of the light streaming from ahead and looked at his watch. It was 4:00 a.m., September thirtieth.

CHAPTER TWENTY
Phantom Children

IN THE CLAYS' HOUSE, THE CLOCK IN THE SECOND FLOOR hallway chimed four times. Nancy's anxieties over the safe return of her sons had kept her awake. Unknown to her, Jeff was also experiencing the same frustration. Accepting the fact that a peaceful night's rest would be impossible, she crept from the bed so as not to disturb her husband whom she presumed was asleep.

"What's wrong?" blurted Jeff.

"Sorry. I thought you were asleep."

He pushed himself to a seated position and voiced what he knew was troubling her. "I've got the boys on my mind too."

Nancy stopped short of the bedroom doorway. With her back facing her husband, she declared, "It's hard to believe that within the next fifteen hours or so either our family will be reunited or half will remain forever in another world."

"Honey, you shouldn't talk that way. It's not an all or nothing situation. If for some reason the boys don't return later tonight, I'm sure we'll see them during the October full moon."

Jeff's optimism failed to comfort her. She had a feeling that the oak on the church lawn would not remain indefinitely. She disregarded his comment. "It's almost too much to grasp that the coming hours will shape the rest of our lives."

"They're resourceful kids. I'm sure we'll see them during tonight's full moon," he comforted.

"I hope you're right." She walked into the hallway.

Jeff jumped from the bed, snatched his robe, and darted from the room.

In the meantime, Nancy had entered the kitchen. In a stunned state, she opened a cabinet and grabbed the coffee.

Jeff stepped into the room. After years of marriage, he knew the inner turmoil she was battling and imagined that she was wrongfully blaming herself. He placed his arm around her. "We'll see them later tonight," he reiterated.

She wept bitterly.

He helped her to the kitchen table while cautioning, "Dwelling on something that we have no control over won't help our situation."

"I know." She reached for a tissue on the table. "But if I had just kept a closer eye on—"

"Nancy, don't torture yourself," he insisted.

She blew her nose, rose from the table, and resumed the breakfast preparations. "I'm sorry. I don't know what's come over me." She filled the coffeepot with water. "Ever since the boys' disappearance, I've tried to remain hopeful that they'd return safely. But this morning—"

"I know," he interrupted, "but this morning is more difficult than most because it's the day of their return. It's been rough. There's no question. But that's normal."

Nancy looked at the wall clock. "I'll probably feel better after the early Mass."

During their meal, Jeff did his best to comfort his emotionally-spent wife.

As she agonized over the loss of her sons, Jeff reached a decision on a dilemma that had been nagging him for several days. For his wife's peace of mind, he knew that he had to make the transworld journey later that night if their boys didn't return.

As Nancy dressed for church, he secretly loaded a packed knapsack in the car's trunk.

•

In the sinister realm, the seven travelers sneaked up the tunnel in complete silence. The mysterious voices ahead had not faded as they had hoped.

"What's with all these boulders?" asked Jimmy.

Sam knew that even the softest reprimand could alert the unknown beings to their presence. He spun and delivered a stern look at Jimmy.

The unusually large number of boulders scattered throughout the cavern was unlike anything the group had seen in the underworld. The area reminded Jimmy of an obstacle course.

With his sights fixed on the forward torches, Dan unknowingly kicked a rock against the tunnel wall. The sound echoed up the cavern.

The explorers came to a complete stop and waited to see if Dan's blunder would be detected by the chatty beings ahead.

Cindy tapped Sam on the shoulder and pointed ahead.

Sam nodded. He also saw the illuminated side cave—fifty feet ahead—on the cavern's left wall.

The quiet march resumed.

Opposite the cave's entrance rested a long boulder. Sam led his friends to its safety and concealed themselves between it and the cavern wall.

"What do you mean torches are missing?" was yelled from inside the lit cave.

"Pardon me. Be merciful," immediately followed.

From behind the protective boulder, the travelers viewed a section of the cave's interior. Though they heard the heated conversation, they couldn't see the inhabitants.

"That's it," whispered Jimmy.

"Shh," warned Sam.

Jimmy was not deterred. "That's it," he said again.

Sam glared at his young companion.

"That's the wooden carving," blurted Jimmy.

Sam jerked his head and stared inside the cave.

Positioned against one of the cave's walls was a tall wooden chair with a six-headed serpent carved at the top of its back support.

"Are you sure?" asked Sam under his breath.

"Positive," Jimmy replied.

Cindy overheard their hushed voices. She leaned into the boulder and looked beyond William and Dan to Jimmy. "What's wrong?" she asked.

"Jimmy said that's the wooden carving on the chair," said Dan.

Cindy looked inside the cave.

"Summon the legions to the open cavern," was ordered from within. "Whoever has escaped will pay the ultimate price. The prisoner will beg for my mercy."

Unlike his traveling companions, Father James believed that the cave before them would be more difficult to conquer than the others. Overwhelmed by the horrible stench coming from the cave, he turned his head and vomited behind the boulder.

"What was that?" came from within the cave. "Check it out—now!"

Father James made eye contact with Sam at the opposite end of the boulder. "Stay here, Sam, and make sure that everyone escapes," he whispered. He glanced inside the cave. "This is my battle." He stepped from behind the rock and had advanced only eight steps when he was nabbed by the light keeper and Cerberus.

One of the hound's heads sank its fangs into the priest's thigh.

He wailed in agony.

The travelers covertly watched the attack from behind the boulder. It took unmatched self-control for them to remain hidden. Each knew that any attempt to rescue the priest would endanger the lives of everyone.

After the three-headed hound was yanked away, the light keeper grabbed the priest by the throat and dragged him inside the bright cave.

Six heads poked from behind the boulder.

The priest was shoved against a cave wall beyond the travelers' vision.

"Ah, a Catholic priest," was heard from inside the cave.

Father James trembled at what stood before him. His leg injury forced him to the ground.

Cerberus eyed its helpless prey and lunged a second time. The priest suffered a gash on his calf. A scream reverberated throughout the chamber.

The light keeper tugged on the chain and pulled the hound from the priest.

"Let Cerberus be," commanded the second being. "Let it have some fun."

Cries of torment filled the inner rock world.

Between the tunnel wall and the protective stone, Sam was enraged. As much as he wanted to rescue his pastor—even if it meant risking his own life—he knew that stepping into the cave would put his five friends at the jaws of the hound.

The travelers finally heard the rattling sound of the chain being jerked again. The hound yelped.

Sam breathed a soft sigh of relief.

From the cold ground, the priest raised his sights to the creature before him. He quickly refocused his attention to his leg injuries. The being's appearance was unforgivable.

"Look at me!" ordered the being.

Father James refused to offer another momentary glimpse at the cave dweller.

"Do you know who I am?" shouted the being.

The priest was silent.

"Answer me!"

"Lucifer!" yelled Father James.

On hearing the priest's response, Dan toppled from his squat position.

Sam stared at the teenager and placed a finger over his lips, motioning for silence. A fluttering noise caught him by surprise. He faced the front of the rock.

Two winged beings stood before the group demanding their audience with the king of hell.

In Sam's efforts to shield Cindy from the demons, he unintentionally left his lance resting on the ground. Certain that Cerberus would attack the first person who entered the cave, Sam stepped ahead of his friends. Dan immediately trailed.

"Kneel before me, priest!" demanded Lucifer.

Father James remained on the ground, praying with the greatest fervor.

Sam and Dan raced to the injured priest. They were just three feet into their sprint when they were smashed against a cave wall by the slightest rotation of Lucifer's finger. Skeletal arms burst from the wall and wrapped around the men's necks, waists, and legs.

"The priest is not to be touched!" ordered Lucifer. "He still has to learn the consequences of failing to pay me fitting homage."

Having witnessed the outcome of Sam and Dan's dash to the priest, the other travelers postponed their rescue mission.

Queasy at Lucifer's appearance, Cindy diverted her stare and scanned the royal chamber.

The one-hundred-foot-high ceiling was noticeably void of stalactites.

As Cindy continued surveying the throne room, William collected his courage and looked at Satan who stood almost seven feet atop a deformed goat frame. Clothed in a tattered sleeveless tunic, the chest of the beast was covered with animal fur. Two oversize ears arched backwards and extended nearly three inches beyond the back of his head before terminating to a point.

Of all his facial features, the eyes and mouth were the most hideous. Each eye was midnight black with a white horizontal slit that extended the length of the eyeball. Unlike anything they had seen on earth or in the parallel world, Lucifer sported two mouths—one above the other—below his hooked nose.

Father James believed that the ruler of the underworld was intentionally disfigured with two mouths since he was the Father of Lies. In his opinion, the demon was sentenced with the pair of mouths to correspond to his crime of speaking contradictory statements from either mouth whenever it furthered his diabolical cause.

In a display of power, the Master of Darkness unfolded his black wings which spanned nearly fifteen feet. At once, the explorers noticed that they were composed of thousands of interlocking dung beetles. They were repulsed at the sight.

Seven smaller versions of Lucifer—each clutching a sword and shield—were stationed around the perimeter of the throne room. *Cilohtac* was engraved along the border of each shield.

Lucifer sensed uneasiness on Cindy's face when she glimpsed the lesser demons. "These men are members of my elite force—the Cilohtac Legion," he revealed. "They've sworn eternal allegiance to me.

The pleasure of their existence is to serve me." He offered a quick look at Sam and Dan captured on the wall.

Cilohtac, I wonder what it—thought the priest. "My God," he whispered.

Satan returned his attention to Cindy and divulged, "The rest of my legions patrol within the cavern walls and other undisclosed regions in my kingdom."

William moved toward Father James who was staggering to his feet. The young man was hurled to the wall and seized by the skeletal arms.

To avert a fall, Father James grabbed a charcoal burner that was close at hand. To his surprise, its metal bars were ice cold. Though a fire was burning, it refused to release heat. Instead, a damp cold was produced. He noticed the oddly-shaped black coals. The foul odor of the burning embers was intolerable. He cupped his hand over his nose and mouth.

Just as Father James was convincing himself that the coals—like everything in hell—were a peculiarity to the realm, Lucifer hobbled on his goat frame to the priest's side and looked intently into the charcoal pit. "They exist only in my empire," he divulged.

Father James remained silent. He redirected his gaze to the wall where Sam, Dan, and William remained captive.

The skeletal arms tightened their grasp around the prisoners' necks.

The faces of his dangling friends turned blue.

"Stop!" shouted the priest.

Lucifer gazed at the wall. With another rotation of his finger, the men fell to the ground. The Father of Iniquities looked into the charcoal burner and restated, "The coals are found only in my empire." He withdrew from the priest's side and approached his royal throne. "Eons ago, six hundred inferior demons dared the impossible. They tried to usurp my eternal dominion and power." He sat upon his wooden chair and elaborated, "What fools. As I was debating their penalty, it occurred to me that their everlasting punishment should reflect their crime. Since they tried to steal my power, I stole theirs."

A puzzled expression emerged on the priest's face.

"Since your Almighty gave everyone—including the six hundred traitors—an immortal soul, I ripped the souls from their bodies and discarded them in the seven charcoal burners throughout my royal chamber. Since their souls of pure evil are eternal, I enjoy unending light."

Throughout Lucifer's explanation of the sentence imposed on his former subordinates, Sam, Dan, and William inched their way to the center of the cave and stood alongside their companions.

Lucifer rose from his throne and neared the group. "Once their souls were dropped in the charcoal pits, I banished their rebellious bodies to the lowest realm of my kingdom where they remain to this very day howling for mercy and reprieve. Trust me, there's no greater misery for angels—fallen or not—and mankind than to lose their souls." The Father of Lies stared at the priest and declared, "I find their cries of anguish most entertaining." He glanced through the cave opening and listened for the screeches of his former underlings before explaining, "You see, with the loss of their souls, they also lost their will power to escape and attempt another mutiny." Lucifer took two goat steps closer to the explorers. "Perhaps you've heard them screaming during your journeys."

So those were the shrieks we heard in the abyss when crawling over the ceiling, thought Dan.

Sam and Cindy also recalled their escape over the chasm.

Satan labored on his bowed legs to Dan's side. "Speaking of banishment to the lowest realm—so this is the famous Dan Clay who was instrumental in banishing the Reclaimers to the lowest realm in the parallel world."

Dan displayed a confused look.

"Don't look so surprised," exclaimed Satan. "My tempters are everywhere—including the parallel world—and they keep me informed of everything. I learned of you and the fate of the Reclaimers the moment they were buried in the gorge."

Dan remained silent, gazing upon the undying coals. Lucifer's looks were too nauseating to endure for an extended length of time.

"But trust me, Dan, you and your friends won't be as lucky as the Reclaimers. After only a few seconds in the dark abyss of hell, you'll be begging me to throw your wretched bodies into the lowest region of the parallel world for all eternity." He altered his tone and declared, "But I wouldn't be overly concerned. Since you never experienced bodily death before entering my kingdom, you'll die of old age before hitting the bottom. Once dead, your souls will have no choice but to experience the horrors below forever." He shot a fiendish glare at Dan and foretold, "Your false act of heroism in the parallel world will cost you and your friends your immortal souls." He returned to his throne.

"By the power of the Almighty, you will not prevail!" shouted Father James.

To everyone's surprise, Lucifer was not annoyed with the priest's outburst. Rather, he seemed amused.

His shouts, however, provoked the Cilohtac Legion. They approached the group.

The explorers stepped closer to a glowing charcoal burner.

Satan raised his arms. The seven demons ended their advance and returned to their former posts.

"Your God permitted you to enter my kingdom," declared the Prince of Darkness with a chuckle in his voice. "But there's no escape from my realm. So you see, I have prevailed." He took notice of Dan's fixed gaze at the wooden carving above his head. "Ah, the enchanted oak," he exclaimed. "And you think that's your means of escape? No, my pathetic humans, the carving will not be your exodus from hell."

With its head lowered, a member of the Cilohtac Legion flapped its wings, flew to its master, and hovered three feet above the ground. As its rapid wing motion decreased, the lesser demon descended to its knees.

"Rise, Folly!" ordered Lucifer.

Folly motioned to the wooden carving above the monarch's head. "Master, the time draws near," it announced.

The two-mouthed ruler nodded.

Folly returned to its station along a cave wall.

Father James looked at his watch. The full moon would rise soon. It was already 7:00 p.m.

Satan pressed his body firmly against the throne's back support. "No, there's no escape," he said again. "When I'm finished amusing myself with your subangelic intelligence, I'll throw your bodies and souls into the dark abyss below where—" He paused and corrected himself. "As a constant reminder of my triumph, I'll rip your souls from your bodies and drop them in a charcoal burner. Then I'll have the pleasure of hurling your pitiful bodies into the subterranean world of my empire where you'll remain for all eternity with my former would-be usurpers."

Father James was convinced that he and his friends had nothing to lose. "Lucifer, you will fail!" he prophesied. "God will protect and deliver his children from your crafty wickedness. Yes Lucifer, you will fail. But we—with God's help—will not."

"But your God has already failed you!" shouted Satan. "Your presence here is proof of that."

"Lord, your love endures forever. Never forsake the work of your hands!" prayed Father James.

Infuriated with the priest's constant reference to the Almighty, Lucifer jumped from his throne and roared, "How dare you quote Scripture to me! I've heard the supposed sacred words uttered down through the centuries. I've even heard them spoken from the mouth of your God's alleged Son. The words are meaningless." He seated himself before ordering, "You are forbidden to quote Scripture in my presence!" The Master of Sin regained his composure before divulging, "Countless Christians in previous ages refused to surrender to my temptations. Sadly, many remained steadfast in their faith to the point of death. But your generation is exceedingly easy to influence. Such little time and effort are needed to plant the seed of doubt in you present-day Christians—doubts that your God lives and doubts that my kingdom exists." He plucked a dung beetle from his battered left wing that still bore the scar of the lightning strike that hurled him from heaven's heights millennia ago. He tossed the insect into his lower mouth and boasted, "I have humans eating out of my hands."

"That's where you're wrong," insisted Father James.

"Am I?" he posed. "Are your churches overflowing with people wasting their time worshiping your God?"

"Even when I walk through a dark valley, I fear no harm for you are at my side; your rod and staff give me courage," prayed the priest. He was slammed to the ground, gasping for air. His internal organs were being twisted and yanked upwards.

Dan witnessed Satan's piercing stare at Father James. "Stop!" he shouted.

"I ordered no Scripture to be quoted in my presence!" He removed his glare from the priest.

Father James recovered his breath.

As Sam and Dan sat on their heels beside the priest, Lucifer rose from his throne and hobbled to a charcoal burner. He turned to face the group and touched the cold—yet blazing—coals. The light from the burner cast his shadow on a nearby wall. "Flee!" commanded Satan.

The travelers were shocked.

Lucifer's shadow broke free from his body, soared to the ceiling, and vanished. During its separation from Satan's body and its flight, the Prince of Demons remained completely motionless.

"Thanks to the souls of my previous inferior demons, I have endless shadow tempters who prowl the earth enticing and corrupting anyone they encounter," he explained.

"This can't be happening," remarked Dan in disbelief.

"Welcome to my kingdom!" howled Lucifer. "Whatever evil thought or deed I wish to inflict upon humanity, I simply conceive the idea and my shadow—avarice, in this case—performs my bidding by ascending to earth and waiting in darkness until a human crosses its path."

"That's impossible," said Dan.

"You humans are so feeble-minded," accused the fallen angel. "The shadows in your world that are created by trees, mountains, and manmade objects provide the perfect cover for my phantom children to lurk. Since they despise natural light, they hide in darkness until someone steps into the shadows. Once a human nears, my offspring invade the soul—the farthest point from natural light. In a very real way, my children are a natural extension of me." He touched the demonic souls in the charcoal pit and created two more shadows of temptation to further illustrate his point and convince the explorers. Moments after the second shadow tore itself from his side and vanished overhead, Lucifer posed, "Surely you've stepped into a dark alley and felt a strange presence."

The group remained silent. All had experienced the eerie sensation many times.

The stillness was interrupted by a growl from Cerberus.

"Resume your patrols!" ordered Satan.

The light keeper bowed and left the cave, but not before the hound made an unsuccessful charge at the group.

Lucifer paced his royal chamber. Eventually, he neared a member of the Cilohtac Legion. "Impiety, gather the Nacilgna Legion and the other legions to learn how our prisoners escaped the seven caves," he directed.

Impiety genuflected before flying from the throne room.

"It was Dan's selfless act that permitted him to escape the first cave," explained the priest.

Satan approached the group. "So Dan's the hero again," he said.

"And not only that—the group's ingenuity and determination to break free from the caves were crucial to our reaching this point," informed Sam with a hint of fear in his voice.

The Prince of Darkness ignored Sam's comment and delivered a callous glance at Father James. "What do you humans know about selfless acts? Your selfish ways, greed, and pride have been the root of your sins and your downfall." He snatched another dung beetle from his wing and swallowed. "In fact, it was pride that ushered in the first sin and mankind's fall from grace. In your world, many humans refuse to accept the story of creation. They refuse to believe in sin or in the existence of hell. So few recognize that it was my tempting of Adam and Eve into believing they would be like gods that led to their disgrace. Before Eve gave birth to Cain, she and Adam gave birth to pride. Throughout human history, pride and its countless variations have degraded your race."

Again, the group was speechless.

The silence, however, was brief. The back support of the throne shook.

As the explorers focused on the chair, Lucifer approached his seat. "Your eternity in my kingdom is preordained." He rested on his throne and spread his wings to hide the portal. With a mystified look on his face, he asked the priest, "Why does your Almighty have such great love for a species so vile and egotistical? Why do humans—obviously inferior to angels—hold a special place in the eyes of your God?"

Father James refused to answer. He knew that any response would be misconstrued and used against him.

Dan had a hunch that the portal was not yet fully activated. He gathered his courage to stall for time. "How does it work?" he asked.

"How does what work?" demanded Lucifer in a domineering voice.

Dan rose from the priest's side, stepped several feet in front of the group, and asked, "When someone is thrown into the oak, who or what determines which cave that person will spend his or her eternity?"

Lucifer was pleased with the young man's interest in his kingdom. He was equally intrigued with his resourcefulness in escaping his assigned cave and in his heroic efforts—though against evil—in overpowering the Reclaimers. "I'm beginning to understand why your winged friend Michael has taken such an interest in you."

"What's so special about the wooden throne?" asked Dan.

The Father of Lies lowered his wings, exposing the portal. "This wooden throne was carved from the tree of knowledge."

"The tree of knowledge?" blurted Father James. He struggled to his feet.

"Of course," replied Lucifer. "Surely you didn't think I'd let one of your God's greatest acts of creation in the Garden of Eden to remain inactive and unexploited?" He stepped from his seat and turned to view the back support. "I plundered it from the Garden of Eden shortly after the exile of your first parents."

"What's the tree of knowledge?" asked Jimmy.

"You've never heard of the tree of knowledge?" exclaimed Lucifer.

Jimmy shook his head.

The Father of Lies brushed aside Jimmy's intolerable question and walked clumsily toward Dan. "Ever since the Garden of Eden was abandoned, whenever humans die and are judged worthy of my kingdom, they are drawn through my throne—the tree of knowledge—which instantly discerns their predominant sin or fault and sends them to their fated cave. The deciphering and banishment processes are so instantaneous that they are unaware of their sentencing and oblivious how they arrived in their place of torment. To them, it's identical to a dream where fact and fiction are often indistinguishable and where details and memories are never recaptured."

The throne rocked with greater intensity.

"But we didn't die," reminded Dan. "We were thrown into the oak."

"That's your misfortune," roared Lucifer.

With all eyes glued to the sovereign's chair, the travelers watched an oak leaf drift through its back support and settle on the ground.

Lucifer's black eyes met Jimmy's.

"Why wasn't it sent to a cave?" asked Jimmy.

Satan glared at the young man before shouting, "If stupidity were a sin, you would have been doomed to my empire long ago." With a twist of his wrist, the leaf rose and landed in his hand. "Only humans are judged and confined to caves when they pass through the tree of knowledge," he explained. The Father of Falsehoods neared his throne.

Father James was slowly yielding to despair. He pulled the prayer book from his pocket to draw strength from its inspired pages. His leg injuries caused him to stumble. While successful in grabbing the cold charcoal burner to prevent a fall, he dropped his prayer book in the process. It fell on top of the glowing embers.

Though the coals were incapable of producing heat, they retained their burning qualities.

Lucifer and the six remaining members of the Cilohtac Legion fell to the ground, screaming streams of profanities. Throughout their uncontrollable spasms, they tried to shield their large ears with their hands and wings. Their attempts offered only minimal relief. Blood dripped from their ears and pooled on the ground.

"What's happening?" shouted Cindy.

"I don't know," admitted Father James. He looked into the charcoal pit and saw his prayer book ablaze. He presumed that the burning pages were the source of the demons' agony.

The unearthly qualities of the hellish coals eluded the group. They were unaware that as the sacred Scriptures and prayers were reduced to ashes, each word was echoed throughout the royal chamber at a frequency above the range of human hearing but audible to the demons.

The Scriptures and prayers were absolute torment to Satan and his inferior fiends.

The explorers' wide-eyed gaze at Lucifer and his subordinates was interrupted by another jolt from the throne.

"Come on! It's time!" yelled Sam.

The pages were being consumed at an accelerated rate. Once Sam and William had secured the injured priest between their shoulders and the group was stepping closer to the throne, the last page of the book was incinerated.

Lucifer and his underlings regained their former powers and rose to their goat hoofs.

Dan jumped. He felt the familiar warm touch on his shoulder that he had experienced in the parallel world. The arrival of the presence signaled the departure of his fears. He knew that he and his friends had the powers of heaven on their side.

"Your souls are mine!" shouted Lucifer. He had just raised a finger—prepared to rip the souls from the travelers—when a dazzling oval light appeared at Dan's side. Satan was taken by surprise. He lowered his finger.

The light faded and revealed a well-known figure.

"Ah Michael, what an annoying surprise," ridiculed Lucifer.

Next to Dan stood the six-and-a-half-foot-tall heavenly warrior who was graced with a pair of eight-foot-wide, semitransparent wings. He was clothed in a leather tunic and brandished a golden shield and sword in one hand. With his free hand resting on Dan's shoulder, the archangel heralded, "Lucifer, you have no eternal right on these humans."

"Michael, Michael, surely you know that you're greatly outnumbered in my empire."

The six remaining members of the Cilohtac Legion obeyed the secret hand gesture behind Satan's back and inched nearer the archangel—but with justifiable fear.

"At a moment's notice, I can have legions upon legions of my loyalists vanquishing you and your human companions," dared the Father of Deceit.

The archangel offered a mere sweeping glance at the six-member

Cilohtac Legion. They vanished. Satan, however, remained unaffected by the heavenly being's gaze.

Clanging sounds echoed throughout the throne room as the six unmanned swords and shields crashed to the ground.

Lucifer trembled, though he was quick to turn and conceal his panic.

With Dan protected at the heavenly messenger's side, the other travelers sought refuge behind Saint Michael.

Satan boiled with rage at the thought of the archangel defeating his elite legion with simply a glance. He sank his raptor-like talons into his chest and tore open his flesh. He spun, yelling, "Enter your eternal abode, Dan Clay!"

A paranormal wind tunnel instantly materialized. Its origin and destination were the core of Lucifer's exposed soul.

Father James passed out and fell to the stone floor.

The archangel quickly extended his wings to shelter the travelers behind him.

Dan's feet were pulled out from under him. He was being pulled into the wind tunnel.

Saint Michael grabbed Dan's arm; the teenager clasped the wrist of the heavenly being.

Dan remained elevated four feet above the ground in a horizontal position. He was slowly being drawn into the wind tunnel in spite of Saint Michael's hold.

The intense pull yanked the archangel one step forward.

Behind the heavenly messenger, five explorers tried to release Father James from his dazed state. Sadly, only seconds before Saint Michael spread his wings to block the view of Satan's vile soul, the priest had peered into its dark recesses. In that brief moment, he witnessed the re-enactment of all sins committed since Adam and Eve's expulsion from the Garden of Eden.

In their efforts to revive the priest, the travelers gawked at Dan's predicament. William and Sam bolted to their feet. For their own safety, Saint Michael knocked them to the ground with his wings.

Dan's grip on the archangel waned. As he looked at his clenched hand around Saint Michael's wrist, he eyed a peculiarity. Within the mighty wind tunnel, he watched a partially transparent image of his hand slide to his forearm. It reminded him of a snake shedding its skin. The sensation was similar to one's hand falling asleep. He released his hold on the archangel. His lifeless hand went limp.

Saint Michael tightened his grasp on Dan's arm.

Dan lowered his gaze to the ground.

Though Dan was mystified with the physical abnormality, Saint Michael had observed firsthand the postmortem sight many times—but never on a living being.

Dan's soul was being ripped from his body.

"Pray!" screamed the archangel.

Dan remained silent.

"Pray!" he yelled again.

Dan raised his head. Their eyes met. The teenager's left eye was midnight black with a white horizontal slit that extended the length of his eyeball. A demonic possession had begun. Dan lowered his sights a second time.

Whereas no humans are completely immune to occasional despair, Dan was suffering isolation and spiritual desolation at the deepest personal level. He regretted the many missed opportunities in his young life to inflict hatred and harm on his neighbor.

Aware that the extraction of his soul would soon be irreversible, Saint Michael placed a death grip on his friend's arm. "Pray!" he demanded.

Dan raised his head, offered a devilish look, and screamed, "Hail Mary!"

With the proclamation of the two words—though shouted with insincerity and in rage—Dan's left eye immediately took on its normal appearance. Life returned to his hand. He grabbed the archangel's wrist. Although his soul had been reclaimed, he still remained at arm's length from Saint Michael and within the pull of the demonic wind tunnel.

Towering above Dan's fluttering body, the archangel spit into the wind tunnel.

The saliva entered the core of Satan's sinister soul. The contact of saintliness with unadulterated evil caused the Master of Lies to undergo brutal spasms and foam at both mouths. He crashed to the ground, shrieking profanities.

With his collapse, the wind tunnel dematerialized.

Dan fell to the floor on his stomach.

For several minutes, the Prince of Darkness remained face down and motionless, allowing his torn flesh to repair itself supernaturally.

With his sword and shield still clasped in one hand, the archangel helped his young friend to his feet. "Dan, we must act quickly," he instructed. He looked at the huddled group behind and warned, "Lucifer's loss of power won't—" He noticed Father James's dazed state and quickly placed his healing hand over the priest's eyes.

The moment his hand was removed, Father James blinked and then shuddered.

Saint Michael fixed his eyes on the motionless Prince of Evil and cautioned, "Lucifer's loss of power won't last long." He refocused his attention on the recovering priest and stressed, "Father, never forget what you witnessed. Always remember that sin and its effects are real. Pray for the conversion of sinners."

Still shocked speechless, the priest nodded slowly.

"How long will Lucifer's condition last?" asked Sam.

"Not long," informed the heavenly being.

The archangel and the travelers had taken only four steps in the direction of the throne's portal when the demonic spasms ended.

As the Father of Lies rose to his two goat legs, the travelers jumped behind Saint Michael.

The archangel instantly spread his wings to shield them. He glared at Satan and proclaimed, "The Almighty has charged me to release this group from your wrongful hold."

Lucifer took three backward steps while wiping the foam from his mouths. "But the only escape is through the tree of knowledge," he reminded. Satan plopped on the throne. "And they'll have to get past me—an impossibility."

"With God's help, they have the means to outwit and overpower you," declared Saint Michael.

"Me?" he replied with a trace of laughter in his voice. He shook his head. "Michael, Michael, do you actually believe that these insignificant humans can defeat the pure essence of deceit, decadence, and depravity?"

The explorers trembled. They knew that Satan had regained his previous powers and cunningness.

"Really Michael," declared Satan, "I think you've been hovering dangerously close to the glow of your God far too long."

Without removing his stare from Lucifer, the archangel ordered Dan to his side. "Your pocket," whispered Saint Michael.

Lucifer leaned over the left arm of his chair and watched Dan reach into his jeans.

The throne suffered its worst shakes.

The Father of Darkness was thrown to the ground again.

From his pocket, Dan pulled the three ripped pages from Father James's prayer book.

"The only way to escape the heart of hell is by the Word of God," proclaimed the archangel.

The battle for the eternal possession of seven souls waged on.

CHAPTER TWENTY-ONE
Canopy Chaos

THE CLAYS, THE PARKERS, AND SARA SOMER REMAINED IN CONstant prayer throughout the day below the statue of Saint Michael the Archangel. The only time they left the church was for a late lunch at the local diner.

At 7:00 in the evening, the families entered the last pew to accommodate the mourners who had arrived for a funeral Mass. Just three days prior, a senior parishioner had passed away of natural causes. From the back of the church, the parents watched Father Andreas descend the sanctuary steps and sprinkle holy water on the draped casket. Weeping was heard from the first pew.

Nearly ninety minutes later, the parents returned to the kneeler below the statue.

Father Andreas placed the censer that held the burning incense used during the funeral Mass on the church steps to cool. He approached the parents. "May I join you?" he whispered.

"Oh please, Father," replied Nancy.

Although initially disbelieving of the parents' outlandish stories, Father Andreas was amazed with the resolve of the families to deepen their prayer life and attend daily Mass for the safe return of their loved ones. Moreover, since there hadn't been any reported sightings of Father James or the recovery of his body, he found himself mulling over their claims with greater frequency, though he still entertained considerable doubts.

The moment the final prayer was recited, Jeff raised his sleeve and announced that it was 9:00 p.m.

As much as the parents had longed for that particular sunset for weeks, they trembled at the thought that their children might not return.

Father Andreas rose from the kneeler. "It's time," he announced.

The parents and the priest walked to the doors in total silence. In the chilly night air, they descended the church steps.

Sara accidentally kicked the hot censer. It wobbled.

"Careful," warned the priest. "I set it out here to cool."

The families and Father Andreas stepped off the sidewalk and advanced three feet nearer the oak.

Jeff, on the other hand, turned in the opposite direction and headed to the parking lot.

"Honey, what's wrong?" asked Nancy.

"Nothing. I'll be right back."

The group reduced the distance between themselves and the ominous tree by another few feet.

Nancy heard movement from behind. She looked over her shoulder and saw her husband moving toward the group with a backpack strapped to his shoulders.

"What are you doing?" she asked.

While positioning the backpack squarely between his shoulder blades he replied, "I can't take the chance of the kids not returning tonight. I refuse to be left in limbo for another month." He glanced at the tree. "I'm going after them."

"I'll join you," insisted Tom.

The wives looked at their husbands in dismay.

Despite the fact that Marie had mentioned to Tom the possibility of the men taking on a rescue mission, now that he had volunteered, the reality of the dangers disturbed her deeply.

The women faced the ultimate dilemma—choosing between their loved ones. While they knew there was the likelihood that their husbands might not return, they couldn't bear the thought of never seeing their children again.

Nancy rose above her internal conflict and compromised, "Jeff, I can't prevent you from doing what you feel you must do, but let's give our boys a little more time."

"What do you mean?"

"Let's give them a couple more hours," she proposed. "If they don't return by midnight, then you and I will step into the oak."

"You?" he blurted. "Absolutely not. It's far too dangerous."

"Jeff, I can't live without you and the boys. My place is at my family's side, regardless of the dangers."

He reluctantly agreed to his wife's offer.

The vigil commenced several feet from the sidewalk.

Few words were spoken. The stares at the sixty-foot-high oak—nearly fifty feet away—remained unbroken.

At 10:45, Jeff moved closer to the tree.

"Jeff, it's not midnight," exclaimed Nancy.

"I know, but I'm curious if the tree's soft," he said. "If it's not, then we're wasting our time."

Sara screamed.

A single limb thrashed wildly at the treetop.

Sara immediately recalled Officer Moore's dream about the overactive branches. Thankfully, the limb never reached low enough to pose serious danger. But the group wasn't taking any chances.

Tom, Marie, Sara, and Father Andreas sought safety on the sidewalk.

Nancy, however, remained on the lawn, entreating her husband to return to her side.

"But I have to touch the oak," he explained. "I need to know if I can walk through it."

"Honey, please step out of harm's way," she implored.

After another pleading, Jeff returned to her side. Together, they joined the waiting party on the walkway.

All eyes focused on the tree's canopy.

"Maybe it was just the wind," remarked Sara.

"I thought that too," said Tom. "But if it was the wind, then why'd only one branch move?"

"And the wind wasn't strong enough to swing a branch that size," claimed Marie. "It's awfully large."

Jeff paced the sidewalk before stepping into the street. He viewed the oak from all angles.

"What do you think, Jeff?" asked Father Andreas.

Jeff lowered his gaze from the tree's heights to its base and answered, "I guess it's active." He neared the group. "I tend to agree with Marie. It's odd that a large limb shook in a gentle breeze."

The events of the previous full moon gradually replayed at the top of the oak as the midnight hour drew closer.

Within minutes of noticing the single branch whirling aloft, several more limbs whipped overhead. With each passing minute, the branches lowered their reach.

Near darkness blanketed the group after a bold limb shattered the streetlight. Fortunately, the families and Father Andreas were beyond the reach of the branch. In the poor light that filtered from across the street, the party remained watchful from the security of the sidewalk.

After several minutes of uninterrupted stares at the tree, Sara was becoming impatient. "What time is it?" she demanded.

Jeff shouted that it was 11:15.

"Sara, I know it's close to midnight, but we must keep our hope alive," encouraged Nancy.

"I know; you're right." In confusion she added, "But it's strange."

"What's that?" asked Nancy.

"I've been waiting for this night for a month. And now that it's here, I'm absolutely terrified."

"So am I," admitted Nancy. "I never thought I'd—"

Her remark was cut short by a disturbance on the street. The group was blinded momentarily by the high beams of a car pulling alongside the curb.

Officer Moore stepped from her police car.

"Good evening," greeted Father Andreas while walking to the curb.

"Hello Father." The policewoman wasted no time. She approached the parents. "Good evening, folks," she said. "I was on patrol when I noticed—" She was caught off guard by eight twirling limbs and a broken streetlight. "What on earth!" she exclaimed.

"The branches only recently started tossing about," informed Jeff.

"And the streetlight?"

"A limb hit it just minutes ago," replied Nancy.

"We decided to wait for our kids on the sidewalk—out of the limbs' path," explained Marie.

The officer compared the distance between the sidewalk and the tree against the reach of the limbs. "We should be safe at this distance," she predicted.

"Officer, you said that you were on patrol when you noticed what?" asked Jeff.

"I was on patrol when I noticed the full moon. I thought I'd swing by to check out the area."

"Thank you," said the priest. "We could use your protection."

The policewoman grabbed her portable radio and informed headquarters of her location. There was a moment of silence before she concluded, "No backup is necessary." She silenced the radio and turned to the parents, asking, "If your children vanished through the tree as you claim, when do you expect them to return?"

"There's no way of knowing exactly, but sometime before sunrise," answered Jeff.

"Well if we're going to be here for several hours, I suggest we make ourselves comfortable." She, along with the parents and the priest, sat on the sidewalk.

•

In hell, Lucifer sprang from the ground and plopped on his throne. He refused to leave the chair's back support in clear view.

Under the protection and direction of Saint Michael, Dan dropped one prayer sheet on top of the burning embers.

Satan tumbled from his throne and wailed aloud. He was experiencing another series of intense spasms.

"Cindy—go!" commanded the archangel.

She gave a quick bow to the heavenly messenger and began her sprint. Her leap to freedom, however, was delayed.

Sam had grabbed her by the arm and warned, "When you're free of the portal, stay clear of the limbs. If they're lashing about like you said they were the night you were thrown into the tree, I don't want anyone ending up back in a side cave."

She resumed her dash to the throne and jumped into the back support. After a surge of bright light, she disappeared.

•

On the other side of the portal, Sara and Jeff bolted to their feet. They were the first to spot Cindy emerge from the tree.

As the other parents and the priest scrambled to their feet, Officer Moore remained seated on the sidewalk, staring at the oak's base in a stunned state. She—who prided herself on being well-read on virtually all phenomena—was traumatized. Not even her previous dream prepared her for the unexplained event.

Unlike Officer Moore, Father Andreas—though admittedly startled with Cindy's sudden appearance—never slipped into a shocked condition.

To Cindy's surprise, she experienced only minimal crossover effects. She looked overhead and was thankful that the limbs—although swinging wildly—were not nearly as hostile as they were the night she was abducted. Mother and daughter embraced beneath the enchanted oak.

A limb plunged halfway down the tree.

Jeff grabbed the women and guided them to the safety of the sidewalk.

Minutes after Cindy's return to Lawton, Brad stepped from the tree's base and collapsed to his knees. The physical effects of the crossover had left the newest traveler breathless. Tom raced across the lawn and helped him to the walkway.

The group stood on the sidewalk's border, nervously awaiting the arrival of the remaining travelers.

•

In the throne room, the last words on the prayer sheet were proclaimed throughout the chamber before being reduced to ashes.

Lucifer tried to muffle the pronouncement by covering his giant ears with his hands and wings. Blood trickled down his arms.

Dan dropped the second page into the charcoal burner.

"William, go!" ordered the archangel.

He made his dash.

•

Nancy and Jeff ran across the church grounds to their son.

Several limbs extended their reach within feet of the ground.

The parents embraced William for nearly a minute.

A sudden crash on the lawn surprised them. The family narrowly escaped being captured by two diving limbs. They reached shelter near the church steps.

As the full moon rose in the heavens, more aggressive limbs fell to the earth.

"Where's Jimmy?" screamed Marie.

"He's coming. He needs more time," said William.

"What time is it?" she demanded.

Jeff yelled that it was 11:45.

Just feet behind the group, Officer Moore's condition remained unchanged.

•

In the sinister realm, Saint Michael ordered Jimmy to flee the land of perdition.

After unintentionally trampling Lucifer's left wing and flattening a handful of dung beetles in the process, Jimmy darted to freedom. Another family reunion took place below the hostile limbs of the oak. During the gathering, the limbs displayed their most violent behavior. Amazingly, the family dodged three aerial assaults and reached their friends on the sidewalk.

Jimmy immediately noticed the unresponsive police officer sitting on the sidewalk. "What's wrong with her?" he asked.

During the uproar of the rescue efforts below the canopy chaos, no one noticed the police officer's dazed state.

Father Andreas knelt at her side and tapped her face to release her from her condition. His attempts failed.

•

In hell, Dan dropped the third prayer sheet into the charcoal pit.

"Sam, help Father James through the portal," commanded Saint Michael.

"Please," implored the priest, "Sam and Dan should go first."

A quarter of the last prayer sheet was incinerated.

In a calm but commanding voice, Saint Michael directed, "Go Father. Your vocation is vital in battling and conquering the rampant wickedness on earth."

Father James gave a respectful bow and stepped with Sam on the throne's seat. They had raced only a short distance across the church lawn when the priest's leg gave way. He fell face forward.

Sam jerked his gaze from the dangers above and helped Father James to his feet.

Two daring limbs were quick to take advantage of the men's temporary helplessness. The branches nose-dived, wrapped around the escapees, and dragged them nearer the oak's base.

William, Jimmy, Cindy, and Brad disregarded their own safety and raced to the captured men. With careful footing, they sidestepped several crashing limbs and reached their friends. With eight hands tugging against the grasp of the two limbs, the branches surrendered their prey and sprang to the moonlit sky. After three more close calls, the six travelers were panting on the sidewalk.

"Where's Dan?" screamed Nancy. "Where is he?"

"He'll be here," promised William.

•

Dan stared at the third prayer sheet that was now reduced to half its original size.

Saint Michael rested his hand on the teenager's shoulder. "Why do these thoughts consume you?" he asked.

Dan was astonished that the archangel knew something was

troubling him. The teenager looked at Satan in agony on the ground before divulging, "This trip was nothing like our journey in the parallel world. Here, the dangers and consequences were eternal. Here, our souls hung in the balance. But you weren't with us this time, like you were in the parallel world."

"Dan, just because you didn't see me, hear me, or feel my touch doesn't mean I wasn't at your side," corrected the saintly being. "Both your guardian angel and I have been with you since the moment you were thrown into the oak. You were never alone."

Dan lowered his head, ashamed of his doubts. With his sights cast downward, he saw that barely a quarter of the final prayer sheet remained. In terror, he looked up at the archangel who was staring into the burner. Dan followed his gaze. He was shocked. The combustion had stopped.

"You see, Dan, the entire group—but you especially—received an extraordinary gift," revealed the heavenly being. "You and your friends were permitted to visit hell and experience its horrors. Now you know that hell exists. And now it's your responsibility to warn others." There was a deliberate pause before the archangel posed, "I think you know what God's will is for you." Saint Michael glanced at the prayer sheet again. The burning resumed. "But your time has come. Your parents are waiting."

The two stepped over Satan and jumped on the wooden throne.

Dan turned and took an unlimited view of the royal chamber, committing the appalling surroundings to memory.

The final amen on the final prayer sheet was obliterated.

The archangel and the human leaped through the portal.

Dan's feet had just touched the church lawn when he fell to his knees. He watched a streak of light cross the sky. The angelic departure happened so quickly that it eluded the families near the church.

"Dan!" screamed Nancy. She and Jeff darted off the sidewalk.

It was midnight.

At the height of the full moon, every limb exploded with rage. Dozens of branches slammed against the ground.

For her safety, Jeff pushed Nancy beyond the reach of the combative limbs.

The priests restrained her. She was denied to step foot on the battlefield.

Jeff resumed his dash and was successfully dodging the limbs en route to his son.

Dan was experiencing greater crossover effects than normal. He dropped from his knees to his stomach, trying to catch his breath. Fully aware that his quest wouldn't end until he was beyond the reach of the limbs, he lifted himself and was crawling on all fours when his ankle was seized. He looked behind, expecting to see the limb that had grabbed him. He gasped.

Lucifer's hand was sticking through the tree and pulling him back.

"Dad!" screamed Dan.

Jeff raced the remaining feet and dived to the ground. He took hold of his son's left hand.

"I said there was no escape!" roared Lucifer.

As Dan squirmed to free himself from Satan's clutch, Jeff got a glimpse of the demon's face. "My God," he whispered. Were it not for his determination to rescue his son, he—like Officer Moore—would have fallen into a state of shock.

Even though Sam, Jimmy, William, Tom, Cindy, and Brad made numerous and heroic efforts to help Jeff, the overactive limbs kept pushing them away.

As Father James watched the branches knock the potential rescuers back to the sidewalk, but without capturing them, he knew that the oak was interested in only one victim that round—Dan. And nothing would foil its mission.

A limb wrapped around Jeff's leg and pulled him farther from the tree. Father and son were separated.

Lucifer made the most of the setback. He dragged Dan closer to the portal.

Jeff wrestled free of the limb's hold, leaped four feet, and re-established the one-handed bond with his son.

Lucifer, however, refused to relinquish his grip on his victim.

The would-be liberators on the sidewalk made no headway.

A hysterical Nancy continued fighting to escape the priests' hold.

Her high-pitched screams snapped Officer Moore from her dazed state. The policewoman instinctively focused on the commotion nearly fifty feet ahead. Drawing on her physical training from the police academy, she dodged the falling limbs until she was on her stomach at Jeff's side. "Dan!" she yelled. "Give me your other hand!"

Dan rolled onto his side.

The officer saw what Jeff had spotted minutes earlier. She shuddered at Lucifer's appearance, but only briefly.

Another falling limb caught Jeff and the policewoman off guard. It coiled around Jeff's neck and dragged him from Dan.

With one hand gripping Dan, Officer Moore pulled her pistol from its holster, took aim above Jeff's head, and pulled the trigger.

The limb released its victim and sprang to the treetop.

The officer and Jeff pulled Dan from Lucifer's grip.

Before rising to his knees, Dan glanced behind. With Satan's head still poking through the oak, Dan smashed his boot against his face.

The Prince of Darkness was knocked through the tree and toppled from his throne.

With extreme caution, Jeff, Dan, and the officer reached the safety of the sidewalk.

The priests released Nancy who ran into the arms of her son and husband.

As the family members embraced, Father James—though still in a great deal of pain from the injuries inflicted by Cerberus—knew that he had to kill the tree. *But how?* he thought. He had a hunch that the Father of Lies would step through the oak at any moment. Time was crucial. The hot censer on the church steps gave him an idea. He limped the several feet and grabbed it.

"Father, what are you doing?" asked Father Andreas.

"We need to destroy the tree!"

"I doubt the hot incense will do much good," predicted Father Andreas. "The oak's enormous."

"With what exists inside that tree, this blessed incense may be our best and only hope."

Four limbs targeted the group. Fortunately, the families were beyond their reach.

"But we have to act fast," insisted Father James. "Lucifer could step from the oak at any moment."

"Lucifer?" blurted his brother priest. "Do you realize what you're saying?"

With the exception of Jeff and Officer Moore, terror surfaced on the faces of the parents and Father Andreas.

"I'll explain later," snapped Father James.

Sam reached for the censer. "No disrespect, Father, but you're in no condition to race to the tree."

"I suppose not," he yielded.

"But Sam, the branches are still crashing to the ground," warned Dan.

"I know!" Sam turned and stared at the oak's trunk. "But we don't have a choice. It's too far away to throw from here and expect a direct hit. And we've got just one shot."

Cindy offered an alternative. "Maybe a few of us should—"

"You're not stepping near that tree!" ordered her mother.

"Cindy, I'll be fine," assured Sam.

"Sam, you and I could—"

"Forget it, Dan!" shouted Sam. He stood on the sidewalk's edge, waiting for the opportune time to strike. The moment five low-hanging limbs bounced back to the canopy, he charged through the path of destruction.

The onlookers remained on the sidewalk, holding their breaths. The priests prayed.

The five branches that had only recently soared overhead, plummeted when Sam was barely halfway to the oak.

Jeff stood behind Dan with his arms folded across his son's chest.

"Dad, he needs my help!" he shouted.

As much as it pained Jeff to remain idle and watch Sam risk his life for his family and friends, he knew that any attempt at heroism on his part would free Dan to race into danger. After cringing and watching Sam narrowly escape the five limbs, he promised, "He'll be fine."

Just ten feet from the oak, Sam came to a standstill and took careful aim at its base. Sadly, moments were all the limbs needed to launch another airborne raid.

One branch wrapped around Sam's chest and another around his pitching arm.

Sam was leveled to his back. In his fall, the censer rolled beyond his reach. As he fought to free himself, he stretched a leg to nudge the censer.

On the sidewalk, Dan and Cindy broke free from their parents. Though initially making progress at diving and rolling between the dropping limbs, they soon suffered the same fate as Sam. They were captured by four branches.

Jeff, Nancy, and Sara raced across the lawn.

Sam heard screams from behind. He wrenched his neck and witnessed the tragedy unfolding. Faced with the real possibility that his friends would be hurled into the possessed oak and imprisoned in a side cave, Sam made a final reach for the censer. It rolled within inches of the oak.

Understandably preoccupied with freeing their children, Jeff, Nancy, and Sara were oblivious to the situation at the tree's trunk.

The hot embers jumped to the oak's base.

From the sidewalk, Father James suspected that the tree's rapid combustion had nothing to do with its flammability, but everything to do with the blessed coming into direct contact with pure evil.

The tree's instinct for survival prevailed over its desire for prey. The branches released Sam, Cindy, and Dan. In the limbs' rush to the oak's base to quench the flames, they scattered the hot embers.

Jeff raced to Sam who was resting on his elbows, mesmerized with the rising flames. "Come on," he ordered, before yanking Sam to his feet. Within seconds, the men were standing on the sidewalk.

Nancy, Sara, Cindy, and Dan also made a safe escape without incident.

From the distance, they watched the flames climb the tree.

Without warning, the oak shook violently. The ground quaked.

Cracks on the soil near the tree's base raced outward in all directions.

In panic, the group raced across the lawn in the opposite direction of the dying oak.

"What's happening?" shouted Cindy.

Extending from the oak's trunk, the soil breaks grew in width and depth until the ground between the oak and the sidewalk resembled a war zone that was marred with countless rifts. From the distant lawn, the travelers, their families, the priests, and the policewoman watched the oak sink into the soil.

"Dan!" was yelled from below the earth.

Fear overwhelmed the teenager.

His father pulled him close.

The tree continued its rapid descent. Within a matter of only minutes, the church grounds had swallowed up the lofty oak and censer.

Cracking sounds immediately followed.

"Cool," exclaimed Jimmy as he watched the soil heal itself and erase all evidence of the recent battle.

The group was silent and completely awed by the oak's demise.

Father James's near collapse broke the stillness.

Thankfully, Father Andreas was close by to prevent his brother priest from hitting the ground. It was only then that he noticed Father James's bloodstained pants. "I need to get you to the emergency room," he insisted.

"I'll be fine," claimed Father James.

Nancy rested on one knee and examined her pastor's injuries. "Father Andreas is right," she seconded. "You need to get these wounds checked out."

"Later." He directed his attention to the church, saying, "First things first—I'd like to make a visit. After all, I haven't been inside a church for a month."

There was no denying the fact that his gashes needed attention, but they weren't life threatening. The group agreed to his wishes.

On the second step, Father Andreas turned and looked to the sidewalk. "Officer, aren't you coming inside?" he asked.

"I suppose a brief visit wouldn't hurt." She raised the volume on her portable radio and alerted, "But I may be called away."

"That's fine; we understand," said Father Andreas.

Inside Saint Augustine of Canterbury Church, the group dropped to their knees below the marble statue of the heavenly rescuer. Father James's wounded calf and thigh required that he sit in a nearby pew.

After a few minutes of silent prayer, Cindy rose from the kneeler and sat with Father James. "Something still puzzles me," she said.

"What's that?" asked Father James.

"The lesser demons—the Cilohtac—where did they go?"

Her question drew everyone from their prayers.

Sara stepped alongside the pew. "Honey, what on earth is a Cilohtac?"

"They were Lucifer's elite servants."

"Lucifer?" she exclaimed. "Cindy, that's not a name you should toy with—especially in a church."

"But she's not toying with it," corrected Father James. "She's telling the truth."

"From what I saw poking through the oak a few minutes ago, I have no doubts," remarked Jeff.

"Look everyone, come sit in the pew. We'll do our best to recount our journey," suggested Father James.

"But Father James, your leg needs to be checked out," implored his brother priest. "I can see blood dripping from here."

"I appreciate your concern, but it's not that bad," played down the pastor. "Besides, it's not the first time I've lost blood in this church."

"So it was your blood at the Communion rail—like in Officer Moore's dream," said Nancy.

"I don't know anything about the officer's dream, but yeah, it was my blood." He glanced at the Communion rail. "I guess that's the best place to begin the story."

Halfway through his account of the travelers' adventures in hell, Nancy interrupted. "What do you mean the guardians rose from the dead?"

"Just that. There was no way to kill them—at least not forever," stated Father James.

Nearly an hour later, Dan concluded the story by describing Satan's throne room and his departure with Saint Michael.

A crime in progress was broadcast from Officer Moore's portable radio. She reduced the volume. "It appears there's been another home burglary on Crawford Lane," she disclosed before exiting the pew.

She had walked only several feet up the aisle when she stopped and turned. "Before I go, um—"

"Yes officer," prompted Father James.

"Before I go, I owe all of you an apology."

"Officer, you owe us nothing," assured Nancy. She looked at Dan and reminded, "You saved our son's life."

"Be that as it may, I still owe everyone an apology." She rested her hand on her holster from which she drew her strength. "I guess it goes without saying that I was very skeptical of your story at first. I started to believe when I found Dan's house key in this very church. But as time passed, I found myself questioning your story more and more. Doubts crept in and refused to leave."

"I also owe everyone an apology," admitted Father Andreas.

"An apology?" questioned Father James. "For what?"

"The families met with me one morning after Mass and asked that I not remove the oak," he explained. "When they told me why, I refused to believe their story. It was too—I don't know—unearthly. Even when I read your letter I still doubted."

"You got my letter?" asked Father James.

"Yeah," he replied. Father Andreas lowered his head.

Father James sensed that his brother priest and the officer were harboring needless guilt. "Look," he said, "I hold nothing against either of you. Anyone would have thought our story was unimaginable. Anyone would have reacted the same way."

The families voiced identical sentiments.

Officer Moore expressed her regrets a second time and left the church.

After the door slammed behind the policewoman, Cindy spun in the pew in Father James's direction. "You never answered my question," she said.

"What's that?"

"Where did the Cilohtac go?"

"Oh, the Cilohtac," he recalled. He rested his aching leg on the kneeler and admitted, "There's no way of knowing for sure. But I'd imagine that Saint Michael relocated them to a remote part of hell."

"What kind of a name is Cilohtac anyway?" asked Jimmy. "I mean, you can hardly pronounce it."

"I also was intrigued with the name," said Father James. "I couldn't figure it out. But then it hit me."

"What?" asked Cindy.

"Cilohtac is Catholic spelled backwards," he explained. "And the other legion that Lucifer mentioned—the Nacilgna—is Anglican in reverse."

"Wicked!" exclaimed Jimmy.

"And I wouldn't be surprised if Satan's other legions also were named after Christian denominations, but backwards," guessed the priest.

"Come on, Father James, we need to get you to the emergency room," implored his brother priest.

"Give me a few minutes." *Minutes,* he thought. Father James glanced at his watch. To his delight, the date was accurate. "The throne room also was full of contradictions," he added, "like the two demons of the Cilohtac Legion whom Lucifer called Folly and Impiety. Folly is the opposite of understanding and impiety is obviously the opposite of piety—two gifts of the Holy Spirit. I'd wager that the other five members of the Cilohtac Legion also have names that are opposite the other five gifts."

"It's also weird, Father, that the charcoal burners produced cold and not heat," said Dan.

"I can only surmise that the souls of iniquity in the burners were the source of the cold," said the pastor. "Remember, there's no warm feeling in evil." He noticed a perplexed look on Dan's face and suspected that something deeper was disturbing him. "What's on your mind?" he asked.

"Why did Lucifer grab my ankle when I left the oak? I mean, why didn't he use his powers to throw me back into his throne room, like he hurled Sam, William, and me against the cave wall in his chamber?"

Father James scratched his chin. He also was baffled. "I suppose he couldn't use his complete supernatural powers because he was partially outside of hell," he eventually proposed. He eyed a look of doubt on more than a few faces in the group. "Don't get me wrong," he quickly clarified, "Lucifer has incredible powers on earth. But in hell, everything is complete evil with a total absence of anything even remotely good. On earth, however, all of God's creation—especially humans—possess some degree of goodness and beauty which counteracts or diminishes Satan's control in the world. Never underestimate the power of prayer."

William shook his head. "But why—"

"That's enough," interrupted Father Andreas. "We can continue this conversation later. Right now, I need to get Father James to the emergency room."

The pastor agreed to his demand.

After Father James was buckled up in Father Andreas's car, he looked at the families on the street curb. "I'll see you at Mass on Sunday," he promised.

"That's presuming you're well enough to celebrate Mass," cautioned Father Andreas.

"I'm sure I'll be fine by Sunday."

As the priests sped away, the families neared the parking lot.

"Mom, Dad, I also owe you an apology," confessed Dan.

The parents stopped in their tracks.

"What for?" asked Nancy.

"During the last full moon, William and I sneaked out of the house and walked to the church. We just wanted to be there when Sam got back. But we didn't break our promise. We didn't jump into the oak."

"We know," said Nancy.

"You do?" exclaimed Dan.

"Of course," she replied. "Officer Moore had a dream about the wild limbs. Anyway, after she shared her dream and then told us about her find at the church, we put the pieces together."

"What did she find at the church?" pressed Dan.

"A twig and an oak leaf behind a loose brick."

"I don't understand," said Dan.

"We'll explain later," promised Nancy.

Once farewells were exchanged between the families, they headed home—except for Sara and Cindy who offered Brad Blaze a ride across town.

At 2:30 a.m., the Clays pulled into their driveway. After another hour of storytelling around the kitchen table, they retired.

In his basement room, Sam was asleep within minutes. Nancy

and Jeff welcomed the peaceful slumber that had escaped them for weeks. William, resting on top of a comforter in his travel clothes, dozed in the middle of a conversation with his brother.

Dan stretched out in bed and mentally replayed his last conversation with the archangel. He was determined to discern God's will for him. At 4:00 a.m., exhaustion won out. He closed his eyes.

CHAPTER TWENTY-TWO
Guarded Grin

THE MORNING SUNLIGHT STREAMING THROUGH THE WINDOW stirred Nancy from her sleep. She crawled from the bed and tiptoed across the bedroom floor, careful not to wake Jeff. Knowing that her sons hadn't eaten in a month, she decided to treat her family to a bountiful breakfast. Before descending the staircase, however, she neared the boys' shared bedroom and opened the door where she remained motionless—leaning against the doorjamb—lost in her gaze at her sons. She reflected on their innocent childhood and how circumstances forced them to adulthood in just a few short months. She closed the door and headed to the kitchen.

An hour later, she jumped while cracking an egg.

Dan had slipped into the kitchen unnoticed and squeezed her shoulder from behind.

She spun. "Dan, you scared me nearly half to death!"

"I know; I meant to," he teased.

She shook her head before looking at the smashed egg on the floor.

Dan turned and caught sight of the spread on the table. "Who's coming to breakfast?" he asked.

"No one." She grabbed a paper towel and bent down to clean the mess on the floor while explaining, "I thought it would be nice for the family to enjoy a hot breakfast together. I guess you could call it your second homecoming meal."

GUARDED GRIN

"I haven't eaten in so long, I hardly know what to eat first." He opened the refrigerator door.

"Honey, what are you looking for?" she asked.

He reached for the milk carton.

"Since you're there, grab the orange juice." She tossed the dirty paper towel into the trash can before suggesting, "Go downstairs and wake Sam."

"Sure."

Dan was only four steps down the staircase when William entered the room. "What's the special occasion?" He approached the table.

"Good morning honey," she said. "The special occasion is that my family has been reunited—that's what."

He took a swig of milk from Dan's glass. "Where's Dad?" he asked.

"He's still upstairs. He hasn't been sleeping too well during the past month. I debated on waking him earlier, but then thought that the extra rest would do him good."

"Obviously not enough rest." He watched his father step into the kitchen. "Hey Dad," he greeted.

"Morning son. Where's your brother?"

"I don't know. He wasn't in his bed."

"He's downstairs waking Sam," informed Nancy.

A familiar creak was heard at the top of the basement staircase. Sam and Dan stepped over the doorsill.

"Wow! I've never seen so much food—at least not in a month or so," exclaimed Sam.

"Come on everyone, let's sit down before it gets cold," directed Nancy.

Following a prayer of thanksgiving for the meal and the travelers' safe return, the family enjoyed the feast.

"Boys, your mother obviously has put a lot of time into this breakfast," observed Jeff. "But considering you haven't eaten in a month, I'd be careful about overdoing it. We don't know how your bodies will react."

"I never thought about that," said Nancy.

"But Dad, it wouldn't be right to disappoint Mom," said Dan in a joking manner.

"Yeah, we can't upset her," seconded William. "Like you said, she's put a lot of time into it."

Nancy looked at her husband and grinned.

As the brothers and Sam filled their plates, Nancy and Jeff sipped their coffee and glanced from son to son. For a month, Nancy had secretly feared that she'd never witness the family around the table again. There were no words to describe her joy. Jeff, on the other hand, was astounded with the amount of food the men devoured in record time.

Nancy was drawn from her bliss and Jeff from his astonishment when Dan muttered something with a mouthful of eggs.

"Honey, swallow your food," advised Nancy. "We can't understand a word you're saying."

He gulped. "What about Jimmy?" he said.

"What about him?" asked Nancy.

While filling his plate with another pile of eggs, Dan replied, "Shouldn't someone tell him to go easy on the food? I mean, it's no secret that he's rarely missed a meal in his life until a month ago."

Nancy set her coffee cup on its saucer before stating, "Let's let Marie and Tom worry about that."

Jeff failed miserably at concealing a smirk in his napkin.

"Jeff, there's nothing wrong with Jimmy having a healthy appetite," reminded Nancy. She reached for her coffee cup, raised it to her lips, but quickly pulled it away. "Still, how on earth did he survive an entire month without food?"

"And it doesn't look like he's lost any weight," added Sam.

Nancy realized that her comment was only encouraging the conversation. "I'm sure that Tom and Marie will keep an eye on his intake," she concluded.

The rest of the meal involved more chewing and less conversation.

Once the three travelers had emptied the six serving dishes and pushed their plates aside, they rested their elbows on the table and captivated Jeff and Nancy with more stories of the guardians that patrolled the caves of hell.

At the mere mention of Lucifer, Nancy blurted, "Okay, that's enough for now." In truth, just the idea of Satan horrified her. Her sons' encounter with the Father of Lies was too much for her to bear.

She looked at the empty plates and changed the subject. "Let's clean this mess and figure out what to do today."

"Let's check on Father James," blurted Dan.

"I was just thinking the same thing," said Nancy.

By 11:00, the Clays and Sam were welcomed at the rectory door by Father Andreas who led them to the living room where Father James was resting on the sofa. After nearly two hours of exchanging hellish war stories, they excused themselves. The priest needed his rest.

The remainder of the afternoon was spent relaxing at home. An early evening visit was paid to the Parkers and the Somers.

Shortly before 10:00 p.m., the Clays and Sam were sound asleep.

To Nancy and Jeff, it seemed that they had just dropped their heads to their pillows when the 7:00 a.m. alarm rang.

"Come on, boys!" yelled Nancy from the hallway. "Get up or we'll be late for Mass."

By 7:30, the family was pulling into the church parking lot. They froze halfway up the sidewalk and stared at the spot where the oak once stood. To the parents' surprise and relief, neither son made an attempt to cross the lawn to examine the area. The family stepped into the church where they joined the Parkers and the Somers in the pew closest to the marble statue.

"Jimmy, this isn't a funeral," taunted Dan.

"What?"

"Your suit," he clarified. "What's with the suit?"

Jimmy ignored his neighbor's sarcastic comment.

The prayers of gratitude offered by the families were interrupted by the clanging of a bell. Mass had begun.

Father James limped across the sanctuary, kissed the altar, and made an unhurried sign of the cross. When trapped in hell, he promised himself that he'd embrace his Catholic faith and vocation with greater fervor. Every word and gesture evoked humility and reverence.

Fifteen minutes later, the congregation relaxed on the wooden pews as Father James opened his homily.

After asking forgiveness from the faithful for his unexpected absence—though careful not to reveal any specifics about his whereabouts—Father James continued, "Moments ago, we heard Saint

Paul's words, 'What eye has not seen, and ear has not heard, and what has not entered the human heart, what God has prepared for those who love him.' But have you ever stopped and reflected on this passage?" He looked at his former co-explorers near the statue. "These words hold special significance to all of us as pilgrims—travelers as it were—on our earthly journey to heaven. Essentially, Saint Paul is telling us that no one can possibly imagine—even in their wildest dreams—how glorious heaven will be for those who love God."

Standing only a few minutes brought on intense pain. Father James would have collapsed had he not grabbed the pulpit. After regaining his balance, he proposed, "But I believe the passage can be viewed from another perspective. On a personal level—and I stress that it's my own belief—I feel strongly that the opposite also holds true." He looked again to his traveling companions. "What eye has not seen, and ear has not heard, and what has not entered the human heart, what God has prepared for those who do *not* love him. It's impossible to imagine how vile, wretched, and insufferable hell can be." In a fraction of a second, he relived all the horrors that he and his friends had suffered. He cleared this throat and leaned into the microphone. "Please, my brothers and sisters, waste no time in taking the path to holiness. Avoid all occasions of sin, for Satan never rests and never tires in his efforts to lure us from sanctity to iniquity. And don't be fooled—even the smallest sin can mushroom into a serious one. Though sometimes we may feel defenseless and vulnerable to Lucifer's slightest temptations, always remember that our guardian angels are at our sides shielding us from his onslaughts and those of his lesser demons. We just need to call upon our heavenly protectors. They will always guard us from the evil one."

Never before had such a brief homily impacted his congregation so profoundly.

Nancy glanced at a neighboring pew and saw that her fellow parishioners were equally awestruck with their pastor's guidance and counsel.

Within thirty minutes, the Mass had ended. The worshipers were greeted by Father James at the back doors. Father Andreas purposely remained close at hand in case his brother priest needed assistance.

As Father James attempted to explain his previous adventure in deliberately vague terms to a prying elderly couple, the travelers and their families waited within earshot for the pair to leave the church.

To pass the time, Nancy scanned a bulletin. At regular intervals, she looked at Father James who was still cleverly dodging questions about his month-long absence from the parish.

The couple eventually blessed themselves with holy water and stepped into the sunshine.

"Father, your homily was exceptional," complimented Nancy as she walked to his side.

"Thank you," he acknowledged. "The idea about Saint Paul's—" He cut his remark short and cocked his head. "Jimmy, why the suit? I've never seen you—"

"He's afraid of going to hell," interjected Cindy.

"Cindy!" snapped her mother.

"Well, why else would he wear one?" she asked.

"Anyway Father," continued Nancy, "from the expressions on the parishioners' faces around us, I'd say your homily made quite an impression."

"I hope so. It's so important that I educate my congregation on the eternal consequences of sin."

As Nancy and her pastor discussed his homily, Dan was engaged in an internal conflict.

Father James noticed the distant look on the teenager's face. "Dan, what's wrong?" he demanded.

"Father, I was planning on telling my family first, but—"

"What is it, son?" asked Jeff.

Dan struggled for the right words to open the conversation.

Father James wanted his hunch confirmed. "Dan, what was said in the throne room between you and Saint Michael after we left?" asked his pastor.

"I also want to educate people on the consequences of sin and the existence of hell," disclosed Dan.

"That's music to my ears," congratulated Father James. "I think that a man your age can accomplish—"

"But I want to do it from the pulpit," he interrupted. "I think I want to be a priest."

Everyone was stunned—except Nancy.

"In Satan's throne room, Saint Michael explained to me—in so many words—the importance of combating evil and warning others of the effects of sin," related Dan.

Nancy expressed her wholehearted support of Dan's interest in the priesthood.

"Dan, like your mother, I'm also pleased that you're thinking about your calling," declared Father James. "From what I've seen, you'd make an excellent priest." He took a panoramic view of the church's interior to confirm they were alone. "But I have a concern."

"A concern?" questioned Dan.

After an uncomfortable moment of silence, the priest disclosed, "Some priests and religious are occasionally ruthlessly tempted—mentally, emotionally, and spiritually—by Satan, since he knows of their desire to convert their lives and those they serve into lives of holiness. Although I'm thrilled with your decision, I have some—" His comment trailed off.

"Yes Father," urged Dan.

"I'm sorry, but while I have no doubts that the calling to the priesthood is a great blessing, I have some uneasiness about your decision," confessed the priest.

"What do you mean?" prodded Dan.

"I'm sure that Satan will tempt you like no other priest," revealed Father James. "Your earthly life could be a living hell. As I just said, it's not uncommon for priests and religious to be tempted greatly at the hands of Lucifer. And…well…ever since I saw Satan trying to pull you back into the oak the other night, I can't shake the feeling that he's determined to win possession of your soul—especially since he knows that you were partly responsible for the downfall of the Reclaimers in the parallel world and that it was your resourcefulness that led to our escape from hell."

Another hush prevailed.

Dan broke the awkward stillness. "I know, Father. I've thought about that too. But I've also thought about the unending life of the soul and how nothing is more important than preventing anyone from being sentenced to hell. The last thing I would want is for anyone to endure for an eternity what we suffered for only a month."

"Well, I can't argue with that," said the priest. "It appears that your mind is nearly made up. However, I suggest that we meet regularly to talk about your potential vocation." He reached for Father Andreas's shoulder. The acute pain had returned.

"Father James, let me help you to the rectory," offered Father Andreas.

"Do you need any help?" asked Jeff.

"Thanks, but we'll be fine," replied Father Andreas.

Moments after the priests left, the families stepped outside and headed down the sidewalk.

"Dan, even though I'm not Catholic and I don't know much about the priesthood, I also think you'd make a good priest," said Cindy.

"You do?" he remarked in amazement.

"Of course," she replied. "You've got all the qualities."

"What do you mean?" he asked.

"Well, you're clearly unselfish, considerate, and you genuinely care about other people," she elaborated. "Heaven knows that you put your life on the line more than a few times for the group. Those traits are obvious with you. But with other people, you have to look for them."

"And you really know how to get under Lucifer's skin," blurted Jimmy.

"Jimmy!" yelled his father.

As the families approached their cars, an unexpected gale swept through the parking lot and ripped the bulletin from Nancy's hand.

Dan watched it become airborne before settling alongside the church. He raced after it. Dan had no sooner grabbed the bulletin when he was plagued with doubts about the priesthood—doubts about his worthiness, his piety, and his ability to convert lives. A foul odor immediately filled the air. He froze. A fiendish chuckle was heard from behind, seconds before a penetrating cold rested on his shoulder. It was only then he realized that he was standing in a shadow cast by the church building. He flicked a dung beetle from his pants, jumped from the shade, and raced to the families.

Jeff detected more than a trace of fear in his son's eyes. "What's wrong, Dan?" he demanded.

"Nothing. I'm fine—really."

Though his father was certain that something was troubling him, he decided to drop the issue until they were away from the group.

After agreeing to meet up at the local diner, the families stepped to their cars.

Dan sat in the back seat with Sam and William. He rested his head against the window and stared into the cloudless sky. After the disturbing encounter with Lucifer in the church's shadow, he knew that Father James was right—he knew that the Prince of Darkness would hound him incessantly until his dying breath. Despite the fact that he would be pursued from the pit of hell, he was comforted knowing that his angelic companion—who had accompanied him to hell and back—would remain forever at his side. He also drew consolation knowing that every time a person resists a temptation, he or she grows in spiritual fortitude. Aware that the rest of his life undoubtedly would witness heavenly interventions along with hellish temptations, Dan displayed a guarded grin.

e|LIVE

listen|imagine|view|experience

AUDIO BOOK DOWNLOAD INCLUDED WITH THIS BOOK!

In your hands you hold a complete digital entertainment package. In addition to the paper version, you receive a free download of the audio version of this book. Simply use the code listed below when visiting our website. Once downloaded to your computer, you can listen to the book through your computer's speakers, burn it to an audio CD or save the file to your portable music device (such as Apple's popular iPod) and listen on the go!

How to get your free audio book digital download:

1. Visit www.tatepublishing.com and click on the e|LIVE logo on the home page.
2. Enter the following coupon code:
   95d6-97e9-c6e9-086c-6b5c-c53a-0a6c-0eb3
3. Download the audio book from your e|LIVE digital locker and begin enjoying your new digital entertainment package today!